HEART
OF THE
MOUNTAIN

HEART OF THE MOUNTAIN

LARRY CORREIA

A Baen Books Original

Baen Publishing Enterprises
P.O. Box 1403
Riverdale, NY 10471
www.baen.com

ISBN: 978-1-6680-7239-4

Cover art by Kurt Miller

First printing, February 2025

Distributed by Simon & Schuster
1230 Avenue of the Americas
New York, NY 10020

Library of Congress Cataloging-in-Publication Data

Names: Correia, Larry, author.
Title: Heart of the mountain / Larry Correia.
Description: Riverdale, NY : Baen Publishing Enterprises, 2025. | Series: Saga of the forgotten warrior series ; 6
Identifiers: LCCN 2024048859 (print) | LCCN 2024048860 (ebook) | ISBN 9781668072394 (hardcover) | ISBN 9781625799999 (ebook)
Subjects: LCGFT: Fantasy fiction. | Novels.
Classification: LCC PS3603.O7723 H43 2025 (print) | LCC PS3603.O7723 (ebook) | DDC 813/.6—dc23/eng/20241105
LC record available at https://lccn.loc.gov/2024048859
LC ebook record available at https://lccn.loc.gov/2024048860

Printed in the United States of America

10 9 8 7 6 5 4 3 2 1

To George R.R. Martin. See? It's not that hard.

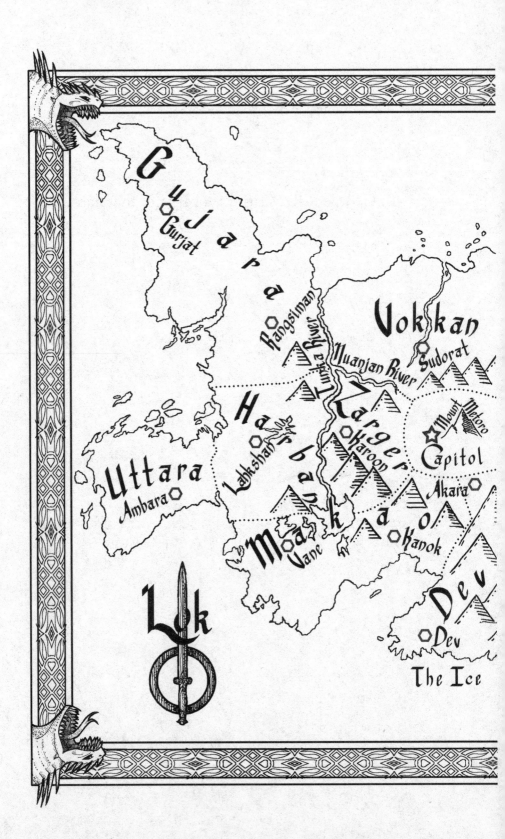

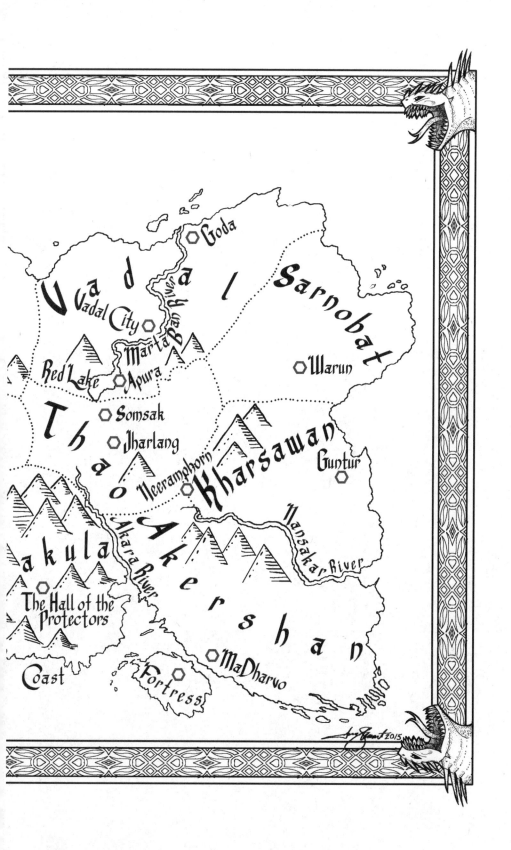

Prologue

The Testimony of the Traitor Ratul
Recorded 7 years ago

I have been called many things, like Ratul the Swift, or Ratul Without Mercy, and much later I was known as Ratul the Mad, or Ratul the Traitor. I have held many offices, most notably the rank of Master within the Protector Order, a title reserved for only the fiercest defenders of the Law. Yet that mighty office paled in importance to my illicit calling, when the Forgotten appointed me the Keeper of Names. I gave up one of the mightiest stations in the land to become a fugitive, and did so gladly, for I truly believe the gods are real.

Some say I am a fool, and all say that I am a criminal. Religion is illegal, preaching, as I have done, is punishable by death. My time will come. I embrace my fate, for they are the fools, not I. It is the world which has forgotten the truth. Soon they will be forced to remember, and it will be a most painful event.

Yes, I have been called a great many things, from heroic leader and master swordsman to fanatical rebel and despicable murderer, but young Ratul Memon dar Sarnobat was a kindhearted child, nothing at all like the jaded killer I would become.

Those years are long distant now. I was born on the moors south of Warun, second son of a vassal house, and second sons of the first caste are commonly obligated to serve the Capitol

1

for a period of time. It is said the houses keep their eldest close to prepare them to inherit and rule, but offer the rest of their children to the Capitol to demonstrate their total commitment to the Law. In truth, it is in the hope we can secure offices of importance within the various Orders to siphon wealth and favors back to our families, but I was naïve then, and did not yet understand the hypocrisy and rot within our system.

Young Ratul dreamed of being obligated to the Historians' Order to maintain the relics in the Capitol Museum, or perhaps the Archivists' Order, to spend my days organizing the stacks of the Great Library, for young Ratul loved stories and books. I also had a great talent for music and dance, as did all in my house, but I was the most graceful child. Perhaps I would be best obligated to an artisan's school, and go on to compose great plays? Maybe I would be an Architect, raising mighty monuments to the Law, or something odd and secretive like the Astronomer, tracking the moons and cataloging the sky? Regardless of where I was obligated, I looked forward to living in the magnificent Capitol, where it was said all the women were beautiful, the food was rich, and the waters pure and free of demons.

As a gangly boy with thin arms, a narrow chest, and a sensitive disposition, it never even entered my mind that I might be obligated to one of the militant Orders. But, upon the flag of Great House Sarnobat is the wolf, and such a cunning predator is a fitting symbol for the family which mine was vassal to. I shall not delve into the petty house politics which resulted in my obligation going to the Protector Order, but basically, my father had given some inadvertent insult to our Thakoor. Thus it amused our leader to give me to the most infamous Order of all, the brutal enforcers of the Law, where it was common for their young obligations to die in their unforgiving training program.

I recall my mother sobbing as I left our house, because she knew in her heart that her soft summer-born child would fail and die miserably.

At fourteen years old—which, by the way, is a little old to become a Protector acolyte—I traveled, not to the glorious and wealthy Capitol, but to the austere and miserable Hall of the Protectors, near the top of the world, high in the unforgiving mountains of Devakula, in the distant frozen south. I was despondent the entire journey there. All I knew of the Protectors was that they did nothing but pursue and execute lawbreakers... That, and they were one of the few Orders whose members were not allowed to wed until their obligation was fulfilled, so they lived a life of stoic solitude. At that age I was a silly romantic, so the idea of being bereft of female companionship until my obligation was done filled me with dread. My service was to last for a period of no less than ten years. And let us be honest, the odds of me surviving ten years of murderous village-burning butchery were slim as my waist.

We crossed a great many narrow bridges over deep chasms on the way to the Hall in Devakula, and I contemplated hurling myself off every single one. Those I traveled with would surely tell my family it was an accident, for slipping on ice and falling to your doom—though ignominious—was a more honorable end than suicide. Hitting the sharp rocks would've been a much faster end...

Except it was during this journey that I found I possessed a great stubbornness, for I would not give my Thakoor the satisfaction of expiring so quickly. To the ocean with him.

Though he was the focus of my great hate at the time, honestly, I can no longer even remember my Thakoor's face—he is as forgotten by me as the gods are to man—but that initial spark of defiance which flickered into being on a swaying bridge high in those mountains has remained with me ever since.

Decades later, that tiny spark would grow into a great roaring fire.

Later that fire would help ignite a conflagration which would threaten to burn the entire world... But I get ahead of myself. Gather close, my children. I must tell you how I believed in those days, for I still had much to learn.

The Law required there to be three great divisions within our society: the caste that rules, the caste that wars, and the caste that works. Every man has a place. Some said that there was a fourth division, meaning those without caste, but such speech could be considered subversive, for the Law declares that the casteless are not really people at all.

The first caste is the smallest, yet obviously the most important of all whole men. They are the judges and the arbiters of the Law, the members of the various Orders of the Capitol, and the great house families.

Each great house has an army to defend its interests. These are the warrior caste. They are more numerous than the first, yet far fewer than the third. I thought of them as a bloodthirsty, boisterous lot, with their own odd customs and a peculiar code of honor, but they were kept in check by the Law and the will of their great house.

The worker caste was the largest in number, yet the simplest in direction. They exist to labor. The structure provided by the Law and the wisdom of my caste had shaped Lok into a land of industry and wealth. It was the worker who dug the coal, weaved the cloth, and grew the crops. They paid taxes to the first caste, and paid again for the warriors to defend them, but in turn they required payment for their toil and their goods, for the callous worker is often more motivated by greed than allegiance to the Law.

The castes were the great division, but there are many—perhaps innumerable—lesser divisions beyond that, for each caste had a multitude of offices and ranks, and only members of that particular caste could hope to decipher where they all stood in relation to each other. Every duty or achievement bestowed status upon the individual who held it, and status determined everything else. A miner and a banker were of the same caste, only one could sleep in a mansion and the other in a hovel, yet both would bow their heads in deference to the lowliest vassal house arbiter, for he was closer to the Law.

Usually caste was determined by birth, but on rare occasions the Law might require a man to be assigned to a new caste. I'd heard of a particular worker who'd shown great strength, who the warriors had claimed, and in the opposite direction, of an inept and cowardly warrior who'd been ordered to trade his sword for a shovel. A particularly brilliant man could be promoted into the first, but a member of the first would cut his wrists in shame rather than accept the humiliation of leaving his caste.

It turned out my new Order was one such place where warriors could become members of the first, albeit temporarily, for when their obligations ended, they would return to their place. It was during my induction ceremony that I stood among children of the warrior caste for the first time. Every one of them, even the ones who were two or more years younger, were far bigger and stronger than I. To the Protectors, the new acolytes were all equally nothing. For the first time in my life, the status I had been born with had become utterly meaningless.

Our training began. Previously I had thought that I understood what hardship was. That had been a delusion. The Hall was as gray and stark as my house was bright and colorful. I'd lived in a land of song, but our only song was groans of weariness and cries of sudden pain. Our instruments were wooden swords. Our drums were our sparring partners' helms.

Over and over we were broken, physically and mentally, and constantly remade, not just muscle and brain, but also with magic. It is said Protectors are more than man. This is true. I shall speak no further about this, for there are some vows which even the vilest traitor still holds dear.

I know now that the program is a thing of beauty. It is so cruel, not because the Protectors hate their acolytes, but because we love them. Great suffering prepared us to overcome any obstacle, to face any challenge without flinching, even unto death.

The Order is not so different from the gods in that respect.

As I'd been warned, many of the acolytes perished. However, I would not be among them. For despite being the weakest of the acolytes, I was also the angriest, and in my heart was a great capacity for hate. Hate fueled me. It kept me warm through the cold nights, and every night in Devakula is cold.

At first my hate was directed at that now forgotten Thakoor, who had robbed me of my dreams of idle comfort. Then my hate shifted to the few acolytes who saw in my frail form a victim to be bullied. Tormenting me provided them a temporary distraction from their own torment. But the stupid and morally weak do not last long in the program, so after I outlived those, I needed a new outlet for my hate.

Thus I began to hate the enemies of the Law.

It was the reasoning of a bitter young man. If criminals did not exist, then there would be no need for the Protector Order. If every man kept to his assigned place and did as he was told, then those of us obligated to the militant Orders would be free. When it came time for the acolytes to be given lessons in the application of the Law, I excelled, as I always pronounced unhesitating condemnation upon every infraction, and I unfailingly recommended the harshest sentence allowed.

My teachers thought it was because I was smart enough to

grasp the nuances of the Law, that I was impartial and calculating as a Protector should be. This was not the case. I was filled with hate. Luckily for me, so was the Law.

It is curious that it is the softest ore which can be forged into the hardest steel. After three years of training, my long limbs had turned wiry strong and my already quick mind became sharper. Most beneficially I discovered that the unconscious rhythm and grace of the dancer was not so different from the timing and agility required to master the sword.

Upon obtaining the rank of Senior Protector I went forth into the world to dispense cruel justice.

It turned out that I was rather good at it.

This was the era in which I became widely known as Ratul Without Mercy. None were as devoted as I. Wherever I was assigned, criminals became afraid. From the jungles of Gujara to the plains of Akershan, I spilled blood. I shall spare you the litany of the many sins I committed in the name of the Law. It is a long list, and we have not the hours left before dawn.

Upon my tenth year, my mandatory obligation expired. I had the choice: retire and return to the house where my service had brought them great honor, to do any of the many artistic or intellectual things I had once aspired to, have a marriage arranged for me, create my own house, and raise my heirs...or voluntarily continue as a Protector.

Strangely enough, this was not a difficult decision, and I remained with the Order. I'd never have a wife to love me. I would make do with the loveless company of vapid pleasure women whose names and faces were forgotten the next day. I would never have heirs. There would be no sons to carry my name. I would never have a house of my own. The only symphonies I composed were the sounds of battle and my instrument was my sword. I had forgotten how to dream, but I had not forgotten how to hate. I knew that for every criminal I'd executed there was another still in hiding, and I would not be able to rest until every last lawbreaker was dead.

For a righteous hate can be addictive as the poppy.

It was as Protector of the Law, Eleventh Year Senior, that I, Ratul, encountered the lawbreaker who would start me on my path of rebellion. Of the many types of criminals Protectors hunted—rebels, rapists, murderers, unlicensed wizards, smugglers of bone and black steel, and so forth—none were more hated than religious fanatics, for it was those who practiced illegal religions who were the most nefarious. The others were motivated by things most of us could understand because we'd felt glimmerings of them in our weakest moments, like greed, lust, or jealousy. But the fanatic was motivated by something inscrutable: a belief in invisible forces and imaginary beings. Such foolishness was infuriating to the Law-abiding man.

For many weeks I had searched for this particular fanatic in the hill country of Harban. There had been reports of a nameless man—probably of the worker caste—going about and preaching of gods and prophecies, trying to rouse the people to rebel. As was usual with these types he'd found some success among the casteless. I thought of the non-people as gullible, and a few of them had risen up and struck down their overseer, proclaiming their actions as "the will of the Forgotten" even as the hangman's noose had been put around their necks.

I'd killed many such fanatics. I expected this one to be cut from the same cloth—a raving lunatic, bug-eyed and foaming at the mouth, filthy and unkempt, leaping about and cursing me with the wrath of his unseen gods. But when I finally tracked down my prey, I found a calm, soft-spoken scholar instead. Not of the worker caste as alleged, but like me, born of the first. He didn't live in a muddy cave, or a hollowed-out tree. He lived in a small but sturdy cottage, on a hill overlooking the city of Lahkshan.

Unlike most—guilty or innocent—who answer a knock at their door and discover a Protector waiting, this man showed no fear. If anything, he seemed resigned, as if weary from his labor. He was just old enough to be a grandfather, no more. There was a sadness in his eyes. I remember this clearly.

"Come in, Protector," said he without preamble.

I had no time for foolishness or a fanatic's tricks. The cottage was humble, but big enough to conceal several enemies. He made no comment upon my drawing my sword as I followed him inside.

There was no rebel ambush waiting therein, just a cot, a pair of comfortable-looking chairs, a kettle warming on the small stove, and a shelf *full* of actual books. That, I marveled at, because it would still be another year before the Order of Technology and Innovation approved the sale of printing presses. Only men of considerable wealth and status could obtain such a library in those days, and those were usually prominently displayed in a great house, not a one-room abode in the hills.

I had not even declared the charges against him, when the fanatic admitted, "I am guilty of all the crimes you suspect, and probably more. I will not resist, and I accept my punishment without protest."

"The penalty for proselytizing is death."

He simply nodded. Even though I was about to slay him, this fanatic was so polite that I almost felt bad for not taking off my shoes before entering his home.

Curious, I went to the shelf and started checking the books. Some of them were new, approved volumes purchased from the Great Library of the Capitol, but others appeared to be ancient. I opened one of those, gently, for its binding felt as if it might crumble to dust. I skimmed a few pages, at first thinking it was a history of some kind, and instead discovered the most heinous of crimes. These were religious tomes.

They were *scriptures*. There was nothing more illegal in the world.

I dropped the book as if it had burned my fingers. "Saltwater!"

"Though still forbidden, these are not originals, Protector. Those rotted away long ago. These are copies of copies, handed down in secret."

"Why would you keep such terrible things?"

"To learn about our past and our nature. The people of Lok had many different religions before the demons fell from the sky, each believing different things. I have gathered the holy books of several of those over my travels. The books disagree on more things than they agree, but all are fascinating in their own way."

I'd seen the various rough-hewn idols of the fanatics scattered about Lok—the four-armed man, the elephant-headed man and his mouse, the smiling fat man—and I'd broken each one I'd found, but I'd never before seen one of their books, because the Order of Inquisition had burned most of them long ago.

"I am curious, Protector. You've not yet set my home to the torch."

"Oh, I will."

"I know, but you hesitate. I have a feeling that you are a student of history."

He had guessed well. "As much as the Law allows."

"Then that is why you wait. May I ask of what house you were before joining your Order?"

I do not know why I answered truthfully, but I had never before engaged a madman in a conversation. "Sarnobat. Of the Vassal House Memon."

"Ah!" The fanatic went to the shelf and picked out a particular book. "Your people were a rare minority in old Lok. This was the holy book your ancestors used." Upon its cover was a crescent moon and a star. I'd seen such a symbol before, in my childhood, when a farmer had unearthed an old stone, and the Inquisitors had come and smashed it to dust with hammers. He held the book out to me, like he was offering a gift, but I did not take it. Seemingly disappointed, he put the illegal tome back on the shelf. "Of course you would not want that one anyway, Protector. That is not why you are here."

"I'm here to execute you for violations of the Law."

"You are here because the Forgotten wanted you to be. There were many religions before, but only one that mattered after the demons came." He picked out a different book, bound in gray, narrower than the others. I did not accept it either, but he left it standing alone. "This one is a copy of a book written during the Age of Kings, from after the demons were driven back into the sea. The Forgotten wants you to have it."

Genuinely baffled, I asked, "All these gods are forgotten now, so why speak of this one as if it's special?"

"I did not choose him. He chose me. And now he has chosen you."

I grew tired of this talk. The time had come. He did not so much as cringe as I raised my sword.

I could not help but ask, "Why are you not afraid?"

"Because in a dream the Forgotten showed me the man who would claim my burden and my life. Farewell, Ratul."

I had never told the fanatic my name.

Strangely enough, I did not hate this man. I stabbed him in the heart because it was expected of me, but I did not hate him.

I would have returned quickly to my duties, but the hour was late, and a cold rain had begun to fall, so I decided to spend the night in the fanatic's cottage and return to Lahkshan in the morning. I ate the fanatic's dinner of curried goat, and sat in his comfortable chair, as he lay dead on his floor.

My sleep was plagued with strange dreams. I awoke with a great unease.

My eyes kept drifting back to the shelf, and that book. Not the one of my ancestors, but the strange gray one which had come after. A sick curiosity gnawed at the back of my mind. Part of me desired to read this lurid tale from the Age of Kings, an era whose records were declared mostly off-limits to us. The Law was clear that I should not so much as let my gaze touch those pages, but I have already established that I was not a being of Law, but rather a being of hate.

I'd dealt with fanatics before, but I had never once been tempted to understand their superstitions beyond what I needed to know to better kill them. The Law said I should not, but my defiance said I should. I've fought many battles, but none were more difficult than the one I faced that night as I tried to decide between looking inside and placing it in the stove. Eventually I decided I would look briefly, and *then* I would burn it, so it could tempt me no more.

I lit an oil lamp and retrieved the book.

The brief glance I allowed myself stretched into hours as I read all through the night.

It was the forbidden history of our people, and all that came before. It did not read like the ramblings of madmen, or the lies of charlatans. I was pulled along, seemingly against my will, as I read of things strange, yet somehow familiar.

It struck me as true, and that was troublesome.

The book told of what had been, what was, and what would be. How we would rise, and fall, and rise, and fall again. It was in that last section, filled with dire prophecies, that I stopped, suddenly afraid, as I realized that centuries ago, this writer had been *writing about me*.

I speak not of generalities, or vague mumbling that could be about anyone if you squinted hard enough, but of a man without mercy, an enforcer of an unjust code. Who would stab a faithful servant in the heart and then read this very book while sitting next to his cooling corpse.

Suddenly furious, I threw the book on the floor. Then I dashed the oil lamp against the wall, setting the cottage ablaze. I stormed outside... only to be tempted to rush back in to try and save that damnable book. But I did not, and instead watched the cottage burn to the ground. Once I was satisfied all was ash, I walked back to Lahkshan in the dark and rain.

In the days that followed, I devoted myself to the Law and did my best to forget all that I had read. Ratul Without Mercy was the scourge of criminals everywhere. Rebels and fanatics fell to my sword.

Yet no matter how hard I worked, or how many criminals I killed, I could not shake the feeling that book had imparted to me. My dreams were haunted. If they were visions from forgotten gods, or figments of my imagination, I could not tell. I told no one, not even my closest friends in the Order, about what was troubling me.

As the years went on, I saw more distressing things, events which could be taken as signs of dire prophecies, indicators of a looming apocalypse. *If* the book was true, and *if* the prophecies were true, then drastic action had to be taken soon or man was doomed.

I had been taught that before the Law, there was only madness. That it had been created by the first judges to save Lok from the chaos that was the Age of Kings. The Law was all-encompassing. All things are subject to the Law. Even the demons of hell must obey. They remain in the sea and man stays upon the land. Those who violate are guilty of trespass and will be punished.

But the Law could give me no answer. Merely voicing my concerns would have resulted in my being hanged upon the Inquisitor's Dome, to cook to death beneath the sun, my flesh devoured by vultures, and my bones swept into a hole. Though my faith in the Law was shaken, my loyalty to my Order remained strong, for I loved my brothers. There is a kinship that can only be found in hardship. Yet even among them, there was none who I could confide in. To do so was to condemn them as I was condemned.

I began to question my assumptions and everything I believed. I required knowledge. Using my status as a Protector, I was able to access parts of the Museum and the Great Library, which were off-limits to all but a select few. In secret I studied the black-steel artifacts which had survived the Age of Kings. I consulted with the Historians. I learned what the Astronomers were really watching for. My desperate search across the Capitol was a grotesque version of the dreams once held by Young Ratul.

My sustaining hatred did not die, but once again shifted its aim. My fixation became the judges who had kept us from the truth for hundreds of years. I began to despise the Capitol for the things it had me and my brothers do. As I lost respect for those who wrote and interpreted the Laws, I began to delve into more forbidden areas of research.

It was in a cavern, deep beneath the world, that I met a giant. I speak not of a large man, like Protector Karno, who stands a head above most, but of a true giant. Ten feet tall, with skin blue as a Dasa, who'd slept through the centuries, but had been born when kings still ruled.

The giant told me of a place in the steaming jungles of Gujara. There I sought out a legendary temple with carvings upon the wall where the last oracle of the Forgotten had prophesied of those who would be gathered to once again lead the Sons of Ramrowan in the final battle against the demons. There were three old symbols: the Priest, the Voice, and the General, representing those who must be found and prepared before the last days. Then there were three symbols in opposition, vague warnings of those who would wage war against the Forgotten's chosen, such as the Crown, and the Mask, and finally there was the sign of the Demon, which surely represented the entire host of hell.

Each of these roles had to be fulfilled to bring about the gods' great plan. Without them, hell would consume the land. Mankind would be eradicated.

In the distant south, in the coldest winter, I waited until the ice froze enough for me to walk across the ocean without being eaten by sea demons, so that I could knock upon the impenetrable gates of Fortress. They tried to blast me to pieces with their terrible magic before I convinced them that I too was a seeker of truth. I spoke with their Guru and discovered that I was not alone in preparing for the end.

Yet, doubts remained.

Despite all my quests for forbidden wisdom into the darkest corners of Lok, the truth was finally revealed to me, not by a wall in a distant jungle temple or a fantastical being, but by one of my fellow Protectors. For it was I, Ratul, twenty-five-year master of the Protector Order, who discovered the secret identity of one of our acolytes. A secret which would shake the very foundations of our society should it be revealed, for a lowly casteless had been chosen to bear the most powerful magic in the world.

It took this clear fulfillment of prophecy to finally convince me, and through conviction at last came my conversion.

The prophecies were real. *The gods were real.*

It took more research before I was certain that this boy was meant to be the Forgotten's Warrior. I could never tell him who he really was. To do so would be to destroy him. And selfishly, in the meantime, I did not wish to deprive the Protectors of this powerful weapon which had revitalized and strengthened our waning Order.

As I tell you that tonight, I know it seems senseless that even after being converted I would still try to help the very Order which has done so much harm to the faithful. They may be misguided by the Law, but the Protectors are the best of men. They do more good than harm. Though they despise me now, and they will surely take my life soon, they remain my brothers.

After that I lived two lives simultaneously: Lord Protector beneath the eyes of the Law, and rebellious criminal in the shadows. While I still had faith the gods would show their General his path, it was my duty to search for the Voice and the Priest. I carefully checked every report from my Protectors involving religious fanatics. I did everything I could short of revealing my treachery to save what worshippers I could, ordering my men elsewhere, giving faulty intelligence, or even sneaking messages to the faithful to run.

That was how I found the genealogy and secretly became the Keeper of Names.

It was twelve long years after my conversion before I found the Voice in Makao. Yes, children, a true prophet walks amongst us once again. For their safety, I will not speak here of this person's identity, but know that the Voice lives, and I give you my word, that the Voice is real. The Forgotten speaks to us once more, and he requires great things of us before we may have our reward.

Unfortunately, there were witnesses to my discovery. Word of that event spread to my Order. I was required to explain my actions. Why had Ratul Without Mercy spared the life of an illegal wizard? I told the closest friend I've ever had the truth.

He turned his back on me.

My treachery was at last revealed, and I had to flee.

My name is worth saltwater. I am the most hated man in the history of the Protectors... for now.

I have hidden among the casteless and continued my search. It is here, in the borders of Great House Uttara, that I believe I have finally found the man who is to be the Forgotten's High Priest. He is clever, but driven by anger and bitterness, like I once was. Yet it is his ambition which will finally free our people.

We are out of time.

Ratul had suddenly looked to the south, eyes narrowed dangerously. She knew that Ratul's senses—augmented by the magic of the Protector Order—were far superior to those of anyone else present. Maybe he had smelled the smoke of the burning barracks, or the blood of warriors being shed. Perhaps he heard the screams of the dying as the rebelling casteless attacked the warriors.

"That damned fool," Ratul muttered, sounding now like the tired old man that he was. "I must go and save Keta's life. Farewell."

He said that, not to the mob of dirty untouchables who had been clustered around him, listening intently to his story, but to her. His testimony had really been intended for her alone. These casteless didn't realize it yet, but they would probably all be dead by morning, caught up in the bloody purge that would follow Keta's inevitably failed rebellion.

She would live, as she always did.

Ratul rushed out the door of the shack. She got up and followed. There was a faint orange glow in the distance as the arson fires spread.

"There is a Protector there," she warned him.

"I know. I can sense the magic in his blood."

"Does it tell you which one?"

"No, but I suspect who it will be..." Ratul turned back to face her, grim. "Since my treachery was revealed, each night as I have dreamed, the Forgotten has shown me the same vision. I am wading through waist-deep snow, in the mountains of Devakula, and I know that I am being pursued by a mighty predator. It is one of the great southern bears, white as the snow, powerful and proud. In the dream, there is no escape. And every night, the bear gets closer and closer. Last night, it was so near I could feel the hot breath upon my neck, and when I looked up, it had a bloody scar across its face."

"Devedas." She knew of him, but she knew a great many things, more even than Ratul. "Then if you go, you will surely die."

"There was one thing I didn't speak of tonight. The last prophecy in that gray book I read in that dead man's cottage all those years ago, which enraged me so. It foretold my death, cut down by a man I'd love as a son, who would love me more than his own father... That knowledge... comforts me." The condemned man smiled. "I have no hate left."

"May the gods lift you, Ratul of many names."

"Thank you for all of your help, Mother Dawn."

Then Ratul went to seal his testimony with his blood.

Chapter 1

The Capitol had been the magnificent home of the Law, the jewel of the desert, the grandest city in the world, and the ultimate monument to the glory and hubris of the first caste. It had existed in a place so harsh it should have been devoid of life, but fed by aqueducts that were incredible feats of engineering, the Law had made the desert bloom. Isolated and aloof, the first caste had ruled from their prestigious city, for it had been built in the center of the continent in order to be as far away from the corrupting influence of the ocean as possible.

That had not been enough to save it.

In a single morning, the Capitol had fallen. Using tunnels dug by the ancients, now flooded by the sea, the demons had swarmed from below. The dead had been too numerous to count. The vultures had feasted.

Now glorious palaces and gigantic government buildings lay empty as columns of refugees fled back to their native houses. Priceless treasures and family heirlooms had been carried out of the city, only to be abandoned along the road when they had grown too heavy. Between those treasures could be seen the occasional body, as escaping members of the First had collapsed from heat or thirst, or simply given into despair and lay down on the sand to die. Such a death did not take long in the central desert.

Two armies marched northward from the ruins of the Capitol. One was an army of Law, the other of rebellion.

Ashok Vadal had to remind himself that the Sons of the Black Sword were no longer considered criminals, thanks to the decree of one man, Maharaja Devedas. The destruction of the Capitol and the demonic invasion had turned old enemies into new allies. It was an uneasy agreement that could only exist because the threat of demons was so much worse than anything the Law could do against rebels, or rebels could do against the Law. What were the disagreements of men when compared against the unrelenting savagery of hell?

The trade roads near the Capitol were well maintained so the armies made excellent time. Normally this route catered to the endless merchant caravans that had kept the mighty Capitol nourished for centuries. Now that great city lay gutted and mostly abandoned, so the caravans were turning back, but luckily there remained a great many settlements where the armies could resupply along the way. Leaving nothing to chance, the Maharaja had sent messengers ahead to make sure that there would be resources sufficient to keep his soldiers fed the entire march to Vadal.

The prophecy of the god who lived inside Thera Vane's head had declared that the Great City of Man would be the location of the final battle where the fate of all mankind would be decided. According to Archivist Radamantha, Capitol scholar and wife of Maharaja Devedas, Vadal City was what the ancients were referring to as the Great City of Man, for it had been the greatest city of the prior age. It was believed the demonic army that had attacked the Capitol would need time to clear debris and dig their way through the vast tunnel system that the ancients had built beneath Lok in order to reach their next target. How long this would take the demons was a mystery. It could be weeks or months, but the armies of man set a brutal pace because this was a race that mankind could not afford to lose.

They marched with tireless determination because they had seen the fate of the Capitol. Tens of thousands had been slaughtered in a single morning and the home of the Law had been left crippled.

The Law-abiding army was in the lead. The rebels brought up the rear. This was not meant as an insult, but rather practicality. The Maharaja's forces were made up of Protectors, who were feared or respected in every land, and warriors obligated from all the great houses. Compared to them the rebel army—the Sons of the Black Sword—looked like a mob of mismatched mercenaries, casteless, and foreigners armed with illegal magic who would surely provoke violence at every checkpoint. Word had gone out about the sudden and drastic changes to the Law that granted status to the casteless and clemency to the religious, but it would take time for that new reality to take hold...if it ever did.

Despite that, Ashok still sent scouts to range far ahead, because it appeared that the mysterious Mother Dawn had once again predicted their path and sent more fanatics his way. They kept finding secret worshippers who had been warned by Mother Dawn *months ago* to present themselves in certain locations, on this specific date, so they could follow their prophet into battle. After the first batch of those fanatics—made up of warriors from as far away as distant Gujara—had nearly gotten into a battle with the Protectors, Ashok had made sure there was always an element of Ongud's cavalry riding a mile or two ahead of the main body.

That poor young officer had a difficult job. If the men he spied waiting along the trade road appeared to be fellow fanatics, then he would hurry and greet them to explain the situation before the Law-abiding army arrived. If it was an official patrol, then his job was run away, and hope that they didn't catch up to what surely looked like a gang of bandits before the Maharaja's banners came into sight.

To make this task easier, Ongud had made a simple banner to fly, bearing symbols that all of the faithful would surely recognize. Painted upon it was a red meat hook and a black sword.

After several days on the trade road, the rebel leaders had been summoned to the Maharaja's camp that night.

Ashok alone accompanied Thera, serving both as her general and bodyguard. He trusted Devedas to be a man of his word and keep the peace, but he had far less faith in the goodwill of the rest of the Law-abiding. There was a great friction between the two armies. Neither side trusted the other, for obvious reasons. There was so much history of bloodshed and betrayal that even the looming threat of demons couldn't make the wronged entirely forget what had been inflicted upon them by the other side.

Now that they were walking through a camp surrounded by Protectors and warriors who had recently been hunting them as if they were vermin, Thera whispered to him, "It's a good thing they need us more than we need them."

"If your gods are to be trusted, we need each other. All will be essential."

She eyed some of the scowling warriors. "I just hope they remember their king's promise to us."

"If any are so foolish, then I will give them a harsh reminder." Bitter eyes were upon them, but Ashok doubted any of them would try anything. They respected Devedas, they feared Ashok, and they were united against the demons. Hopefully that would be enough to keep the peace.

Ashok was effortlessly intimidating. Even without his reputation as the finest combatant alive, he was a tall man, lean and broad shouldered, who confidently walked through the ranks of his recent enemies without showing the slightest bit of fear, because he had no fear to show. The ability to experience fear had been ripped from him as a boy, in a vain attempt to artificially shorten his life. The warriors did not know this about him, but they could see that the man who carried deadly Angruvadal was not to be trifled with.

Thera was not so confident, but she hid it well. She was an attractive woman, but she'd spent so much time hiding from the Law that trying to avoid notice was her first instinct. Normally she walked with her hood up and her head down, but not here, not tonight. For she commanded a mighty army and a thousand Fortress guns, so she held her head high, defiantly meeting every contemptuous gaze with a patronizing smile.

"We're their only hope to survive the demons and they know it," she told Ashok. "It's sad it took the fall of the Capitol to gain their reluctant acceptance, but I'll take what I can get."

One of the Maharaja's Garo bodyguards loudly announced them as they approached the center of the camp. "It is the Lady Vane." The Law-abiding would tolerate their presence, but they certainly weren't going to call her by the titles her people used, like Voice or prophet. "And Ashok Vadal." Whatever titles they had for Ashok here, the bodyguard was smart enough to not say aloud.

Devedas was in council with his advisors and officers. He had forgone the lavish tent due a man of great status. He was a king now, the first in over eight centuries, holding the status of a hundred judges by himself, yet he sat upon the dirt before a humble campfire, eating regular rations of stale naan and dried meat and drinking the same watered-down wine as his men, which had been claimed from a caravan that day. Say what you would about prideful southerners, but they were always quick to forsake their own comfort when there were more important matters at hand.

"Let them through and fetch my guests some dinner. The rest of you, leave us." The men who had been meeting with Devedas did as they were commanded, some grudgingly, and a few of the brave ones gave Ashok looks of sneering disdain as they walked past. They stopped a polite distance away, waiting and watching to make sure the criminals did nothing to harm their beloved Maharaja. Ashok took no offense, because when he had been them, he had been taught to hate and distrust criminals too.

"Have a seat. Should I have a servant get you a pillow, Thera?"

"You spoil me with your hospitality, Maharaja," Thera said as she sat on a nearby rock. "This will do. I'm just glad to not be on a horse for a minute."

Ashok remained standing as he studied his former brother. Devedas was obviously weary, and not just from the march. He had haunted eyes and a face haggard from stress, yet retained about him an aura of grim determination. Ashok understood now that the gods had conspired with black steel to make Devedas into what he was today. Perhaps it was a good thing the gods were so cruel, because a lesser man surely would have collapsed beneath the weight Devedas had to carry now.

"What're you waiting for, Ashok? I know you don't expect a cushion."

Ashok sat on the ground. "You do not look well, Devedas."

"And to think, I was always the pretty one of us. I suppose I look like a man who knows he holds the fate of the entire world in his hands."

"You sought out that burden."

"And lucky for you that I did. It appears my belief that the casteless can exist as whole men and religious fanatics should be spared is in the minority among men of status."

Thera dipped her head in thanks. "Luckily for us, your opinion is the only one that matters."

"Will you still feel that way when one of the decisions I make as Maharaja is different from what you and your so-called gods want?"

"I suppose we'll find out when that day comes," she answered coyly. "My people are honored to be given the chance to exist under the protection of the Law, but let's deal with the demons first. Politics later."

"Yes, why worry about things that won't matter if we all get killed in the north and demons devour everyone else?" After his men delivered plates of food and cups of wine to Ashok and Thera, Devedas wasted no more time on social frivolities. "I need to update you on the situation in Vadal."

"Have you come to a diplomatic solution to end your war with them?" Thera asked.

Ashok was curious as to what the answer to that would be, as Thera had already told the Maharaja that her rebels were happy to fight demons, but they wouldn't shed a single drop of human blood on the Capitol's behalf. From the annoyed look Devedas gave her, Ashok doubted his answer would be a satisfactory one.

"I sent messages via demon bone to my forces that have Vadal City surrounded, as well as the armies of Vokkan and Sarnobat. I've commanded all the invading forces to cease hostilities, end the blockade, pull back, and hold position at the border awaiting my further orders. The Army of Many Houses has done as they were told. But Vokkan and Sarnobat pretend not to hear me."

"Of course they don't obey," Ashok said. "The Vokkan are bold liars, and it is Sarnobat's character to crave conflict. Both have hated Vadal forever. Your invasion gave them opportunity."

"It was a fine plan, until demons cut our head off. I've also been trying to reach the Vadal leaders, but we've burned pounds of demon bone trying to talk to those stubborn bastards . . . Oceans know the only resource we don't lack for right now is demon bone, we killed so damned many of them in the Capitol. But despite my show of good intent, the Vadal have ignored my calls for peace."

"It's because Vadal's winning, isn't it?"

The Maharaja clearly didn't care for Thera's tone as she pronounced that uncomfortable truth, but Devedas was not a weak leader, and had no aversion to facing cold reality. "They're no longer losing. They're still outnumbered, but word spread quickly about the attack on the Capitol and its current, nearly abandoned, state. My Army of Many Houses reacted poorly to the news. Hundreds, if not thousands, of soldiers abandoned their obligation to return to their own houses. The morale of the loyal remainder is awful."

"Desertion's not unexpected, considering that if sea demons could attack the Capitol sitting in the middle of the desert in the middle of the continent, then surely they know their own families might be in danger. I bet Vadal saw this collapse, and going from being outnumbered three to one, to only two to one, they rallied."

"I've got to remember before you were a criminal, you were warrior caste, daughter of Vane."

"I will take that as a compliment, Maharaja."

"It is," Devedas assured her. "So I'll not hobble my words. I still have a great army in Vadal, but they're paralyzed with fear and indecision. The Vadal proved to be tenacious foes but now that they've heard the Capitol is weakened, they fight like never before. They most assuredly believe that my warnings about the demon army coming for them next to be some kind of trick."

"Can you blame them?"

Devedas nodded at that harsh, but fair question. "After the Capitol's response to the Scourge? I wouldn't believe me either. Sarnobat and Vokkan still press Vadal despite my call for peace, I assume because those ambitious houses see my words as nothing more than the barking of a toothless dog now. While these houses continue their fight, the demons dig."

Fortress Collector Yajic was their expert on the ancients' underground tunnel system the demons were using to travel beneath Lok, but his guild had been cut off from the northern section for a very long time and had no idea of the state of things here. Based on how long it had taken them to get from Kanok to the Capitol, Yajic's best guess was that they only had a few months before the demons dug their way through.

"I've got three houses squandering lives and resources for gains which will become meaningless once the demons drown us all in blood. I've left my wife to run what's left of the government while I try to gather an army sufficient to defend a city from the entire might of hell, except I can't do that if I'm outside besieging their gates trying to starve them into submission. All

I'll do is deliver up an easier target for the demons to take. As of now it appears I'm powerless to stop the war I started, but I have an idea. The Vadal hate me, but they might listen to you."

Thera laughed at that. "My words are saltwater to those people!"

"Not you." Devedas nodded toward Ashok. "Him."

Ashok looked up from his wine and scowled; for breaking their sword and dishonoring their name, surely Vadal despised him more than anyone else alive. "Has the desert sun driven you mad?"

There were very few men who could talk to the Maharaja like that and live. "Sadly, Ashok, this plea is being made by a rational man. The heirs of Harta blame me for their father's death and refuse to believe me now, but the armies of Vadal are led—rather capably—by a phontho named Jagdish. I think you know him."

"I know a Vadal warrior named Jagdish, but he was a mere risalder, much lower in rank and status than a supreme phontho."

"They're one and the same. He's not too shabby a commander for a prison warden. I attended his wedding. Despite Jagdish trying to hide it from his first caste, the man clearly respects you as a mentor and loved you as a friend."

The idea that poor, disgraced and dishonored Jagdish had not only successfully redeemed his name, but also risen to the mightiest of ranks in his caste actually made Ashok smile, which was a rare event.

"Good for Jagdish!" Thera exclaimed. "A phontho, you say?"

"A phontho, and a damned good one, from the reports I've gotten from my army, at least. He's a master tactician, unbound by tradition, who inspires his men to greatness. He's routed Sarnobat in the east and now that the Army of Many Houses has retreated to the south, he's turned his attention toward Vokkan in the west."

"He was our first risalder," Thera said with pride. "You're fortunate Jagdish no longer has the fearsome Sons of the Black Sword under his command, or he would have pushed that army of yours into the sea a long time ago!"

Devedas let that slight against his troops pass. "I must ask you, do you think Jagdish is a man of honor?"

The truth was so obvious, Ashok didn't even need to think about his answer. "Jagdish would have made an excellent Protector."

For the two of them, that was all that needed to be said. "Good.

It will take a warrior of character willing to put aside glory and risk his name for the sake of his house's future. I know I can't command you to do anything, so all I can do is ask. Will you go to Jagdish and get him to listen to reason? If you can convince him the demons are on their way, then he might convince his Thakoor. The sooner we can bring an end to this war, the better off we'll all be when the demons show themselves again."

Ashok looked toward Thera. It seemed a logical request to him, but he had pledged to serve her and no one else. She was pondering the proposal, probably thinking of what boon she could ask for in return for this service, but Ashok already knew what she would decide, because to Thera, doing the right thing would be more important than squeezing one more concession from the Law.

"You can't hardly defend a city you're at war against, and I didn't bring all my fanatics and foreigners this far just to watch you fight. I think it's worth the attempt."

Ashok nodded at their wisdom. "Very well. I will take Horse, and I request the fastest steeds from your Zarger cavalry. If I rotate between mounts and then use the Maharaja's authority to claim fresh animals along the way, I should be able to get to Vadal City over a week before you do."

Devedas inclined his head toward one of the many banners that flew over his camp. "I had in mind something much faster."

Upon that flag was the symbol of the Capitol's wizards.

Chapter 2

"Your orders, Phontho?"

Jagdish looked out over the mighty army Great House Vadal had entrusted him with and was pleased.

"My orders are to purge these Vokkan scum from our lands once and for all. Move to the secondary positions. *Forward, Vadal!*"

His command was relayed. Flags dipped. Horns blew in response.

Across the field waited over fifteen thousand men of Vokkan. On this side a mere three thousand warriors of Vadal began marching toward them. The ground trembled as a line of fifty war elephants lumbered along, armor clanking, while archers and spearmen rode in howdahs upon their backs. Normally those great beasts would be in the lead, where their charge would hopefully cause the greatest amount of terror to the enemy, but for now Jagdish held them in reserve. Gotama had more experience with elephantry and had warned him they were skittish animals who were often too smart for their own good. Jagdish would not inflict on such sensitive creatures the discomfort he had planned for the Vokkan.

Jagdish's horse cavalry moved toward the flanks, awaiting his signal. The Vokkan commanders saw this, and their cavalry moved to match.

Phontho Yaduvir Vokkan was no fool. Judging by the successful campaign he'd waged in western Vadal thus far, he was a solid commander. Even if he had been a dullard, Yaduvir still had numbers more than sufficient to counter anything Jagdish might attempt. With the mighty river Martaban at their back, Jagdish's army had nowhere to retreat. If they failed here, Vadal City would be totally cut off from the last of its unthreatened provinces, to be inevitably starved into submission.

Jagdish had led many battles against Great House Sarnobat in the east, but few against Vokkan in the west. The house of the wolf were born raiders, boastful, always prefering to hit and run rather than stand and slug it out. Jagdish had used their pride against them many times, tempting the Sarnobat with what seemed to be easy victories, only to lure them into certain defeats. The warrior caste of Vokkan, on the other hand, tended to be patient and methodical. The house of the monkey took the long view, carefully considering the consequences of every maneuver and the cost of every decision. Dishonest themselves by nature, the Vokkan suspected everything they saw to be a ruse and were thus untemptable. Vokkan slowly took ground, held it, consolidated their gains, and then pushed for more. They never outran their supply chains. They always left themselves an escape route. Whatever territory they took, they stripped of value, leaving nothing behind that could be used against them later. What the Vokkan lacked in imagination, they made up for in thorough cruelty.

As Jagdish had achieved victory after victory in the east, Yaduvir Vokkan had defeated the armies of Vadal one after the other in the west. Treacherous fate had smiled on Jagdish on one front, but would she allow him to win a second?

The odds were not in his favor. Vadal was badly outnumbered today. His men were still weary from the journey here while the Vokkan were rested since their last battle. This was the entirety of the Vokkan warriors left in Vadal lands. Jagdish had help coming, as the armies of phonthos Girish and Kutty were marching this way, but it was doubtful they would arrive here in time. If Jagdish's army had held back to wait for reinforcements, the Vokkan would have been able to destroy the rest of the bridges across this southern Martaban with impunity. Such cowardice would cut the city off from its southern supply routes and likely starve them into submission.

It appeared that the flat, dry ground of these farmers' fields granted neither side an advantage. It seemed that the pleasant sunny day presented no weather to use against his enemies... but Jagdish knew better.

When the main bodies of the two armies were still several hundred yards apart, the traditional dance began in earnest. Teams of horse archers from both sides began harassing the enemy as paltans of infantry changed course to try and take advantage of the limited terrain features the farmland presented. In a battle like this, a simple livestock fence or drainage ditch could turn out to be a huge advantage. From his far-off vantage point, Jagdish was unable to discern such things, so he could do nothing but trust his junior officers to do the right thing as he'd taught them. Close eyes made better decisions than distant ones. Trying to meddle in the little things now would only confuse matters, and that was truly the most difficult thing about being a phontho. His heart yearned to be out there when the spears crossed and steel met steel. His mind told him his place was to command from a position of safety, surrounded by officers, bodyguards, and messengers, who were all willing to lay down their lives to protect him.

Except Jagdish was a warrior, born to fight. It was in his blood. He was an exemplar of his caste. When the time came, he would inevitably join in, and every man in his army knew it, and respected him all the more as a leader for it.

Through his spyglass he saw that Yaduvir's troops were gradually moving into range of his trap. "This will do. Signal a halt. All paltans hold position." His officers began shouting orders. Satisfied that his infantry would get the word and not blunder into the dangerous area, he commanded, "Send word to Mukunda's wizards to begin their spell."

Jagdish hadn't smuggled a wagon full of demon bone across half the continent to not use it. So far during their illegal house war, all that magic had been held in reserve, just waiting for an enemy ancestor blade to take the field, but since none ever had, he might as well use that magic now. The battle wizards were eager. Fate had given them a calm day. Jagdish would make it howl.

A different, very specific tone was blown on the signal horn. A moment later, there was an answering signal, as the wizards confirmed they had gotten it.

Jagdish checked his pocket watch. As expected, it took a few minutes for the wizards to form their pattern and begin twisting the elements to their will, but gradually the crops just ahead of their front lines slowly began to bend toward the Vokkan. Then a sudden gust made the few trees shake. He put away his watch and got out his spyglass. Rather than letting up, the wind was slowly growing in intensity until leaves were being stripped from the plants. Dust devils sprang into existence between the armies, and went whirling through the enemy ranks, stinging eyes.

It was rare for the warrior caste to have wizards so blatantly manipulate the battlefield on their behalf. Such meddling wasn't seen as *honorable*. But Jagdish had spent his entire life being sneered at by supposedly honorable types who seldom left the safety of the courts, who'd never had a callus on their palms or a brother die in their arms, so he didn't particularly care to be lectured by such men about what they thought honor meant. He had a war to win.

"Have the archers begin."

Vadal and Vokkan bows were very similar in design, so were of comparable capability...at least until one side tried to launch their arrows against a mighty wind while the other was equally strengthened by the same. Suddenly, the Vokkan range was halved, while the Vadal's doubled. Hundreds of arrows fell among the distant Vokkan, while their return fire floundered uselessly from the sky.

The officers around Jagdish saw the tumbling arrows and cheered.

But not everyone on his staff approved. "Of course it takes cheater magic to make a Vadal bowman's arm as strong as any wolf of Sarnobat."

"It seems my ears are deaf to your whining today, Najmul," Jagdish told the fanatic, who was just sore that Jagdish had so thoroughly humiliated his brothers in the east. It was a testament to Najmul's fierce loyalty to his secret illegal gods that the Sarnobat man hadn't murdered Jagdish in his sleep yet, but had instead proven himself to be an excellent bodyguard. "Even if I could hear you over this glorious wind I'm paying for, I'd give a fish about the moral perspective of a raider who thinks it is fine to set houses on fire with children inside."

"Alright, alright," Najmul muttered, for if there was anyone the fanatic disliked more than the Vadal, it was their inferior cousins, the Vokkan. "I'm happy as long as the wretched Vokkan die."

"Oh, they will," Jagdish assured him, before turning to one of his roiks. "Light the fires."

During the night, his skirmishers had built piles of brush and whatever else they could find that was flammable, and then soaked those piles in oil. As long as they were burning demon to fuel this magical hurricane, they'd use that wind to blind and irritate their enemy. Vokkan would surely have wizards of their own among such a vast army, but as Mukunda had explained to Jagdish, it would take more energy for them to effectively counter the patterns the Vadal wizards were already using, than it would for the Vadal wizards to maintain their spell. In the meantime, Jagdish intended to smoke them out.

The wind whipped the many bonfires into a roaring frenzy. Black smoke quickly filled the space between the armies and engulfed the Vokkan lines.

Even from here, far upwind, the smell was intense enough to make Jagdish's eyes water.

"Oceans, that's truly nasty stuff!" exclaimed one of his officers.

Which was as Jagdish expected, since the primary crop grown in this area was the unforgiving Vadal viper peppers. Eating them hurt the mouth in a blissful way. Getting the oil of one on your fingers and then touching your eye was excruciating. Now bushels of those hostile peppers were burning, and he would force an entire army to stew in the caustic vapors until they were blind and coughing their lungs up, all while their arrows did nothing and Jagdish's fell among them like rain.

"A dirty trick," Najmul said. "I am impressed."

"Fate presented us with an even field, so I have made it uneven. Serves the invaders right." Keeping up this wind had to be costing a fortune in demon, but he'd rather spend bone than lives. Jagdish waited until the entire enemy side was fully shrouded in obscuring smoke before ordering, "Send Zaheer's cavalry up the side while they're good and blind."

Yaduvir Vokkan was logical, but he was not creative. With his army suffering and his wizards scrambling to push back, he would have to retreat, hold, or move forward. Those were his only choices. Jagdish had a plan for each possibility. He guessed with the Vadal army pinned against the river, Yaduvir would be hesitant to retreat as that would give Jagdish room to maneuver, and he would be too suspicious to blindly rush forward. Even as Jagdish knew his enemy's reputation, surely they knew his, and crafty Jagdish might have prepared another trap for them. Yaduvir would likely do the safest thing, which meant holding and suffering, searing their eyes, breathing poison, and occasionally being struck by arrows, because the enemy phontho would assume that Vokkan hardiness would outlast Vadal's supply of magic.

Of course Yaduvir assumed correctly about that, and after twenty minutes had ticked by on Jagdish's little pocket watch, gradually the howling wind calmed to a breeze as Mukunda's wizards exhausted themselves. Jagdish had already had his infantry and archers return to their original positions and wait back where the air was clean. "Have the skirmishers quench the bonfires and fall back."

As the smoke cleared, Jagdish saw that the entire Vokkan army had gone prone, getting as low to the ground as possible and hiding from arrows behind their shields. They'd wrapped their scarves around their faces in a vain attempt to keep the smoke from their lungs, and now they were pouring their canteens in their eyes. He imagined he could hear the coughing from here. Their cavalry was in complete disarray, as they'd lost control of many of their horses.

"Look at them—pathetic. You should charge and destroy them now."

"Calm down, Najmul. That impatience is why I beat your house. It's the little things that win wars."

"Strength and courage win wars. Those are not little things."

"Neither are elephants, and our trainers told me their beasts have an aversion to peppers. They rub viper oil on their fences to keep the elephants inside. Let all the smoky air out first. *Then* we can stomp on them."

Another tense half an hour passed as the Vokkan composed themselves. It always amazed Jagdish how battle maneuvers were so slow, until the terrible moment they were fast. Even with his overwhelming numbers, Yaduvir remained cautious. As he rightly should, as this was the bulk of Vokkan's military might assembled in one place. If he somehow lost here today, his house would be terribly damaged. If he failed to destroy the bridges now, Jagdish would be reinforced, and Vadal City would be safe.

Sarnobat had failed. The Army of Many Houses had retreated for unknown reasons. Yaduvir had to trust in his superior numbers and push onward, because it was doubtful Vokkan would ever have a chance to defeat their hated rivals like this ever again. No phontho worth his stars could ever let such an opportunity pass.

The Vokkan began to march.

Then they abruptly stopped.

A sudden halt had been called. Jagdish spied a great deal of commotion around Yaduvir's banner. Messengers were leaping from horses. Red-eyed men were yelling and waving their arms. Jagdish recognized fear when he saw it.

"They're unnerved!" one of the officers who had his own spyglass exclaimed.

"Looks like Zaheer's riders made it past in the smoke unseen, and from their reaction, I assume that right now our best cavalry are busy slaughtering the Vokkan baggage train."

Jagdish always tried to learn as much as he could about his adversaries before meeting them in battle. From Vadal spies sitting and listening to warriors complain in Vokkan taverns, to interviewing prisoners and deserters, and even reading the enemy phontho's writings when available helped paint a picture of who they really were. Yaduvir never neglected his logistics. He never outran his support. This particular war dog would only go as far as his chain allowed. The farther Yaduvir got from home, the more he jealously guarded his supplies, and the Vokkan were very far from home right now. By sending Zaheer around to harass those supplies, Jagdish had hoped to divide Yaduvir's attention, to make him worry about the future, for in the moment of crisis a warrior who was more concerned about his journey home than his battle ahead would surely fail. Warriors had to accept death in order to overcome it. On the battlefield only those prepared to die might live. That was why Yaduvir was the one trapped here, not Jagdish.

"Forward, men of Vadal! *Forward!*"

Jagdish's officers repeated his commands. Banners dipped and swayed. The battle horns blew. They all knew what to do, because Jagdish had seen to it that they were exceedingly well trained. They believed in him as he believed in them. He had been born to lead men and make war against his enemies. Today Jagdish dictated his own fate.

He bellowed so as many men as possible would hear his words and take heart. "No mercy. No compassion. They tread upon our land! Do your duty for Vadal! Attack! *Attack!*"

Roiks bellowed commands at their risalders and then every paltan was on the move back to the positions Jagdish had let them study earlier. They'd been taught what to do. Now they would perform or perish.

The massive opposing army hesitated, confused, as their commander was torn between the real threat before them and the mostly imagined one behind, but when they saw Vadal was moving forward, the Vokkan were once again given the order to proceed. Only their momentum had been lost, and it appeared Yaduvir was overestimating the size of Zaheer's force, because far too many of his paltans split off to go and protect their support companies.

Jagdish smiled at that great fortune, yet an incredible force still remained.

Against such odds Vadal would need every sword it could get. Even if they started to lose, there would be no retreat for him to call. As always, Jagdish's head told him to command and his heart told him to fight, but with no commands left to give, he climbed atop his horse and followed his warrior's heart. His personal bodyguard consisted of five handpicked Vadal swordsmen and one Sarnobat fanatic. When they saw their leader mount up, they immediately did the same. Each of them had accepted this obligation knowing that that this was no typical elderly phontho, content to give orders from the safety of the rear. Today, their only safety lay through victory.

"Follow me, boys. It's time to cause some trouble."

"For Vadal!" they responded.

Since he'd strictly forbidden Najmul to ever mention his illegal gods in the presence of Law-abiding men, the fanatic shouted, "For glory!" instead, but Jagdish knew what that madman was actually fighting for. Gods weren't real, but in the off chance they were, let them be praised as glorious because Jagdish would take all the help he could get.

As the two armies marched toward each other, the distance between them rapidly shrank. Skirmishers rode back and forth between the lines. Men and horses were struck with arrows. Cavalry wheeled back and forth at the flanks, though the Vokkan horses still seemed panicked from the smoke. To keep from being totally encircled, Jagdish's infantry was spread thin. It appeared the Vokkan were about to engulf them like a mighty wave anyway.

Then his elephants struck the middle.

There was nothing in the world quite like the charge of a war elephant paltan. The world shook as they ran. Vokkan infantry readied their spears, and that sometimes worked, as elephants were intelligent animals, and intelligent things did not willingly stick their faces into hornet's nests, but Vadal war elephants were fed a narcotic plant by their handlers immediately before battle to calm their nerves. Each of the beasts had been trained from birth by respected specialist families within the warrior caste, and every elephant was clad in armor of interlocking plates and mail backed with thick padding, crafted as finely as that of the great house's Personal Guard. Elephants were born and died, but that precious armor was well maintained and handed down through the generations. Such was the benefit of being the wealthiest house.

Most of the Vokkan spears did nothing against the charging animals. Some pierced armor and found flesh, but even mortal wounds couldn't stop their momentum. Dozens of warriors were trampled underfoot before the dying beasts toppled over, crushing even more men beneath. The rest of the elephants trudged onward through the Vokkan ranks while their Vadal riders continually launched arrows down from their howdahs. The disciplined lines of Vokkan shields and spears disintegrated beneath the shadows cast by the twelve-thousand-pound animals. Bodies were sent flailing in every direction.

A moment later, the Vadal infantry followed that bloody path, carving their way deep.

Jagdish's seven rode behind Roik Joshi's infantry, looking for their opportunity, but not too close, because even war horses tended to balk around elephants. There was a hole in the Vokkan center. If they could exploit this, they might have a chance, so Jagdish rode into the chaos.

Far ahead, an elephant reared up on its hind legs, front legs wheeling. Ropes snapped and the howdah slipped from its back, spilling men onto the ground. The mighty animal came back down on top of more Vokkan warriors. Even brave men lost their nerve and ran as they saw heads pop like grapes, or the guts being stomped out of their brothers.

As Gotama had explained to him, elephants were not horses, and could only be controlled for so long before they decided to do whatever they felt like in the pandemonium of battle, and when they did there wasn't much their riders could do but hold on and go wherever they were taken. The timid elephants would be overcome by the noise, smell, and pain, and try to turn about and flee back the way they'd came, and Jagdish watched in horror as one did so, running straight through a paltan of Vadal infantry. But the fiercest male elephants would often descend into something only one step shy of demon frenzy, and Jagdish marveled as another one veered off to the side, chasing after a flapping Vokkan banner that had somehow drawn its wrath, swinging its brass-capped tusks to and fro, snapping the bones and cracking the skulls of a great many Vokkan warriors along the way.

The elephants had fulfilled their purpose. Orderly line against orderly line, the side with the numbers would prevail. Turn that into a bloody mess, and the day would be carried by whichever side had the most skill and will to violence. Jagdish was betting on Vadal.

He went into the fray, charging against the light infantry, laying about him with his sword. It clanged off Vokkan helms, but each man knocked over by his horse became easy pickings for the Vadal infantry to finish off.

Suddenly, his mount was killed out from under him. Unable to escape the stirrups before he went crashing down, Jagdish bellowed in pain as one leg was smashed between his horse and the ground. As he struggled to drag himself free, a Vokkan warrior rushed him, mace lifted high in one hand, ready to kill.

That warrior's arm came off in a spray of blood.

Najmul stood protectively over Jagdish. "You cannot threaten the gods' chosen!" The disarmed Vokkan screamed and tried to escape the fanatic, but Najmul followed, snatched up the dropped mace, and caved in the back of the warrior's helmet with a mighty overhand blow. "He is the gods' to kill! Not yours!"

Jagdish grunted and tried to shove the horse up enough to extricate his leg. "I told you no religious nonsense."

"Yes, sir!" Najmul went back to him, grabbed the saddle horn, and pulled hard.

Knee throbbing, Jagdish struggled the rest of the way out and stood up. A Vokkan rushed him, but Jagdish parried the strike and then thrust the tip of his sword with perfect accuracy through the armpit gap in that warrior's armor. He wrenched it free and a gout of blood followed.

"I'll not have that illegal foolishness in this army!"

"Won't happen again, sir," Najmul replied, though that was certainly a lie. Then he stabbed a Vokkan soldier in the throat, and smashed another over the head with the mace in his other hand. The rest of Jagdish's bodyguard went about thoroughly destroying every enemy around them, because no fury burned hotter than that of a proud people who had been invaded.

The Vokkan wore dark armor, brown to nearly black, with only the fronts of their helms painted red. The Vadal colors were blue-gray and bronze. They were two very different styles, yet within a few minutes they were all so covered in gore and dust it was difficult to tell who was who, and Jagdish had to pause between his mad slashes to make sure he wasn't hitting his own men. Hot tears were flowing involuntarily from his eyes because of all the pepper smoke that lingered on the Vokkan uniforms. It was nasty for the Vadal, but the poor Vokkan bastards were still half blind and desperately wheezing for breath.

The fighting was intense. Jagdish had never been in a battle of this size, as such events were rare in Lok. It turned out a big battle was much like a small battle, but *more*. Or in this case, it was a hundred small battles rolled into one bloody catastrophe.

But by sheer weight of numbers, Vadal was losing far too many of those.

Jagdish rallied his nearby men and kept fighting. It was a blur of chaos and brutality. His muscles burned. His army fought like demons, yet with a great and growing dread, Jagdish began to realize that would still not be enough.

Black shadows flashed by overhead, and Jagdish barely had time to look up and see that they were being cast by what appeared to be two huge birds, except there was a searing unnatural light to the shapes that stung his eyes even more than the pepper dust.

He had once seen the assassin Sikasso melt his body into the form of a great bird and soar away. That had to be what these were.

Those were not Jagdish's wizards.

"Wizards incoming!"

As the wizards circled over the battlefield, it appeared that one of them carried something in its talons. *No. Not something.*

Someone. That bird came back around, lower now, swooping just out of range of the uplifted spears. When the talons released, the man it was carrying dropped, and the bird soared upward.

The man hit the ground a mere ten feet from Jagdish, rolling through the dust and blood, but quickly rose from among the dead bodies, seemingly unhurt by his fall.

The newcomer was tall, dark of skin and dread of countenance, dressed not in the finery of a mighty wizard, but in humble worker's attire, stained from travel and bleached by sun.

"Ashok?" Jagdish whispered as he saw the ghost.

"Look out!" Najmul roared as he protectively stepped in front of his charge. "Wizards attack!"

"That's no wizard!"

But it was too late, and the fanatical bodyguard hurled himself at the new threat.

Najmul was one of the fiercest combatants Jagdish had ever met, but Ashok merely sidestepped the thrust meant for his heart, and then ducked the mace meant to smash out his brains, before catching Najmul by the throat with one hand and sweeping him effortlessly to the ground. The rest of Jagdish's men reacted a bit slower, but they too rushed forward to protect their phontho.

"Stop! Hold!" It was a testament to their training that his men could still hear and heed him in the middle of a desperate battle, and they stopped before Ashok had to put them down too.

Jagdish lifted his visor to reveal his face. "Oceans! Ashok, is that you?"

"It is I, Jagdish." Ashok nodded in greeting as he stepped on Najmul's sword arm to trap it until the bodyguard realized he wasn't an enemy. "I have come to warn you that you must stop your war."

"What?" Jagdish had to shout to be heard over the screaming and clashing of swords and shields all around them, and even more disorienting, he was still reeling at seeing his old friend here, alive, and falling out of the sky. "Can't you see we're in the middle of something?"

"I am too late." Ashok looked around, scowling, and his disappointment was perhaps the most frightening thing on the battlefield. Then he focused upon Yaduvir's command banner in the distance. "Perhaps not... If I force their phontho to call for a retreat, will you let them go?"

"What?"

"When I defeat their army, will you spare their lives, Jagdish?"

That was madness, even for a ghost. "Sure." They were all about to die anyway. "Why not?"

Ashok turned back toward Yaduvir's banner and drew his sword.

It was Angruvadal!

All of the Vadal men gasped. Not only did Ashok live, but so did their lost sword?

It was an inconceivable revelation, but then Ashok was away, nearly as suddenly as he had arrived. He leapt effortlessly over the Vadal lines and plummeted into the Vokkan, black blade singing. Warriors were cut down. Steel armor split as if it were paper. Stunned, Jagdish could only track Ashok's progress by the carnage. Where Angruvadal went, spears dipped, banners fell, men died. Five. Ten. Twenty.

It really was him!

Ashok was cutting a swath through the Vokkan ranks, directly, inexorably toward where their phontho watched. Jagdish only knew a few things with absolute surety in this life: the love of his family, the love of his soldiers, what it meant to be a warrior... and that if Ashok Vadal said something was going to get done, it was going to get done.

Cursing himself for following his heart and ignoring his nagging mind, Jagdish grabbed his nearest bodyguard by the shoulder and shook him. "Gather runners. Find the bannerman and horn! When Ashok takes the enemy's head, we must break contact and *let them go.*" He made sure they could all hear him, which was difficult through the padding of their helmets, even when the blood wasn't thundering in their ears. *"Get to it!"*

Jagdish caught a passing horse. The animal was frightened, rider lost, but Jagdish took the reins and vaulted into the saddle. He needed the higher vantage point so he could see better, find who needed to be found, and reassert control. Jagdish picked out roiks and risalders and tried to get their attention. That was difficult since they were all up to their elbows in Vokkan blood, but he managed to catch a few.

In the time it took Jagdish to dispense a handful of commands, Ashok had dropped more bodies. An entire paltan of heavy infantry broke apart before him and he reached Yaduvir's personal bodyguard and command staff within minutes of his strange arrival. Jagdish couldn't see exactly what happened beneath Yaduvir's banner, but heads and hands were severed and sent flying high into the air. A moment later, the banner fell.

A moment later, an unfamiliar, panicked sound blew from a Vokkan horn. That must have been their signal to retreat.

Only that surrender must have been insufficient for Ashok, for in the heat of battle that desperate noise might be missed by too many of the combatants, because then Jagdish saw his old friend *climbing onto the back of a rampaging elephant!*

The animal had lost its howdah somewhere along the way, so had no controller. The big bull was simply running along behind the Vokkan lines, crazed, and scaring their horses.

As blood-drenched Ashok effortlessly stood on the back of the bucking creature, he roared with a voice that shook the heavens. *"Men of Vadal! Men of Vokkan! Heed my words! I am Ashok Vadal, bearer of Angruvadal!"* As he lifted the terrifying black steel blade for all to see, the elephant reared up on his hind legs and trumpeted, surely alarmed that someone with a voice worthy of a fanatic's god was upon its back shouting, yet Ashok was not shaken from his place. *"I declare this battle is over."*

The fighting just . . . stopped. All eyes were upon Ashok.

"It's really him," whispered a nearby Vadal warrior with awe.

"Spill no more blood today. If any among you still wish to fight, then your fight will be against me."

No one was foolish enough to accept that challenge.

The bull elephant quit rearing and went back to stomping about in an angry and confused circle.

"This war is done. Depart in peace or not at all. I have spoken."

Ashok leapt off the animal's back and started walking calmly back the way he'd come.

The Vokkan army fearfully parted before him.

Chapter 3

His old friend Jagdish had achieved much since Ashok had last seen him, carrying demon bones into a swamp on a mule train with Gutch. Night had fallen as the two of them sat on the banks of the swiftly moving Martaban. Ashok had listened to Jagdish's tale and had to admit at the end, "I am truly impressed you went from risalder of a gang of criminals, to commanding all the armies of Great House Vadal. I should never have doubted when you told me you would redeem your name. I was certain Harta would have you killed."

"Well, he was sorely tempted! I can't say there weren't a few bumps along the way. I got to spend some time in Cold Stream."

"As warden again?"

"Naw, as a prisoner. I much preferred being the warden!"

The river was wide here and deep enough to easily conceal demons, but Ashok did not sense their foul presence nearby. He still maintained his distrust of water, for it was the home of evil, but this was the only place the two of them could speak freely away from the ears of Jagdish's men.

"Do you think your new Thakoor will heed my warning?"

"Ah, yes, the warning of the man who is responsible for his grandmother cutting her own face off and bringing years of shame and disorder and eventually war to our house?" Jagdish took a drink from his bottle of wine, thought it over, then took another. "Most certainly not. Thakoor Bhadramunda is young, but he is no fool. Now me, on the other hand, the unlikely war hero entrusted by his wise father Harta to save their house in its direst hour, who has resoundingly done so, outwitting not one, but two rival great houses in battle...? Maybe, he'll listen. So I'll do the talking while you stay in the distance, being your menacing criminal self."

It was a good plan. "You seem far more astute in the ways of the courts now, Phontho."

"Not really, but politics is a sport to my new wife, so I've learned a thing or two from her."

Jagdish had grown melancholy as he'd told Ashok of Pakpa's death during childbirth, but he seemed to take great joy in the companionship of her replacement. "That is good. You should seek her insight before you approach your Thakoor."

"Oh, I surely will. Though she's probably going to tell me I'm a fool, having once again established my name, to promptly taint it once more by association with *you*."

Ashok spread his hands apologetically.

Jagdish snorted. "Though what can Vadal's First say now, after the dreaded Black Heart arrived in our house's darkest time of need to turn a battle in our favor? Perhaps that will make them hate you *slightly* less."

Ashok had scrubbed the blood from his body, but not his conscience. He had been carried across the sky by wizards—a most disconcerting journey—in order to keep warriors from killing each other, so they could be better spent fighting demons. Instead, he'd killed or injured over a hundred of them himself in a matter of minutes. Yet he knew that if he'd not acted with such swift and overwhelming brutality, the death toll from allowing the battle to continue would have been far higher. Life had been simpler when such thoughts had never troubled him.

"From above I could see that one army was far bigger than the other. It was an interesting perspective. I did what was necessary."

"Being alive and victorious right now rather than dead or a Vokkan hostage, I'm inclined to agree." Jagdish chuckled. "I thought I had them there, though. It pained me to let Yaduvir walk, but I trust you."

Ashok would not have his efforts be in vain. "You must convince your Thakoor, Jagdish. In Kanok, there were dozens of demons. In the Capitol, there were hundreds. I do not know what manner of hell will rise from beneath Vadal City, but I fear all the seas will empty, as every demon in the world makes its way here."

"You know, this is a lot to take in, Ashok. You gave me all of a few minutes to rejoice I'd won one war, just so you could tell me there's a new, worse one looming. Why Kanok and then the Capitol? If our hometown is this Great City of Man from the olden times as you say, and that thing in Thera's head declares this is that pivotal place where all must be won or all is lost, why not hit Vadal first? If there's a tunnel that crosses all of Lok beneath our feet, why didn't the demons invade from the northern coast instead of the south?"

It was a sound question. Jagdish had always had a head for strategy. "The Fortress folk have an Order of treasure hunters who explore those deep roads. They are called Collectors. I asked the one who has joined my army this same thing. He said that the ancients sealed the north end of the main tunnel with an invisible barrier to keep the demons out long ago. That barrier must still stand, otherwise they could have entered there. The ancients sealed that northern passage after the other continents were lost to the rain of demons."

"Other continents?" Jagdish mulled that over, then took another drink, not knowing what to think of that strange concept. "What are those like, I wonder?"

Ashok shrugged. "Who knows? The collectors say the entire world was once connected by these unseen routes, but they are lost to us now."

"The same way man used to cross the oceans in big boats and had harbors to put them in, like the ruins we saw in Bhadjangal, before it got flooded and turned into the House of Assassins... Our ancestors really got around before the demons wrecked everything, didn't they?"

"The ancients also built cities far beneath the world, protected by these same impenetrable barriers. I have seen one, gone to rot and decay, but still standing, row upon row of buildings grander than anything in the Capitol. I fought and killed a mad god there."

Jagdish looked at the bottle. "I'm going to need more wine."

They had both been busy since they'd last ridden together. "Regardless of what powerful magic the ancients left behind to safeguard their descendants, most of those measures have been used up now. The demons must understand this and that is why they are attacking. It is up to us now."

"I know a bit about those safeguards and shields myself, Ashok. I stood beneath a pillar of fire that shot down from the sky so hot it melted the rocks around us while my beard was not so much as singed." Being a proper warrior, Jagdish could not be outdone by his friend dueling a mad god. "See? You're not the only one who can share tales of seemingly outlandish events."

Jagdish was trying to make light of the situation, but Ashok knew all these events had to be intertwined. "A warrior girl was struck by a bolt from the heavens which enabled her to channel the Voice. Around the same time, a casteless blood-scrubber boy was chosen by an ancestor blade. The only bloodline which was prophesied capable of stopping the demons was nearly eradicated, and now the demons are upon us. For good or ill, this is the end, Jagdish."

"Sadly...I do believe you. It's a terrible failing of mine that I keep believing you—no matter how much trouble it causes me—because you have an annoying tendency to be right. Now it seems all I must do is convince Thakoor Bhadramunda Vadal to trust in the seemingly lunatic tale of the greatest criminal who has ever lived."

"He must also trust the Maharaja."

Jagdish laughed until he wheezed. "Sure! The would-be king who supposedly came to help Vadal, but invaded us instead, and then sent assassins to my wedding to poison our leader...Wait. Are you actually suggesting...?"

Ashok had not yet had the chance to explain his current alliance. "Devedas is on his way here now to fight the demons. He brings with him what is left of the Capitol's forces and has been gathering more along the way. He has also summoned all the Protectors and remaining Inquisitors to meet in Vadal."

"You can't be serious...Damn it. You *are* serious...Devedas sent murderers into my *home*, Ashok."

"I do not think he did. Devedas tried to conquer Vadal, yet he denies sending assassins. He swore to me those were minions of Grand Inquisitor Omand, who has since fled. His location is unknown. I make no excuses for Devedas' actions, but I believe that to be the truth. Condemn Devedas for what he has done after the demons are defeated, for if they are not, your offense—no matter how righteous it may be—will not matter."

It spoke to Jagdish's character that was able to control his anger. "The last time the Capitol said they were coming to help against demons, we ended up with their army strangling us, only this time they promise to be good? Are there any other potential invaders you wish for me to make excuses for?"

"Before leaving the Capitol, Devedas issued a proclamation to every house, asking for them to send warriors here to help repel the demons. Having witnessed firsthand the difference Angruvadal makes against demons, Devedas made a special plea for the bearers of the ancestor blades to come here as well."

Would any of the other bearers actually do so? Ashok didn't know. Even if they respected Devedas, which was doubtful now with the Capitol being gutted, what great house would willingly risk such precious treasures in a distant land?

Jagdish sighed, resigned to his fate. "So, it's merely the legendary criminal who has wronged us and his infamous Sons of the Black Sword, a thousand Fortress maniacs armed with their illegal alchemy, wizards, Protectors, Inquisitors, houses both friend and foe, and even other ancestor blades? Oceans, Ashok, should I tell my new Thakoor that you intend to call Keta's gods down from the sky to fight alongside us too?"

"I have extended the invitation to them. I do not know if they will reply."

Jagdish grimaced, unable to tell if that was one of Ashok's rare attempts at humor or not. "Alright. I promise nothing, but I'll see what I can do."

That was all Ashok could ask. Jagdish was one of the few people in the world Ashok considered a friend, and, more importantly, an honorable man. It seemed time had not changed his nature. "Thank you. With your permission, I would travel with you to Vadal City. I will send the wizards who brought me here back to report."

"That would be for the best. Have them tell that snow weasel Devedas he'd best be prepared to kiss the feet of Thakoor Bhadramunda Vadal to beg forgiveness for all the offense he's given." Jagdish spit on the ground. Someone in the army camp began calling for their phontho, because a good commander's work was never truly over. "Sounds like I'm needed. If you'll excuse me, we'll have to continue piling more onerous details onto my already insurmountable task later."

"It has been good to see you again, brother."

Jagdish stood up with a grunt and limped away on a swollen knee. It was the same leg that Ashok had broken once. "Welcome home, Ashok."

Ashok just shook his head at that and went back to watching the light of Canda reflecting off the river.

"Indeed...Welcome back to Vadal, Ashok who stole its name."

Angruvadal warned Ashok that he was in the presence of an incredible danger.

Glancing over, he saw a dark figure standing on the bank only a few yards away, dressed in a voluminous black cloak, with his face obscured by a hood.

"I stole nothing. That name was given as a replacement for the one which was taken from me."

"Tell yourself whatever you will. This land is where life began for you. This is where it will end. Vadal was where a non-person was born and where a hero will die."

Though Ashok had been alert as always, he hadn't heard the stranger's approach, which suggested he was dealing with a wizard of some sort. Strangest of all, the instincts embedded in his sword offered no suggestions how to counter this potential threat, because none of the previous bearers of either ancestor blade had ever encountered someone—or perhaps *something*—like this.

Most curious.

"Who are you?"

"Do you not recognize me?" The hood turned, and from the shadows beneath was revealed the leering face of the Law. It was the golden mask of the Grand Inquisitor.

"I have met Omand Vokkan. He is middle-aged and gone to softness."

"Your cruel words wound me."

From the voice, this man was in the prime of his life, and even wrapped in robes, Ashok's experienced eye could tell that this stranger carried himself like a fit and experienced combatant. With the Capitol in exile, Devedas had certainly not had a new Grand Inquisitor appointed in the day since Ashok had last seen him. "You are not Omand Vokkan. Name yourself, imposter."

"I am truly he. Only I have been forever changed into something greater than before by immersing myself in the font of all magic."

Ashok sensed no lie. So if this was truly the Grand Inquisitor himself, then this immersion he spoke of was sufficient to make Angruvadal nervous. "What have you become, then?"

"Something greater that you can understand. Though now that I see you in person, Ashok, it appears you too have been turned into something more than you were as well. We are both unique specimens. You have come a long way since I condemned you in a stinking prison cell, casteless fraud."

"Unlike you, my fraud was unwilling." Ashok had been waiting a long time for this meeting. He wasn't even angry. It was more that for the world to go on, some men were so evil it was simply necessary that they die. "Offense has been taken, Grand Inquisitor."

"You dare threaten me? My, you have changed not just in physical capability, but in temperament as well. The old Ashok was subservient. A slave to the Law. An unthinking, witless, tool whose only purpose was to be used as a weapon by his betters."

"I chose to live for something other than the Law." Ashok supposed he had Omand to thank for that, for if he'd not commanded him to serve Thera, Ashok would surely have gone to some miserable purposeless end by now. Except that accidental kindness was not nearly enough to make up for Omand's crimes. "The punishment you meant to destroy me, saved me instead."

"A terrible miscalculation on my part. It would not be the last time I underestimated just how tenaciously the casteless would cling to their meaningless lives. You were useful to me once. I have come to see if you might be of use to me again, or if I should just destroy you and be done with it. Though it appears you were of use to others during that time as well. I suspect you were one of those guided by the Mother of Dawn?"

"She appeared to me at times."

Omand spoke with smug pride. "She is gone now. I destroyed her."

That was unfortunate. Ashok had never understood what Mother Dawn was, or her true motives, but her actions had always provided aid to Thera's rebels. Most of the loyal fanatics who had joined the Sons had found them because of her directions, as somehow she always knew where they would be, long before they decided to go there.

"Then her name will be added to the list of those who will be avenged when I take your life."

"What a long list that must be...I listened to you make your plea to that warrior. Do you wish to know the real reason the demons have chosen to attack us now, after all these centuries? It's because I deceived them into believing the bloodline of Ramrowan had been almost entirely wiped out by the Great Extermination."

"Many of the casteless have survived despite your best efforts."

"The demons do not know that. The casteless served their purpose to me, the same as you did. I would have been able to stop the demons easily by myself if Mother Dawn's treachery had not robbed me of the rest of my birthright."

"What is that?"

"I speak of godhood, Ashok Vadal." Omand raised his gloved hands and curled them into fists before him. "My life's work has been to seize for myself the power of the ancients. I procured only a small part of that inheritance before she tricked me, and the rest has been locked away. The power I hold now is beyond your comprehension, yet it is not limitless as intended. That's why I've come here to examine you instead of simply willing all my potential competitors into oblivion."

Ashok recalled the prophecies of the Fortress monks about the forces who would compete to rule the next age. "So you are the Night Father."

The mask tilted to the side, curious. "I do not know the meaning of this title."

"No matter. You will not be the first god I have killed. I pitied the Dvarapala. I despise you."

The robed figure floated a bit closer. The black-pit eyes of the golden mask studied him. "Ah, I can see now that the Forgotten has taken the Law's weapon and turned it into his own. Magic fills your blood. It infuses your bones. Perhaps you may still be of some use to me after all, Black Heart. Maybe the old gods' contingency plans might even prove sufficient to defeat the armies of hell."

Ashok took one last look at the river, then stood up and placed his hand on the hilt of his sword. He turned toward Omand. "I said offense has been taken. Accept my challenge and make this a duel, or do not accept, and it will be a murder. Either way, I intend to kill you."

An evil laugh echoed from behind the golden mask. "I will

admit that great offense has been given by me against the laws of both man and gods, and I have only just begun to offend."

Lightning quick, Ashok drew and slashed.

The black robes parted like smoke before Angruvadal. The Grand Inquisitor broke into bits and drifted away on the wind.

There was no one there.

Omand's voice came from somewhere far across the water. "You cannot harm me, Ashok. Only a god can kill a god. Yet, why should I slay you now when I can let you and the demons kill each other for me? They are compelled to slaughter. You are compelled to protect. Your battle is inevitable. The winner will be weakened, and then I will have my reckoning."

Ashok sheathed Angruvadal and growled at the darkness. "I will be waiting."

Chapter 4

~~~~~~~~~~~~~~~~~~~~

Amid the ruins of Kanok, Javed Zarger, the Keeper of Names, taught those who had been humbled.

The crowd listened intently as he preached to them of the gods and their great plans for the people of Lok. He told them that he was a priest of the Forgotten, dispatched to share the truths that had been stolen from the people by the Inquisition, which he had once served. Javed warned them that the demonic bloodshed that had consumed this great southern city had only been the beginning of the invasion, that there was still a great and final battle yet to be fought, and that only through the bloodline of Ramrowan might man be spared from extinction. Javed chastised them for their wickedness, for if Great House Makao had not been so eager to exterminate their casteless, then there would have been children of Ramrowan still here to defend them. The people wept and begged forgiveness for offending the gods, but such forgiveness was not within Javed's power to grant. Their only hope was to change their ways and follow the counsel of the gods' chosen from now on.

To be seen by as many eyes as possible, Javed preached while standing atop a plinth in the middle of a vast courtyard. The plinth had once held a statue of a famous Inquisitor, but the locals had recently torn it down after their Thakoor had banished that Order from his lands. The bronze Inquisitor had been replaced by a priest of flesh and bone.

The mob was enthralled by his words. He dragged them along, varying his tales in pitch and intensity as he read their mood and adjusted accordingly. Javed had always had a gift for manipulating the emotions of others. The Inquisition had honed this into a weapon. Now he tried to use that weapon for good instead of evil, not to obscure the Forgotten's wisdom but to share it.

When this sermon was over, the crowd reluctantly dispersed. Experience had taught him those who were ready would understand his words and obey. Others would try to but fail. The rest would fill their hearts with bitterness and deny the truth they'd seen with their own eyes. So be it. He had done his best and could linger here no more.

Javed hopped down from the plinth and walked toward the back of the courtyard, where an ornate palanquin was waiting, guarded by half a paltan of fearsome Makao warriors. The bodyguards knew to part before him and let Javed through, because their master was a frequent and avid listener to Javed's sermons, and had become one of the priest's most ardent students. The Personal Guard might take offense at aiding this criminality, but they knew their place.

Thakoor Venketesh Makao swept open the palanquin's curtain and stepped out into the fresh morning air. "A fine lesson today, Keeper. Must it really be your last among us?"

Javed stopped before the boy ruler of Great House Makao, but he did not kneel. No offense was meant, or taken, because they both understood that they were freemen, bound not by Law, but by gods. "It's difficult for me to abandon the newly converted, but the time has come for all of you to stand on your own. The gods have whispered to me that I'm needed elsewhere."

Venketesh had already tried to talk Javed into staying, offering him wealth and status as a court advisor, but he understood that a priest answered to a master greater than any mortal Thakoor. Venketesh was still a child, yet he possessed great responsibility, and many of the advisors he had relied upon since the untimely death of his father had been killed during the demon attack. When all had seemed lost, Javed had inspired the young leader with new purpose, and no fire of religion burned hotter than that of a recent convert.

It was outlandish to imagine that a Thakoor of a great house had openly embraced illegal religion, yet Venketesh had allowed

Javed to use his house's printing press to mass-produce illegal scriptures, *The Collected Prophecies of the Forgotten's Voice*, and then helped send them out into the world. In defiance of the Capitol, Venketesh had driven the Inquisition from his lands. The members of his court who had protested had been dealt with harshly, for though Venketesh was young, he had proven himself to be incredibly ruthless.

The demons had torn Kanok's heart out. His people had lost their faith in the Law. They had been despondent and defeated. Javed had offered them a new belief to cling to. Like a drowning man, desperate to hold onto anything that floats, the people of Kanok now clung to the gods.

Javed prayed that they would survive without him.

"It has been an honor to preach to you and your people."

"I understand. Know that you will always have the eternal gratitude of Great House Makao. You saved my life and helped save my house."

"I merely did what the gods wanted me to do. They allowed me to wield a black sword for a time, and it was their will that I gave that sword up. I was called to be the Keeper of Names, not a bearer."

"You let go of an honor that no one has ever willingly given up before, but I don't speak only of you taking up Maktalvar and slaying demons with it, Keeper, but what you did in the days afterward. The demons killed thousands. Entire districts burned. My family mansion, which had stood for centuries, was swallowed by the ground! Our monuments toppled. My people despaired, until your words set a fire of religion in their hearts. In *my* heart. We do not wallow in pity for the past but look to the future. For that, you have my thanks."

Javed didn't know if he had done these people a favor or not, because the path of the faithful was a difficult one, and it was a path they would have to tread without him. "You'll still face many challenges. The Law hates the truth."

"It doesn't matter who the Law hates, but what the gods demand. You taught me that, Keeper. We are armed with your holy books. Carry your holy message to the rest of the world. When the great and final testing of man is near, Makao will serve."

Javed left Kanok.

Chapter 5

Hidden in the tall grass, the tiger waited and watched.

The gods had blessed Javed with an abundance of demon bone in Kanok, because in the brief moment they had allowed him to bear one of their sanctified black-steel blades he had harvested enough demon to manifest and maintain the tiger pattern a thousand times over. The gods would not have given him such a bounteous gift if they'd not intended for him to use it up in their service.

The tiger form was quick, but more importantly, could move unseen from town to town, even while Inquisitors relentlessly searched the countryside for the troublesome priest who had been spreading illegal mass-printed scriptures from the liberated press of Kanok. By day Javed ran and by night he preached to the secret faithful and anyone else who would heed his words. By the time the Law learned of his presence in a specific place and came looking for him, he had already moved on to the next location.

He went without sleep for days at a time. Sleep brought him no rest, just time for bad dreams and regret. Javed was sustained by magic, faith, and the tearful thanks of the believers he visited. Run and preach and run and preach, Javed had repeated that process for weeks by the time he had been informed that the Sons of the Black Sword had been seen openly marching north from the Capitol, flying the banner of the red hook and black sword.

It was a sign.

The gods didn't speak to Javed directly, for he was but a priest, not a prophet. Yet he knew that his place was among the Sons of the Black Sword. The end of the age was upon them. The last decisive battle was at hand. The prophecy said the Voice would have need of her Keeper of Names, for the priest was one of the six whose presence was required at the final reckoning. Thera surely hated him still, and it was likely she would have him killed on sight—and rightfully so—but that was a risk he would have to take. Javed would present himself before Thera for judgment and the Forgotten's will would be done. If she executed him, then that meant his duty was fulfilled, and at last he could rest.

Javed had been pursuing the Sons ever since.

The tiger form was swift, and could cover an incredible amount of ground. After following their trail for several days, he finally caught up to the Sons in the forests of southern Vadal.

It was odd, seeing the forces of the Law setting up camp alongside the rebellious followers of the gods. The two armies should have been mortal enemies, but here they were, cooperating as if the Law hadn't been brutally silencing the faithful for centuries. Javed knew that obligation well, for Witch Hunter Javed had slit a multitude of faithful throats.

But now Protectors and Inquisitors were bedding down only a few hundred yards from where the brazenly religious were saying their prayers out loud. *What was going on here?* Javed had heard rumors about a demon attack on the Capitol, and he had seen the columns of refugees proving that at least some of the tales were true. Believer and persecutor—Javed had been both—the two groups that inhabited this camp must have hated each other as much as Javed hated himself, but fear had united them against a greater menace.

It was a miracle that the gods could even use demons to further their great work.

After spotting the banner he searched for, the tiger stalked through the undergrowth unseen. Deer sensed him and fled. The prey animals were as nervous as Javed was, for in a moment he'd present himself to the prophet Thera, and then she would do with him as she wished. Service, exile, or death, regardless of her decision there would be no protest from his lips.

The Sons had posted many guards, and though they were

extremely wary, they were no match for the tiger's stealth, so Javed slipped between them easily.

Near Thera's tent, he paused, feeling as if he was being watched.

"I told you all I sensed magic coming. If that cat's natural, I'm the Chief Judge," a man whispered from farther inside the camp. There was a metallic *click* as a Fortress rod was cocked and the man shouted, "Stop where you are, shape-shifter, or I'll blow a hole in you big enough to watch the sunrise through."

Four wizards who had been waiting in the space between worlds appeared all around Javed, with bits of demon already clutched in their fists, ready to immolate him.

It was good to see that Thera had learned her lesson since he had captured her, and improved her security. The tiger held perfectly still.

"Thanks for the warning, Master Gutch, but we've been tracking him too," a young female wizard said, before addressing the intruder with authority. "Nobody gets close to the prophet without us knowing. Show your real face so we can see if we've caught us an outsider assassin, or if your master is Devedas and he has violated our agreement to not spy on the Sons."

"Either way he answers I should just shoot him and be done with it. But you heard the wizard, tiger. Undo your spell."

Javed let the pattern fade and melted back into his true form. Slowly, he rose from a crouch and spread his open hands wide to show he had no weapon or magic ready. He must have been quite the sight, with his clothing little better than filthy rags, his hair and beard long and unkempt, and his body coated in dirt from the harsh journey.

The man with the Fortress weapon walked out into the forest a bit to see better. He was huge and rotund, and dressed in the finest of robes and enough gold chains and rings to suit a banker, but the deadly rod he had pointed at Javed's chest never wavered as he got closer. There were several workers behind him, all armed with rods or spears. If he did anything to provoke him, he'd be dead in the span of a few heartbeats, for even a tiger couldn't outrun a bullet.

"From the looks of this scrubby miscreant I'd say we caught a beggar, but beggars don't carry ten pounds of demon bone in their packs. Take that off and throw it on the ground."

So the big man could sense magic. "I'd rather not," Javed

stated calmly. "There are things in this bag far more precious than demon bone and I'd hate to damage them."

"Shows what you know, stranger. Going rate per pound, very few things are worth more bank notes than demon bone. Well, at least not yet taking into account the adjustment in cost given the rapid increase in supply as a result of Ashok killing so damned many of the things in the Capitol, but we're not here to talk economics." He aimed the rod at Javed's face and his voice went cold. "I said drop the pack."

What a strange man. "This pack contains a collection of the gods' holy scriptures, compiled by me as commanded by Mother Dawn. Their words are far more precious than anything that can be bought with mere bank notes."

That was when the wizard girl recognized him. "You!"

"You know this fool, Laxmi?"

"I do." And she seemed even more prepared to strike him down with her magic as she said that.

"It's Keeper Javed." One of the other wizards remembered him as well. "He assisted Keeper Keta."

That wizard looked somewhat familiar to Javed, and then he realized the last time they'd met he'd been no mighty magic user, but rather a drooling simpleton, capable of nothing more complex than mucking out the horse stalls.

"I see that the slaves freed from the House of Assassins have finally reclaimed their minds from the fog. It is good that the Forgotten has healed you."

"We've been truly blessed," that wizard responded.

"Enough!" Laxmi shouted. "Not another word out of you, murderer."

Javed nodded politely. At least one of the wizards knew who he *really* was, or rather had been.

"I'm going to get Thera. Don't listen to the honeyed words that come from this filth. He's a killer and a liar. If he tries to talk before I return, shoot him, stab him, and burn him to ash." Laxmi ran off between the trees.

"Oh, well now I'm really curious!" Gutch shouted after her, "You can't leave me in suspense like that, girl." He turned back to Javed. "Can you believe that? That's downright unfair to establish such an air of mystery without any resolution. So who are you now?"

"Laxmi said—"

Gutch cut that wizard off. "Oh, this intruder can go ahead and talk freely to me if he wants. Laxmi's *your* boss. She's not the boss of me. I'm an independent associate of the Sons, bit outside the old chain of command, you know."

But as directed by the prophet's maid, Javed said nothing.

"Alright then, I suppose the threat of gruesome fiery death at the hands of angry wizards will cause a man to bite his tongue. Not me. I'm a dedicated conversationalist even in the most tumultuous of situations. But anyways, give me that pack so I may search it for danger or valuables." Gutch let the end of his Fortress rod swing downward menacingly. "Or I'll shoot your cock off. I won't ask again."

Javed took the strap off his shoulder and tossed the pack to Gutch, who caught it with one hand. He backed away, should Javed try anything foolhardy, before checking inside.

"Well, I'll be... This book's bound in real demon hide. Is that Keta's book? The one he was always writing casteless names in?"

Javed had been one of the few entrusted with the location where Keta would hide the genealogy should the Creator's Cove ever be threatened. Javed had retrieved the sacred book during his traveling ministry and kept it safe. If Thera killed him tonight, then at least the precious book would be placed in worthy hands of her choosing, and not left to rot away, hidden in a hole in the rock.

"I saw Keta scribble in this thing whenever we found casteless outcasts hiding in the woods, and then when we met those who ran the barges of the Nansakar he interviewed them about who their fathers and grandfathers were and wrote the answers in here. A curious little man... I wonder what its purpose is?"

For generations the Keepers before him had recorded births and traced lineages with these sacred tomes. As those Keepers had found direct descendants of Ramrowan in distant houses, they had guided those heirs to new homes, to take wives and make sure Ramrowan's line would never die out. It was said even Mother Dawn herself had used the book to move her children about Lok in order to keep that blessed bloodline strong. But Javed said nothing.

A few minutes later, a group of people approached through the forest. Since it was growing dark, some of them were carrying torches. Thera Vane was in the lead, hood up, eyes cold.

She was a beautiful and strong daughter of the warrior caste.

When he had first begun spying on her band he had thought Thera was just another false prophet, a charlatan like all the others who had come before her, but she was so much more than that. This was the vessel chosen by the gods to bear their holy Voice. He went to his knees and bowed his head.

"Javed Zarger." The fury was apparent in her voice.

"Hello, Prophet."

"Why are you here?"

"I've come to serve you."

He knew most of the Sons behind her. These men had considered him family once. He had broken bread with them. He'd tended their loved ones while they were sick. He had even officiated the wedding ceremony of one of them. In this moment of what should have been joyous reunion, there was obvious confusion on their faces about their prophet's angry reaction to their beloved priest's return.

The Inquisition had taught him how to read the emotions of a crowd, in order to better manipulate them. Javed realized that she'd not yet told the Sons of his transgressions. For whatever reason, she had spared his name from ridicule and hate. They didn't know him as Javed the traitorous witch hunter, but as Javed the priest and friend. Her mercy toward his reputation shouldn't have mattered so much to him, but for some reason, it did.

"I thought you were dead in Kanok, until your books started showing up everywhere."

"Please forgive me for my absence, Prophet. I continued to serve the Forgotten as best as I could. While we were separated I recorded all the words of Keta and Ratul, and then I sent them out into the world."

"I bet that flood of propaganda's irritated some Inquisitors," Gutch quipped, but Thera glared at him, and the big man wisely closed his mouth. Outside the chain of command or not, Thera was in charge here, and she was clearly very angry.

"There are no more Inquisitors in Kanok. I saw to that. Thakoor Venketesh has become a true and faithful servant of the gods. It's a safe haven now for the faithful, where the religious may pray openly and not be punished for it."

"That's soon to be the Law everywhere now. I've made a deal with Maharaja Devedas: the Sons' help for the Law's clemency. Religion is no longer illegal in any house."

That couldn't be. "The Law has changed?"

"Only because I held its feet to the fire."

"It's a miracle!" Javed cried.

Thera looked around and found that most of her people were agreeing with that. "The ink's still wet. Don't get your hopes up. We're on our way to Vadal City to make sure the deal sticks."

Truly, to accomplish so much in so little time, the gods had chosen their servants well. "For the faithful to come so far is a gift. I can die happy."

"As long as you die," Thera snapped.

The Sons shared confused glances over that, baffled by their' prophet's unexpected wrath toward their beloved priest, and who could blame them? If she'd spared his name, they had no idea of his crimes.

"Wait!" Javed shouted. "She's not wrong. I have come to beg for forgiveness, for I do not deny that I deserve death for my sins."

"Do you really think a confession will help you now?" Thera demanded.

"I don't care about what happens to me, but if you're going to execute me in front of the Sons, my confession will help *you.* If you kill me and they can't discern the reason, it'll shake their faith. These men have followed you through so much, Thera, not just because they've heard the Voice, but because of who you've shown yourself to be to them. They trust you with their lives. Don't throw that away over scum like me! Let them know who I really am, so if you decide to spill my blood on the ground, they'll know it was a righteous execution."

"What's he talking about?" asked Ongud, the cavalry officer. "Why would you kill one of our priests?"

"Javed's a—" Then Thera stopped herself from revealing his true nature in front of so many witnesses. "No... I'll not let you manipulate me again, Javed. You'll not get some public spectacle to crush their spirits. Laxmi, keep that demon ready to strike him down and remain here. The rest of you return to camp. *Now.*"

The Sons were confused, but obediently did as they were told, and began walking away, with many glances sent back over their shoulders.

Another of Thera's men approached, having arrived late, surely curious what all the commotion was about. Javed recognized Toramana, once chieftain of the fearsome swamp folk who had given the Sons shelter through the winter, and now one of Thera's commanders. The savage was a proud man, a true believer, a strong leader, and a loving father.

And Javed had murdered one of his sons in cold blood.

Surely the gods had brought Toramana here to make Javed fully appreciate the suffering he had caused.

"What's going on?" Toramana asked when he saw Javed there on his knees. "The priest returns?"

Thera glanced back and grimaced when she saw it was the chief. "Saltwater . . . You at least deserve the truth."

"I don't understand. The new fat priest told us Javed took up a black-steel blade in the name of the Forgotten and fought demons with it. Why are we not celebrating?"

"A crime's been done, and I'm not talking about the Law."

Gutch also remained there and sat his bulk on a fallen tree, giving no indication that he intended to go anywhere. Thera looked toward him and frowned.

"Oh, don't mind the presence of little old me, Lady Vane. I don't believe in priests or any of that godly nonsense. I'm just here to supply you with more guns."

"Fine. If Javed tries anything, please shoot him dead."

Gutch looked toward Laxmi. "It appears our young wizard friend there is practically seething with murderous intent, and is likely faster than I am, but I'll gladly blast him after she sets him on fire or whatever other violence it is she intends."

When it was just the five of them, Thera turned back to her ragged prisoner. "You wanted to make a confession?" She pointed at Toramana. "Make your confession to him. The Chief can decide how you die."

Toramana had ruled a village far from civilization. In the swamp, he had been the Law. It wasn't the first time he'd decided an offender's fate, but he had clearly not been expecting to do so tonight. "You know I live to serve, Prophet, but what's this all about?"

There would be no hiding from what he'd done, so Javed spoke clearly. "Great offense has been given, Chief. I was a senior witch hunter, sent to spy on the rebellion. I was your secret enemy until the Mother of Dawn appeared to me in the desert and ordered me to repair the damage I'd caused. Since then I have been true and faithful, but before that conversion, I did many terrible things to your people."

Toramana stared at Javed, speechless.

"I spent my life hunting the faithful and killing them whenever possible. I committed acts of torture, arson, and a great many assassinations on behalf of the Law. Then I was sent to infiltrate this rebellion by Grand Inquisitor Omand. I was told to become trusted and indispensable. By killing the assassins who were hunting the faithful in the snow, I became a hero to the survivors. That was calculated. I served the Creator's Cove, doing whatever needed doing, tirelessly working so the people would come to trust me and rely on me. When the Grand Inquisitor needed the rebellion to be quiet for a time, I poisoned the Cove's water supply to keep everyone sick."

"That plague was your doing as well?" Thera asked, surprised.

Javed nodded. "The Voice showing you how to heal them was my first indication that you might be something more than a fraud. All witch hunters are masters of poisons. That was a potent one."

"Many people died before Thera cured them, though," Toramana spat. "You are a monster!"

"Yes. And I felt nothing as I carried the bodies of those I'd murdered onto the pyres I built using the wood I gathered because the gods had not yet taught me the pains of guilt or shame. I did my obligation, unquestioningly. Then I lied to Keta in order to become his friend, so he would trust me and name me a priest, all while I reported to the Inquisition your every move in secret via magic. These communications were discovered once, which is why I murdered Parth and Rawal."

"My son..." Toramana blinked a few times, and then reached for the axe at his belt.

Thera placed one gentle hand on Toramana's arm and shook her head. "Let him finish the story first, Chief, so we can finally have the whole truth."

"He stuffed his body in a hole." Toramana was blinking rapidly, but he did not draw the axe yet. "That was my boy."

It was difficult to see such profound sadness on a man's face, but Javed met Toramana's gaze. "I make no excuse. My obligation was an evil one. I began to understand how wrong I had been when I heard the Voice for the first time myself. Then at the battle of the aqueduct, the Grand Inquisitor decided that the rebellion was no longer of use to him, so my Order captured Thera in the hopes that we would be able to rip the Voice from her head and get some use from it. I was transporting her to the Capitol to be interrogated and then dissected when Mother Dawn appeared to me in her giant many-armed form and commanded that I help the prophet instead."

"The Mother has appeared to many of us." Toramana's eyes were filled with tears. "She told my people to help the prophet too. You are not special!"

"You are right, there's nothing special about me. Your people were chosen because you pleased the gods with your courage and will to survive. I was chosen because I was all they had left. I was told they still needed a priest to carry on their work, and with wise Keta dead, I, a worm, lower than fish, would have to do. I know now what I have done is wrong. I've been trying to make amends ever since."

"It's not enough."

"I doubt it will ever be enough, and I will spend eternity suffering for my evil. I have seen hell once before. Not the ocean. That is a false hell. I speak of Naraka, endless torment for those who give offense to the gods. That's likely where I am going now."

Toramana stalked toward him, pulling out his axe. "Are there no more crimes? Is that the end of your story, then?"

"It is. I have changed. I am a true believer in the gods, so I accept whatever fate you bestow on me, Prophet."

"Don't look at me," Thera said. "This is Toramana's decision now."

What other decision could a grieving father make concerning the murderer of his son? Javed bowed his head. He would meet his end with resigned acceptance.

"I thought a tiger killed my boy. That's an honorable death for a hunter. Tigers are dangerous foes. They're kings of the forest. Witch hunters can take the shape of tigers, but they are only kings of lies. Look at me. *Look at me.*"

Javed did so. The chief towered over him, axe at his shoulder.

"Wait!" A thin man in orange robes was running toward them through the forest. "You must not kill him!" He tripped over a root and fell hard, but quickly got back up and staggered in their direction, desperate. "You need him! The priest needs to be alive!"

"Your Fortress monk seems rather riled up," Gutch remarked nonchalantly.

"Hold, Chief," Thera cautioned, and it was a testament to the barbarian's faith that he didn't simply split Javed's skull anyway. "What is it, Lama Taksha?"

The stranger was casteless thin and had a shaved head except for an odd topknot of hair. He was out of breath from his run and had scraped his forehead when he'd fallen. Heedless of the blood dripping into his eye he asked, "This is your Keeper of Names?"

"The fake one," Thera said. "Keta was the real Keeper."

"But Ram Ashok says Keta is dead. If this one was appointed by Keta, then he *is* the Keeper of Names." He wiped the blood away with the back of his hand. "You must not kill him! The priest must be present at the end or else."

"Or else what?" Laxmi asked. It was plain the wizard girl really wanted to kill him, and Javed suspected it was because she was afraid of him. "Why do you need this assassin?"

"I don't know, but this is on all the writings. Every prophecy embedded in metal. Every Guru agrees the six can all die there, or afterward, for by those who live in their vision will the next age be shaped, but they must *all* be present. Guru Dondrub thinks that if all the pieces are not there, then the demons will win and mankind will be hunted to death soon after."

"What about you?" Thera demanded. "You're some kind of priest. You take the book."

"The calling is different. I'm of the workshop, servitors of mighty Ramrowan's legacy, preparers of the Avatara's return. I'm no Keeper of Names. There's only one Keeper of Names at a time. Just as there is only one Voice. Or one Forgotten's Warrior, or the King, or the Mask. And the last Keeper chooses his successor. Please, you must believe me. We are almost at the Great City of Man where all will be decided."

"The Voice pronounced the same thing once," Javed recalled. "Check the Testimony of Ratul. It was the third prophecy of Thera's that he recorded."

Toramana kicked Javed in the stomach so hard it curled his body around the boot, and he collapsed, retching and heaving.

"Evil will be silent when the faithful talk, Witch Hunter. Do you really expect us to believe the words you wrote, that conveniently say we're supposed to let you live?"

Thera swore under her breath, before saying, "Sadly, the

bastard's not lying. I know the one he's talking about. It's from the same manifestation that declared the Voice has to be sacrificed at the end... Damn it."

The foreigner begged, "The danger is too great, Voice. Gods old and new have spoken. You must spare this Keeper. If you take your revenge now on him, the demons triumph. All our homes, gone. All our temples, razed. All our kin, dead. In your land and then in mine. Lost forever."

Javed could tell that Thera was torn. She herself was not a convert. She was a slave. Yet she knew her master was real, and though the Voice's proclamations could be confusing, they were never, ever wrong.

"Oceans." Thera took a deep breath, held it for a long time, and then exhaled angrily.

"No..." Toramana said slowly.

"We can't risk it. We've got to spare him for now, Chief."

"After what he confessed, you expect me to *let him live*?" Toramana was livid. "He killed my boy, Thera!"

"And a great many others, and I tended them and tried to comfort them as they withered away, crying tears of blood from what I thought was a natural plague, not some witch hunter trick. And he'll pay for all of them soon enough. Their blood cries from the ground for vengeance, Toramana! I want him dead too, but we're not far from Vadal City, and the demons won't be far behind."

"You said it was my decision to make!"

"I did..." She eyed the axe in his hand, then slowly nodded. "And it still is... Now I'm asking you to make the best decision for our people. We're both leaders. You know it's not about our desires, but what our people need. Let Javed live for now. Then after the last battle, he's all yours."

Wincing against the pain—Toramana was an incredibly strong man and had a kick like a horse—Javed struggled back to his knees and managed to gasp, "I'll do whatever you want. Imprison me and kill me when your tasks are done, as the Forgotten wills it."

Toramana paced back and forth, before growling at him. "The Keeper's obligation is to write down the prophecies and put the names in his book. What hand do you use to write with?"

"My right."

"Hold out your left."

Javed did so without hesitation.

"Wait!"

But the chief was done listening to Thera, and his axe was *very* sharp.

Javed's left hand went spinning off into the forest. Blood spurted from the stump.

"Oceans!" Gutch jumped from his log.

The pain was beyond comprehension, yet Javed did not scream. He didn't so much as cry out. He simply brought the stump close to his chest and tried to squeeze shut the severed artery with his other hand.

"Take the rest of my limbs if you need them," he gasped. "It's a small price to pay to prove I'm telling the truth."

"The one limb will do ... *for now*." Toramana simply turned and walked away.

Gutch shook his head in wonder. "No wonder they banned religion. You people are insane."

The world was getting very dark, but in his heart, Javed praised the Forgotten. He had come here believing his life would be spared, and it had been, because his work was not yet done.

"Looks like that hurts," Thera told Javed, then she snapped at the foreigner, "Hurry and help me tie this off before the gods are out another prophecy."

"Pinch the big bleeder," the wizard girl said completely without pity as the demon bone in her hand glowed brighter. "I'll cauterize the rest."

Javed passed out ... until the fire woke him back up.

Chapter 6

~~~~~~~~~~~~~~

Rada had never wanted to rule anything. Even the idea of someday assuming her father's obligation as head of the Order of Archivists hadn't been something she'd dreamed about, even though that was her likely fate, and there was no one better suited for the responsibility. She'd been content with her books. Life had been simple. She'd always believed it was better to leave leadership in the hands of those who were inclined for such endeavors, dedicated members of the first caste who had been raised to command.

Oh how naïve she had been.

It turned out those who sought after power were the absolute worst at letting them have any. Rada had not asked for this, but she was going to do her best to fix the excesses of those who'd come before her.

"With these judges as my witness, I swear that if those food supplies aren't delivered by next week as obligated, I'll have you branded a scoundrel and publicly flogged as we auction off all your property as restitution for the damages caused by your fraud."

As expected, the merchant bowed and scraped and made excuses. "I didn't intend to deceive you, Maharani. It's just that the latest caravan was delayed and—"

"And nothing." Rada had already investigated and knew that there was no *delay*. Because the Capitol's grand bazaar had been destroyed by demons, this merchant had thought it would be more profitable for his caravans to divert to Karoon first instead. The arbiters this merchant usually bribed to sabotage his competition had been killed by demons; unfortunately for him, the Capitol wasn't entirely abandoned, and she still had people to feed. "You signed a legally binding contract. The Law did not cease to exist when demons wounded it, and the work of the Capitol Orders must continue. They can't do that if they're hungry. I don't care if you have to walk to Uttara and pick the beans yourself, you will bring the Capitol what you have promised, or else."

"It will be done, Maharani Radamantha."

"Good. Go." She waved her hands at the merchant like she was shooing off an unwanted pest. Warriors took the merchant by the arm and escorted him from the room. "Next."

"That's the last item for this morning," the court scribe informed her.

"Oh, thank goodness. It seems there's no end to our problems."

"There are another ten petitions waiting to be heard after lunch, though."

Rada sighed, because of course there were.

Though she was ostensibly running the government in her husband's absence, Rada sat behind a humble wooden table in a simple wooden chair, not a throne. Instead of meeting in the legendary Chamber of Argument in the once glorious Capitol, her court in exile was held in a spare room of the Astronomers' Order in the wilderness north of Mount Metoro. Seated to her right and left were the few remaining judges who'd survived the demon attack and been willing to continue serving.

Yet the work had to go on.

"Thank you for your time, honorable judges. We shall reconvene in a few hours." Rada rose, eager to escape the stuffy meeting room. She had letters to write, reports from the various Orders to read, and somehow she hoped to find the time to continue studying the select works she'd brought over from the Capitol Library, hoping to find more tidbits of information that might aid Devedas in his preparations against the demons.

Except one of the judges intercepted her before she could get out the door. "May I have a moment of your time, Maharani?"

Chiranjeet Zarger was a dignified old man. Scholarly by nature, he had been a regular patron at the Library during her time there, which inclined Rada to like him. His decision to remain here, maintaining the Law, rather than retreating to the safety of his house like so many other men of his rank and status had done after the fall of the Capitol, made her respect him even more.

"What is it, Judge Chiranjeet?"

"First, I must admit that I was a bit apprehensive when our new Maharaja left a librarian to oversee his entire government while he was away, but I have been pleased by how well you have done. I should not have been surprised, as I respect your father greatly, and he has always struck me as a man of keen intellect and character. He clearly raised you well, as you have governed with meticulous wisdom and a surprising amount of care."

"I just threatened to have a merchant whipped over beans."

"The first caste is required to deal with unsavory things at times." Chiranjeet glanced around the room. "On that note, I'd like to take a moment to discuss Maharaja Devedas' rather lenient tax policy with you."

Rada died inside, because nobody sane wanted to listen to discussions about the details of taxation. She'd woken up feeling ill and unrested and didn't think her nerves could withstand a topic of such profound boredom. "My husband needs the houses' warriors right now more than he needs their taxes, and it's not as if we have any extra Protectors to send to collect if they decide not to pay, but I'd be happy to schedule a meeting to discuss the details with you later. I'm really rather busy right now."

Except it appeared that the crafty old judge had simply been stalling until the other courtly types had left, and only Rada and her Garo bodyguards remained. "I honestly don't care about that at all. I just require privacy to speak with you about something of a more sensitive nature."

Rada nodded toward her warriors. "These are trustworthy men, handpicked by Devedas. Anything you can say in front of me, you can say in front of them."

"Very well. It concerns Historian Vikram Akershan and the artifact of black steel he entrusted you with."

That piqued Rada's interest, as she kept the mysterious Asura's Mirror with her wherever she went, but very few people knew it existed. "What do you know of it?"

"I served on a select council of judges and high-ranking members of the scholarly Orders, including the Historians, the Astronomers who are now our hosts, and your own Order, the

Archivists. That is how I became acquainted with your father, who also served on this council. Our purpose was to oversee those Orders'—shall we say—more discreet duties."

"I've never heard of this council."

"Very few have, and it was kept that way on purpose. It is an obligation rooted in old tradition which has existed since the founding of the Law."

"Who chaired it?"

"The Chief Judge himself."

That was odd. If a man of such immense status controlled it, belonging to such a council would bring its members great prestige and notoriety in the Capitol. Surely, Rada—even with her distaste for all things political—would have heard of it growing up, especially if her father was a member.

"All of the various organizations that fell under the Chief Judge's responsibilities now report to the Maharaja, or they were dissolved."

The crafty old judge smiled. "We still exist, though we may have neglected to inform the Maharaja of this fact because his rise to power was rather sudden. Even the Grand Inquisitor did not know about us. Despite that secrecy, several of our members still had to flee the Capitol during Omand's purge."

Rada nodded, for her family had been among those, and she still did not know if they'd gotten away or not. "This is unfortunate."

"Worse, an unlucky few of us died atop the Inquisition's foul tower. Those of our council who remained felt it was prudent to observe the Maharaja for a time in order to understand his nature first, to see what manner of man he was. Sadly, he did not get to reign for long before the demons interrupted this process."

"I'll tell you what manner of man Devedas is: He is the best of you. So, you approach me now instead?"

"We debated how to proceed. The majority felt it was prudent to speak with you, but only after I assured the others that you were no tyrant who would abuse our knowledge for evil. Please, do not make me a liar."

Rada didn't know if she should take offense or not. With so many tumultuous events in such a short period of time, who could blame these men for being cautious? There had been nothing but chaos since their leader had been assassinated on the steps of the chamber. She could not fault them when she herself had spent months hiding from the Inquisition with her Protector turned dear friend, Karno.

At times Rada missed those simple days. "So what are these discreet duties of the scholarly Orders, and what does that have to do with the mirror?"

"The mirror's former caretaker, Vikram Akershan, is part of our council, Maharani."

"Last I heard he was running from the Inquisition. Vikram is most likely dead."

"I assure you he is not. He's a wily one. He was a noteworthy warrior once, before he was promoted to the first caste due to his intellect. In fact, Vikram has recently returned to his estate, which is not far from here."

Rada knew it well, for that was one of the many places she'd hidden from Inquisitors and bounty hunters. It was good to hear that old Vikram had survived, even if he had done so by shoving his secret obligation off on her. But to be fair, she'd had reliable Karno by her side to keep her safe and Vikram had not. "I look forward to seeing him, and I hope his family is well."

"They are, and I assure you he wishes the same for yours. I will send for Vikram. As for the purpose of our council, it is better to show you than to try and explain it. Would you please meet us at the main observatory at midnight tonight?"

Though she'd been a guest in their holdings for weeks, Rada had been far too busy to become acquainted with any of the Astronomers, as they were an odd, secretive bunch. "Are we going to gaze at the stars?"

"There is far more up there than just stars, Maharani. Let me demonstrate to you the true purpose why our Orders were formed to begin with."

Chapter 7

The government in exile had come to this place because it was not too far from the Capitol but was far more secluded and defensible. Only a token force of warriors remained in the Capitol itself to guard the priceless treasures kept there from opportunistic bandits, while the remaining first caste had gone to the other side of Mount Metoro, where supposedly the ground was too hard for demons to burrow beneath.

The Order of Astronomers was headquartered in a small town in the desert whose only real industry was to stare at the sky. It was usually a quiet, sleepy place, but was now overflowing with officials from all the other Orders who were still trying to fulfill their obligations. Estates that had once held a single family were bursting at the seams housing refugees from the Capitol. High-status arbiters were living in homes meant for workers, and those workers had gotten shoved into the barracks that had up until recently housed casteless.

Above all that crowded restless mess, built where the mountainside shielded it from the polluting lights of the Capitol, was the Observatory. It was an edifice that was as sacred to the Astronomers as the Great Library was to Rada's Archivists, and the Capitol Museum was to the Historians. But those places were open to anyone of sufficient status to come and study. The Observatory, on the other hand, was exceedingly private, for the

Astronomers were a peculiar and insular Order, and outsiders were forbidden. The only extra funding they ever asked for was to buy more Zarger glass to be used in their telescopes. For the most part, the Astronomers were overlooked and ignored in the bustle of Capitol politics. Unimportant, because their only obligation was to look at stars. What was the point of that?

Rada was about to find out.

Chiranjeet had met her at the main gates to let Rada and her escort in. At Devedas' insistence, she rarely went anywhere without at least a dozen guards in tow. All of them put together were no Karno, but they were good soldiers obligated from Vassal House Garo, and so loyal to her husband that they'd rather die than allow any harm to befall her.

The judge led them through a courtyard toward the Observatory itself, which was an imposing sandstone edifice with a great dome atop it. It had once been as finely decorated as any structure in the Capitol, but the harsh desert wind had worn the carvings down over time until all that remained were blobs that had once represented constellations. It seemed the Astronomers were too preoccupied looking upward to care much about their surroundings at ground level.

"We are on a tight schedule, but as we walk allow me to explain that this is the third observatory that has been constructed on this spot since the beginning of the Age of Law, with each one being larger and more advanced than its predecessor. As you can see—"

"I mean no offense, Judge, as normally I would find this all very educational, but it is very late, and I'm very tired." Rada had been cursed with a weariness lately that seemed beyond even what running an entire government should cause. Every Order of the Capitol clamored for her attention, but all she wanted to do was nap. The inability to do so had left her grumpy. "I've come to learn about the Chief Judge's private council, not to take the Historian's tour."

"Of course, Maharani. Right this way. Though your guards must wait outside."

"By the command of Maharaja Devedas, that's not going to happen," said the nearest Garo, a proud risalder by the name of Kumudesh. He'd been one of the men who'd fought to save her from the demon in the Library, and his left arm was still in a sling from the wounds he'd taken that awful day.

The judge ignored the warrior and spoke to Rada as if the lesser caste wasn't there. "The matters we are about to discuss are beyond the capability of the uneducated to comprehend. This knowledge has been kept secret from the overwhelming majority of the First and shared only with a select few declared trustworthy by the Chief Judge himself. This has been the tradition since the dawn of the Law."

"The Chief Judge still got murdered by a fish-eater with Fortress alchemy, so that's not the compelling argument you think it is," the warrior said. "Where she goes, we go."

Rada was in no mood for pretentious foolishness. "Risalder Kumudesh."

"Yes, Maharani?"

"Pick three men who can keep a secret. They will accompany me. The rest will stay here and guard the doors."

"As you wish." Kumudesh pointed at two of his soldiers. "You're with me."

Chastised, Chiranjeet opened the door. "Forgive my impertinence, Maharani. Your reputation for respecting the other castes is well known. I am elderly and forget that tradition has been trampled by recent circumstances... Welcome to the Observatory, honored guests."

Most of the interior was taken up by one exceedingly large room, but it was hard to tell just how big it was because it was so dim the opposite end could not be seen. The only illumination came from a handful of scattered candles. In the center of the space was a marvelous contraption of steel and brass. Complex and gigantic, the telescope appeared to be moved about the room by giant gears, controlled by teams of Astronomers pulling upon big levers. There were also hundreds of smaller levers mounted upon plates along the telescope's sides, probably to provide much finer adjustments while aiming the device. The huge tube was pointed upward through the dome, which appeared to be made of movable panels. There were more Astronomers working up there, tied to scaffolding by ropes. Rada was unused to seeing members of the first caste doing so much manual labor, but she supposed it wasn't that different from her people stacking books. Either Order would rather die than let mere workers handle such sensitive things.

"Behold, the pride of the Astronomers' Order. This is the finest telescope of this age. It is said the ancients had devices ten thousand times greater than this, but the knowledge of how to build such things has been lost to us."

"As so much has. Still, this looks impressive," Rada said, even though she knew very little about such things. Her knowledge of using glass to aid vision was limited to the kind she wore on her face.

As her eyes adjusted to the dim light, she saw that upon the walls were thousands of drawings of constellations. These appeared to be very complicated maps of the sky. There were desks for scribes, and shelves full of paper with what had to be generations worth of observations recorded upon them. There was a large wooden cabinet on one wall, inside of which were many clicking gears and a swinging pendulum, and atop that cabinet was the largest clock she'd ever seen. Rada was surprised to see that this particular clock had three hands for measuring time, which was most impressive, as the finer ones sold in the Grand Bazaar of the Capitol had but two.

"The astronomical clock is the most precise device of its kind in the world," Chiranjeet said with quite some pride. "The nightly phenomena are recorded with great accuracy to watch for anomalies."

Several men of obvious status were waiting for her by the telescope. Introductions were made, for among them were judges and senior obligations Rada had not even known were still alive.

Historian Vikram Akershan was also in attendance. He gave her a very deep and respectful bow as she approached. She returned the gesture.

"It has been a while. Congratulations on your marriage and your promotion, Librarian."

"It is good to see you're still breathing, Vikram. Is your wife still angrily ranting about my Order?"

"Despite the Inquisition's best efforts, I live, and my family is safe." The canny old warrior-turned-Historian gave her a kind smile, for he had been a friend of her father and known her since she was a child. "I've been told you put the treasure I entrusted you with to good use."

"An Archivist never shirks her obligation, whatever it may be." She patted the satchel, which rarely left her side. She'd carried the Asura's Mirror across the continent in a bag made of leather so it wouldn't accidentally eat her fingers, but now it rode in a purse made of fine silks and decorated with jewels, as befitted her office. Most would assume it was simply a lady's fine purse, and not that it held a deadly implement of black steel.

"Don't worry, Maharani. Everyone on this council is aware of the artifact's existence."

"It's a bit worse for wear. I'm afraid it got a crack in it."

"A small price to pay for calling down fire from the moon sufficient to cauterize demons from the land. Yes, I was informed of that. Most impressive. All those years I kept it safe, I never thought it could do *that*. Has it spoken to you?"

The odd occasional whisper directly into her mind was something she'd told very few people about. So rather than answer directly, she asked Vikram, "Did it speak to you?"

"Yes, albeit rarely."

"What did it say?"

"That I wasn't the one." Vikram spread his hands regretfully. "Yet it also implied that I would know the bearer when we met. It is good to see that I guessed correctly."

She'd never asked to be a bearer of a black-steel artifact, especially one so obstinate. She'd gotten tantalizing glimpses of the knowledge contained within, but that all seemed locked away except for in times of the direst emergency. "It contains an incredible amount of information, thousands of pages, if not more, but it is very stingy as to what it chooses to reveal."

"According to the Historians' Order, that has been the case since the beginning of this age," Vikram explained. "The mirror deciding to participate in the affairs of man once again should have been a warning that the end-time was drawing near, but sadly our council had lost our way, and too many of us sat useless as the world changed around us."

"Agents of our own government were our undoing," said another Historian. "Curse Omand to the sea."

"Regardless, we were supposed to be a council of vigilance, and we became a council of complacency." Chiranjeet hurried and made certain that Rada was familiar with the rest of the members. Alas, no one knew what had become of the Library's representative, as her father, Durmad, was still unaccounted for, as was the rest of Rada's family. Hopefully, they had escaped Omand's purges and made it back to Nems safely.

That thought left her in a sour mood. "Every one of you is an illustrious and respected man. So what was the secretive purpose of this council? If it was to watch for signs warning us the demons were coming back, it certainly failed there."

"That was part of it," Chiranjeet admitted. "Except we were too suspicious of the sky, and not the ground beneath our feet."

"Sadly, it seems the only voice of warning about the Capitol's fate came from a man all the Law-abiding world had dismissed as a mad criminal," Vikram said. "If we had listened to Black-Hearted Ashok, many lives would have been saved."

That was a somber thought, but a true one. "Lessons have been learned. The truth is more important than the source. Proceed, councilmen."

One of the Astronomers glanced toward the loudly ticking clock. "It's nearly time."

"This way, please." Chiranjeet directed Rada toward a cushioned seat beneath the telescope. "Place your face against this leather cup. The adjustments have already been made so the telescope is pointing in the right place."

Rada tapped her glasses. "Will these matter? I need them to see things up close."

"This is the most distant thing you will have ever seen, Maharani, but if the view seems blurry to you, turn that dial there beneath your right hand until it seems clear to you."

"Very well." The device's operation seemed straightforward enough, so she peered into the eye tubes. It took some moving her head about to get a clear image, and then she suddenly giggled with joy—which was an undignified sound for a Maharani to make—but she had never known there were so *many* stars. It was astoundingly beautiful. Growing up in the Capitol with all its lanterns it wasn't until she'd been camping in the desert with Karno that she'd realized just how many stars there really were. Yet this wonderful device revealed that even the darkest blank spots between those desert stars were secretly filled with lights.

"This is a truly lovely light, but I don't understand the importance."

"Fifty seconds," warned the Astronomer who was watching the clock.

Chiranjeet explained, "Demons nearly destroyed mankind, but it did not take long for religious fervor to nearly destroy us again afterward. The Law was created to prevent us from going down that fanatical path once more. However, some of the ancients' works were so great, so astounding, that it is impossible for lesser men to look upon them and *not* worship."

"Thirty seconds."

"For this reason, the Historians had to hide many artifacts, your Archivists had to lock up some books, and the Astronomers have managed to keep telescopes this potent as illegal as Fortress rods to the masses. To do otherwise would be to paint the ancients as gods. It is said when the demons came to this world, they fell from the sky. That is *partly* correct."

"It should be in view now."

A black shape blotted out some of the stars as *something* came into Rada's view.

Her gasp was so loud that it startled her bodyguards and made them reach for their swords.

She hurried and twisted the knob to try and bring clarity to the oddity. Having it come into focus more clearly only made matters worse.

"The religious fanatics talk of there having once been castles in the skies, where their imaginary gods once dwelled. Perhaps there is some truth to that foolishness, but it is a simplification. The Astronomers track the path of our two moons, Canda and tiny Upagraha, but we also look far beyond them. You are a learned woman, so surely you know there are other planets which appear to be nothing more than bright stars to the ignorant."

"Of course." She had read a book on astronomy once, though it had no mention of anything like this.

"Not so distant as those planets, is the anomaly which we call the broken circle."

It was a ring of black, its shape revealed by the stars in the middle and the stars all around, as if it was defined by the absence of light. Yet that circle was incomplete, as if pieces were missing.

"What is it?" she demanded of the judge, still struggling to comprehend what she was looking at. "What is this vast thing?"

"Its true nature is lost to us, Maharani."

"Not entirely," Vikram stated.

"Don't be tempted to stray into illegal religion, brother," warned one of the other Historians.

"Call it what you will. Our cowardice has been our undoing so far. If Rada's husband is our Chief Judge now, and she is his proxy here, then she must know all that we've theorized, whether we're certain it's true or not."

"Speak, Vikram," she ordered, because no matter what he

had to say, it couldn't be more unnerving than what she was staring at right now.

"There were legends once that said the circle used to be unbroken. It was a gate, through which man first arrived on this world."

"From *where?*"

"Unknown. The many religions which used to exist all had their own myths concerning the creation, but all we do know is that centuries after we arrived, the demons followed us."

"Could the circle be some kind of natural phenomenon?"

"We do not know, Maharani."

If this was some manner of construction, then it was of an immensity beyond comprehension. When she'd studied the ancient forbidden tomes, locked deep in the basement of the Library, she had read about the so-called war in the heavens. It had seemed like fanciful tales to her, but what if those ancient historians hadn't been exaggerating. Was this the aftermath of that war?

"Was it the demons who damaged the ring?"

"It is said that our ancestors did that to protect us."

She remembered hiding in the Library with an angry demon right outside. "They closed this door so no more demons could come here."

"That's the theory at least, Maharani," Chiranjeet said. "And as the Protectors watched the shores for danger, the Astronomers have watched the skies. It was all for nothing as we got slaughtered by those who had burrowed beneath the ground. The belief had been handed down from the judges of our council, through the generations, that if the demons were to make war against us again, there would be signs in the heavens first."

Rada's frustration was apparent in her voice. "There *were* signs! While our people wallowed in self-imposed ignorance, keeping secrets from each other, the demons prepared for war. The religious fanatics are quick to brag about how they got their prophetess from a fiery bolt from the sky, the arrival of which was seen across all the west!"

"We recorded that event as a simple meteor," said one of the Astronomers apologetically.

"A meteor that gives the gift of prophecy! And what of Upagraha?"

"What do you mean?" another of the Astronomers asked.

"If your purpose is to watch and warn, why didn't you speak up when Upagraha launched its cleansing fire against Vadal? Surely your marvelous machine was able to see the pillar of fire that the entire world could see with just their naked eyes."

"Upagraha did appear to be a slightly different shape afterward," he admitted. "Except at the time—"

"Your leader had just been killed, the Chamber of Argument was in shambles, and you were scared of what manner of leader Devedas might prove to be." The fear and uncertainty her beloved had caused in his rise to power had silenced this particular warning. "Oceans."

Would knowing about these ancient rumors beforehand have changed the Capitol's fate?

There was no way to know now, and Rada had no room left to carry any more guilt. Ignorance of these signs had left the Capitol vulnerable. Ignorance of their history had allowed a casteless genocide. As every Order kept its secrets, any group that might have understood what was happening had been cowed into silence by another. Their insular nature had been their undoing. None among them had possessed full vision, and there was no wheel to turn to make the truth come into focus.

This sight had filled her with awe at first, but now that was replaced with anger.

She forced herself to look away from the terrifying enigma, back toward the council. "Is there more secret knowledge out there that any of you have been hoarding in wait for these signs?"

"It is difficult to say. Each Order has specific things it has been entrusted with, Maharani," Chiranjeet answered. "Our number were scattered. Of those present, the answer is no."

This offended Rada, not just as the ruler and responsible party, but as a scholar. "The Capitol fell as a result of our corruption. The time for hiding from our past is over. Summon all your obligations, from each of your Orders—all of them. Whatever you have in your vaults, or your secure collections, or hidden in some Historian's basement in the desert, gather it *all*. If it pertains to the ancients or the demons, bring it here."

"There are surely things which have been concealed because of the Inquisition," Vikram said. "But their fangs have been removed."

"To the oceans with the Inquisition and all the useful knowledge they destroyed with their zealotry. If they'd deem it religious, all the more reason for us to study it now. What's forbidden religion to us was just life to the ancients. Knowledge is a weapon our people have deprived ourselves of for too long because we were scared of the wrong thing. We hid the truth from ourselves because it pointed us in uncomfortable directions. It shouldn't matter. Truth is truth. If any warrior had failed in his duty as thoroughly as our scholarly Orders have failed our people, he'd cut his own throat because of the dishonor."

The warrior Kumudesh grunted in agreement at that, and all the high-status men looked down in shame.

Rada understood what they were feeling right now better than they could possibly understand, for she had once violated her oath of honest scholarship, and millions had suffered because of it. All that could be done now was to try and put things right. She'd certainly tried. It wasn't enough, but it was something.

"Forgive us, Maharani," one of the Historians wailed. "We abandoned our watchtower when we were needed most."

"The enemy is here, but the war's not lost yet. Knowledge is a weapon. So let us arm our people as best we can."

Chapter 8

Maharaja Devedas stood before Thakoor Bhadramunda Vadal and his entire court. All the highest-status men of Vadal had turned out in the hopes of watching the usurper king debase himself. They did not realize that Devedas was far too proud to give them that satisfaction.

Many hateful eyes were upon him, for the visitor in golden armor had recently brought war and bloodshed to their vibrant land. Everyone here had suffered to one degree or another because of his decisions. Let them despise him. Devedas didn't care. His purpose today was to make them understand what was at stake. Then they would either do the sensible thing and accept his help or they would die.

The Thakoor sat silently upon his throne, studying his nemesis. Only a few years past twenty, Bhadramunda—named for his grandfather, the previous bearer of Angruvadal—was young to hold such an important office, but it was said that he was the most capable and intelligent of Harta's children, and a worthy successor. The reports Devedas had received from his spies here had all warned him that Bhadramunda had inherited his father's pragmatic cunning and was not to be underestimated.

"Recently the Maharaja's forces surrounded this great city and tried to starve us into submission, yet here you are before me, all by yourself." Bhadramunda even sounded somewhat like his father when he spoke. "It is a curious decision to place yourself in such danger."

"A decision I felt was appropriate, considering I'm on a mission of diplomacy."

"You were not so diplomatic when you had the might of the Capitol at your back. But now that your great city lies abandoned, while mine prospers, *now* you are petitioning me for aid."

"This is not a petition, Thakoor. I come to offer help in Vadal's time of need, and I will ask for nothing in return."

The small army of advisors who were clustered around Bhadramunda all began to whisper and mutter at that, because the Capitol never did anything for *free*.

Bhadramunda lifted one hand to silence the chattering old men. "Need? I am not the one in *need*. We have no evidence of this looming threat against us beyond the word of a notorious criminal."

Devedas didn't know if the criminal Bhadramunda alluded to was Ashok, or him. The first caste were very good at delivering cutting insults in a manner indirect enough to give offense while denying intending it. That was a skill Devedas had never developed. When he insulted someone, there was never any doubt whether it was intended or not.

"The evidence is Kanok, the evidence is the Capitol, and the towering piles of corpses left behind in each. There's no denying that the demons have launched an offensive unlike anything seen in modern times. They will not stop until mankind is extinct, and they are coming here next."

The Thakoor's court was held in Vadal's great house itself, which was quite possibly the finest building in the world, including even the greatest palaces of the Capitol. Everything here was a testament to the wealth, power, and history of Great House Vadal. It was gilded opulence atop carved and painted glory, and though Devedas—being an austere southerner—had no use for such things, it would still be a shame to see demons destroy it all.

"Assuming those two attacks were not an anomaly, and the demonic rampage will continue, why should we believe that Vadal is their target?"

"Why wouldn't it be? Is this not the greatest city left in the world?" Devedas wasn't trying to flatter the Vadal—he was simply stating facts—but the advisors seemed pleased at the compliment anyway. Even when they were actively looking for offense to take, the Vadal remained a most prideful people.

"There have been many debates over which city is finer, this one or the Capitol, with arguments to be made in either's favor. Alas, I believe that contest has been settled for us."

Devedas frowned, for if young Bhadramunda had seen the slaughter in the desert he wouldn't be so flippant about it. "The finest minds in the scholarly Orders are certain that Vadal City will be the demon's next target."

"Does that include Ashok?" Bhadramunda asked pointedly. "Phontho Jagdish told me of your alliance with the Black Heart and his gang of criminals."

"No one has ever accused Ashok of being a scholar of any subject other than violence, Thakoor. However, Ashok also swears to this danger based upon the black-steel magic that pumps through his veins."

"Oh, the untouchable who broke our sword and murdered my grandmother in this very room swears to it? Well, that settles it, then! Let's throw open the gates and have a party for all our former enemies."

The pack of advisors and courtiers all laughed at their Thakoor's bitter humor.

Devedas had not realized that this was the same hall where Ashok had confronted his supposed aunt about his true identity. These stones had seen some blood. Hopefully they wouldn't see any more today.

"I won't attempt to defend any of the many evil things traitorous Ashok has done against the Law-abiding, but when the greatest killer who has ever lived says he smells blood in the air, then it would be wise to prepare for blood."

"We were also told you'd killed him!" exclaimed one of the judges.

That question galled him, for he'd certainly tried. "I *thought* I had killed him. I cut his throat and threw him in the ocean. Except, Ashok laughs at death and the great nothing keeps sending him back."

The Thakoor scoffed. "Your animosity was legendary, yet now you ride with him?"

"It is an alliance of circumstance, made tolerable only because of the severity of the danger."

"Some claim Ashok is a bigger threat to us than demons."

"Having fought both, they would be wrong. Anyone who says a rebel with a magic sword is the greater danger has never seen the devastation an army of demons leaves behind. For now, Ashok would rather shed white blood than red. He tried to warn the Capitol of what was coming, but we didn't listen. I implore you, Thakoor, do not make the same mistakes I did. I missed the warnings. I failed my city." Devedas' voice broke a bit as he admitted that, and even the jaded members of the First must have been able to tell the emotion was genuine.

Pity temporarily softened Bhadramunda's hardened heart. "I offer my condolences for the multitude who perished in the Capitol. I traveled there several times with my father. It was a beautiful place."

"It will be once again. We will rebuild it after the demons have been destroyed." Devedas took a deep breath and composed himself before continuing. They were both powerful men, but their ultimate purpose was to protect their people. They were both trying to do right by their obligation. "If I am wrong, and this threat isn't real, your house will be defended unnecessarily. If I'm right, then your people are in danger from a menace beyond anything humanity has seen in a thousand years."

His words hung heavy over the court.

"Still, you must understand my hesitancy, Maharaja. Once before the Capitol used the excuse of a demon attack to trespass an army into Vadal lands, where you remained, threatening us, long after our capable warriors had defeated that scourge." At that, Bhadramunda nodded toward Phontho Jagdish, who was standing off to the side, trying his best to remain unnoticed.

Jagdish could have taken the praise and remained silent, but Devedas suspected he was far too honest for the courts—and his own good—because the phontho cleared his throat and then spoke the truth. "The reality is we should have died, my Thakoor. We only survived the scourge because we had the magical aid of the Maharaja's future wife on our side."

Bhadramunda frowned. "Ah yes, when my father's favorite librarian brought down a pillar of fire that charred miles of our valuable countryside into ash, taking many lives, and causing untold amounts of property damage."

Jagdish spread his hands apologetically. "I never claimed it was a pretty victory, Thakoor . . . but having seen and fought demons far more than anyone else in Vadal, I still decided to bring this man before you because I believe his warning to be true."

"You would stake your reputation on this belief, Phontho Jagdish?"

That was a very dangerous question in a place like this. Few men of status would risk their name. Getting it wrong would result in dishonor, exile, and possibly even death.

Jagdish didn't so much as hesitate. "Yes. To deny it would be to endanger our house and all our people."

Bhadramunda nodded slowly, digesting that promise. His advisors clearly didn't like what was happening but the First often hated warriors who became too popular in their courts. They preferred to keep the lower castes in their place, and that place certainly wasn't speaking unequivocal truths to their master.

One of those advisors spoke up. "The Capitol plays us for fools, Thakoor Bhadramunda. Devedas spit on our hospitality once before and sent Sarnobat assassins against us. Against your very father!"

"I did no such thing," Devedas snapped.

"How the kicked dog barks!" that arbiter shouted back.

Thoughts of diplomacy fled as a dark anger consumed him. "If your intent is to label me an animal, I am no mere dog. I would be a white southern bear. The bear does not bark. It rips the head off any prey stupid enough to challenge it, and then roars his victory so loud the world may hear. Do you challenge me, Arbiter?"

His words were so cold that even the hardened warriors of the Vadal Personal Guard took an unconscious step back.

"I apologize for this inadvertent offense," the arbiter stammered.

The advisor having quailed, Devedas turned his attention back to the only man whose opinion truly mattered, and spoke with a passion born of desperation. "Yes, Thakoor, I invaded you. I occupied your lands. I led men into battle against the armies of Vadal, where both sides fought with courage. But I did not send those assassins against your house. That was the work of Grand Inquisitor Omand, whom I have since declared a criminal who is to be killed on sight. Once I received the invitation to approach your city, I left my army behind and rode here by myself, without fear of being killed or taken hostage because I know the Vadal hold their honor dear. I came to speak to you, face-to-face, ruler to ruler, admitting my mistakes in the hopes that you recognize my sincere regret, and do not make the same mistakes I did. These are not the actions of a man who has something to hide. Please, hear the truth in my words. Vadal must prepare for war once more, or the demons will consume us all."

The court had come expecting a swallowing of pride from a hated enemy, and instead they had received an offer of friendship and an ultimatum that appealed to their accountability. It was not often the First were so obviously confounded.

Bhadramunda pondered Devedas' words for a time, his expression unreadable, before announcing, "I would speak with my advisors for a moment."

"Of course," Devedas answered.

The Thakoor got up and walked out the back followed by his entire entourage, leaving Devedas standing alone in the middle of the vast space. The lesser members of the court remained in their chairs, but none of these were important enough for him to care about. There were warriors stationed at each door and upon the balconies above. If Bhadramunda was going to have Devedas killed to avenge a murder that wasn't Devedas' fault, now would be the ideal time. But the only people who approached him were the house slaves to offer refreshment and a chair to sit on. He refused both.

A minute after the slaves had left, an unnatural silence settled upon the great hall. The gentle breeze that had filled the room abruptly stopped, leaving the air unnaturally still. Oddly enough, Devedas' vision grew blurry, but no amount of blinking could clear it. He didn't have the gift for sensing magic like sword master Ratul had, but this change was so abrupt that it was obvious wizards had to be involved somehow. It was more disappointing that Bhadramunda would be too stubborn to listen to reason, than it was that he'd send wizards to attack him, but Devedas did not react, just in case this was something other than an assassination attempt.

That theory proved correct when a man in black robes and a golden mask stepped out of thin air, directly in front of him.

"Hello again, Maharaja."

"Grand Inquisitor Omand..." Devedas deliberately placed his hand on the hilt of his sword. "We were just talking about you."

"About how you've declared me a dangerous criminal fugitive? Oh yes, I was listening to that part. It amused me to hear your biased version of events."

Smug and aloof as ever, this was clearly Omand, yet there was something different about him. Devedas had never once seen his fellow conspirator's real face, but he looked leaner and sounded younger... and somehow more dangerous. Omand had always been a powerful wizard, but now his presence made the hairs on Devedas' neck stand up. His eyes flicked to the side, toward where the Personal Guard were watching over the hall, except they seemed oblivious to the fact that there was an intruder. It was as if their eyes were unfocused, and their ears couldn't hear the conversation taking place only a few yards away.

"They see what I want them to see and hear what I want them to hear. There will be no witnesses unless I require some. I come and go as I please, with even wizards and bloodhounds none the wiser. We may speak freely."

"We've nothing to speak about, criminal."

"*Criminal?* You say it as if we are dissimilar in that respect. Are we not both criminals?"

"No. Because *I won.* Our arrangement ended when you decided to rule over the Capitol like a mad tyrant. I came back to put an end to your excesses, and the people loved me for it."

"True, albeit a brief rule. You selfishly reaped the benefits of my labor, betrayed me, and now call me the villain. I find that delicious. Now I get to watch you grovel before your enemies, begging them to help you save a people you cannot. Come, Devedas, you said I was to be killed on sight. Are you not a man of your word?"

When Devedas tried to draw his sword, nothing happened. It was as if the steel were frozen inside the sheath. He pulled harder, but to no avail. When he tried to let go in order to reach for his dagger instead, his hand remained involuntarily curled around the hilt of his sword, as the muscles of his fingers refused to unclench.

"Ah, it appears I am beyond your reach, backstabber."

Even calling upon the Heart of the Mountain for strength, Devedas could barely move against the magical paralysis. Straining with all his might did naught but make him shake.

Devedas was too angry to be afraid.

Omand could have easily ended his life, but instead he walked in a circle around Devedas, gloating. "That's right. While you played at being king, I was occupied with unlocking the power of the ancients. The mysteries of magic are mine to exploit. The very fabric of reality is mine to distort as I see fit."

He couldn't move his body, but Omand had left him his ability to speak, probably in the hopes of hearing him beg for his life. He'd give Omand no such satisfaction. "If you're so mighty now, then use that magic to help stop the demons."

"And why should I aid those who neither love me nor serve me?"

"This is more important than amassing power!"

A cold chuckle came from behind the golden mask. "How disappointing! There's nothing more important than *power*, foolish Devedas. I thought you of all men might understand that fact. Your inability to truly commit to that ideal is why you will ultimately fail." Omand gave a theatrical pause, and then turned his head side to side to take in the sights of the magnificent hall. "Do you realize the significance of this place?"

Devedas didn't answer, because he was busy grinding his teeth, struggling like he was trying to lift a boulder in the vain hope of breaking the spell so he could wrap his hands around Omand's neck to wring the life out of him.

"This . . . *this* is where Angruvadal chose a casteless of the bloodline of Ramrowan to be their champion. On this very spot." The eyes of the mask lingered on the floor before them, as if searching for signs of the blood that had been scrubbed away decades ago. The black holes of that mask turned back toward Devedas. "That quiet event—seemingly only consequential to this one great house—was the death knell of this age. That black-steel choice was the culmination of centuries of calculation and preparation. I have a much better vision of the true nature of things now, though even my great understanding is cursedly incomplete. Damn Mother Dawn for her clever meddling. Other parts of their plan were already in motion—I had already met my demonic guide, for example—but what is time to the gods?"

"I don't know what you're talking about. You speak in mad riddles!"

"No. There is no madness in what the ancients prepared for us. It was the coldest of calculations. Dispassionate, really. Many of us had an unwitting part to play. As did I. As did you. How can I be upset by the unrelenting ambitions of someone designed to be king centuries before he was born? How I marvel at the ancients' foresight."

Devedas spat, "Kill me and get it over with, wretched spider."

"I intend to, eventually, but not quite yet. The predictive engine declared the end of this age required a king. It said nothing about needing one for the beginning of the next. Also, for my own enjoyment, I would like to watch you suffer more first. As the demons tear apart everything around you, and the people look to you with tears in their eyes pleading for you to save them, and you cannot, remember that you asked for this heavy crown."

"To the ocean with you, Omand! Ashok said black steel wanted me here. You say it was by the gods' design. I don't care. No matter how heavy that crown may be, it's mine now, and I will use it to protect Lok from evil, whether it's from the sea, or from the filth like you."

The darkness on the other side of the mask studied him for a time. "It is a pity that our time is up for now. The Thakoor returns, his decision made. He will accept your help, but his command will be structured in a way that humbles and insults you, so the people of Vadal know their would-be conqueror has been put in his place. You will accept this, because you know of the darkness that is coming, and your honor leaves you no choice. I would advise not telling the Vadal that I was here, for I leave no trace of my existence. If you begin babbling of Inquisitors turned into dark gods, the Vadal will surely think you are hallucinating and reconsider their agreement. Goodbye, Devedas."

In the blink of an eye, Omand was gone. Sound returned. The air began moving again. Devedas' limbs unlocked, and he nearly toppled over from the sudden freedom. Flushed, he hurried and wiped the sweat from his face with his hands and composed himself before the high-status men entered the room. *Weakness must never be shown.* It was a lesson hard learned in his youth.

Omand's predictions proved accurate. Bhadramunda welcomed the Army of Many Houses to his city, but he had a great list of demands first. It didn't matter what he wanted, no matter how insulting or degrading, and the Thakoor's speech was like the buzzing of insects in his ears. Courtly things were meaningless now. Devedas cared only about beating the demons and then figuring out if there was a way a king could slay a god.

Chapter 9

Jagdish had not specifically forbidden him from entering Vadal City but Ashok had decided it would be for the best if he waited outside. His presence would only inflame fury or invite fear. Devedas was already hated in this house. His diplomatic delegation would face enough challenges without the specter of Ashok riling up Vadal's first caste even more than they already were. Honorable Jagdish had given his report and made his appeal to Thakoor Bhadramunda Vadal, Harta's son and successor, but would that be enough to sway this prideful house to action?

Judging by the reactions Ashok had seen on the journey here, Jagdish was beloved by the common people. To worker and warrior both, Jagdish was the hero who had stepped up again and again to lead their house through a time of crisis. They had even written songs about him; Ashok had heard several being sung along the road. Vadal's demon-hunting wizard slayer had gone on to be a master strategist who crushed other houses in battle. Because of his humble origin and disgrace—and dare they even mention his association with criminals—the members of the lower castes saw something of themselves in Jagdish. He'd been just like them once, and even in his current glory it was obvious he never forgot where he came from. As one of the songs had declared, Jagdish remembered his roots and lived by his code.

It seemed even the casteless loved Jagdish. Unlike the other great houses, Vadal had never fully implemented the Great Extermination, and the armies commanded by Jagdish had ignored it entirely. Ashok had never seen casteless sing about a whole man before. It was odd to him, seeing casteless quarters still occupied here, because everywhere else he had been recently, those all lay abandoned or ruined.

Yet the devotion of worker, warrior, and especially untouchable meant nothing to the first caste, and only they would be able to decide the future of Vadal City. If Jagdish could not convince them with words, then Ashok would be left with no choice but to convince them by the sword and a thousand guns. He would prefer not to, but time was short, and the demons many.

It was a beautiful day, as most days were in Vadal. The sun was warm, but not too hot. Birds sang from every tree. Vadal City was vast and sprawling across a dozen hills, stretching far beyond its original walls. The mighty Martaban River passed through the city, for though water was the source of evil and the home of hell, it was necessary to sustain life, and this much life required an incredible amount of water. Vadal City never really stopped, it just tapered off as the buildings got smaller with more space between them. It was surrounded by dozens of small towns and villages that had all grown together over the centuries.

Ashok had picked one of those villages on the outskirts to stay in, with his identity concealed, and his location known only to Jagdish so he could be sent for if needed. He hid, not out of fear of the Law—Ashok was far past caring about that—but rather because once word got out that he was still alive and somehow in possession of an ancestor blade, the hungry duelists would inevitably arrive to challenge him in an attempt to seize Angruvadal for themselves.

Ashok was weary of killing normal men. They no longer presented a challenge. He'd prefer to save his wrath for demons and dark gods.

The inn he was staying at was a humble one, but the food was hearty. Ashok sat outside beneath the shade of an oak tree and ate his curried chicken and rice in peace, his face hidden beneath a big straw hat, with Angruvadal wrapped in his merchant's cloak by his side. It was doubtful any random worker here would recognize him, but it was better to be careful.

Ashok passed the time listening to the workers as they went

about their business. Women gossiped. Children played. All these humble people knew was that a great war had just ended in victory, and life would be good for them once more. Mostly they rejoiced that the rationing was over, and trade could resume. They praised Jagdish and spit on their idea of Devedas. They had not heard about the devastation of the Capitol or Kanok. The greatest enemies they could imagine were Sarnobat, Vokkan, and hunger, and those had just been crushed. He heard not a single mention of his name, probably because they all thought he was dead. Ashok would enjoy this moment of peace, because if Jagdish failed to sway Bhadramunda Vadal, it would be ruined soon enough.

He heard a man approaching. Ashok could tell that he was very old from the shuffle of his feet and the thin wheeze of his breathing. He walked with a cane, which made a *thunk* each time it was ponderously placed into the hard dirt. Ashok expected the old man to pass him by, but instead, he stopped a few feet away.

"May I join you, Ashok?"

This man was clearly too old to be Jagdish's messenger. Then he realized that the stranger had brought an odd stillness with him. The nearby chatter had nervously ceased. The children ran away. A dog barked at the scent of the odd stranger. It was as if when the villagers saw this new arrival, they all decided they had somewhere better to be and hurried to get there.

Ashok lifted the brim of his hat, and scowled when he saw that the old man was dressed as a wizard, in dark robes decorated with feathers and bones. The wizard's back was crooked, and his hands were so thin that they weren't that different in appearance from the dried bird talons that hung from the necklace around his wrinkled neck. The wizard's eyes were clouded so gray he must have been going blind.

Despite the decades since they had last met, Ashok recognized him almost immediately.

"Kule."

And in that brief moment, Ashok was a fake boy again, an amalgamation of parts and beliefs, stitched together with threads made of Law, stripped of his memories and fear, and presented to the Protector Order so that he could die as quickly as possible for the greater good of this house.

This was his creator.

"It has been a long time, hasn't it, my boy?"

The moment of weakness was over, and Ashok was once more the man he had become. "Over a thousand lives have passed since you left me with the Protectors."

"Mind if I sit?"

"That depends. Would you prefer to die standing?" Ashok asked that without animosity.

"So that is how it must be?"

As one of the conspirators who had perpetuated the great fraud that was Ashok's life, Kule needed to die for his crimes. It was that simple. If Kule had been present at Bidaya's party, he would have died along with his master.

"Do not pretend there is any other possibility."

"Well then, at my advanced age, one recognizes that every possible way I'm likely to die is equally undignified, so I will sit and rest." There was a wooden stool beneath the tree. Kule tottered over to it and groaned as he lowered himself into place. "Ah. Much better."

Ashok hadn't been prepared for this unexpected meeting, so it took him a moment to decide how to proceed. When he had confronted Bidaya, he had been filled with the righteous fury of the offended and a profound sorrow for the loss of things he couldn't even remember. Suddenly placed before him was the man who had stolen those memories. It turned out that his anger remained, but it had long since cooled from a boil to a simmer.

"Explain why you are here, wizard. Then once I am finished with my lunch, I will kill you."

"You always were direct. Even as a child you never wasted time on frivolous nonsense. That's probably one reason Angruvadal picked you."

Ashok went back to eating his rice.

"If you can't tell, the time I have left is already short. I have lived a very long life. Recently my health has taken a precipitous turn for the worse. Dying in bed or dying by the vengeful sword of a boy who once took shelter in my home, either way I'm dead. My dying today should not make much difference, and at least one of us will get some satisfaction from the event."

Ashok kept chewing.

"Very well." Kule had never been given to displays of emotion. He must have passed that trait on to his creation. "I have come to tell you that Thakoor Bhadramunda listened to Jagdish's earnest request, but his distrust of Devedas—and you—seemed insurmountable. Bhadramunda believed honorable Jagdish had been tricked by the Capitol's guile, and this alleged demon invasion is another elaborate scheme to conquer us. After all, didn't the Capitol use the threat of demons against us once before?"

"This time it's no trick."

Kule nodded. "Of course. And you are no Devedas. Which is why I stepped in. Young Bhadramunda has known me his entire life. As the only one of Harta's many children who was magically gifted, I was assigned to be one of his tutors. He is not a very capable wizard, but that's not his purpose in life. As the wisest of the heirs, his purpose now is to see to the well-being of this house. Given time, I'm sure he will grow into a fine leader. Our new Thakoor is named after his grandfather, whom I also served. You know, after you picked up Angruvadal, Bidaya believed that her husband Bhadramunda must have been your real father? The prior bearer having his way with some random casteless woman and leaving a half-caste bastard offspring made far more sense to her than the idea that our ancestor blade would pick a non-person to wield it."

Ashok savored a bite of his chicken.

"You accentuate that your plate is nearly empty. I see my time is short...Though if Bidaya had guessed true that would make you our new Thakoor's uncle, and Harta's half brother, a thought which surely troubled Harta a great many times."

"It shouldn't have. My true father was a casteless named Smoke. His obligation was the cremation of bodies."

"How do you know this? The casteless quarters you came from were all wiped out."

Those barracks—and all their residents—had been burned to keep Ashok's true nature a secret. "The casteless keep a secret genealogy. My birth was recorded in this book."

"Hmmm. Curious. I didn't know the fish-eaters had such a thing." Kule seemed amused at the idea of illiterate fools doing something so odd. Who cared about the birth of non-people? "Though it really doesn't matter which of them sired you, whether it be bearer Bhadramunda or cremator Smoke, since I'm the one who made you into who are."

"Do you expect my gratitude?"

"Shouldn't there be gratitude to the one who dropped a thing to watch it shatter against the ground, but who then picked up the shards and carefully glued them back together into something better and stronger than before?"

Ashok took a drink of his wine. The wizard's audacity was impressive.

"Your construction was a painstaking labor. Everything you have ever believed was only there because I whispered it into your ear. Then I used magic to brand those ideas onto your mind forever. I am no mere father, Ashok. I am a *sculptor.* You are my masterwork. My only regret in my long life is that I couldn't ever brag about my greatest single accomplishment to my wizard peers, because what I had done was so very illegal. I came here to see you in person, because I wanted to marvel at my art one last time."

Ashok almost killed Kule right then, but he had already said what he was going to do, and he would not waste perfectly good food. "You said you stepped in with the Thakoor. How?"

"I told Bhadramunda that I thought you must be telling the truth, because I did not build Ashok *to lie.* I reminded him that our spies had confirmed the demonic attack against the Capitol, and that the damage was as great as you claim. Most of all, I planted seeds of fear and doubt into his heart by reminding him demons were the greatest threat of all. Man can be reasoned with. Demons only kill."

"So he has agreed to Devedas' proposal?"

"He has agreed. It took great effort on my part, but the rest is details for the Arbiters to work out. Luckily our house is already mobilized for war."

These workers would surely be saddened to hear that their food rationing would continue, but that was a far better fate than being devoured by demons. "Good."

"Devedas and the Capitol will have to make many concessions to Bhadramunda to earn our cooperation, but ultimately Vadal will stand united with you against the demons. You may begin building your grand defense here. This would not have happened without me. You are welcome."

Ashok kept eating.

"There is to be no thanks from you at all, then? Nothing?"

"Why should the sculptor care what his clay thinks? Today you did what was best for your house. That should be sufficient."

Kule snarled, and in that moment Ashok could once again see the younger, meaner, more ambitious wizard he had known. "I have *always* done the best thing for my house. I suppose I just wanted to hear the words *thank you* come out of your mouth once before I departed for the endless nothing."

Ashok watched the happy people pass by and knew that soon enough their joy would be replaced by fear, as word of the demonic invasion spread. But that knowledge would give them a chance to prepare. Kule was a thief of memories and master of lies but, at least at the end of his miserable life, his words to his Thakoor had helped give these people a fighting chance.

Insufficient.

"You will receive nothing but contempt from me, Kule. My family died quickly. You failed at murdering me slowly."

"Such ingratitude. Oh, well . . . What a foolish goal for an old man to have." Kule took a small vial out of his robes and swallowed the contents. "Ah . . . So bitter . . ."

"What is that you drink?"

"A deadly poison."

"Hmm . . ." Ashok didn't like being robbed, but dead was dead.

"Even now I help you, Ashok. If the demons are truly on their way, having the fallen bearer who our house must reconcile with murder a respected court wizard would only create more animosity. Someone will find my body here in the shade of this comfortable tree and suspect I sat to rest my feet and my tired old heart finally gave out. I knew once you found out I was still alive, you would certainly kill me. How could I expect anything other than a relentless pursuit of justice from you? I made you that way."

Ashok grunted in acknowledgment. "Are all the other conspirators dead?"

"You know of Bidaya and Harta. Chavans died of a fever years ago. I am the last."

"Then the matter is closed."

Kule looked down at the frail hands resting in his lap but seemed unable to move them. "This poison . . . works quickly. I have only one question left for you, Ashok. I built you not to survive, but to die. I took away your fear and left you . . . impossible responsibility." It was becoming increasingly difficult for Kule to speak at all. "Everything. Everything I did . . . was designed to make you perish. To court... death. To love... death. How... do you still... live?"

Ashok understood why now, but even if he told Kule, he wouldn't have grasped it in time. Assigned a higher purpose, Ashok had been designed to be its perfect servant. The purpose had changed. Indomitable Ashok had not.

"You have deceived yourself all these years, Kule. You are no artist because you do not comprehend what you have done. Now you will die without ever having your answer."

"I was the one... who taught you... such cruelty..." The wizard smiled, then his head lolled forward on his frail neck. Propped up on his cane, his body remained on the stool rather than sliding off into the grass.

Ashok finished his lunch and left Kule to die alone.

Chapter 10

The fortification of Vadal City began.

The war council met at an estate in the warriors' district. It was a fine mansion, but by the importance of those assembled, they should have been meeting in the Thakoor's mansion itself. Except the last time Ashok had been there he'd ended up in a dishonorable knife duel against the Personal Guard and their Thakoor had died messily at the end. So, he took no offense at his lack of invitation there.

The council was assigned representatives from each force present. As part of their agreement with Devedas, the Vadal had demanded that Phontho Jagdish be in command. This was a slight against the Maharaja, who by his office was supposedly the supreme arbiter of all of Lok, but Devedas had no choice but accept Jagdish as their ultimate decision maker. There would be many such abuses before this was through, but Ashok reasoned that insults were a small punishment for Devedas starting a war he could not finish. The loser of most wars ended up with his head stuck on a pike outside the winner's front gate.

By the size of the army they had present, Jagdish led Vadal. Devedas commanded the Army of Many Houses, or at least what he had managed to reassemble of it after their retreat. And Ashok represented the Sons of the Black Sword. Each of those three had brought a few of their officers as well as anyone else they suspected might be of some use.

Jagdish had caught Ashok by the arm as soon as he had arrived in the meeting hall and whispered, "Watch yourself. This could turn hostile. We're assembling a lot of men who've been enemies to each other in the same room. There's bad blood here."

"At least they are all united in hating me," Ashok agreed.

"There's that too. I'll handle things, but stay wary."

"What if any of the Capitol's men question your authority as their commander?"

"Then they can challenge me to a duel... Speaking of which, if that happens, do you mind if I name you my champion? That should sort out even the dumbest of them right quickly."

There were two dozen people assembled in the meeting room so far, clustered into knots based upon their faction and status. Most of them were warriors, but there were also workers representing the industries vital to their logistics, and even a few members of Vadal's first caste who had invited themselves, probably in order to meddle. Ashok wasn't too worried about those. The preparations would take time, and the important men would drift away as they lost interest in the mundane issues of city defense. If those members of the First stymied them at all, Ashok expected Jagdish to stomp on them. The Thakoor had declared that Jagdish operated with his full confidence. It was rare for a warrior to be so trusted, but Jagdish had proven himself to be a phontho above reproach who cared only for the well-being of his house. Insulting him would be the same as insulting Bhadramunda.

From the corner, Ashok watched as more Vadal men arrived. Very few of them would even look his direction. Those who met his gaze did so with naked contempt or outright disgust. No offense was taken. Ashok understood he had brought them nothing but pain.

However, those same men obviously adored Jagdish, and it was obvious they would gladly follow him into battle against the hordes of hell. They clustered around their natural leader, hanging on his every word. If the Vadal loved Jagdish a bit more than they hated Ashok, that might be balanced enough to keep them in line.

Jagdish abruptly stopped his conversation with the warriors when he spotted an enormous worker hesitantly pause at the council room doors. "Oceans! It can't be. *Gutch?*"

When Gutch saw Jagdish he shouted, "Why did someone put a phonto's turban on that fish-eater?"

"Come here, you magnificent bastard!" Jagdish abandoned

his confused officers and rushed toward Gutch. "Good to see you, brother!"

Overcome by genuine emotion, Gutch engulfed Jagdish in a bear hug, effortlessly lifted him off the ground, and shook him. Jagdish had a fearsome-looking bodyguard who moved to intervene, until he realized that the big worker wasn't about to snap his charge in half, and backed off.

Gutch held Jagdish out at arm's length. "How're you not dead?"

"I'd ask you the same." He thumped Gutch in his considerable gut. "Life's clearly been kind to you! What're you doing here?"

"I asked him to join us," Ashok stated. "Gutch possesses knowledge that may be very useful to Vadal."

"Were you riding with the Sons again then, Gutch?"

"Eh, affiliated. Loosely, and in an entirely non-criminal manner."

Jagdish laughed, for there were very few things Gutch did that weren't a violation of the Law somehow. "That doesn't sound like you at all."

Gutch looked to Ashok, before nodding his head toward where a masked Inquisitor was sitting in the back by himself. Nobody willingly associated with members of that Order, especially now that their leader had brought them so much dishonor. "Before I say another word about my recent endeavors before these fine Law-abiding men, Ashok promised to discuss a pardon for any potential wrongdoing which may or may not have happened in the past involving yours truly."

"We will get to that," Ashok assured him. It stood to reason that if Devedas could make casteless into whole men by decree, then he could just as easily choose to overlook Gutch's fabrication of illegal weapons on the mainland.

Ashok had brought a few of the Sons with him: Ongud Khedekar dar Akershan and Eklavya Kharsawan for their strategic cunning, Laxmi as leader of his wizards, and the Fortress envoy, Praseeda Jaehnig. Ashok had ordered her to abandon her strange uniform and wear clothing made in Lok instead, so as to not be a distraction. The men of Vadal were still coming to terms with the insulting idea that they were supposed to ally with criminals. He would not overwhelm them with a curiosity like a foreigner... especially one who was a master of illegal alchemy. The Fortress folk looked the same as regular people, until they opened their mouths and their strange accent revealed them to be oddities.

Nervous, the Sons stayed close to Ashok. It had taken them great courage to come here and surround themselves with warriors who would gladly fight them in normal times. The Law granted them status now, but that was nothing compared to generations it had been legal—even mandatory—to kill religious fanatics on sight. They were trusting in the reputation of Ashok, the word of Devedas, and the honor of Jagdish to keep them safe.

The Maharaja's contingent were the last to arrive, and were the most numerous, as they had officers in the colors of every house who had contributed soldiers to the Capitol's army, including men of Sarnobat and Vokkan. The Vadal greeted those with nearly as much sneering hostility as they had Ashok. It would be a miracle if no duels were fought today.

"It takes some nerve for the monkey and the wolf to show their faces here," a Vadal warrior whispered to his friend.

Jagdish silenced the complainer with a scowl.

The room went totally quiet as Devedas entered, dressed in a plain uniform lacking any ostentatious badge of office. The Maharaja took one look around the assembly and nodded, satisfied. He dispensed with the usual pomp and fanfare the arrival that a man of such considerable status would demand and simply announced, "The army of the Capitol is present and ready when you are, Phontho."

Jagdish was no statesman, but rather a warrior's warrior who understood that their caste lived or died based upon respect. There could be no effective defense without cooperation. This petulant animosity between their forces would not do.

"Welcome, Maharaja Devedas." Jagdish looked around to make sure everyone was listening. When he confirmed that they were, he continued. "I wish to say, and let it be heard before all of these witnesses, that what's behind us is done." As the silently glaring crowd watched, Jagdish walked directly to his former foe and gave him a bow, which was the traditional style of greeting in the north. "That was a damned good fight."

"It was a most impressive defense." Devedas returned the bow, and then he extended his hand in the southern style. "Do you think Vadal can do as well against the armies of the sea?"

"Easily. What's the ferocity of demons when compared to you?" Jagdish shook Devedas' hand. "All of the offenses between us will be as forgotten as these fanatics' gods have been."

"Perhaps that is not the best analogy," Ashok said.

"Maybe." Jagdish gave him a wry grin. "But if we can hold our grudges quietly and in secret for a few hundred years before remembering them in public again, that's sufficient for me!"

Ashok mulled that over and had to admit that Jagdish was more clever at politics than he gave him credit for. His new wife had tutored him well. "The supreme phontho of Vadal is a wise man."

"I'm glad you are here, brothers. All of you." And Jagdish specifically looked toward Ashok's criminals as he said that as well, which would serve as a subtle reminder to his officers that anyone who'd lift a blade in defense of Vadal City was to be welcomed. "Together, we'll send the demons back to hell, where they belong."

"We'd be better off without their kind," spat a young warrior, who could apparently no longer contain his disgust.

With surprising speed Jagdish moved to where that warrior stood and grabbed him by the sash so hard he nearly pulled him off his feet. It was an incredibly insulting gesture, but gone was the jovial welcoming leader, to be suddenly replaced suddenly by a commander who was hard as nails. "How many demons have you fought, Risalder?"

"N-none, sir," he stammered.

"I've fought one to the death!" Jagdish shouted in his face. "The bravest soldiers I've ever known barely took it down, and it still took everything we had. When I saw a bare handful of the things working together, it was a terror beyond comprehension, and we lived only because of him." Jagdish pointed at Ashok.

"But we are Vadal. We are—"

"A bump in the road to them," Jagdish snarled. "Twenty or thirty demons was all it took to rip Kanok apart. Lord Devedas, how many demons did you face in the Capitol?"

"Hundreds of the things. Their numbers were so thick their crossing blotted out the desert sand."

"Then that's the kind of force we can expect here. Listen to me carefully, boy, for I will only say this once. I will tolerate no dissent. You will set aside your pride until after this battle or I will set aside the rest of your life. *That goes for all of you!*" Jagdish looked around the room to make sure he was understood, before turning back to the warrior. "This is not just a challenge to us, or our house, or even our caste. It is a challenge to our species. This time we don't make war for land, or wealth, or the whims of the offended first. We make war to *survive*. We make war so our wives and children might live. We make war so there is a tomorrow. Do you understand me?"

Shamed, that young man nodded.

"On second thought, keep your pride. You will need it to fight. But temper it with the wisdom to accept help when it is offered." Jagdish let go of his sash, then walked to the center of the room and raised his voice. "Now listen up. We don't know how long we've got until the enemy arrives, so we'll waste not a single minute. If any of you here are yearning for a righteous vengeance against anyone else here, you'll have to wait your turn. At this dinner party the demons get the first serving before anyone asks for seconds. You have all heard now of what happened in the south and in the desert. That cannot be allowed to happen here. *I* will not allow that to happen here. I require every sword arm! Every wizard! Every illegal weapon and rod and bomb! If there's a stick, we'll sharpen it. If there's a place for a trench, we'll dig it. Whether they be fish-eaters or judges, everyone in this house will fight when and how I tell them to! Do you understand me?"

"*Yes, sir!*" all the Vadal warriors shouted in unison.

"Good! Men of the Capitol, Sons of the Black Sword, the same goes for you. From now until the demons show their ugly faces you will not care what the man by your side believes in, or which banner he follows, only that he is willing to stand with you against hell! I have ridden with the Sons of the Black Sword. I have led the armies of Vadal after being thrown in a Vadal prison. I have fought with and against the forces of the Law. Our loyalties before today do not matter for this fight. All that matters is what we do now. *Would you be remembered as the men who crushed the demon menace forever?*"

Every warrior, regardless of house or lack thereof, roared in affirmation.

"Then you are with me! Together we fight. Together we win!"

As the warriors of many houses cheered, Ashok nodded his approval. Jagdish had always had a natural gift for leadership. It was good to see that it had not been squandered. It was ironic that the gods had prepared for this battle for so long, molding their chosen leaders with black steel and prophecies, that now their fate depended upon the character of one humble warrior who had ended up where he was simply by constantly trying to do the right thing.

"Let's get to work. We have a city to defend."

Chapter 11

Days passed. Plans were made. Supplies were stockpiled. Combatants were gathered. Pardons were issued.

"I can't believe I'm flaunting the Law like this in public," Gutch muttered as he inspected his wagon full of guns, in a busy district, surrounded by thousands of witnesses. "I feel like surely this is a test for shameless criminality, which I have undoubtedly failed, and any moment now the Inquisitors are going to swoop down upon me in the form of glowing black buzzards to pluck out my eyes and carry me back screaming to be roasted to death upon their terrible dome."

"Calm yourself, Gutch," Jagdish assured him. "You said so many things there that're wrong I hardly know where to begin correcting you. The Inquisitors answer only to Devedas now, and he's declared if the weapons are intended to be used against the demons, we can make whatever Fortress alchemy we feel like. And apparently it's not called the Inquisitors' Dome anymore, it's called the Tower of Silence, I suppose 'cause that sounds scarier. Only the Capitol lies mostly abandoned anyway except for the small contingent of firsters there led by his lovely wife."

Ashok stood next to Jagdish and Gutch. "I have met this Maharani. She seems rather capable."

"Indeed. Rada's sweet too. My daughter adores her. She's also the main reason Vadal still has casteless. And, Gutch, let's be reasonable.

The Inquisitors could hardly be expected to transform into birds and carry a man of your considerable density all the way back to the Capitol. Can you imagine the expenditure in magic it would take to move such a great weight such a long distance that way?"

"Hey, now!"

"This is likely true," Ashok agreed. "The wizards who carried me to find Jagdish asked that I leave my armor behind due to the weight."

"Alright, alright. Enough already. You don't need to pile it on."

"That's surely what the poor Inquisitor who was expected to fly Gutch all the way to the desert would cry!" Jagdish quipped.

"Such disrespect as I am brutalized at the hands of my alleged friends." Gutch sighed and pulled the cover back over the back of the wagon. Legal or not, it was reflex for a smuggler to hide his cargo. "Alright, boys, they're all yours. Don't have too much fun all at once," he told Jagdish's men, who were there to take delivery of the temporarily not-illegal weapons. Those poor warriors still seemed nervous to be around such dishonorable things, but they would do as they were told, and the guns would be issued to the city's sepoys—worker caste obligated to serve as a city militia.

"Alright, Jagdish, that's twenty more Gutch-quality rods delivered to aid your defense, and more should be arriving by the day."

Jagdish had told Ashok that though the warriors hated such untraditional weapons, his Thakoor was not so bound by tradition, and had directed Jagdish to collect as many Fortress rods as possible while he could. *If* the demons were defeated, Ashok suspected there would be a rebalancing of power in Lok...but that was not Ashok's concern.

"Well done, Gutch," Jagdish said. "With the aid of the Sons' gunners and foreigners it shouldn't take too many days to teach the conscripts how to stand on a wall and make noise and smoke in the demons' general direction."

Gutch watched the wagon roll around the corner out of sight, before gesturing for Ashok and Jagdish to walk with him. "Those rods of my usual excellent quality at a heavily discounted price I reserve only for friends and family, but this humble delivery isn't what I asked you fellows here for today. Come on."

They followed Gutch as he led them deeper into the workers' district. The big man moved with surprising speed for his size and had a spring to his step.

"You walk with purpose, Gutch," Ashok said.

"Us workers would call it hustle, General Ashok. That's what my caste does when we see a golden opportunity before us. I merely require your support to make this dream come true."

Many of the people here recognized Gutch and seemed happy to see him. The rest of the workers knew who Ashok and Jagdish were. They loved Jagdish. They feared Ashok.

"This was one of the districts where I worked before my unfortunate brush with the Law that sent me to Cold Stream. As a Forge Master Smith I had to become very familiar with the city's many industries and how they work together. With your permission, illustrious Phontho Jagdish, whose turban is now heavily burdened with stars, I would like to take over some of these facilities in order to commission a great work which has the potential to make even the armies of hell tremble."

"This ought to be good," Jagdish said.

"Of course, I will require a few things from both of you, but as you know, honest Gutch always provides a good return on your investment."

This district was a loud, busy place. Throngs of workers rushed about, attending to their odd affairs. There were sparks and smoke, and draft animals bellowing over the endless banging of hammers.

"What do you need from us, Gutch?"

"I have already borrowed from Ashok his Fortress envoy so I could pick her brain. She knows a surprising amount about mechanics and physics for a female. Her tales are fascinating. Did you know the islanders have used their rods against demons before? Though deadly against humans, they're lacking in power against demons. Lead balls don't work much better than us beating them with clubs, only they can do it from farther away. Most of the projectiles flatten and bounce off their iron-tough hide uselessly. Their gunners have to hit a demon hundreds of times in the off chance of inflicting a deadly wound upon one, so their success against the beasts isn't much better than our warriors'."

It appeared Gutch was taking them toward a gigantic foundry facility. In Vadal, even the workers' holdings were artistically decorated from top to bottom, and this one was no different. The carvings of trees, animals, and peaceful nature scenes seemed out of place on a structure devoted to noisy industry. The three steaming towers of this place were capped in bronze, and a massive bell hung over the entrance.

"The Fortress folk make special rods to be used against demons which fire pointed, hardened steel bullets, loaded from the rear of the barrel rather than the front, and they do slightly better at penetrating hide than their regular designs, which aren't so different than the ones shown to me by Mother Dawn, which I've been producing. Sadly, there's no way I could switch over production to such a wild and untested new design in all my many facilities across Lok fast enough. By the time we got the problems worked out, we'd surely be up to our necks in sea demons. So, I got to thinking to myself, and said, 'Master Gutch, applying your great knowledge of manufacturing and demon anatomy to this problem, working only with what resources we have available here in Vadal today, what is the solution?'"

"So you've appointed yourself an expert demon surgeon now too?" Jagdish asked.

"Well, we butchered several of them in the swamp. I wouldn't say 'surgeon,' as I don't need to know how to put them back together, just take them apart. Nonetheless, stymied in my quest, I proposed this same question to Envoy Praseeda, as her Weapons Guild has asked themselves this same thing many times. The answer they came up with was something called cannonry, which was rather innovative, based on old drawings from their so-called workshop, and they forged some prototypes to test the concept, but unfortunately for Fortress their poor little island lacked the materials to build very many of the things. And then where would they put them? They are very heavy. With so much coastline they have no idea where the demons would strike, and they were too big to be very mobile, so the idea was abandoned. However, Vadal does not lack for resources, and in this case, we know where the demons are going to be because they have to come to us. I can simply put them on wheels."

"You've lost me, Gutch," Jagdish said.

"Ah, Jagdish, being lost is the story of your life. You have often gotten lost when you've not had your humble servant Gutch there to lend you his wisdom...Look up."

They had stopped under the shadow of the giant bell. To Ashok it appeared to be made from the same bronze that decorated Vadal's armor.

"Alright...and?"

"The Thakoor said you could obligate whatever you needed to save his city, Jagdish. Turn this bell metal foundry over to my control, as well as anything else I deem essential, and all the notes necessary to pay the best craftsmen, along with some of Ashok's knowledgeable Fortress folk, and I will provide you with guns so powerful that even if they don't pierce demon hide they'll still hit those salty bastards hard enough it should break their bones and pulverize their flesh into a demonic slurry."

"So, your great idea is go bigger?"

"Bigger is always better, my friend. If you warriors have been told otherwise it's because the ladies were trying not to hurt your feelings. I'm talking about Fortress rods that will launch metal balls big around as your noggin, faster than the eye can see. The Weapons Guild of Fortress has the knowledge of projectiles, powders, and pressure. Vadal has the tools and materials. Give me the keys to this district and time to work and I'll give you splattered demons in return."

This was not Ashok's decision to make, so he looked to Jagdish, who appeared to be mulling the offer over.

"Time I can't promise, Gutch. When they'll attack, your guess is as good as mine. Bank notes? Devedas has pledged the support of his banks, so money isn't an issue for now. But taking over the city's industries and interrupting our trade—which has already been stalled for so long—will anger all the high-status men who've already got doubts the demons are coming at all. I know those snoots are whispering in my Thakoor's ear that I'm delusional for listening to *him*." He nodded toward Ashok. "You've seen these Fortress things used far more than I have, Ashok. Your opinion?"

When he had met Gutch, Ashok had thought of him as nothing more than a selfish criminal, motived only by the basest greed, but Gutch had since proven Ashok wrong a great many times. In his own peculiar worker way, Gutch was a visionary man, as stalwart as any of the Sons. If he said it could be done, then it could be done.

"Give this man his factories."

Chapter 12

Weeks had passed since his arrival in Vadal City, and Devedas had spent much of that time writing letters and composing messages to be sent via demon bone. It had been a challenge to run the government in the best of times. It was proving far more difficult to do so isolated on one end of the continent, while the base of his power sat empty, and all the Orders that served him were in shambles.

Many of his recent pronouncements had not been well received. His requests for aid in the north had mostly been ignored. Very little help had been promised so far. Had he fought this hard to become king of a great heap of nothing? Were the great houses—barely tamed beasts in the best of times—going to forsake the Capitol and blunder off in their own direction? All the things that traditionally kept the castes in line had been weakened. The Inquisition was a husk of itself after the shame Omand had brought to it, and every Protector had been ordered to travel to Vadal as fast as they could to meet the demon menace. It didn't matter what edicts a Maharaja made, if there was no one he could send to enforce them.

And damn the demons most of all. Normally a day without demons was a good and normal thing, but the more time that passed without any sign of them the more people began to doubt that an invasion was happening at all. It was easy for the naïve to say two attacks on two different cities was a fluke. Coastal raids were infrequent, but it was as if those had ceased entirely. Many took that as a sign the demons' hunger had been sated by their feast in the Capitol and the sea would be content to leave them be. Devedas knew this was merely the calm before the storm. He could feel it in his bones. There were no raids because all the demons in the world were on their way here.

He did not believe in Ashok's silly gods, but only a fool would deny that there was something to Thera Vane's prophecies. It was no coincidence the rebel prophet had used the ancients' name for this place, only to have that corroborated by his own wife. Rada was incredibly intelligent. She was often naïve, and her good intentions got her into trouble, but she was quite possibly the smartest person he had ever known. She believed Vadal City had significance to both the demons and the ancients. So this was the place. Of that Devedas had no doubt. The issue was how to convince—or force—the other powerful men of Lok to believe the same.

A Thakoor's responsibility was to his house. They would reason that if there was another underground attack coming, it could be against them, so why should they send troops to distant Vadal rather than fortifying their own lands? He had tried his best to persuade them, but Devedas could never admit that his strategy was based upon the prophecies of a rebel witch, a foreigner's memory of an ancient map, and his own wife's interpretation of the prior age's symbology.

Instead, he had written to the eleven distant Thakoors that the Capitol had discerned Vadal to be the demons' next target based upon ancient wisdom—which was partially true—and the deduction of the finest minds of the scholarly Orders—which was entirely a lie, as most of those scholars had already fled or been devoured by demons when he had made the decision to march here.

Yet doubts nagged him. What if he was wrong? What if it wasn't Vadal City, but Lahkshan or Warun they were burrowing toward? What if there was nothing to Thera Vane's mystical Voice or Rada's cracked mirror? By leading his remaining forces north, Devedas had made the wounded Capitol appear even weaker to the houses. A king who could not command respect was no king at all.

The one good thing that had come from this mess was that it appeared the demonic threat had finally brought an end to the various conflicts fueled by Omand's machinations. There had been tensions and even outright war among several different houses, but with demons on the prowl none of them wanted to end up like the Capitol, with the bulk of their troops off on some distant campaign, and their homes unprotected.

Devedas sighed as he read the latest note that had been delivered to him. The Thakoor of Harban had responded. He had already obligated many of his warriors to guard the Capitol, and those had been conscripted into the Army of Many Houses. Was that not enough? He had his own lands to defend, and his neighbors in Makao had recently descended into a fever of religious fanaticism. Why did he pay taxes to the Capitol if the Inquisition and Protectors would not fulfill their responsibilities of keeping the houses safe from such madness? The judges would never have let criminals preach of gods and sow division in his lands. He did not care for Devedas' sudden ruling that religion should be allowed. How could eight hundred years of criminality be reversed so suddenly? And what was he expected to do with his remaining casteless? How did the Capitol expect to turn savage animals into whole men? What next? Would the Maharaja declare on a whim that there were no more castes, and the workers should wage war while the warriors plowed the fields? Was the Capitol going to proclaim that pigs and goats were now whole men too? All of these questions required satisfactory answers before the Thakoor of Harban would even begin to consider the Maharaja's request for more warriors.

Devedas threw that note on the pile with all the others. Some of the responses had been polite. Others had been as rude and disrespectful as that one. He had no good answers to their angry questions, and in some cases he even agreed with their assessment. Only, none of those sheltered fools had watched a horde of demons plucking the limbs off women and children like they were flower petals. No one who had survived the Capitol doubted what was at stake.

Rather than compose a response while he was frustrated—because the way he felt right then it might result in another war—Devedas picked up the one letter that he had received that day which had actually brought him joy, and he read that one again instead.

Dearest Devedas,

    I have sent detailed reports about everything I have found in the oldest histories about the nature of demons and the prior conflict against them, as well as an update on the affairs of the Capitol in exile and the state of each of the Orders therein. I hope these letters will be of use to you. For this letter in particular I would prefer to write of personal matters.

    Though the days have been grim and spirits are low I am happy that we have managed to salvage most of the Capitol's books, papers, and historical artifacts. I have been trying desperately to get the first caste to do what is best for Lok. I have managed as best as I can this authority which I never endeavored to hold. In your absence I govern an empty city in your name and despite that emptiness somehow an entitled mob still bothers me, incessantly nattering away asking for help and favors I cannot give. All while I am not you and they do not respect me accordingly.

    That is only one of the many reasons I eagerly await your return. My heart yearns to be reunited with you once again. I regret every harsh word which has ever passed between us. I miss you greatly, my love. I know you are doing what you must to protect us all. I know it is by trust in my scholarship that you have gone to the north. I know that goodness will prevail and evil will be vanquished back to the sea.

    It is with great joy that I inform you that I am with child. The Maharaja will have an heir. Only my maids know of this so far. If all goes well the baby should be winter born, like his father.

                    Be strong for both of us.
                      With love,
                      Radamantha

It was good to have a reminder why he needed to keep fighting.

"Maharaja, you have an unscheduled visitor," Rane Garo called from outside the tent.

What remained of the Army of Many Houses was camped on the eastern outskirts of Vadal City, in a pasture that Phontho Jagdish had chosen for them because it was as out of the way and unthreatening to Vadal's first caste as possible. Despite their location, Devedas still had an endless parade of visitors trying to waste his time and curry his favor. Rane knew to turn most of them away, so this must be someone important.

"Who is it now?"

"Former Protector Karno Uttara wishes to speak with you. He's right outside."

No wonder the uninvited guest had made it so far into the Maharaja's camp. It wasn't like anyone here had the stones to turn Karno aside. He was an imposing giant. Karno was not an angry or boastful man. On the contrary, there was a perpetual calmness about Karno, but he obviously possessed so much nonchalant capability for violence that it cowed even the most bombastic warriors.

Devedas carefully folded Rada's letter for safekeeping and put it away. "Let him in and give us some privacy."

Karno had to duck to enter the humble tent, and when he saw Devedas was sitting on a straw mat, using nothing but a plank as a desk to write his correspondence, he seemed to approve of the austere spectacle. The Maharaja's fine armor was on its stand and that was the only thing in the tent with any shine to it. His quarters were as stark and uncomfortable as the barracks they'd shared as children.

"I expected more opulence for a man of your towering station. Where are your legion of servants?"

"Digging defensive trenches and building fortifications, probably. There's a time and a place for that ostentatious nonsense, Karno, but I've got an invasion to stop. Have a seat."

Karno looked around and then sat on a patch of grass. At least he'd been polite enough to leave his war hammer outside with the guards.

There was an uncomfortable silence between the two of them. Devedas fought with emotion. Karno fought with indifference. They had long been friends, but the last time they had truly spoken things had become very heated, and they had parted, not as enemies but with an anger between them. Devedas had talked with Karno only briefly in the aftermath of the demons' attack on the Capitol, but that had been reserved, and they'd both been distracted. Devedas had seen very little of Karno since then.

"I'm told you ride with the Sons of the Black Sword now. Has the legendary Karno Uttara gone fanatic?"

"I find the religious to be superstitious fools, but at least they are honest in their dealings."

"And I have not been."

Karno shrugged. He'd not said it.

"Before you say anything else, Karno, I never had the opportunity to thank you for your service in the Capitol."

"I was not there to serve you."

"I'm aware. Regardless, thank you."

Karno nodded at Devedas' sincerity.

And sincere he was, for Rada was going to give Devedas a child, and the only reason she was alive to do so was because of the fearless devotion of this man. "So, what brings you to the Maharaja's splendorous tent, Karno? Have you come to mock my hubris in thinking one man could run the entire world?" He gestured bitterly at the pile of letters before him. "It seems all the Thakoors do."

"Those who mock will mourn when the demons consume us because they refused to listen to the truth."

"You really think Ashok's woman is right about this being the place?"

"I've been among the fanatics for a while now. They are sincere. A fraud might deceive them, but Ashok?"

Devedas nodded at that wisdom. "Unlikely."

"You must make the Thakoors understand what is coming, Devedas. You must defend Lok. It is your responsibility."

"I'm doing everything I can."

Karno scowled. "Are you?"

So *that* was what had brought Karno here to face him finally. It had certainly taken him long enough. "You want me to tell the Vadal about the second Heart. Is that it?"

Karno said nothing—as was his manner—which said everything.

"They don't know what kind of treasure they have, Karno. Even if they did, their wizards lack the understanding to use it properly. Only Senior Protectors grasp what that artifact is capable of or how to awaken its power. If it's got a fraction of the magic in it that our Heart of the Mountain once did, then it could change everything. No one house could ever be allowed to have such power unchecked. Can you imagine what would happen if Vadal could create its very own army of Protectors?"

"They could fight demons better."

"And afterward they could conquer every other house with ease. Such power in one Thakoor's hands would destabilize all of Lok. Vadal City would become the Capitol and every other house would be enslaved."

Karno shrugged again.

Devedas laughed, as if life was as uncomplicated as Karno made it out to be. "Of course, I realize none of this will matter if demons kill us all before that. Believe me, that thought has crossed my mind." In reality, it was more like the idea had tormented Devedas' dreams and robbed him of sleep the entire journey north, but he would not admit to such weakness. "Once I knew I couldn't seize Vadal's Heart by force, I thought about how I might trick or coerce the Vadal into giving it to me, so I could use it to revitalize the Order, to create many more Protectors who could help against the demons. But given our recent history, the Vadal aren't going to grant the Capitol another inch."

Karno mulled that over before responding. "You know, the religious fanatics constantly tell tales of this ancient warrior, mightier than any man, who came down from the sky to fight the demons. It's their favorite story. They will not shut up about this Ramrowan of theirs."

"So?" Devedas didn't know why Karno would bring up some old myth right then.

"Except...this story is at least partly true, for I have been inside his tomb. It was Ramrowan who founded our Order, not to serve the Law, but the people. *The people,* Devedas. I do not like the idea some religious king created the Protectors. It leaves a sour taste in my mouth even saying the words. But Rada's old books confirm them. It was in this Ramrowan's secret tomb that I found the other Heart, hidden among the ashes of the Protectors who came before us. This Heart belonged to them. You cannot let their descendants perish in ignorance while such a mighty weapon sits unused."

As the Capitol had been torn apart around them, the only combatants who had held their own against the demons had been those who had touched the Heart of the Mountain. Devedas, Karno, Bundit Vokkan, and Broker Harban, with Ashok and his killing sword, fighting side by side had proven equivalent to hundreds of regular soldiers in effectiveness. Devedas had sent for every Protector in Lok to get here as quickly as possible, but even if they all arrived in time, they were still comparatively few in number.

"You must realize that simply giving a Heart to Vadal is madness. If we show them how to unlock its power, we *might* survive the demons, only then Vadal would surely rule the world afterward."

"I don't care for the Vadal over any other house, but they do not eat human flesh. This does not seem a difficult choice to me."

"Choices are easier when you're not the one responsible for the well-being of the Law and every other great house, Karno."

"I'm not the one responsible... and I am thankful for that. This is the duty you sought, Devedas. You wished to rule. So rule. Do what is best now, while there is still a future to worry about."

Devedas gave a bitter laugh. "So you come here pressuring me to do what you think is right, putting it all on me. Except you know about the second Heart too. Why haven't you told the Vadal about it yourself?"

Karno scowled at that absurd notion. "My oath as a Protector forbids me from sharing the Order's secrets. I am no longer a Protector, but you know that oath holds until death."

"So, you can ask me to gamble the future of the Capitol, and the continuation of the Law itself, and all the traditions of our people, of every other house, forever and ever... but flawless Karno can't break an oath? You'd put this difficult choice on me, after shirking it yourself? You ride with Ashok now. Ratul showed him how the Heart works, same as either of us. Yet you didn't tell Ashok so he could use it to empower his ferocious Sons of the Black Sword. Instead, you're here, placing this choice on *my* head, I think, so you can be free of the cost yourself. Then stalwart Karno Uttara never has to ask himself *what if I'm wrong?*"

Karno seemed to take offense at that, but he was never quick to anger. Instead, he pondered Devedas' words for a moment before nodding slowly as he decided there was some truth to them. "That's not entirely wrong. I shouldn't expect someone else to bear the brunt of history's judgment for my bad decision. If in a generation we live with Vadal's boot on all our necks, let the people curse the name Karno for it. I will remedy my weakness of character immediately and notify the Vadal... Will you have me killed to protect your secrets, Maharaja?"

"No." Devedas wasn't even offended by Karno asking such a thing. That was a wise question when dealing with a man of his station. "That is not my way."

"Good. Then I shall go to Phontho Jagdish and tell him what his house truly has in its possession. If you will excuse me." Karno stood up.

"Hold on."

As the giant paused, Devedas went through his pile of letters, picked one in particular, and held it up. "Before you go off stirring up outrage, read this first."

Karno took the letter in one big hand and scanned it quickly. "The Maharaja has declared that a new elite militant Order be formed?"

"That I have. The Protectors serve the interests of the Law. That's so ingrained in our nature I don't think it could ever be changed, no matter what I pronounce. So the Protectors will always serve as the Law's enforcers. The Inquisition's mission was to stamp out religion, the practice of which is now legal, so they are without greater purpose. Also, after we deal with the demons—*if* we deal with the demons—I'm having the Inquisition disbanded and their members sent to other Orders as fitting to finish off their terms of obligation."

Karno actually smiled, which was a very rare thing. "The masks will not be missed."

"They will not. Of the many world-shaking pronouncements I've made recently, ending the Inquisition will probably be the least controversial one among them. The Capitol has always had two militant Orders seeing to its interests. With the Inquisition ended, there would be one. So there will be another Order formed, equal in might and scope to the Protectors, only they'll not answer to the Capitol but rather to the will of every house and every caste."

"Curious. You propose a rebalancing of power?"

"I do."

"Such an Order might have stopped your rise."

"Most likely. It's also a shield against any future excesses by me or my heirs. The Protectors' weakness is we...or now I should say *they*...serve the Law even when the Law is subverted. As the people were tormented by Omand, their houses had no recourse except risking a war they couldn't possibly win, so they allowed the Law to become corrupted. Vadal alone was rich and stubborn enough to stand against us. Having another Order equal in might to the Protectors, answering to a council of the houses and castes, would prevent such an abuse of authority in the future. Every individual the houses obligate to this Order, who is judged worthy by that Order's master, will be granted physical gifts equal to those of the Protectors."

"Empowered by the second Heart..."

"Yes. Check the date."

Karno frowned. "Two days ago."

"That was when the message was sent, in secret, by magic to every Thakoor and by letter to the ranking warrior and worker in every great and vassal house, as well as Thera Vane on behalf of the religious, and to Ashok, who I reason should speak for the casteless as well as anyone else, at least until all the fish-eaters out there realize it's illegal to murder them anymore and they form their own organizations to represent them. I composed that letter the week before that, but I needed to be able to see the second Heart for myself, to be absolutely certain it was as you described it to be, so I wasn't making any promises I couldn't keep. Your report was accurate. Now all the houses which doubted me about the demons and refused to send help, will rush to obligate their best fighters so that they'll have an opening stake in this powerful new entity."

Karno thought through the repercussions of Devedas' actions for a long moment. "So rather than simply giving this power to the Vadal as I impatiently would have done, you've sacrificed some of your own power and used it to recruit more defenders from every house to stand against the demons here."

Devedas spread his hands in mock apology. "You came to persuade me to do something I had already done, Blunt Karno. I was just trying to do it in a way that accomplished the most good while causing the least harm...as a good ruler should. Sorry to waste your time."

"Hmmmm..." Karno pondered that, before giving Devedas a respectful nod. "Learning about your own weaknesses is never a waste. I have been humbled. Accept my apology."

"Despite what you think of me, I'm not evil."

"I do not think that," Karno stated flatly. "I believe you to be ruthless and determined. Sometimes misguided. Often too prideful for your own good. But not evil. That is different."

Devedas would accept that description. "As part of the agreement I made with Phontho Jagdish and Thakoor Bhadramunda, the first obligations to this Order will be from Vadal. The next will be from the Sons of the Black Sword, because I want it known that even the fanatics will be respected under my rule. If some of the First want to whine and kick against me giving status to certain kinds of criminals, then they will do so as hypocrites, as they send their finest to join the same powerful new organization so as to not get left behind."

It was a rare thing, but Karno actually seemed impressed. "You have done the honorable thing, and in a way that is wiser than I would have. Perhaps you will not be a terrible king after all."

"On the contrary, all kings must be terrible in some way. Trading arcane knowledge for the Maharaja's political gain was a simple equation, but there are still matters to attend to. Though it's hidden beneath this city now, the second Heart must be entrusted to a caretaker of a different house to maintain balance. Just as the Master of the Protectors set the standards and determined our traditions and code, so will the newly appointed master of this new Order. This must be a man of honor and integrity, who can't be swayed or bought, because surely the houses and castes will try. He alone will judge the individual obligations and decide who among them is worthy to be magnified."

"This is wise," Karno agreed. "This method has always worked for the Protectors. Assuming their Heart works as ours does, it can only be used on a handful of obligations over the span of a few days, before requiring time to recover as those connections are strengthened. For now, we will need as many warriors empowered and taught how to use its gifts as quickly as possible, but men of poor character must be weeded out before being entrusted with such might. Such precious magic should never be wasted on the unworthy."

"I'm glad you agree. I would have you start then immediately, *Master* Karno."

The big man was silent for a very long time as he pondered the implications. "You cunning bastard."

"Add that to your list of descriptors for me—determined, misguided, and a right cunning bastard, but rarely evil. Regardless, your Maharaja has spoken. Karno Uttara...will you accept this obligation?"

Devedas already knew what the answer would be because he had trapped Karno as surely as he had trapped all the great houses with the creation of this Order. The bait to catch Tha-koors was the fear of being excluded from prestige and power. The bait to catch Karno was his sense of responsibility, for he would recognize that there was no one else available here and now who was as uniquely suited for this duty as he was.

"What'll it be?" he asked.

"If we survive the demons, will this master still be able to mold the Order as he sees fit?"

"What are your terms?"

"They must serve among the people of their houses and castes, against any and all outside threats, whether those threats come from the sea or land. This includes the Capitol should it ever again become tyrannical."

"I'd expect nothing less."

There was nothing there but the canvas wall of a tent, but Karno stared into the distance as he outlined his vision. "They will serve among their people, because being separate and above makes even good men aloof. I would make them guards, not conquerors. Champions, not overseers. The Protectors should never have been made into tools of punishment. We are the best among men, yet the people don't love Protectors. They fear us. Because even as we kept them safe, we took their property with impunity. What difference does it make to the farmer if he's robbed by bandits or by the Law? He's still getting robbed. We were supposed to protect the people, yet they live in fear that the smallest perceived infraction means we could destroy their lives. That mistake must be avoided."

Devedas considered Karno's words. The Protectors of the Law had been the Law's finest killers since long before either of their time. "I trust you with this foundation. Build it as you see fit."

Karno bowed his head. "Then this Order has my obligation. I will serve."

Giving up the second Heart had been a very difficult deci-sion. Who to entrust it to had not. "Per our agreement, the first obligations must be from Vadal. They will present candidates—"

"I already know who will be the first from the Vadal."

That was unexpected. "You've not even seen who their Tha-koor is going to send."

"I don't care. He can save those for the next batch. I spent time among this people. I have observed the character of a few of them under pressure. Such a test is more accurate than any amount of questioning I could give them. I know the ones who stood with me against the Scourge and beneath the pillar of fire. Also there are a few who aided Rada and me, even though it risked dishonoring their names. Assuming they lived through their war against you, those will be the first called."

Devedas couldn't argue with that logic. It wasn't like they had the time to train them mercilessly from childhood at an isolated fortress, before making them climb a frozen mountain to fight Dasa to test their mettle. "Then you must choose an equal number from the Sons of the Black Sword."

"I have ridden with them long enough to know each by deed and reputation. There are several who I think would do. Then I must pick from your Army of Many Houses, I assume?"

"Yes. I would offer suggestions, if you would trust them. Though once their obligation in this battle is through, they'll be released from the Capitol's army and get sent back to defend their homes."

"Hmmm...I like that. Does this Order have a name?"

"Not yet."

"Then let the Defenders of Lok be both check against, and ally to, the Protectors of the Law, and together we will fight for our people."

Chapter 13

"Stop whatever you are doing, Ashok Vadal, and come out to fight me!"

Ashok had been conferring with two of his officers inside the Sons' camp. He looked over and saw Jagdish quickly approaching, and wondered why the phontho of Great House Vadal was carrying a pair of wooden practice swords. Several of his officers were trying to keep up with their leader, but Jagdish was clearly too excited to worry about decorum.

"What's all this?"

"It's time we had us a rematch, old friend."

"Right now?"

"Yes, right now." Jagdish tossed one of the wooden swords Ashok's way.

He reflexively caught it. "Does Vadal's supreme commander not have anything more important to do?"

"I've got a long list of duties that need attending to." Jagdish grinned as he spun his wooden sword a few times to stretch the muscles of his arm and wrist. "Which is why I'm going to make this quick."

Most encounters against Ashok were over fast, yet he had always enjoyed sparring against Jagdish. While he had been confined to Cold Stream Prison, Jagdish had been a relentless challenger and dedicated student, testing himself against his undefeatable opponent nearly every day. Those sparring sessions had been the only enjoyable thing about the miserable time he'd spent in prison while awaiting his sentence.

Jagdish was grinning like a fool. "Trust me, Ashok. This will be a good fight."

Perhaps it would be good to take a break from the monotony of preparing for an invasion. "As you wish, Phontho."

"You heard your general, fanatics!" Jagdish shouted at the nearby Sons. "My challenge has been accepted. Now stand back and give us some room."

The men were eager for the show. What soldier wouldn't enjoy unexpectedly watching his commander fight? Especially when one was a noted swordsman, and the other was a living legend. Warriors of both factions hurried out of the way, leaving the two commanders alone on the grassy area between some tents and wagons.

Most of the Sons only knew of Jagdish by reputation, but Shekar Somsak and Eklavya had been there since near the beginning and had both served under Jagdish when he had been the Sons' first risalder. Ashok knew they loved the man like their flesh-and-blood older brother. Those two officers shared an excited glance, because they had watched this match play out many times before. They too had trained against unstoppable Ashok, especially in those early days when their numbers had been few. Though none of the men had ever come anywhere near besting him, Jagdish had come the closest. It had still been a vast gulf between them, but all things were relative.

"I always loved these beatings," Shekar crowed, before bragging to the gathering crowd. "Back when there weren't so many of us, we all got to try ourselves against Ashok to get humbled. Watch and learn, boys!"

One of the men who had come with Jagdish was wearing a Vadal uniform but with a wolf pelt over his shoulder like a warrior of Sarnobat. "It is an incredible honor to finally meet the Forgotten's Warrior, but please, Lord Ashok, do not kill foolish Jagdish for daring to challenge you. I think the gods might still need him."

"Not now, Najmul!"

"You have begun collecting your own religious fanatics?" Ashok asked.

"It's a long story." Jagdish brought his wooden sword up in a salute. "Cold Stream rules?"

Those had been the agreed-upon terms for their sparring sessions in prison. It meant he would not use Angruvadal and would try his best to not injure Jagdish too severely. The prison had needed its warden conscious and with unbroken bones. There had never been a corresponding consideration for Jagdish to try not to injure Ashok, because frankly, it was highly doubtful that he'd ever be able to anyway, no matter how hard he tried.

"Cold Stream rules." Ashok returned the salute. "Let us begin."

The two of them circled. As expected, Jagdish's stance seemed competent as ever. He had always been strong, but his footwork would never be considered graceful. Jagdish had never been a naturally gifted swordsman but had become a very proficient one through tireless effort. There were never any shocking breakthroughs for a warrior like Jagdish, just an endless grind to become a bit better somehow. Stick with that long enough and even a clumsy man could become a good duelist, and Jagdish was certainly not clumsy.

Ashok was still curious as to what had brought about this sudden challenge. He got his answer when Jagdish launched his first attack with Protector speed.

Narrowly avoiding a sudden thrust, Ashok had to pivot to block the wooden sword inches from his body. Without hesitation, Jagdish struck again. He used the traditional Vadal style of powerful overhead strikes, which could quickly turn into vicious curving slashes. It was a technique Ashok knew well, but Jagdish launched twenty attacks in the same time in which a regular man might send five. Dents were driven into the hardwood as Ashok anticipated and caught each blow. Faster than a man could blink, the wooden sword kept coming. The last was a wide flashing arc that forced Ashok to dive and roll away.

When Ashok came back up, he found that Jagdish was beaming. "I almost got you that time!"

"Nearly so." Ashok nodded respectfully, for Karno had chosen his first obligations well. "Well done, *Defender* Jagdish."

The crowd was gaping at both of them. Even the haughty Sarnobat bodyguard seemed awed by his master's incredible speed, but neither Ashok nor Jagdish could speak about the existence of the second Heart in public. Though Shekar and Eklavya both grinned nearly as wide as Jagdish at the mention of the new Order, for both of them had been interviewed by Karno as potential candidates.

Those two had been around Ashok long enough to grasp just how superior a Protector was to a normal warrior, and it was a nearly inconceivable dream that such magical might could be bestowed upon those who had so recently been disgraced criminals.

"I think I understand you a bit better now, Ashok."

"If you truly understood me, Jagdish, you would not have tried to defeat me."

Jagdish charged again, but now knowing what he faced, Ashok moved aside easily. As Jagdish made himself faster, Ashok easily matched the unnatural speed. When the wooden swords crossed, Ashok shoved his opponent away.

"Impressive, Jagdish, but you have much to learn still. Let us continue your education."

"That sounds menacing."

This time Ashok set the pace, and even drawing magical might to his muscles, all Jagdish could do was try to survive. He managed to counter Ashok's strikes, but Ashok wasn't just physically fearsome. There was so much more to it than that. Fighting was a contest of technique and instinct. Even without drawing upon his connection to the memories embedded in black steel, Ashok could still anticipate everything his foe would do. He knew Jagdish's thoughts before he had them.

Ashok leaned back as the wooden sword flew past his neck close enough to rustle the hair of his beard, and promptly jabbed Jagdish in the ribs for the trouble.

Jagdish staggered away, breathing hard. "Oceans!"

"Fast is better than slow. Strong is better than weak." Ashok tapped the side of his head. "But the battle is won in here."

It would take time and practice for these new Defenders to grasp the full potential of their magic. The Heart could do many things, but it could only do one of them at once. It could make a man stronger, faster, tougher, improve any one of his senses, or even be directed to heal wounds at an incredible rate. Once mastered, anyone who touched the Heart would be capable of incredible feats. Ashok was thankful that Devedas had the wisdom to use such a mighty force against the demons, but for these men to be effective, learning would have to occur.

Jagdish leapt through the air, far higher than a normal man was capable of. Ashok stepped aside and the wooden sword hit nothing but dirt. Jagdish went after him immediately, striking furiously with a series of powerful blows that would have staggered any regular adversary. Ashok calmly caught each, darted around the last, and hit Jagdish in the lower back. The wooden sword left a bruise. If it had been a regular sword it would have sliced through a kidney. If it had been Angruvadal it would have cut him in half.

"*Ah.*" Jagdish winced at the sharp pain. That would give him a chance to practice using the Heart's healing magic. Ashok was benevolent like that. "Saltwater!"

"It was a fine effort."

"I still can't beat you."

"Yet you came closer than ever before."

Jagdish realized that was true and cackled with glee. "That I did!"

Ashok had given that compliment for the benefit of the observers. Let them be inspired by what fearsome combatants their leaders were. The men from both armies would be left awed by the display of martial prowess they had just seen, and there could be no shame in losing to the legendary Black Heart. Then Ashok went over to Jagdish and placed one hand on the back of his head and drew him close so only Jagdish could hear his words.

"Don't let pride trick you, brother. You have twenty thousand men who can swing a sword. They have *one* who can lead them as you do. Do not fall into the trap of thinking this gift is about individual might. Think bigger. Think like the man who once broke an entire army's spirit with smoke from hot peppers. With the Heart you are a commander who can see the entire battlefield, whose orders can be heard across a city, and who can refuse to die from his wounds until the conflict is done. You do not need to beat me, because you are already *better* than I am."

"That's a lie," Jagdish whispered back.

"As a swordsman, yes, but as a leader . . . as a man, you are far greater than I have ever been, Jagdish. Remember that."

Coming from Ashok, that was powerful praise. The witnesses probably thought Jagdish was wiping sweat from his brow, not an unbidden tear from his eye. "I'll remember."

"Good. Use this new power wisely. Do not squander it."

"I still had to try to take you though, didn't I?"

The genuinely made Ashok laugh, and he embraced his brother. "Never change, Jagdish."

Chapter 14

＝〰〰〰〰〰＝

Later, once Jagdish and his men had left the Sons' camp—after a great deal of visiting, back slapping, and telling of boastful tales, of course—Ashok returned to his command tent and found Karno waiting for him inside. It was unsurprising that the giant had been able to sneak in here unobserved. Karno had always been capable of moving very quietly for a man of such size and physical might. Karno was like a bull with the grace of a tiger.

"So you watched our sparring session, I take it?"

"I followed my first obligation from a distance. Where he went with his newfound power was his decision."

"Did you encourage that frivolous challenge?"

"I did not dissuade him. I was curious to see what would happen."

"And?"

"The abilities granted by the second Heart appear roughly equivalent to ours given by the Heart of the Mountain."

Ashok nodded. "That's good. We will need them."

"I believe I can use it to empower five or six a week, at most. Training them to use it effectively will be another matter entirely."

Protectors spent years mastering the Heart's magic, until calling upon it was effortless. Even if they'd had another hundred Senior Protectors in the Capitol, it wouldn't have been enough to defeat

135

that army of hell. Instinct—his own and the shard's—was telling him the force that was on the way here would be even bigger.

"That is insufficient, Karno."

"I'm aware."

The sad fact was that no matter what they did, it was likely all their efforts would be futile. Ashok went to a chest in the corner and pulled out a wineskin. He took a swig—sparring was thirsty work—and then tossed it to Karno. "As for training, I can help the obligated Sons. Devedas has Protectors he can command to help teach as well."

"Our former brothers won't like training their future rivals."

"Do you care?"

Karno drank the entire skin in one continuous movement, then wiped his mouth with his sleeve. "Of course not."

"Who have you chosen so far?"

"For the first batch, Jagdish, and not just for politics."

"He would have made a fine Protector."

"I disagree."

Ashok was puzzled by that. "Why?"

"Because unlike us, no matter how stern the indoctrination, no matter how harsh the training, that man's own code would always matter more to him than the strict interpretation of the Law. When ordered to do some of the cruel things you or I did without hesitation, Jagdish would have looked those judges in the eye and said no, the Law is wrong... and then probably been executed for it."

Ashok had to nod at that assessment. Karno had always been a keen judge of character. Even Ratul Without Mercy might not have broken that man's spirits. "Jagdish might have made for a troublesome Protector, but he is the ideal for what it sounds like you are trying to accomplish."

"Perhaps I am naïve, but should we survive the demons I hope this Order would avoid the mistakes of our past. Then I have called Vadal warriors Luthra, Girish, Zaheer, and Joshi. From your Sons I am inclined to obligate Eklavya and Ongud."

"Why?" Ashok agreed, but he was curious at Karno's logic.

"Their fanaticism does not seem to outweigh their honor. I think they fight for their people more than their gods."

"I've found that the gods the Sons follow wear many different faces, yet they always somehow seem to be a reflection of each man's own character. I think they make for themselves gods that are what they aspire to be, or purer versions of what they already are."

"What does that say about the god who lives in your woman's head who bosses you about, then?"

Ashok scowled. "The Forgotten is commanding, yet remote and uncaring."

"What a coincidence...I am still unsure about Shekar Somsak."

"He's a tattoo-faced maniac of questionable morals from a raider house that's barely one step above bandits, but he is a beast in a fight and remarkably clever."

"Would he have made a good Protector?"

That was so absurd that Ashok actually laughed. "Absolutely not. I trust him regardless."

Karno nodded, because earning Ashok's trust was no small thing. "I have also taken a liking to this Najmul maniac who follows Jagdish around like an insane religious puppy. He's supposedly a combatant of legendary skill. Simultaneously he is a wolf of Sarnobat, who worships your false gods, *and* serves Vadal, allowing me to placate three factions with a single obligation."

"Who could have guessed that Blunt Karno has a gift for politics? Though I note these are all warrior caste so far."

"We're preparing for war, Ashok."

"Accurate...Yet if you want the support of every caste, you'll need members of the First, workers, and yes, even casteless represented as well. There are tensions between the castes here, and the war preparations exacerbate them. Empowering warriors inspires the warriors, but why not give the sepoys someone to look up to as well? Make them feel that they matter too."

"Since when does Black-Hearted Ashok concern himself about the feelings of lesser men?"

Ashok shrugged, for that was a good question. Perhaps this reflection of the Forgotten wasn't entirely uncaring.

Karno was not the sort to disregard any suggestion, no matter how outlandish it might first seem, even if it didn't fit his preconceived notions. "There is some wisdom there. The city needs every able-bodied man to fight and it isn't like demons can tell the difference between us."

"From the Sons I would recommend the worker Gupta, who now leads my gunners. He is intelligent and a man of character.

And then Toramana, who is brave, and an archer of great skill, but more importantly was a chieftain of wild men who lived entirely outside the Law, so has never had a caste."

"The same one who recently took an axe to your priest?"

Despite Thera trying to keep Javed's return and true nature a secret, there had still been talk around the camp. "That particular priest deserved it."

Karno grunted in acknowledgment. "I'll take your recommendations under advisement." He went to leave but paused at the tent's flap. "I do have one last question."

"Ask it."

"Why did you hold back against Jagdish?"

Karno had always been an astute observer. It was one of the traits that had made him so effective at catching lawbreakers. "You are probably the only witness who would even notice."

"Yes. Why?"

"Those were our terms."

"Do not blame it on Angruvadal. I saw how you fought in the Capitol. What you did there was beyond any bearer. The Heart did not enable such feats either. You are changed, far surpassing the capability of any Protector. The difference between you and me now is greater than the difference between me and a normal warrior."

"Don't worry, Karno. I restrained my abilities against Jagdish because he is an honorable man. The demons will receive no such mercy."

"That's not my worry. You were an inspiration to the rebellion with only the powers of a Protector and a black sword. How will they react when the world sees what you have become?"

"Do you insinuate what the *gods* made me into?"

Legal or not, Karno still hated religious talk. "They call me Blunt Karno. I do not *insinuate*. There are no gods. Just because I do not understand a phenomenon does not mean that I will blame its existence on unseen beings, yet somehow you fight like a creature of illegal myth now."

"I suppose you are right to be concerned then, Karno. Most people are not so rational as you."

"I've been looking for you, Ashok." The flap parted and Thera entered, then she noticed the massive Karno standing there, glowering. "Hello, Karno. Or I suppose it's Master Karno now."

"Lady Vane." Everyone else in camp addressed her as Voice or Prophet, but Karno was far too tradition-bound to use a fanatic's terms, regardless of what Devedas declared the Law to be today. "Excuse me. I was just leaving."

"What was that about?" she asked after Karno had ducked out of the tent.

"That's a man who has had a great burden placed upon him, trying to figure out how best to carry it."

"Well, he's certainly big enough to carry plenty. Throw a rope on him and he could pull a plow." Thera seemed rather excited. "Come on, Ashok. I need your help."

"Normally, when you need my help that means someone is in need of killing."

"I've got a list I'd love to get to eventually, but our mission today's not one of violence, but celebration." When he didn't respond to that, she gave him a glorious smile. Her happiness would probably have been infectious to anyone less dour than Ashok. "Didn't you hear? The Vadal arbiters have made it official. The proclamation's been printed and will be posted everywhere around the city by sundown. We've worked so hard for this. I want to be among the casteless and see their faces when they find out that they're considered whole men now."

That was surely a victory, but Ashok couldn't help but wonder about the unpredictable repercussions of such a bold act. "With demons on the way, any joy the casteless feel will be short-lived."

Thera took him by the arm and pulled him from the tent. "Then let's enjoy what we can while we can."

Chapter 15

The Martaban River was reliably deep, swift, and clean, which was one reason Vadal City had become such a densely populated place. That easy access to water for drinking and commerce came with a cost, as demons sometimes liked to swim upriver to raid. So as in most of the other cities in Lok, men of status always built their homes away from the water, while the workers got the stretches useful for their industries. And after everything good was used up, then the casteless quarters were built on the unwanted bits that were left over. That way when a demon did occasionally raid this far inland, little of value was lost.

Because nobody ever cared about losing some non-people.

That concept had always bothered Thera, but it had always been the way things were. Stick the casteless in the mud. If the demons eat them, no great loss.

Across the continent most of the casteless quarters lay empty because of the Great Extermination. Those who hadn't been murdered had fled and were hiding away from the eyes of the wrathful Law. In Thera's travels over the last year, she had seen many heartbreaking examples of this, with row upon row of shacks, once vibrant and full of life, left abandoned and vacant.

Vadal was a stark contrast to this because the Great Extermination had been stymied here. In fact, the quarters along the Martaban were overflowing, as many of the casteless who escaped other houses had sought shelter here. When it became known that Vadal wasn't following the Capitol's bloodthirsty command, the number of untouchables here had swelled by ridiculous numbers.

The quarter before her now was so overcrowded that disease outbreaks were almost inevitable. When the issued barracks had proven insufficient, the casteless had built more. When they'd run out of land, they'd built upward, until some of the tottering structures were three or even four stories tall. These expansions were mostly constructed out of bits of refuse discarded by the higher castes, wood found drifting down the Martaban, and various materials the casteless had managed to steal from the workers. Thera had to marvel at the ingenuity it took to build a town out of trash, even as she cringed at the thought of what would happen to them if Vadal was ever hit by a strong earthquake.

It was the nature of Vadal that even the poorest of the poor here still lived in a colorful world. The casteless in other lands always seemed drab and gray, but these northern lands were so bountiful that even the cast-off rags the untouchables scrounged to wear were still bright with different color dyes. Even dirty, they were still bright. And it wasn't just their clothing. Flowering vines crawled up every structure. From how shoddy the workmanship of their garbage houses seemed Thera assumed the structural integrity of those vines might be the only things keeping the multistory shacks from falling over. All the greenery gave the place an odd sort of chaotic beauty, like a wild sprawling garden had consumed a town. The natural perfume of so many flowers was almost enough to overcome the stench of the overflowing shit trenches. Obviously, the whole men took their drinking water from upriver.

"There are so many of them," Ashok stated as he looked out over the bustling mobs.

"Here, sure. They weren't so lucky everywhere else."

The Sons' camp was on the west side of the city, not too far from the largest casteless quarter in Vadal, perhaps even in the whole world. It surely was the biggest left around nowadays! What better place to see the celebration? By Thera's insistence only Ashok had accompanied her. She still had many enemies in this city, not because she'd ever personally wronged—or even met—any of them, but because of what she represented. No matter how much the presence of a rebel witch angered proper society, she doubted anyone would dare try anything against her as long as she had fearsome Ashok by her side.

As the two of them walked across the sandy open area at the entrance to the quarter, the nearby casteless took note of their arrival and things subtly changed. A nervous quiet quickly spread. The fishers quit throwing their nets into the river. Children were abruptly silenced and then herded out of sight. Though they'd mostly been spared from the Great Extermination here, the casteless were still used to being brutalized and mistreated. Strangers caused fear. Especially in a time when so much overcrowding begged for a culling in the name of public health.

To avoid being recognized on their trek across the city she'd kept her hood up. Ashok's face had remained hidden beneath that big straw hat he'd taken a liking to. Yet somehow everyone still realized who they were. The casteless certainly had a gift for spotting things that were beneath the notice of the Law-abiding.

The whispers began. *It's Fall.* The whispers spread. *The Voice!*

Their fear changed to something entirely different as Thera pulled back her hood to reveal her face.

Though they'd never seen her before, they all knew who she was, either by description or some other sense of things, and a woman shouted, "It's really her!" And that was enough. Casteless who instinctively cowered upon hearing that whole men were among them now looked up with hope. The mob surged toward them. The children who'd been shushed and sent away came running out of their shacks. Within seconds they were entirely surrounded by a horde of skinny gawkers, trying to get close to their beloved prophet. There were squeals of delight and tears of joy because stories about the return of the Voice had sustained this quarter through dark times. Thera had dealt with adoring casteless before, but never this many at once. This was all the population of the Cove and more. It was an overwhelming press of bodies. Trembling hands reached for her.

Ashok promptly growled, "If you touch her, I will cut off your hands."

Luckily, the casteless heeded his warning.

In the middle of the clearing was a pile of driftwood with a corroded barrel on top. Thera reasoned that would make a decent enough stand so more of the mob could see her better. Ashok's scowl was enough to part the crowd for her. He may have been the champion they'd told stories about for the last few years to give them hope, but that also meant they knew not to trifle with him. If Fall said he'd take your hands, then he'd surely take your hands.

She climbed up the pile, made sure she had a stable footing—it wouldn't do for their prophet to tumble down a pile of garbage in front of them—and surveyed the rapidly growing crowd. They called her the Voice, but her own voice was nothing compared to that booming thing. Thera's real voice wasn't even particularly melodic or enchanting like a woman's should be. The warrior caste of Vane was known for knife throwing, not for their singing, and she lacked Ashok's attention-grabbing command voice, but regardless, she'd do her best.

"Quiet, quiet. Listen to me, please."

The crowd fell into a hushed silence, eager to hear.

"It is true. I am Thera Vane. This is Ashok Vadal."

The casteless went mad with delight. There was cheering and leaping and dancing and crying. Their reaction was so unexpected and passionate that it caused Ashok to twitch nervously at the many sudden movements. Thera was uncomfortable with the attention. Ashok was worried about assassins using this opportunity to launch poison darts at her.

"Calm yourselves and listen!" It took her a few tries, but she managed to get the mob to pay attention again. "Listen!" The clearing gradually fell silent, except for the outer edges, where more and more casteless were rushing up to see what all the commotion was about. They reacted much as the others had when they found out that the Voice of the Forgotten and his warrior were among them. Within minutes a gigantic crowd had formed, packed body to body.

"We heard you'd come here!" a women shrieked.

"The overseers told us it was a lie but I had faith!" proclaimed another.

"It is true," Thera shouted back. "The Sons of the Black Sword are camped just outside this very city."

The casteless were ecstatic. "We must rise up and kill all the whole men now!" someone roared. Upon those words about a third of the crowd began chanting for blood and the majority started to panic. Of course, casteless were docile when cowed, but wild once riled up. She looked down at Ashok and spread her hands apologetically, helpless to stop the rowdy mob.

"Heed your prophet's words!"

That bellowed command did it.

"No, you're not killing anyone. The fighting against the Law is over." There was some murmuring at that, as surely they took it to mean the rebellion had lost. "We won. We're already victorious. How else do you think we got here? I've come to give you good news."

They seemed baffled as to what she was talking about. Of course they didn't know about Devedas' proclamation. The criers wouldn't come here, nobody was going to waste good ink and paper on casteless, and it wasn't like anyone here could read anyway.

"The Law gave in to our demands. As of today, all of you are no longer considered non-people. You are whole men."

She'd expected more cheering, but instead all she got was confused looks. They didn't seem to understand at all. "But the Law still exists?"

"Yes, but it isn't going to try and kill you anymore. The extermination is over. Not just like it was here in Vadal, but everywhere, in every house, every barracks. The faithful don't have to worship in secret anymore either. Religion is no longer banned by the Law."

It was such an ingrained reflex that merely mentioning their secret religion caused all the casteless to glance around nervously, looking for the Inquisitors surely hidden among them. Generations of paranoia was soaked into their bones.

"The Law isn't going to be unfair to you like it has been in the past. We are making a new way of doing things. There will still be pushback. Many high-status men will hate this change, but they will obey their Maharaja, and we earned his help. The Sons of the Black Sword paid the price for you." She looked out over a mass of confusion. "Don't you get it? You aren't property anymore. You're people. Real people!"

"But we're *not* people," cried a baffled man.

"A dog can't be a pig," said another.

There were many comments and shouted questions. "No, no, listen. Your status has changed. We won. You are no longer casteless."

"Then what are we?" someone wailed.

"You're *free.*" They seemed lost at that too. The concept was simply too much for them to take in. What she was saying was too far beyond any idea they'd ever considered before for it to take hold in their minds. "You'll be free men and women. Not part of the existing castes. No longer anyone's property, but considered whole by the Law."

"But how'll we eat?"

Now it was Thera's turn to be confused. "What?"

"We're property of the house. If we're not theirs, then they'll not feed us no more!"

"Yeah, Voice! What 'bout our food?"

The casteless she'd commanded had been rebels or refugees, already forced to care for themselves to survive, so Thera hadn't even considered that aspect. "We'll figure that out."

Adoration only went so far, and now the casteless were beginning to panic over potential starvation. Famine was a topic they understood well, as they'd all lived through it at one point or another. She'd come to give them joy, and instead had delivered fear.

Freedom was an abstract concept, far beyond anything most of them had dreamed of before. The casteless she'd collected in the Cove had been those already inclined to rebellion, and the refugees had Keta to guide them toward understanding. Keta had excelled at this sort of thing. Public speaking was extremely difficult for her. This was another reminder how much she missed her old friend, because Keta would have had them enthralled by now, then he'd give an inspiring sermon designed to motivate them into doing whatever needed doing.

Ashok must have been thinking the same thing, because he muttered, "They have no priest to lead them, as we did in the Cove."

"Our priest is rather indisposed right now." She kept her voice quiet enough the mob wouldn't hear her over their cries, but she knew Ashok would. "I don't get it. Why aren't they happier? Don't they understand what this means for them? For their future?" But even as she asked, she knew the answer. She had the perspective of someone raised by warriors, taught from her youth to constantly improve and achieve. Young casteless were taught to be subservient and submissive. Improvement brought attention, and attention brought punishment.

"You spent your life looking up," Ashok said. "Casteless necks are trained to only look down."

It was true, and in that moment, she despaired for them. "How in the world do the gods think this rabble is going to defeat an army of demons?"

"Ask the gods. I do not know." Ashok eyed the wailing crowd with growing disgust. The longer Thera hesitated in addressing each of their hundreds of concerns, the more they began to panic. *"Enough!"*

The barrage of questions died. The multitude were staring at her, wide eyed and afraid.

"I know this is a lot for you to hear, but have faith, everything will be taken care of. The gods have a plan." Sadly, Thera had no idea what that plan was, because surely a demon would go through these dregs like a fox through a coop of chickens, but if she told them that there would be a riot. "I must go, but I'll send priests among you to make sure your needs are met. I promise there will be food. Our priests will help you make your way with this new Law."

Ashok took her hand and helped her down from the trash pile. "What are you doing? The Fortress Lama knows nothing about this land or these casteless. He would be useless here. There is only one other priest among us."

"I know." And Thera cursed herself, because in order to keep the hasty promise she'd just made to Vadal's casteless, she would have to break the one she had made to Chief Toramana. "Let's get out of here."

Still surrounded by casteless, begging for help, shouting their concerns, asking for her to let them hear the Voice. Not her. The *real* Voice. Thera put her hood back up and let Ashok guide her from the quarter.

The casteless stopped following at the invisible line that marked the end of their assigned territory. Even though they were whole men now, they'd been trained to never step across that border unless an overseer had told them to.

They walked uphill for a time, and as soon as they were free of the mudflat and its prying casteless ears, Thera spoke her disappointment. "We fought so hard for them! I'd expected at least a bit of gratitude. Oceans, I'm such a fool. I should've known better."

"You cannot expect to undo hundreds of years of conditioning in a few minutes, Thera. They are who they were made to be."

Ashok paused and looked down at the sprawling quarter and scowled. "Just as I was."

Ashok was always scowling, but in that moment he seemed extra troubled. "What is it?"

"I know this place..." He trailed off.

"Could this have been your home?"

"Those barracks were burned and the inhabitants butchered to contain my secret...but from the way the sun hits the bend of the river here now, the view seems very familiar to me. Kule took those memories, but I think some pieces remain." Ashok raised his hands and stared at his palms, as if he were seeing a stain there that Thera could not, then he gradually lowered them. "I think this quarter is not my home, but it was built atop the ashes of my home."

"I'm sorry."

Ashok shook his head. "I'm not. The conspirators are dead. I'll not waste any more time on bitterness."

Despite that assurance, she could tell Ashok was deeply troubled. It hadn't been much of a life, but it had still been stolen from him. When one had so very little, the smallest treasures mattered even more. "I guess I shouldn't be angry either. At times I ask myself if it's all been worth it, but the casteless are who they are."

Thera heard a baby crying and looked over to see that a young casteless woman was walking down the bank, heading toward the quarter, carrying an infant in her arms. When she saw Thera and Ashok standing there—who from their clothing and demeanor were clearly of some status—she quickly averted her eyes and stepped off the path to give them plenty of room to pass by. She waited there, meekly.

"Since they've been taught to never look up, let's find them a priest who can make their necks stronger. Come on, Ashok."

At the mention of his name, the young mother risked looking directly at him, and a moment later, she gasped, "It's you! I know you!" And the way she said that was different from the others—not the reflexive awe of a fanatic, but something more personal. Overcome, the girl burst into tears and went straight toward them.

Thankfully, Ashok recognized this was no threat, and didn't react as he normally would. Instead, he stood there awkwardly as the young mother wrapped her free arm around him and hugged him tight. It was a strange violation of decorum in a place where that mattered so much. The mother and her baby were tiny compared to Ashok, nearly disappearing into his cloak, and he gave Thera a baffled look as the woman held onto him and began crying.

"What is this?"

"Forgive me, mighty Fall." She broke away, desperately trying to contain her tears of joy. "I never thought I'd see you again. I'm Twig. You saved my life. Of course you don't remember me. You're a great hero and I was nobody and you've done so much since then."

"I do not know what you speak of."

"It was in the village of Jharlang during the big ice storm. The workers went to drown me in a horse trough—as was their right—only you beat them for me!"

It was rare to see Ashok actually surprised. "You're the girl who lived in the barn..."

She nodded vigorously. "Yes, yes. You were so kind to us, even shared your food and gave us blankets, then saved me and my brother from the workers who thought we stole."

Thera remembered that day well, because soon after that Angruvadal had shattered, the Voice had manifested, and she'd ended up being carried off by the House of Assassins. All that had happened because Ashok had revealed his identity when he'd stepped in to save the lives of two young casteless from an angry mob of workers.

"You have grown up."

"I only got the chance because of you." Twig bounced her infant to comfort the poor thing, and thankfully the crying stopped. "You took us to Mother Dawn. She blessed us and commanded us to come live with a new family here. We owe our entire lives to you."

"Thank you, but you owe me nothing. Your life is yours to live," Ashok assured her, and Thera never ceased to marvel that the best man she'd ever known could be so humble. "Where is your brother?"

She beamed with pride. "Soon as he was old enough, he joined the rebels and fought the exterminators someplace out west. He wanted to be brave, like you. He's doing for others the same thing you did for us. If not for you, I'd never have gotten a life and it's been a happy one ever since. I found a good husband. Well, casteless aren't allowed to marry but you know what I mean, and he loves me all the same." She held up her baby to show Ashok, proud of what she'd made, and laughed. "This little one would never have got a chance to get born neither!"

To most observers, Ashok would seem as stoic as ever, but it was only because of Thera's great practice in deciphering him that she could tell this chance meeting had moved him greatly.

"It was nothing," Ashok assured the girl.

That moment of mercy had been one of the first cracks in the seemingly impenetrable wall of Law that had been built around the man she'd come to love. Ashok said it was nothing, but in reality, that small kindness had been everything. It had been a great step in Ashok's journey from unthinking weapon to an actual person, and for that, Thera was incredibly thankful.

"Your baby is beautiful," Thera told her.

"He is strong like the hero we named him after. We named him Fall."

Chapter 16

Thera had promised the casteless a priest, but she'd also promised the beloved leader of some of her most loyal followers justice. It was difficult balancing politics and prophecy. Never mind her own desires, which were to see a lying scum witch hunter hanged by his neck until he was quick-kicking.

Not knowing what else to do with him, they'd kept Javed locked away from the rest of the Sons. Toramana, being a man of honor, had respected her wishes to spare Javed's life until after the prophecy was satisfied. Then he was doomed. She reasoned that if the gods needed her to keep this particular priest alive until the demons were defeated, she might as well put him to work turning the casteless into something useful in the meantime. It seemed a shame to waste the talents of the man who had so successfully whipped the Cove into shape, even if he had been a two-faced lying murderer that entire time. Or at least that was what Thera told herself to feel better about a decision that made her feel unclean.

She had sent for Toramana to meet with her near where Javed had been confined. The chief had kept his word, and never told the other Sons or his swamp folk about Javed's true nature. The reason he'd cut the priest's hand off had remained a secret, but one that the entire camp was guessing at and gossiping over. It must have galled Toramana to keep it that way, because many of the Sons loved Javed—the fake version at least—and they assumed their feud was over some petty thing. Maybe the proud chief had lost his temper over some perceived offense? None of them suspected Javed was guilty of betrayal, poisoning, and the murder of children.

Thera hadn't asked for Ashok to accompany her, but he'd come anyway. Most likely because he was concerned the chief might react violently to the terrible thing his prophet was about to command. Thera didn't expect Toramana to raise his hand against her, but considering how distasteful the thing she was about to ask for was, she couldn't blame Ashok for expecting the worst.

The sun had set by the time Toramana arrived at the miller's shack that served as Javed's prison. "Prophet Thera, General Ashok. I have come as you have asked." He looked toward the humble structure that held his son's killer. "Is it time? I've been sharpening my knife."

"Not yet, I'm afraid."

Toramana was a proud hunter, but more importantly, he had been a ruler. It had been a small village, but it had been isolated from the world and surrounded by danger. He was no fool to the give and take that leadership required, but even then he couldn't hide his disappointment. "If you didn't ask me here to kill him, then there's only one other possibility."

"We have need of Javed's skills."

"What skills? Assassination? Tell me who you need dead and I will put an arrow in them myself."

"We need him for preaching and organizing the city's casteless into something that might actually be useful by the time the demons get here, rather than just a dumb mob that's going to eat itself."

Toramana sneered. "It's not enough to let him linger, but now you'd let this animal roam *free*? Even after all he has done?"

"Only for a time. That hasn't changed. The Voice said we'd need a priest to prevail against the demons, as did the Mother of Dawn, and even the old writings of the Fortress folk. You trusted Mother Dawn enough to have your whole village abandon their swamp and follow the Sons. Surely you still believe her."

"Do not question my faith. Of course."

"Then after that's over, he's still all yours."

"Will he be? Or will he make himself too valuable for you

to do without? That's what he did the last time. It's one thing to keep him in a cage long enough to satisfy the word of the gods, but you'd let that venomous snake out? He poisoned their bodies before. Now you would give him their minds!"

Thera understood exactly how Toramana felt, but on this thing, she was certain. "The same prophecies say the bloodline of Ramrowan are the only people who can truly stop the demons. That might be in a year, or it might be tomorrow. Like it or not, Javed's the Keeper of Names. He's got Keta's book of which caste-less supposedly come from Ramrowan. Right now, the casteless of this city would be nothing but a feast for demons. We need someone who can prepare them and teach them, as Javed did in the Cove."

"If the city folk are so weak, then let them die." Toramana had never even seen a real town until after his people had joined the Sons. By the standards of those who'd survived the Bhadjan-gal trapped between wizards and the sea, the city casteless were pathetic. They surely wouldn't last a day where he was from.

"You know I can't do that. In all the time you've followed me have I ever abandoned anyone who put their faith in us?"

"Then use someone else!"

Ashok spoke for the first time. "There is no one else, Chief. We bought the casteless their freedom before we understood what that entailed. If we do not organize them quickly, they'll be scattered before the demons even get here. Javed has proven he is good at organizing casteless."

"He's good at murder too!"

Ashok nodded. "As was I."

Thera could only hope that Toramana heard the earnestness in her plea. "The gods gave us who we've got. Each of us flawed or awful as we might be, this is all we have. I hate Javed too, but for now we need him."

Agitated, Toramana began to pace back and forth. "You insult me!"

"No, Chief, if I intended offense I would've just given the command, as is my right, and afterward told you to accept it or else. Instead, I respect you and your people enough to talk to you first. He will still die for what he's done, but only after we've wrung all the usefulness out of him we can get."

"That is insufficient!"

"Of course it is!" Thera shouted back. It was killing her to watch a good man suffer so, made worse because it was her fault, and she knew it. "Javed could do good deeds for a hundred years and it still wouldn't be enough restitution to make up for the life of your boy. A hundred years! I only need him for this *one*!"

Toramana took a deep breath, trying to control his rage and grief. "The snake claims he has changed, that his evils were purified by the light of Mother Dawn like a sin doll thrown into the Dahan fire. Do you believe his lies?"

Thera was unsure how to answer that. She'd been around so many criminals and dishonorable sorts that it wasn't easy to earn her trust, but she had seen the fervor in Javed's eyes, both when he'd testified before the Thakoor of Makao, and again when he'd willingly given up his hand. He'd come back to her surely believing she'd have him executed and did it anyway. If the tales were to be believed, he had even picked up a black-steel sword, and then *put it down* in the name of the gods. No witch hunter was a good enough actor to fool an ancestor blade.

Ashok answered for her. "The question is not if we believe him, but does Javed believe himself? I will find out. Do you trust me, Chief Toramana?"

He answered without hesitation. "With my life, Ashok. Through fire and death I would fight for you."

"Then you know I do not give oaths lightly. The act of saying a thing will be done means it will be done. I know your son begs for vengeance and your heart will never rest until that demand is answered, so I will give you this vow here and now: When our work is done, Javed will die for his crimes by your hand. If that is not possible, then he will die by mine."

"And if the demons get you both, I swear I'll see to it," Thera added.

Toramana was still seething, but he nodded slowly, for Ashok made no promises lightly. "That will do...Only grant me one more thing."

"A priest is going to need at least one hand," Thera warned.

"No. I've taken enough of his flesh for now. I want to take away his peace before I take away his life. Make sure he knows of this vow. Make sure he knows that every day that remains of his miserable life was only granted to him by the intervention of the gods and the faithful patience of Toramana. And after he dies, I will shout until the whole world hears his crimes, so that his name will be worth saltwater forever. Javed will only be remembered enough to be hated."

"I will see to it," Ashok said.

"I have waited this long. I can wait longer." Toramana stomped off.

"That went well," Thera muttered.

Ashok watched the chief walk away. "He is a better man than I."

They went to the shack. Thera had dismissed the guards—who worked for Gutch, as she didn't need the Sons wondering why their priest was being held captive—but they had already left her the key to the stout lock on the door. She opened it.

A haggard Javed was sitting on the floor, writing with a glass pen by lantern light. There were fresh bandages wrapped around the stump of his wrist. Filthy, unkempt, still in bloodstained clothing, he looked as miserable as the casteless she needed him to lead.

"Hello, Javed."

"Prophet." He stood up and bowed, then took note of Ashok, and then gave him the same gesture of respect. "General."

Javed looked to be in such a sorry state she couldn't help but ask, "Are you well?"

"I have so many comforts here. There's a pile of straw to sleep on and a bucket to shit in," he said sarcastically. "What more could a traitor ask for?"

"It's more than you deserve."

"I do not disagree."

She took note of all the papers. "You're writing more scriptures?"

"The workers who bring my food took pity on me after I begged them to bring me something to write with." Javed gestured at the pages scattered across the stone floor. "These are merely the philosophical musings of a man with time to spare and no distractions. My ruminations will never rise to the insights of Ratul or Keta, but maybe someday these words might be useful to someone."

"Ratul and Keta were good men. You're not. What's this new book about?"

"The Book of Javed will tell of my life before and after finding the Forgotten's truth. I'm including a full confession of all my crimes, the tale of my encounter with Mother Dawn, and everything I've done since, both in Makao, and to spread the word across the rest of Lok. It also contains my thoughts on some doctrines which neither the Voice nor the Keepers have expounded upon yet."

"Do you think this work you do now absolves you of the evil things you did before, Witch Hunter?" Ashok asked.

"I could ask you the same, Protector. But no...Only the gods offer absolution. I'll save you time. I know why you're here."

Thera scoffed. "Did another messenger from above reveal it to you?"

"There are holes in the walls of this shack. I could not help but overhear Toramana shouting. I will serve however you wish. I'll help the casteless of this city, and when the demons are defeated—gods willing—then I will gladly bare my neck for the sword."

"You accept this fate?"

"I embrace it. Toramana wanted to take my hope. That's understandable, but he fails to realize there's nothing left for him take. There's no hope to strip from me. I've already consigned myself to Naraka. Only the gods can free me from suffering forever for my crimes. I know that of a surety." Javed held up his bandaged stump. "This pain pales in comparison to that knowledge. All I can do now is make the most of what time I have left. It probably won't be enough. Still, I must try."

Ashok walked over to Javed until they were face-to-face, only a few inches apart. A lesser man would have quailed. Javed did not.

"You truly believe all this."

Javed actually met Ashok's terrifying gaze, unflinching. "I swear to it."

Ashok scowled. "I couldn't see it in you before, because I did not know to look, but you have always been broken inside."

"Yes," Javed snarled. "You also understand what it means to never question your assigned purpose. It makes for a fine witch hunter, and a terrible everything else. It took Mother Dawn's wrath to teach me how to feel. Now I am cursed with knowledge."

"Yet you were somehow judged worthy by an ancestor blade."

"For a time. Not because I was good, but because I was available."

"Sounds familiar," Thera said.

Ashok continued to study Javed, and honestly it seemed a miracle to Thera that the traitor priest didn't wilt beneath that judgmental stare. If there was anything more unforgiving than the gods, it had to be Ashok.

"You believe your own words. You will do. When the work is done, one of us will kill you. If you are fortunate, it will be me. I will make it quick. I suspect Toramana would not."

Javed nodded. "I accept this obligation."

"Then you'll go among the casteless to teach and help them, but you'll stay away from the Sons." Thera pointed at the pages on the floor. "And don't share this confession of yours yet either, because when the Sons find out that you were the one who poisoned their friends and loved ones, they won't pause to think about how our prophecies require us to have a priest like I have. They'll just kill you on the spot, and I don't want to have to punish a good warrior for doing something that I've longed to do myself."

"It will be done."

Ashok opened the door for Thera, and she walked out. As Ashok went to follow, Javed called after them.

"I have accepted my obligation, Prophet, but have you come to terms with yours?"

Thera paused just outside. "What do you mean?"

"The Voice itself has declared its sacrifice will be required. Keta tried to find other meanings for this, or to avoid thinking about it at all, but that was only because he was afraid. Keta loved you. The meaning of this prophecy is clear to the rest of us. Are you prepared to willingly give your life to unlock the power that lurks in the blood of Ramrowan?"

Ashok crossed the shack in the blink of an eye and wrapped his fingers around Javed's throat. His fury was so sudden that it took Thera a moment to realize he was about to kill their priest and cried out, "Ashok, wait!"

"Even the gods do not threaten my woman with impunity." Ashok shook Javed hard. "Never speak of this again."

The priest's eyes were wide, but in desperation, rather than fear. The threat of death could no longer sway Javed, and he managed to croak, "If you can't abide truth, then kill me now and get it over with." Spittle flew from his lips. "*The Voice must be sacrificed.*"

"Let him go, Ashok...Please."

Ashok grudgingly released his grip, and Javed stumbled away, gasping. "Hate the gods all you want, think them cruel, but I'll not hide from the truth ever again. Prophecy can't be thwarted."

"Watch me."

"I need him to speak honestly, without fear of you promptly killing him for it," Thera said. "Leave us, Ashok, please."

Ashok hesitated, for he was her husband and protector, but she was his sworn commander. It was not often those two roles clashed. "Very well." Ashok turned and walked out of the shack.

Javed rubbed his bruised throat with his remaining hand. "I didn't say that to wound you, Prophet, but to prepare you. I know you've given much, but you've got one last great work to do. No matter how much I help the casteless, only the willing sacrifice of the Voice can grant them the power of their birthright. The gods have been preparing them for this day since the last great war, since before the gods were struck down from their palaces in the sky. The children of Ramrowan are the gods' final weapon against their eternal enemy, their blood refined over the centuries since. The time to reveal the nature of that great work is finally upon us. You alone hold the key."

"Save the preaching for the fish-eaters," Thera snapped, for she'd heard all that prophetic doom before. "Never question my commitment again. I'm a warrior daughter of Vane. I'll do whatever needs to be done."

"That's good. When the moment comes to embrace your purpose, you must not be afraid."

Oh, she was terrified, because unlike Javed, she actually had something to live for. "We're done here."

"Thera . . . Wait."

"What more do you want?"

"There's one last thing, and I must tell it to you and you alone. I don't know if the time is right, and I would wait, because with this knowledge comes agony, but I don't know how much time we have left. This secret was told to me by Keta, who was told it by Ratul, who was told by the Voice itself."

"I've got copies of all the scriptures you printed."

"Yet those are incomplete and kept that way for a reason. I beg you to hear me out."

Damn Javed to hell . . . Yet he sounded sincere.

She let out a long exhalation. "Speak."

"I can't yet," he whispered. "Ashok is still near these thin walls and this is not for him, only for you, because in his anger he would attempt to thwart the Forgotten's carefully laid plans."

She knew Ashok was far too honorable to use his strange ability to hear distant things to spy on her private conversations. "The gods are already calling for the sacrifice of the Voice. I'd be glad to get rid of the damned thing. Except everyone seems to think it's not just the Voice, but me. My life. Yet I'm still here, willing to do whatever it takes. This can't be worse than that."

"Then it's the shattering of your hopes, but it is also the only way forward."

Well, that was just bloody wonderful... except that she was also intrigued. With all the terrible revelations of the Voice, what had Ratul and Keta kept from her all these years? Or was Javed just a liar trying to manipulate her somehow?

"When Ashok is away, seek me out among the untouchables and I will tell you all I was told. You can use that knowledge however you see fit. I pray that that you'll continue to follow the gods' great plan." Javed knelt and began gathering up his papers, a task made far more difficult by only having one hand. "I will go to the casteless quarter now. Their plan for me is to serve, and the work cannot wait another minute."

Thera left the fanatic to gather his things. She found Ashok outside, impatiently waiting for her.

"Do you think we're doing the right thing, letting him out?"

He glared at the shack, still angry that the gods would threaten his woman. "Unfortunately, yes."

The two of them walked in silence back toward their camp. After a while, the awkwardness grew too much, and Thera was compelled to say, "The prophecies are rarely direct, and sometimes they seem to have more than one meaning. We've misunderstood them before. Angruvadal was the servant who died in the ice storm, not me, or you, or Keta. We diverted the Capitol's water, but it was Akershan draining the lake that endangered the Cove."

Ashok was quiet for a long time, before admitting, "I don't want you to die."

She took his calloused hand in her scarred hand and held it gently as they walked. "I know."

They said nothing else as there was nothing left to say.

Chapter 17

Late into the night, Rada studied. Servants refreshed the oil in her lanterns so that she could keep reading and she barely even noticed them come and go. Even with her fine glass lenses her eyes ached from all the strain. Her days were consumed by the tedium of governance, so nights were when she devoted herself into poring over the ancient scrolls, books, and tablets that the scholarly Orders had gathered here.

The room set aside for this endeavor was one of the larger ones that the Astronomers had available, and it had been absolutely filled with materials. Most hours it was crowded with intelligent, hardworking scholars, who were busy doing the same thing she was—searching for any information which might aid them against the demons—only they were all asleep now. She was the only one foolish enough to keep killing herself over an endeavor that had thus far proven futile. Rada knew there might not be any answers to be had in this ancient mess, only confusion and more questions. There was no great secret to be revealed or edge to be had against the demons. The battle would be fought with what Devedas could gather to Vadal City before the demons appeared, nothing more, and there wasn't a damned thing Rada could do to help them.

Such helplessness infuriated her, but it kept her motivated.

The warrior Kumudesh brought her a tray with bits of fruit

and cheese on it and set it on the table next to her. She barely noticed, as she was deep into a rereading of *Indraneela's Comprehensive Biology of Sea Demons*. It was a useful compendium of how to butcher demon corpses in order to harvest the most magic from the pieces, but Indraneela didn't really know much about making the demons dead to begin with. His case studies consisted of finding bodies washed up on shore, or throwing fifty warriors at a single demon and hoping for the best.

"You should eat something, Maharani."

"I will," she assured her bodyguard.

He snorted at that.

Such disrespect! "What was that noise meant to mean, warrior?"

"I mean no offense. Your husband told me to keep you safe from harm. I thought that would mean watching out for assassins, not reminding you not to starve because you're too dedicated to your obligation to eat. Please." He looked around the room conspiratorially, but the only others present were more of her Garo guardians, before he whispered, "When a woman is with child she needs to eat more."

Rada frowned at that, for only her maids knew about that secret, and she was certain none of them had talked. If the courts found out she was pregnant, some might leverage her condition against her. Devedas' rule was tenuous enough as it was without anyone insinuating the woman he had left in charge was too weak or distracted to handle her obligation.

"What are you talking about?"

"I watch over you all day and my wife has given me five children, Maharani. It's not like I'm blind to the signs." Kumudesh pushed the plate toward her with his good arm. "Please at least eat the cheese."

"I suppose it is your job to pay attention." Rada sighed. "Here I was thinking I could simply wear more voluminous robes in the hopes no one would notice."

"Most of the First only see you in court, so they probably won't notice for a while, and by the time they do, your husband will be victorious, so it won't matter. In the meantime, humor a poor warrior who is just trying to do right by his charge."

She relented and took some cheese from the plate. It turned out to be rather good, a small reminder that there was simple joy to be found in the world outside of politics or study...But then she immediately went back to reading because the fate of the world was at stake. Kumudesh, seeming satisfied with that small victory, went back to his chair by the door.

A few minutes later, someone pulled out the seat across the table from her and sat down. Rada looked up to see a man she didn't recognize. He was exceedingly handsome, about her age, lean and stern as a warrior, yet from his haughty demeanor she immediately knew he was of the first caste. The stranger was dressed entirely in black, from robes to sash, and even gloves of silk.

For the life of her, Rada couldn't figure out how he'd made it past her many guards unannounced.

"May I join you?" His tone was polite, but there was an air of menace about him.

Rada looked toward the door, where Kumudesh still sat, yet the warrior showed no reaction to the stranger's presence. Neither did the other guards, who seemed perfectly alert, yet their glances her direction seemed to slide past this man without notice.

"This conversation is not for their ears, Radamantha. This face is not for their eyes."

It was in that moment that Rada experienced something she'd not felt since her adventures in Vadal, as the Asura's Mirror warned her that she was in the presence of an exceedingly great danger.

The stranger shivered as Rada received that warning, as if he had heard it as well. "So you have the device on your person? Of course you would." He closed his eyes and inhaled through his nostrils, as if he was appreciating the fragrance of a fine perfume. "The mirror is a wonderful example of the ancients' craft. Such devices were common once. This is the last of its kind. A pity."

As its bearer, she never went anywhere without the artifact, and it sat in the decorated satchel at her feet. Even if Vikram had asked for it back she would've denied him, as she felt after calling down fire from the moon with the thing it was clearly her responsibility now, but thankfully the Historian had the wisdom to not ask.

"The ancients named these creations of theirs the Asura, after a belief that predated even that world. Each Asura was an independent intelligence, assigned to assist the lord of a particular realm. The purpose of the one you toy ineffectually with now was to oversee the defense of this land from outside invaders, but it was connected to all the others so they could share knowledge."

"Who are you?"

"Though our paths crossed in the Capitol, and I knew your father, I do not believe we were ever formally introduced. Perhaps this will be more familiar to you." One hand had been hidden beneath the table, and it came up holding a golden mask. He gently placed it on the table before him, then slid it toward her. When he took his gloved hand away, the lantern light flickered across the cruel face of the Law.

"That mask belongs to the Grand Inquisitor."

"It does."

To avoid the attention of her guards so blatantly, clearly she was dealing with a powerful wizard of some kind. Despite the mirror screaming into her mind to not provoke this unknown menace, she said, "There is a price on Omand Vokkan's head. Is this mask proof of his demise, displayed to collect your reward?"

The handsome man smiled, but that gesture did not reach his eyes. The show of teeth was as mirthless as a demon's expression. "That reward will go uncollected forever, because forever is how long Omand Vokkan will live."

"A bold claim."

"I know this because I am him."

The mirror let her know this was true, and the blood in her veins turned to ice.

"From your sudden pallor I take it the black steel has confirmed my words," Omand said.

"*Guards!*"

The spell broken, Kumudesh and his men all looked her way.

"I wish you had not done that." As the warriors reached for their swords, Omand waved one hand dismissively.

The room shuddered. Shadows surged from corners. Men died horribly.

By the time Rada blinked, the shadows had retreated, leaving behind splintered bones and mangled bodies. Five Garo had perished in the span between heartbeats. Blood dripped from the ceiling to spatter on the ancient manuscripts. The shadows were just shadows again, places where the flickering lantern did not reach, once more without murderous substance.

Omand had never taken his eyes off her during the slaughter. "Scream louder if you want. Summon more guards. I will gladly paint the entire desert red . . . Or we can continue our polite conversation as reasonable members of our caste."

Her warriors lay in still twitching pieces, but Rada fought off the terror, because her wits were all she had, so she could not afford to lose them. She was trembling uncontrollably, yet she met Omand's gaze and did not flinch away. She understood there was only one reason Omand would reveal his true face to her and that was because he wasn't worried about her ever recognizing him again.

"I am listening."

Omand made a display of looking at what she'd been reading, and then gave a derisive chuckle. "I see that you search desperately for something to defeat the demons. Alas, there are no easy answers for that question. The ancients in all their might tried, yet they still fell. To be fair to our illustrious forebearers they were bombarded with millions of demons, armed with destructive magics the likes of which the army of hell can no longer produce. What we face today is nothing but the dying remnant of that distorted race, risen from the sea in a desperate last-ditch attempt to save themselves from extinction. As our numbers have grown, theirs have remained stagnant, for demons are built, not born."

Even facing death, Rada was ever the scholar. "That isn't in the books. How do you know this?"

"The source of all magic revealed it to me. Both of our races today are but pale phantoms of what we once were, and what we are capable of becoming once again. The Age of Kings was in truth an age of stalemate. The era of greatness has passed for both races, but with the other one dead, then the victor might be able to rise once more."

"We will beat them."

"Perhaps. I truly hope man does triumph, so that I may rule over the survivors. The ancients made a plan for this day. A plan which they knew would take many generations to develop, but which would eventually be capable of eradicating the demons once and for all. This plan requires the king of hell himself to leave the safety of the depths and venture onto land. I do not yet fully understand this plan, for access to that information was stolen from me." Omand uttered that last part with great bitterness. "It is for this understanding I still search."

"I will never help the likes of you."

"I was not asking for your help. Your scholarship is not what has brought me here. As heir to the ancients' systems, I have come to claim what is rightfully my property." He gestured toward where the mirror lay beneath the table. "Then while I am here, I will deprive Devedas of something he loves, as punishment for stripping from me the Order of Inquisition which I worked so very hard to grow. The Inquisition was one of the few things I cared about, and he took it from me. Devedas has surprisingly few things he cares about. You are one of them."

"You intend to kill me?"

"Yes."

Devedas had written to her of his encounter with Omand in Vadal, and she had been searching the texts for references to defeating dark wizards who had so much power they could mimic a fanatic's god, but she had found nothing.

"Unlike you, Devedas is a good ruler. He cares for the people."

"They mean nothing to me. I gave Devedas a city. He put a knife in my back. I went off to claim the power of the gods and returned to find my name synonymous for criminal."

"You were a bloody tyrant and a murderous fool!" If Rada was going to die, so be it, but she wouldn't go quietly. "There was no problem your violence didn't make worse. No truth that couldn't be distorted by your lies. The Capitol was already dying before the demons got here, because you slit its wrists to suck out the blood like a greedy piglet on a teat. You are everything despicable about our caste. You're nothing but a fraud, and when Devedas sends you to the endless nothing all of Lok will cheer!"

Omand smirked. "Such fire you have now. To think that only a few short years ago Sikasso cowed you into silence with naught but a threat."

That was Rada's greatest shame, but she would not admit it to this horrible thing.

"Yet now you goad someone with the power to do *this*?" Omand spread his hands wide, so she couldn't help but take in the ruined remains of her loyal warriors whose lives had been snuffed out in an instant. "You live without fear of dying in a manner that would make the warrior caste proud. Few members of the First ever experience such freedom. It has been quite the journey for you, Librarian. Sadly, that journey must come to an end. You have no part to play in the ancients' prophecy, so I have no reason to let you live. You are an anomaly in a system that is already too chaotic."

Hot tears rolled down her cheeks as she accepted death. "I have tried my best to fix the mistakes I've made. I've fulfilled my obligations to my caste, Order, and family. I go to my death with honor. Will you be able to say the same, Omand?"

"I do not intend to die, so your question is irrelevant. Goodbye, Radamantha."

Defenses active.

The shadows became solid and came for her. She screamed as she was engulfed in black.

Except there was no snapping of bones of rending of flesh as had befallen her poor Garo. The darkness passed by with a feeling like cobwebs on skin, but nothing more, and then they were gone.

Drop.

The mirror hadn't spoken to her directly since Vadal, but she did as she was told without hesitation, flinging herself from the chair.

As Omand rose, the lantern on the table exploded. Burning oil spread across his black robes. Rada snatched up the mirror and crawled toward the wall. Omand effortlessly flipped the heavy table at her.

The wood was smashed to pieces against an invisible barrier.

Wrathful Omand stopped a few feet away and sneered at her through the flames that danced over his face. "After denying me, the black steel has chosen *you* as its administrator? *Outrageous!*"

She'd not even realized that she'd pulled the mirror from the bag and was holding it in her bare hands. The black steel was ice cold, and Rada found that the Asura inside was staring back at her, and this wasn't the faded ghost she'd seen before, but a vengeful matron made of fire and thunder. Ancient texts that had long been locked away were now tantalizingly available.

Just as had happened when the Scourge had attacked, Omand's presence forced the Asura to act.

The Grand Inquisitor made a violent sweeping motion with one arm, causing the fire on his body to leap at her. It splashed off the mirror's invisible barrier. That just seemed to infuriate him even more, and the stone floor shook. An inch of rock was instantly pulverized into chips and dust all about her, except for a circle immediately around Rada's body that remained whole and unharmed. Omand curled one hand into a fist, and all the burning oil and papers were lifted from the ground and compressed into a ball. With an angry gesture, the fire launched toward her, only to spall against the mirror's shield right in front of her face.

The mirror had done something similar for her in Vadal, and that had withstood even Upagraha's wrath. "If a legion of demons couldn't claw their way through, you'll get nothing!"

"Mother Dawn robbed me, and now you taunt me with what should rightfully be mine."

Surely the entire town must have heard that catastrophic pulverizing of stone, so Rada shouted as loud as she could. "Warriors! Wizards! Bring your magic and fight!" Would his shadow magic still be able to kill them in the presence of the angered mirror? She didn't know, but this criminal beast had to be cast from her court. "An evil wizard is upon us!"

"I am no mere wizard."

"I don't care what you are, as long as you die. Begone, fiend!"

Offensive action authorized.

The Asura must have decided Omand was enough of an invader that she finally accepted Rada as her master.

"This is a complication." Omand sneered as he picked up his golden mask. "I do not like complications. I will return for you later."

Then he vanished.

Warriors rushed into the room with swords drawn to find the place on fire, their companions crushed and torn to pieces, and their Maharani lying on the floor in a circle of broken stone and chunks of wood. Despite their desperate attempts to help her, Rada remained focused on one singular purpose. The crack in the mirror had spread even further, but this time she would not let the Asura escape.

The mirror—and all the ancient secrets contained within—remained unlocked.

Chapter 18

Over a month had passed since the Sons of the Black Sword had arrived in Vadal City, and still there had been no sign of demons yet. Tensions ran high. Many high-status men doubted their new Thakoor's decision to ally their house not only with the Maharaja who had recently threatened them, but also with the infamous criminal who had brought shame to their name. Outright violence between the groups had been surprisingly rare, though, partly because the outsiders remained on the outskirts of the city, but mostly because the Vadal warrior caste respected Jagdish enough to honor his wishes for them to remain civil.

But Ashok knew that with three great armies gathered in and around Vadal City, and each of them having new recruits joining their banner by the day, it was only a matter of time before someone did something foolish enough to cause a real conflict between them. The situation was like having too much Fortress powder stored in the back of one constantly shaking wagon. Ashok could feel the static building, and an inadvertent spark would be enough to blow it all to pieces.

As a bearer, Ashok was required to accept all challenges, just in case the sword might find someone better, but oddly enough no one had made an attempt since he had been here. Ashok was thankful for that. Any man he was forced to cripple or kill would be one less available to fight the demons. Still, he could tell that jealousy was growing, and soon, someone would try. All it would take was one prideful warrior of status to spit himself on Angruvadal and their entire alliance could be in jeopardy.

It would be good to remove himself from the volatile mix for a time.

Thera had assured him she would handle things without him. The Sons' officers had preparations well in hand, so Ashok had taken Horse and ridden south following the Martaban, hoping the shard in his chest would help him catch the demons' scent. The map the collector had drawn for them was rough and did not correlate with the landmarks aboveground so Ashok could only guess where the ancients' path lay beneath.

Three days south of Vadal City, Ashok still hadn't smelled demon in the air, and he knew he would have to turn back soon. With the situation so volatile he couldn't risk being away for too many days. What was taking the demons so long? The collector believed that much of the passage beneath the northern part of Lok had been collapsed centuries ago, so perhaps it required a great deal of demonic labor to clear their way through. Did demons have a worker caste? It was an odd thought, but mankind only ever saw the ones who came onto land, and those were clearly warrior equivalents. What manner of society did the vile creatures conceal beneath the waves?

On the fourth day of scouting, Ashok began to doubt himself. Was it possible that the Voice had led them astray? Or that Rada's interpretation of the ancients' terms had been incorrect? Perhaps the Capitol really had been the Great City of Man all along, and they had already failed. If so, the march to Vadal had been in vain and their time was already up. The new age had begun, and it was one where man would be gradually hunted until all their lives were extinguished.

Ashok dismissed such melancholy thoughts because down that path lay nothing but defeat. He would scout for one more day before turning back. Instinct pushed him to follow a certain road.

On the morning of the fifth day, Ashok discovered something odder than demons.

Since the routes had been reopened, the trade roads had been exceedingly busy. As everyone had learned about the demons appearing in the desert, opportunistic merchant caravans that would normally be heading for the grand bazaar of the Capitol were turning toward Vadal City instead, hoping to profit from the hungry armies camped there. To pass among the merchants unnoticed, Ashok had dressed as a worker and kept Angruvadal hidden beneath his cloak. Should he encounter any officials he was armed with official traveling papers, stamped by both Jagdish and Devedas, which should be enough to placate any Law-abiding man.

So Ashok wasn't concerned when he saw a large contingent of warriors riding north on the trade road. However, when he noticed that they were flying the banners of two different houses beneath a flag of diplomatic truce, he became curious. It was odd seeing men of Kharsawan and Thao riding together, as there had been many skirmishes between those houses over control of Neeramphorn recently. So he stopped in the middle of the road and waited for what he estimated to be at least five hundred warriors to reach him. It didn't take long, since they appeared to be in a hurry.

"Move aside or be trampled, merchant," shouted the lead rider, who was dressed in Kharsawani red.

"I am no worker. I would speak to your commander. Where is your Vadal escort?"

"We've left them far behind." The scout's mount trotted toward him, but then Horse snorted angrily at this invasion of his space, and the much smaller animal danced back fearfully. "Whoa!"

"Beware my Horse, warrior. He does not tolerate the insolence of lesser beasts."

"Our passage is approved. We've got no escort but our papers were stamped by the Vadal border guards. You'd best get out of the way for there are high-status men coming through."

"Who?"

"That's a secret, but trust me, friend, you don't want to offend these notables."

"Some consider me notable as well."

The scout was young, clearly inexperienced, and when he looked over Ashok in his humble attire, he must have thought him a liar. "Sure they do."

"Just signal your commander when he nears." Ashok nudged Horse and they moved onto the grass along the side of the road. "I have no time for foolishness."

"Alright, but I'll warn you my commander's not a patient man."

As Horse grazed, Ashok watched the column approach. There were men of Thao and Kharsawan at the head, riding side by side, flying banners of yellow or red with various designs upon them denoting garrisons that Ashok was unfamiliar with. As they rode past, he could tell that these warriors were travel weary, as they were drenched in sweat, covered in dust, and their horses had clearly been pushed hard for many days.

The scout spotted a senior warrior and called out to him. "Sir, this merchant wishes to speak to you."

The roik barely slowed. "Oceans, boy, I told you there's no time for trades. We've got enough supplies to get to Vadal City already. Tejeshwar will have my head if we're delayed one unnecessary minute. We're not stopping for Vadal baubles."

"Are you here to answer the Maharaja's call?" Ashok asked.

The officer pulled back on his reins and broke away from his men to ride toward Ashok. "You know of the call for aid?"

"I was the first one Devedas asked. I am Ashok Vadal."

"Ashok Vadal!"

That cry was repeated over and over. Heads jerked Ashok's direction. Within seconds his name had stopped an army in its tracks. The inexperienced scout may have been confused, but the seasoned combatants took one look at Ashok and knew that this was no mere worker. His wearing a light merchant's cloak was like draping a sheepskin over a tiger. It fooled no one who knew what an apex predator looked like.

The road fell quiet except for the stomping of nervous hooves.

Ashok glanced at the scout, who was now gaping in fear at the greatest criminal in the world. "I told you some would consider me notable." Then he turned his attention back to the roik. "Tell me why you are here."

The man swallowed nervously before responding, "We escort the illustrious Tejeshwar Kharsawan to Vadal City."

A Thao risalder bravely called out, "And we escort the legendary Kaladhar Thao."

Ashok shrugged, as those names meant nothing to him.

Except as soon as two other warriors broke off from the center of the group and rode his way, Angruvadal warned him what he was dealing with here.

It was another bearer.

No. *Two* bearers.

The regular warriors seemed glad to get out of their way. The bearers stopped, side by side, ten feet away from Ashok in order to study him. The Kharsawan man was younger than Ashok, muscular, thick-necked, stone-faced, and wearing finely crafted armor despite the warmth of the day and the length of the journey. The Thao appeared a bit older than Ashok, but short and wiry thin, dressed in a simple robe and turban, but with a gray mustache of impressive length in the fashion the hill folk loved.

They both had ancestor blades.

There was no need to draw them for confirmation, for each of them had surely been warned by the instincts contained in his sword that another deadly threat was present.

The Thao spoke. "You are a bearer." It was not a question.

It would be best to keep this gathering polite, so Ashok slowly moved his cloak aside so they could see sheathed Angruvadal.

Horse, being the only one present who always wanted a fight, snorted derisively at the other bearers' mounts. Horse did not care about black steel. Horse was probably the only animal in the world who might fight a demon if given the chance. Ashok patted Horse on the neck to calm the fierce beast, as he would prefer to not unleash three of the most powerful magical weapons in the world pointlessly on the side of the road in the middle of nowhere.

Nothing else was said for a long time as they sized each other up. Ancestor blades only picked the best among men, so there was no question that everyone here was exceedingly dangerous.

"I heard that Angruvadal had been broken," said the Thao.

"The stories must've got that wrong, because that's clearly an ancestor blade at his side," said the Kharsawani warrior. "Unless this isn't the real Ashok."

"Only a madman would pretend to be me. It is true that Angruvadal shattered. I later claimed Akerselem from Bharatas Akershan in battle."

"That can't be," the Thao scoffed. "Akerselem killed my great-grandfather. Akerselem is curved like an Akershani saber. From the straight sheath, that's the shape of a traditional Vadal long sword."

"I willed the blade into a more familiar form."

"You *willed* it?" he asked incredulously. "We can do that?"

"Yes. Also, my condolences for your great-grandfather."

He laughed. "No great loss. From all accounts great-grandfather was a right bastard...I'm Kaladhar Thao."

"I am Ashok Vadal." He looked toward the Kharsawani bearer, who was still scowling daggers at him.

"We speak to a wanted criminal."

"I have been pardoned by Maharaja Devedas."

"And a casteless in possession of a sword."

"The casteless have been declared whole men. Some whole men are allowed to carry weapons."

"Hmmm..."

"Forgive Tejeshwar, Ashok Vadal. My Kharsawani friend is a devoted stickler for the Law, only the Law's been full of surprises lately."

"I have noticed." Ashok gave a polite bow toward the suspicious young bearer. "I respect your hesitance in showing any courtesy to a known lawbreaker. We live in troubled and confusing times."

Tejeshwar was forced to agree. "That we do."

"I would point out that it is not required that you respect the man, but you must respect the decision of his sword."

The Kharsawani nodded at that wisdom, and then grudgingly returned Ashok's bow. "I am Tejeshwar of the Guntur garrison, bearer of mighty Khartalvar. Let our meeting be a calm one."

The nearby warriors in red all breathed a sigh of relief at that pronouncement. Their bearer must have had a reputation for taking offense. There had probably been a few duels fought along the way.

"I've heard legends about Black-Hearted Ashok," Kaladhar mused. "It's said you've killed a thousand men and a hundred demons."

"The first count is low. The second is exaggerated...Why do the bearers of two houses ride together across a third house's land?"

"We encountered each other on the road south of Apura and we were traveling to the same destination," Tejeshwar explained. "It was logical for us to join forces."

"You go to present yourself in Vadal City?"

The younger bearer nodded. "That we do."

This was good news. One black-steel blade had made a difference in the Capitol. Three would be an incredible help. Still probably not enough to win, but they'd make the demons bleed that much more to earn their victory. "I am impressed that any of the great houses would heed the Maharaja's call for aid enough to risk their bearers."

Tejeshwar gave Ashok an odd look. "My house didn't dispatch me. I was drawn north long before I heard about the Maharaja's plea."

"The same," Kaladhar agreed. "In fact, my Thakoor didn't want me to leave. Said it was too risky. I had to bully the man and tell him if I was forced to choose between his commands and the wishes of my sword, the sword was going to win. If my Thakoor dies angry, he's got heirs to replace him. If our sword shatters in disgust, we're through."

Ashok was puzzled by this. "Your ancestor blades sent you here? Both of you?"

"Did yours not? Otherwise, this is quite the coincidence to find you here."

Ashok had to respect the Thao's wisdom. "Then it was no accident, as it was by instinct I took this road."

"I hesitate to call what I was feeling an instinct," Tejeshwar said. "It was more of an incessant banging of a drum that wouldn't stop until I relented and said I would go. Visions of demons terrorized my sleep and even my waking hours until I set out in the direction Khartalvar desired."

"I thought I was alone in experiencing this, until I heard Tejeshwar's tale. We even had the same dreams about demons rampaging. I think these dreams were really the memories of the first ancestors long ago, when the demons fell from a sky filled with fire. I felt a profound guilt, as if I were shirking a duty I didn't even know I'd been assigned. I knew we would be needed, and soon. I don't know if it is just us being goaded like this, or if all the bearers have been experiencing such promptings."

Since he understood now that all black steel was united in purpose, Ashok hoped every bearer felt that way. He had not experienced this himself, because he was already where Angruvadal needed him to be, but if the rest of the bearers got here in time, they might just have a chance.

"I believe heeding those visions was a test of your worthiness, bearers."

"If so, then we have passed," Kaladhar said. "My sword has been at peace as long as I'm moving in the right direction. From how strong the promptings were, I suspect any bearer who resists

will either be slain by his own blade and replaced, or the ancestors' revulsion at their current bearer's cowardice will be so great
that it will break the sword in disgust."

"Then I hope they heed the warning. The black-steel ghosts
know the final battle of our age is upon us. We will either defeat
the demons there or man's time is done," Ashok explained. "It
was for this purpose we were given black steel to begin with.
Omand's Great Extermination was *nothing* in comparison to
what is coming if we fail. Then the demons will show man what
a great extermination really means."

Tejeshwar glanced nervously toward their unseen destination
in the north. "As much as I'd like to, I can't argue with your
assessment, Black Heart. For the five years I've carried Khartalvar
it has never been so demanding. Never before have I been left
with such a foreboding sense of menace. I know it was for this
moment we were chosen."

The ground rumbled beneath them.

Birds leapt from the nearby trees. While the soldiers struggled
to control their mounts, Horse reared back and then stomped
angrily on the soil that had offended him. After a few seconds,
the trembling stopped.

"Are earthquakes common here?" Tejeshwar asked.

"No." Ashok could sense a distant evil stirring far below.
"That was demons."

The army of hell was making progress.

Ashok could only hope that the remainder of the ancestor
blades were as persuasive as these two had been.

Chapter 19

Among the casteless, Thera watched and despaired.

"They fight and bicker constantly." Javed spoke with great exasperation. "Since they possess almost nothing, they are consumed with petty jealousies that one of their fellows might have slightly more. Some of them are smart, those I have made use of, but for each of those there are two or three who are irrational and easily provoked. Most of them think nothing of their future, only living for the next moment."

"That's your job, priest, to make them care."

"I've been trying."

The two of them sat on a wooden platform on a hill near the river, overlooking the nearby casteless quarter, but unseen by its residents. It was better to observe from afar, because whenever she went down among them, she got mobbed by adoring faithful, begging her for things she had no power to give them and miracles she could not grant. Currently another argument had broken out among the casteless, and two men were shouting and posturing, while a crowd grew around them hooting like Vokkan monkeys and goading the offended toward exchanging blows.

It was odd to see such unruly behavior among untouchables who were normally terrified of drawing the ire of their superiors. "Usually overseers would have stepped in and restored order, except whole men don't have *overseers*, though, do they?"

"No, they do not." Her priest shook his head. "Their overseers have been released from their obligations, leaving these dregs to manage themselves. The castes have rules and traditions. Punishments and rewards, developed over time and handed down through the generations until they become an ingrained way of doing things. The casteless had those things imposed on them. The Maharaja's edict making them whole men, though well intentioned, simply took the small amount of structure the casteless had and tore it away. Without structure to bind them, the fearful cower afraid to do anything, while the bold have descended into hedonistic excess of every manner of debauchery previously denied them."

That sounded like Keta's story about their ancestors. "So is this how priests pass their time? Philosophizing about the nature of man?"

"Your insults fall on deaf ears, Prophet, because I've given this far more thought than you imagine. Witch hunters have to be able to pass for any caste or status as needed. You can't do that without being a keen observer of how people function. You and Devedas cut down a fence. It is not shocking when the once caged animals stray. None of this degradation should have come as a surprise."

To the crowd's great amusement, the two untouchables began throwing fists. A woman, probably the lover of one of the combatants, jumped in and tried to pull her man away. That distraction just made things worse for him, as a moment later he got his nose broken by a wild swing. He fell, and that weakness signaled to a different casteless who must have been holding a grudge to step in to kick the man while he was down. One kicker turned to three, and the poor fool was quickly stomped senseless beneath a storm of dirty bare feet. His woman got pushed into a mud puddle. The mob laughed at her.

"In fairness to the casteless, I've seen workers fight over dumb things too, and if this was my own caste a knife would've come out by now, someone would have gotten cut, offense would be taken, and we'd probably be watching an actual duel rather than this foolishness."

"True," Javed agreed. "Impulsive pride has probably killed as many warriors during times of peace as have died in war."

But at least her people were good at war. These casteless were even more emotional but far less disciplined than any warrior. "How in the world does the Voice expect these fools to beat demons? Have you been doing any philosophizing about that?"

"That's a mystery only the gods know. Some of the casteless are clever. Most are dumb. None are educated. They aren't entirely lazy, but many are directionless and have only the most meager and limited of skills to draw from. Their whole lives, possessing weapons has been forbidden, so they have no martial skill what-soever. As you can see, all they do is flail and jabber. The instant they face real danger, they will piss themselves and run away."

"You sound sure of that."

"Over the years I didn't even bother to count how many fish-eaters my obligation required me to kill, and the tiger form is far less fearsome than a sea demon...yet the descendants of Ramrowan *must* have *some* greater purpose that hasn't yet been revealed to us."

Javed spoke with the certainty of a hateful witch hunter *and* benevolent priest. It was difficult for Thera to reconcile the two. "Other than them being infuriating, how goes your ministry?"

"In the weeks I've been here, I've tried my best to organize them and to teach them what has been forgotten to try and inspire them. About a quarter have listened. The rest refuse. Those who were secret faithful before heed my words but most think this is some kind of scam. I pray for guidance and receive no inspiration in return."

She studied Javed as he said that, and though she still didn't fully trust him, his frustration seemed real. It appeared having a greater purpose had helped him to heal from the terrible wound Toramana had inflicted upon him, as he no longer looked so forlorn and haggard. His missing hand had been replaced by a metal hook bound to his wrist with leather straps, and he used that rough tool to gesture irately at his charges as he continued complaining.

"The untouchables of Vadal City are a mess of thieves and cutthroats. Despite the fact that for centuries the Keepers, who tended the bloodline of Ramrowan, would send here the casteless they found who were offshoots of that lineage from generations before. To this particular city, to rejuvenate the line, so that it never died out."

"Why here?"

"I assume because they knew this was the site of the final battle, where the bloodline had to be strong or else. It reminds me almost of Zarger herdsmen, selecting horses for traits like strength and endurance to breed the next generation superior to the last. But these casteless seem as pointless as all the rest in Lok, their traits no better than any other fish-eaters. Now with the population bloated with refugees of the Great Extermination, all those have become easy victims for the predators already here."

"Better than staying home and getting slaughtered." Thera wondered if the Maharaja's wife realized just how many lives she had managed to save here by bargaining with Harta. If the casteless understood, they'd probably build a statue of Rada out of garbage and worship it like one of their idols.

Javed continued. "The casteless of the Cove gave me some hope because by the time I met them, they had built something remarkable there. So much so that they were willing to die to defend it. But those were ready to listen to Keta and serve because the traditions which controlled them had been stripped away. When they needed something new to believe in, Keta had been there ready to offer them truths to cling to."

Thinking about her old friend brought a sad smile to her face. "Keta was born to preach. Give him a few minutes to tell a story and he'd have even the most listless dullard you've ever seen hanging on his words like he was the greatest storyteller they'd ever heard."

"Keta managed to forge the Cove's casteless into something far greater than they'd been before, so resolute even the armies of Akershan couldn't break them."

"You are no Keta." It still offended her to have this fraud associated with him. As if two men so different in character should ever be allowed to share the same title.

"No...I am not." Javed was quiet for a very long time, staring out at the swift blue expanse of the Martaban. "I am no Keta. He was chosen to be Keeper. I was the unworthy replacement because the gods didn't have time to prepare another. Briefly, I deluded myself into thinking I might become worthy. In the desolation of Kanok when I preached there the people listened— even some of the First—because they'd been humbled. You'd think the casteless would be teachable because they've never had anything to boast of, but it turns out pride is relative. Somehow the casteless of Vadal are as proud as the First just because they rule this mountain of shit."

Thera had to laugh at his indignant frustration. "Herding casteless is a thankless job, isn't it?"

"It is. And my time is short."

She didn't know if Javed spoke of the pending invasion, or that he had many dangerous people waiting in line to kill him. "Ashok gave his word. As a man of honor, Toramana will respect it. He's told no one else."

"That is an impressive restraint."

"If Toramana had talked you'd know because some of the swamp people would've already come here to cut your throat. They're a proud people. You'll live until your work is done. Then you can go meet the gods to apologize to them in person."

"I await that day more than you can possibly know." Javed gave her a resigned sigh. "I was told Ashok is off on some mission. I assume you've finally come to ask me about the unwritten prophecies I warned you about?"

Entertainment over, the mob was dispersing, leaving one man bloody and unconscious, and his muddy woman kneeling next to him sobbing and pulling on his limp arm, futilely trying to wake him up. The casteless quarter was a savage place, but so was the rest of the world, albeit in different ways.

"I put it off as long as I could. It's easier to dismiss you as a mad fool than listen to more prophecies of my doom."

"I've given my testimony. Accept it or don't."

"I'm here, aren't I?"

"You are indeed a very brave woman, Thera Vane. The bolt from the heavens chose well when it picked the Voice's vessel."

"We'll see about that. So tell me about this lost prophecy."

"Very well. The Voice gave it through you, with Ratul as the only witness, sometime not too long after the two of you first met. I was not told the exact date."

Those had been strange days, as Thera had fled war-torn Makao, having been saved by the Protector of the Law—and secret religious fanatic—who had just executed her father, Andaman Vane. "And Ratul told it only to Keta, who told it only to you. Did he say why he didn't tell me?"

"That will become clear, I think. The Voice declared through you with Ratul as the recorder and witness..." Javed cleared his throat. "*The final battle nears. In the Great City of Man the fate of all will be decided. Gather the children of Ramrowan there. In their blood hides my avenging fire, and in that city is buried the fuel. Draw forth my eternal enemy. In his moment of triumph, he will know he has been deceived, then shall he be consumed.* And then Ratul, overcome by the glory of the gods asked, 'How may I start this holy fire, Lord?' The Voice replied, *You cannot. Behold my chosen. Her life is the spark that must be given willingly.* To which Ratul begged, 'She is not ready, Forgotten, she does not believe or understand,' to which the Voice answered, *Hide these words until the hour is upon her, for I shall prepare her through trial. Her death will free me to do what must be done.*"

She wasn't even angry. By the Forgotten's terms, that was remarkably straightforward. "That's it?"

"To the best of my memory, handed down through three Keepers who were forbidden to ever write it."

So that was it, then. There was no way out for her. There would be no giving up the Voice but somehow keeping her life. It was all or nothing. It was one thing to accept the possibility of death so you could keep fighting. It was something else to know that death was certain yet be expected to fight on regardless.

They sat atop the platform with a view of river, squalor, and muck, as she mulled that over in silence for a very long time.

"Are you alright, Thera?"

How could she be? "I see why Ratul didn't tell me that. The Voice had just inspired Vane into a doomed rebellion that got my father killed for it. Had he told me that then, I would've run away from this obligation and never stopped running. I would have said to the ocean with the Voice. All it had accomplished then was to bring me pain."

"And now?"

She hesitated to answer because too much had changed. A lifetime had passed. All those experiences must have been the trials the Forgotten spoke of. Thera wasn't the frightened and angry woman Ratul had saved from her ex-husband Dhaval Makao and a sea demon, nor was she the bitter survivor Keta had tried to drag toward enlightenment. Today she was the mother of a movement, the lover of a hero, and the leader of a free people.

Thera accepted her fate.

She gave the traitorous priest a sad smile. "I don't feel like running anymore."

"I understand."

Thera watched the casteless wade out into the Martaban to capture the discarded trash that was floating by. Anything of value would be put to use. In a land where any water deep enough to stand in and not see your feet might conceal a demon, the casteless waded out there heedless of the danger anyway. It wasn't that they were too ignorant to understand, it was simply the way things were done, and always had been.

"It's good you didn't share this prophecy in front of Ashok. He'd likely have killed you on the spot."

"That's exactly how it was told to me, every last word. I wouldn't lie."

"Oh, Ashok wouldn't kill you for lying, Javed. He'd kill you just to send the gods a message."

Chapter 20

It had been a difficult season for the First.

As summer had passed and the leaves began to turn, tensions had continued to rise in Vadal City. The cooler autumn air did not bring with it calmer voices. Three great armies had grown larger by the day as the city prepared for a war that many whispered was a figment of the Maharaja's fevered imagination. Industry and commerce were continually interrupted as Supreme Phontho Jagdish turned all of Vadal's resources toward defensive preparation. But this was a war without a visible enemy, or a front line, because no one knew where the unseen demons would strike from, and many believed they were never going to appear at all. Harvests that should have been sold were stockpiled. Bitterness grew as merchants left with empty wagons and bankers were left with empty pockets.

Meanwhile, Vadal's still vast population of casteless suddenly becoming whole men, and all that entailed, legally and socially, had rocked the city's elite. Now led by a lunatic priest with a hook for a hand, the casteless were demanding outlandish things like sufficient food and clean water in exchange for labor so cheap that it threatened to undermine the worker caste's importance. Phontho Jagdish had work for them to do now, shoring up the city's defenses, but what about afterward?

Dangerous fanaticism seemed to be lurking around every

corner, as those who had recently been considered the vilest form of criminal now preached their madness on the street corners for all to hear. The fanatics spoke with boldness and impunity, seemingly unaware that they should be too ashamed to spew such lies to the gullible and desperate.

Offense was often taken. At first the commands of Jagdish had kept the violence to a minimum, but an increasing number of duels were fought every week. The warrior sell-swords who made their living by serving as duelist champions on behalf of offended first casters—those who won at least—grew wealthy, but not nearly as wealthy as the workers of the foundry district, who were churning out Fortress rods—a once unthinkable evil—at an alarming rate. It was said that the city known for its perfumes and flowers now stank of Fortress rod alchemy. The peace and quiet was often shattered by sudden test firings of the vile weapons, and reasonable men feared the calamity that would come from the cancerous spread of such evil tools.

Even more frightening than the so-called guns, magic was being traded freely in every market. So much demon flesh and bone had been collected from the attack on the Capitol that the Maharaja's forces paid for their entire expedition off what they peddled to hungry wizards, who were flocking to Vadal to buy vast stores of the stuff at a discount. All that was required for those wizards to procure for themselves decades' worth of magic was to promise to stay in the city for a time, in order to serve the Maharaja should the demons come. It was a proliferation of powerful magic and a collection of wizards the likes of which no one had seen before, and the organization that normally controlled such things—the Inquisition—was a shadow of its once great self.

The Protectors—all of whom were here by now—seemed more worried about preparing for an enemy that might not exist than the enemies who were clearly right under their noses...like the strange Fortress foreigners who wandered about the city, seemingly baffled by color, beauty, and sunlight.

There was also a bold new Order called the Defenders of Lok, but it appeared to the tradition-bound First to be an odd conglomerate of disparate groups, without direction beyond the curt pronouncements of the barbaric giant who commanded it.

As if this chaotic mix was not enough, rumor was that every ancestor blade in Lok had already arrived or was on its way and would soon be here. Bearers were restless and terrifying. What were three great armies gathered when compared to the danger presented by eleven men who it was said could defeat an army on their own?

And worst of all, among those eleven lurked the terrifying specter of the most dangerous criminal who had ever lived. Black-Hearted Ashok—sword breaker, Thakoor killer, the non-person fraud who'd stolen Vadal's name and brought endless shame to their house—now roamed their lands a free man, seemingly bound by neither Law nor decency, and he was wed to the defiant rebel witch who spouted outlandish prophecies while trying to organize all the untouchables into an army.

Such upheaval made it inevitable that the first caste would feel threatened. It was a ripe opportunity. The possibilities to cause strife for his own advantage were endless. The Capitol was weak. Ruled by a librarian in the Maharaja's absence, it was barely clinging to relevance. Rada was beyond his reach for now because the ancients had chosen her to be the administrator of what remained of their systems, but she was too distant and ignorant to stop him from completing his great work.

With the smallest push, he could easily set this entire place on fire, and then rule over the ashes.

It took all of Omand's considerable will to refrain from meddling.

As tempting as it was to pit these fools against each other for his amusement, from the city's shadows he waited and plotted, puzzling over the machinations of the ancients, and biding his time.

For there were demons beneath the Martaban.

Chapter 21

It was time.

Ashok woke with a start. "They're here."

Thera was lying next to him, and she bolted upright, instantly awake. "Demons?"

"Yes." He rose and found his clothing in the dark. *"Guard!"*

One of them appeared at the entrance to the tent. "What is it, General?"

"Sound the alarm. Rouse the camp. Bring me the wizard and the runners who are on duty."

"Right away!" He bolted.

Seconds later, men were shouting as they rushed from paltan to paltan, rousing the Sons of the Black Sword and their Fortress allies from their slumber. Ashok didn't even know the hour, but it felt as if dawn was still some distance away.

"Can you tell where they're at?" Thera was scrambling to get dressed. "Are they aboveground?"

He tried to decipher the urgent twinge in his chest. The shard embedded there was heating up, as if every new scratch of demonic claw through the rock and soil of his homeland gave offense. Somehow he could feel what it was like in the cold depths, and that there was a great weight of rushing water above the demons. They were pushing relentlessly toward it.

"Not yet, but they have found a path directly under the Martaban."

"How do you—Never mind. Is it the whole army of hell or just raiders?"

"It is an army. There's a multitude of them."

"More than were in the Capitol?"

The shard left him no doubt. "Far more."

"Oceans!" Thera cried. "We're not ready."

"It will do."

Thera looked like there was something else she wanted to say, but she hesitated, stricken. She knew he could see in the dark, so there was no hiding her fear from him.

"What is it?"

"It's nothing, Ashok. Just nerves before the fight. If it's to be from the river, then, I'll go to the vantage point like we discussed."

"And you'll retreat if they break through?" He didn't mean that question as an insult to her courage, because demons didn't care about such things, they killed brave or cowardly just the same. He asked because he needed her to live.

"I will. I promise."

Ashok kissed her on the forehead. "Do not fear. This is the moment for which the gods gave you an army and me another chance. We will prevail." He waited for her to nod in understanding. Then he took up his sword belt, threw it over one shoulder, and walked from the tent to see that the camp was already in a frenzy of activity.

One of Laxmi's wizards was on watch at all times, and he had come as soon as he'd been summoned. The wizard stopped before Ashok, breathing hard from his sprint. "Is it time?" Right behind the wizard was one of Shekar's skirmishers who would dispatch riders in case the other army's wizards somehow missed the much faster magical message.

"Spare no bone. Send to every commander and bearer. Tell them the demons have dug beneath the river. They will break through soon."

"Which district?"

The shard's warning wasn't that specific. "I only know the threat will come from under the Martaban."

This wouldn't be like when the demons had attacked the Capitol, emerging from distant Shabdakosh, where the human forces might have been able to intercept them away from the population. This would be more like how the demons had struck Kanok, emerging from beneath the Thakoor's mansion and immediately rampaging outward. Demons appearing from the Martaban had been Jagdish's greatest concern, because the river was gigantic, with miles of city stretching around it on both sides. Demons could swim up and down it with impunity. They could strike a dozen different districts. There were only a relative handful of bridges that spanned the Martaban, and if those fell their forces on either side would be cut off.

Strategy was Jagdish's problem. Ashok's duty was to lead the Sons and kill as many demons as possible. The gods had predicted the Voice would die today, but Ashok angrily dismissed that thought. To the ocean with their proclamations. The gods weren't here. Ashok was.

"*Sons of the Black Sword, Children of Fortress, free men, hear me!*" he roared.

The entire camp stopped to listen.

"*The time has come. To fight for your people! To fight for the brother by your side! To fight for your gods! Let no demon live! Prepare for battle!*"

Chapter 22

Jagdish was not awoken by the messenger, because the truth was, he rarely slept most nights now anyway. There were too many people counting on him to allow for anything more than a few hours of fitful slumber at a time, and the rest was for fretting he hadn't done enough. Closing his eyes just gave him more time to think of the many things he still needed to attend to, of ways he could make this city a tougher nut to crack. There were always more fortifications to enhance, supplies to store, and men to train.

So he was lying on his bed, awake, pondering what else he could do to fight demons better, when the word came that the demons were already here.

It was odd. For just a moment after hearing those warning shouts Jagdish lay there and wondered if he should have been scared, or crushed with a ponderous feeling of accountability, because after all, the future of his people was in his hands. He could even have pretended to sleep for another minute in a vain attempt to deny reality before his guards came rushing in to wake him.

But as always, Jagdish just did what was expected of him, because that's what warriors do.

By the time the bellowing messenger reached the front gates, Jagdish was there to meet him.

The report was dire, and it was from Ashok, who would

not exaggerate. There were demons in the vital artery that ran through his city, in number greater than had gutted the Capitol.

Jagdish had given up his regular quarters in the city to house troops and taken to sleeping in the warrior district's command post. Shakti and Pari had been sent to stay at his estate in the east a few weeks ago, supposedly so that she could attend to the army's affairs on the border, but in truth it was so Jagdish wouldn't be distracted with worry. His lady hadn't cared for that, but Jagdish couldn't afford the luxury of thinking about anything other than his obligation.

Besides, if he failed here, the demons would come for everyone else soon enough.

A cadre of officers rushed to him, and Jagdish wasted no time. "It's as we feared, boys. The demons are using the river, but we've planned for this." In fact, Jagdish had a dozen different contingency plans ready, depending on where the demons emerged. The river had been his most dreaded option. "Have the armies move into their assigned districts along the banks before we sound the evacuation bells. I'll not have the streets clogged with noncombatants trying to run away blocking the warriors from getting where they need to go. Once every paltan has had time to get into position, I'll order the general evacuation of the other castes. If we can't hold them at the banks, then every district has an assigned fortification they can fall back to. Each of you must see to your responsibilities. Am I understood?"

Every one of his aides shouted in affirmation. The officers who'd been obligated to the night watch at the command post tended to be younger and of lower status than those who were here during the day, but Jagdish had drilled them mercilessly just the same. Each warrior in this city had a job to do and it would be done. He knew they would not fail him.

Redundant messages were sent. Everybody with any sort of responsibility would be told to get to it. Jagdish wasn't worried about any members of his caste, whether of Vadal or even the outsiders who'd heeded Devedas' summons and traveled from distant houses to come here. A warrior wasn't going to ride across the whole continent and *not* fight when given such an amazing opportunity for glory. He was more worried about the workers who'd been conscripted and armed to serve as sepoy militia. But he was sending so many runners there would be no claiming afterward from anyone that they didn't know it was time to serve. Anyone who didn't show up to do their duty now would be labeled cowardly shirkers for the rest of their miserable lives.

While his servants helped him into his armor, more officers kept arriving. They'd report or ask questions. He'd bark orders. They'd leave. The cycle repeated. Over his breastplate went his sash of rank, upon which he wore but a single medal, the illustrious *Param Vir Chakram*, the wheel of courage. He wore that in the hopes that when his men saw it they would be reminded of the high purpose of their caste and inspired. Perhaps he was naïve, but Jagdish knew it would have worked on him when he was a lowly nayak. Once fully encased in plate armor and mail painted the proud blue-gray and bronze colors of Vadal, Jagdish went outside to where his horse was saddled and waiting for him.

His personal guard were ready to ride.

Najmul Sarnobat dipped his helm in greeting. "It is for this day the gods sent me to serve you, Jagdish." Since the Maharaja's legalization of religion, the bold fanatic didn't even bother to hide his faith anymore. "I shall keep you alive or die trying."

"I've got no time for your silly gods, Najmul. If any of us survive today it'll be because the men of Vadal do not break."

"And because Master Karno granted some of us Defender might," Najmul quipped, for he too had received the blessings of the Heart.

"That helps too. Now let's go look fate in the eye and tell her we'll allow no demons here."

"You and your talk of *fate*, Jagdish. I swear you fear the gods as much as I do. You just call them by another name."

Maybe that was true... And maybe if Jagdish tried hard enough, perhaps unseen fate would take pity on a poor warrior one last time.

They set out for the river.

Chapter 23

Devedas had once believed that when he marched the Army of Many Houses through the streets of Vadal City it would be as its conqueror, victorious. Not as its guardian, anxious.

Row after row of soldiers drawn from every other house followed the man in the golden armor through the shadowed streets. Among them were Protectors, Inquisitors, and wizards, even bearers of mighty ancestor blades. They were all on foot, because horses would be overcome by instinctual terror and flee as soon as they smelled demon.

Vadal troops made way for the Capitol's army. Most of the soldiers seemed nervous at having such a gigantic force of out-siders present, but the ones who trusted the wisdom of Phontho Jagdish understood that the very survival of their people would depend upon the courage of those same outsiders. Those Vadal saluted him. Devedas made sure to return the gesture every time.

Jagdish's preparations had been so painstaking that every one of Devedas' officers had been supplied with a map of the city, with all the major streets marked and the districts neatly labeled to keep them from getting lost. The battle for the Capitol had taught them that demons were almost impossible to contain in one place and that they tended to split up and spread quickly, roaming as individual hunters instead of remaining in a pack. It was likely that they would have to rapidly divert troops to respond to breakthroughs so every paltan had at least one Vadal guide attached to it. The maps were for when those men died.

The Capitol had only had one ancestor blade there to defend it. Today they had *all* of them. The final bearer had recently arrived from faraway Uttara, drawn here as irresistibly the rest. To each bearer had been assigned Protectors and many warriors from his same house, so that when the bearer was slain, someone who might be considered worthy would be there to try and immediately take up their ancestral sword to keep fighting. He didn't know if this strategy would work, but it seemed the swords themselves wanted to be here, so hopefully they would accept new bearers quickly, and not take offense.

Tens of thousands of warriors had gathered here. If the demons were expecting as little resistance as they'd met in the Capitol, they would be sorely disappointed.

Thinking of the Capitol turned his thoughts to his wife, who was still valiantly struggling to hold the remnants of civilization together. When Rada had sent him a message detailing Omand's vicious attempt on her life, Devedas had been consumed with a fury the likes of which he'd never felt before. It had given him something to hate even more than the demons. Though he was afraid what would happen once the battle was joined, another part of him was eager to see it through to victory, so he could focus on ending Omand's miserable existence.

Vadal buildings tended to be tall and ornate structures, covered in lattice openings to let in the cooling breeze. Having been awakened by the noise of clanking armor and stomping boots, the citizens had gotten out of bed to see what the commotion was about. Now they watched the Capitol's army from their high windows, balconies, and rooftops. So many warriors moving quickly toward the river at this strange hour could only mean one thing.

Some of the people began to panic. "The demons are coming! The demons are coming!"

Grimly, his warriors kept marching. But the cries spread faster than they could walk, and soon the frightened masses began spilling out into the streets ahead of them, gathering their belongings, harnessing teams, loading wagons, and generally getting in the way.

Jagdish had been worried this might happen, because there

were over a million bodies crowded into this sprawling warren of a city, and there was no way to move an army through it even in the middle of the night without alerting them. Terrible conclusions would be made. A desire to survive usually overrode sense, and the citizens blocking the road would end up trapped between the threat and the warriors who were trying to protect them from it. A situation that was stupid, but inevitable. Devedas, though, had already given the order: Anyone who got in their way would be removed swiftly with however much violence was required. Anything that blocked the street would get pushed aside or smashed. He didn't care if it was a banker's carriage, it would get turned into kindling, and his army would march over the splinters. Thakoor Bhadramunda could take offense afterward.

"Make way!" the Garo around Devedas began to shout. "Keep the path clear."

Those who failed to do so were promptly shoved off the road. Most of the rest had the smarts to not get trampled.

They entered a workers' district. The buildings changed from giant works of art to even larger structures that were still decorated, just not as finely. The Vadal simply couldn't help themselves—if there was a blank surface they were compelled to carve designs on it and then paint them. The endless gaudiness offended his sparse southern tastes, but say what you would about the Vadal, they were industrious, because Devedas noted that atop every one of those roofs were workers armed with newly manufactured Fortress rods.

Those weapons still made Devedas uncomfortable. The last time he'd been on the receiving end of such terrible things a single volley had laid low a unit of mighty Protectors. Hopefully the demons would learn to fear them as well.

Despite the late hour, the workers of this district were already scurrying about in great numbers, as if this part of the city never slept anyway. This was probably accurate, at least recently, since they had been too busy churning out rods. Giant metal tubes were being moved about on two-wheeled carts. They appeared to be so heavy that it took teams of hardy workers to manhandle them into place. Everything else in Vadal was decorated, but those huge weapons were plain. For once the Vadal had lacked the time for beautification.

An exceedingly large worker spotted their formation and

approached Devedas. The Garo bodyguards immediately moved to intercept him.

"I know of this one. Let him through."

The worker was an odd sight, as he was dressed in the finest of robes, but with a rough leather apron casually thrown atop them, heedless of the grime. Over each shoulder was slung a Fortress rod, and unlike the other austere weapons Devedas had encountered, the wooden bits of those two had been decorated with rubies and the long metal parts had been plated in gold. They must have been built before the demon invasion, so though it surely wasn't the worker's intent, it was almost as if he was flaunting the illegality of the things.

The big worker gave him a very deep and respectful bow. "Greetings, my distinguished Maharaja. Welcome to the bell metal district."

"You must be the one they call the gun man Gutch."

"That I am, Your Royal Highness. It is a pleasure to be of service."

He knew not what to make of this peculiar criminal. His trade had been the most illegal thing in the world up until the last season, and apparently it had made him one of the secretly richest men in Lok, yet here he was, serving like everyone else. "Jagdish has spoken highly of you, Gutch."

"That's nice to hear. And Ashok Vadal once told me you're the greatest man he's ever known, at least when the two of you weren't battling to the death. So I figure we'll just have to use the recommendations of those luminaries to quickly color our perceptions of each other as we speak."

"Very well." Devedas' army was marching on without him. "But make it quick."

"I got Ashok's message. I'm assuming your men intend to hold this area and the great stone bridges to the north and south."

"That's Jagdish's strategy, but it's a big river. We'll adjust depending on which way the demons go."

"A fine plan. I'd caution you, though, don't get any closer to the water here than the end of that ridge there." He gestured at a wooded hill overlooking the Martaban. "Your men can take the top, but whatever you do, don't go down the other side by the water."

"I don't usually take battlefield advice from a worker."

"You should if he's already got cannons with a fine angle on that area."

Devedas looked toward the vast tubes on the carts. "That is those things?"

"Indeed. Think one of these"—Gutch gently patted one of the ornate rods at his side—"only much, *much* bigger."

"I have seen Fortress rods used in battle."

"Not like this, you haven't. My cannon will blow a hole through an elephant."

"What will they do to a demon?"

Gutch shrugged and spread his calloused hands apologetically. "That's a bit harder to test, though if Ashok's right I suppose we're about to find out. However, if they work as I dare hope they do, then I'd be delighted if you were to keep me and my fine crafts-men in mind for all of the Capitol's future demon-killing needs."

Devedas could hardly believe his ears. "In this hour of apoc-alyptic doom, you are attempting to engage in commerce?"

"There's always time for commerce, Maharaja. It is a rare opportunity for a humble worker such as your loyal servant Gutch to demonstrate the quality of his wares before the biggest potential customer in all the land."

Devedas reached up to place one comforting gauntlet on Gutch's shoulder and kept his voice kindly as he spoke. "I had a friend once by the name of Abhishek. I watched him die, his skull smashed open by a projectile from one of these devices like yours. Despite being a superb combatant who had trained hard his entire life with the finest swordsmen alive, courageous Abhishek never had a chance against a weak, half-blind, mangy fish-eater because he was armed with one of these damned things. Making your foul trade legal—for now—galls me and makes me wonder if I've not unleashed a terrible evil into the world. I want you to know that if the needs of my people hadn't forced me to pardon your kind, I'd spill your guts from your fat belly right now and leave you to die slowly in an agony so terrible that you'd eagerly use one of those ruby-covered guns on yourself to end your suffering."

"Ah..." It was probably a rare thing for this particular worker to be left without words. "Alright, then."

He patted Gutch on the shoulder one last time and then removed his hand. "I will make sure my men don't go down that side of the hill. Carry on."

Eager to escape, Gutch bowed again, and hurried back toward his dishonorable labors.

Devedas thought better of it and called after him. "Gutch."

The worker stopped and turned around slowly, surely expecting to get executed. "Yes, Maharaja?"

"You may prove me wrong by killing a great many demons today."

Chapter 24

"Get away from the river! We must go *now*." Javed, Keeper of Names, ran to where one of the casteless was desperately trying to pull his nets from the water. "Leave those."

"I need 'em. They're the only thing I own."

"You can't use them if you're dead." Javed smacked the back of the obstinate fool's head. He used his flesh-and-blood hand, rather than the steel hook, tempting as that might be.

"If I leave me nets they'll get stole."

"Then stay here and die with your precious trash." Out of patience, Javed kept moving down the shore, roaring at the remaining casteless. "You must go. Follow the others. There are places prepared for you to hide and shelter all throughout the city. You have been assigned to one of those. Go. There you will find sanctuary."

But many of the untouchables were hesitant to leave their quarter. They'd spent their lives being beaten for crossing those boundaries unless a whole man commanded them to. And Javed, being a *priest*, was something new and different from the Law-abiding men who traditionally ordered them about. The faithful trusted him. The rest did not. Besides, they hadn't seen any demon sign yet, so they were far more worried about raising the ire of the Law than getting eaten. The only evidence they had that demons were coming was the word of this crippled priest, and

203

most of the casteless still here didn't even believe in the gods at all, so why should they trust him?

"You must move! Damn you, fools, get out while you still can."

For weeks he had tried to prepare these people for this day, but right now he was so annoyed by them that he was beginning to root for the demons. The faithful had listened, obeyed, and run. Most of the others walked, and they did so reluctantly, worried one of their fellows would steal their meager belongings as soon as they looked away, or perhaps so they could have an opportunity to rob someone else themselves.

Javed had liked the casteless of the Cove far more than these, and he had still murdered a great many of them without compunction. The Vadal City casteless were infuriating in comparison and it took everything in his power to not use the small bit of demon he had procured for himself to turn into the tiger form, so he could terrorize these dregs into moving. Even a three-legged tiger was faster than a foolish casteless.

After several more minutes of pointless yelling, on the verge of abandoning the stubborn remainder, Javed found himself alone in a shadowed spot between the ramshackle buildings. The casteless who'd been crammed into these stinking barracks must have been devout to have left so quickly.

He took a deep breath and then uttered a prayer to try and calm his desperate anger. "Hear my plea, gods. Among these are the bloodline of Ramrowan, blessed among all men. It is my duty to guide them. It is my duty to keep them safe and teach them the words of the Voice. I must record their names and lineage in the holy book. Help me help them, for you have said only the descendants of Ramrowan will be able to prevail on the last day."

"Why?"

He glanced around to see who had asked him that. Very little light made it between the teetering stacks of casteless shanties, so he saw no one nearby. "Who's there?"

When no answer came, Javed shook his head. Surely imagined voices were a sign that exhaustion and stress had caught up to him. He began walking away, because the rest of these fools weren't going to get themselves where they needed to be without him.

"Where are you going, Javed? You asked for a higher power to hear your plea. A higher power has answered."

Javed's blood turned to ice, for that time he recognized the voice.

"I asked you a question, Senior Witch Hunter."

Slowly, Javed turned back, to see there was a hooded figure standing in the shadows of the hovel a floor above him.

"I have forsaken that title."

"No, you have disgraced that title and thus the title has forsaken you."

In the darkness, Javed could just make out the shape of horns and fangs and the gleam of gold...So this was how he would die. "Grand Inquisitor Omand."

"You know it is I, so why do you not kneel before your superior?"

"I kneel only before the gods now."

THEN KNEEL.

The command slammed into Javed's head so hard it felt as if his skull might burst. Reeling, he stumbled and fell onto the sand. Omand's words had smote him, but the shanty was unaffected, as if the thunder had been contained entirely inside Javed's head.

"Kneel, Javed, for I have ascended, obtaining magic beyond your meager comprehension. I have made myself immortal, and the patterns of the ancients are in my hands now."

The world was enveloped in an impossible stillness. The sound of the river vanished, as did the noise of the perpetually bickering casteless. It was only Javed and his vengeful former master.

"I have obtained copies of your so-called *scriptures.*" Omand spat that word with disgust as he floated down toward the sand. "I read them all, marveling as I did so that you threw away your noble obligation to write a work of fantasy and become a groveling worm before the Mother of Dawn. You pledged your loyalty to a slave, whom I destroyed with ease."

Javed struggled to stand.

I SAID KNEEL.

That time the command was followed with a violent rebuke, and Javed was hurled back to smash through the flimsy wall of a casteless hovel. The words had hit like a mace, and he lay there, coughing as accumulated years of dust rained down on him.

"I had such high hopes for you once. Very few men possess our particular gift for detachment. Perfection cannot be hindered by pity or empathy. It can only be achieved through a perfect clarity of thought. Your skills as a witch hunter were second to no one but me. Your future was so very bright...And now look at you, nothing but a scrawny dog herding untouchables instead of sheep."

Javed managed to gasp. "What do you want from me?"

"I'm a god now, Javed. What do all gods want? To be obeyed, of course. Apparently, we gods require priests to do our bidding. I know of only one priest, and you have already served me capably once before. So I offer you this new obligation. You have preached the doctrine of Mother Dawn to the masses. Now you will preach mine instead."

Javed understood instinctively that Omand could crush him like a bug, but he no longer feared death, only failure, so he answered without hesitation. "No."

"What?"

"I said no."

"Such surprising defiance." Omand approached, gliding inches above the ground. "I would grant you anything your heart desires—power, riches, knowledge of a hundred magical patterns and black steel by the pound to fuel them." The darkened eye holes of the golden mask lingered on Javed's pathetic hook hand. "I can restore your body and give you long life and lasting strength. I can make you stronger than a Protector. My priest would have palaces, feasts, slaves, pleasure women. Name your price and I will grant it...or refuse this obligation and die."

Untempted, Javed shook his head. "I will never serve you again."

"What is it about these unseen gods that inspires such devotion? They are distant and aloof. I am right here. They give nothing while I offer everything."

"They are the beginning, the true first. Whatever newfound power you have, you stole it from them. You're nothing but a thief."

"Oh, how little you understand the true nature of things." Omand's mask shook disapprovingly as he chuckled. "The only difference between them and me is the distance of *time*. What seems a miracle to you, was mundane to them. They didn't spring fully formed into existence from the endless nothing. They came here from elsewhere, as builders, designers, architects, creators, artists...most certainly there were some thieves among them. Who are you to judge your betters?"

Again, the priest forced himself to stand, but this time Omand didn't smite him back down. "I know what you are now." Javed leg's wobbled, but he spoke boldly as he recalled the words of the Voice as recorded by Ratul. "You're the Father of Night. The master of lies and corruption who will attempt to thwart the plans of the Mother of Dawn. You are *the necessary evil*. Without your meddling, the great work could not be finished."

"So that's what that name means." Omand paused, as if savoring this new title. "*Night Father*...I find this mantle acceptable."

"The Forgotten's Warrior will defeat you."

"That part remains to be seen, but I suppose we will find out soon enough. Before I kill you for your insolence, Javed, I asked you a question. *Why?* Why was it written that only the descendants of Ramrowan could defeat the demons at the final day? Surely, you must know, for that day has come." With the sudden sweep of one of Omand's gloved hands, the waters of the Martaban were thrown aside in a great wave, a hundred feet wide and fifty feet deep.

And revealed beneath were demons.

Hundreds of demons.

The waters came rushing back, hiding the terrifying demonic army, and striking the shore with a mighty splash. But even as the droplets rained down, they made no noise on impact, as Omand still controlled the world around them. "Why did the ancients think so highly of these untouchable scum? What plan did they put into place that could possibly make pathetic casteless useful against such a deadly foe?"

"If you're the god, why're you asking a mere priest?"

"I already know. I am testing the knowledge of the faithful, to ascertain how badly you're about to lose."

"No...You really don't know, and if there are limits to your omnipotence, you're no god at all." Fate sealed, Javed scoffed at the mask. "You know of the ancients' words, but you don't understand them at all. You took their power, but it is like a child stealing his father's dagger. I hope you cut yourself."

Anger crept into Omand's voice. "The thing you worship is nothing more than a phantom of the past, pushing all of you about like pieces on a game board, directing you toward its ends, no different than how I manipulated the judges of the Capitol. I once thought the great game was politics, but the great game is *everything*, and everything is the prize I intend to win."

"Yet here you are, doing exactly as the gods predicted."

There was movement behind him, and Javed turned back to see that the waters of the Martaban were frothing. The demons were rising.

"Explain yourself," Omand demanded.

Javed began to laugh. Even with demons at his back and an angry demigod in his face, it was a joyous laugh, because Javed trusted in the wisdom of the Forgotten. "Do you think the Keepers wrote down *every* prophecy the Voice gives us? If the Voice revealed to Ratul something that was to be kept secret from our enemies, to be passed down from Keeper to Keeper, to be told only to the Forgotten's chosen at the right time, do you think we would be so foolish as to *write it down*?"

"You will tell me, or I will rip it from your mind."

"I am not just the Keeper of Names, Omand. I am the Keeper of Secrets. Your ignorance will be your downfall. By the Forgotten's will, your suffering will be eternal."

GIVE ME THIS SECRET.

The Night Father's command was so mighty that no mortal could possibly resist it for long.

Rather than betray the Forgotten's chosen, Javed threw himself into the river.

Chapter 25

As the Sons of the Black Sword assembled above the shores of the Martaban, an earthquake shook the city. Men stumbled as it intensified. Bricks fell from nearby walls as mortar ground to dust. Before them was a casteless quarter, and it was fortunate that most of the residents had heeded the warnings to get away from the water, because the earthquake caused many of their feeble shacks to collapse. Anyone who remained inside was surely crushed beneath. The disturbance lasted but a few seconds yet was so intense that only Ashok and those who had touched the Heart were able to remain on their feet.

The tremor abruptly stopped.

There was a moment of strange quiet afterward, and then the city came alive with shouts and wails. Dogs barked, children cried. As his soldiers got back up, Ashok scowled at the distant river, because something wasn't right. All the noises of human fear were slowly drowned out, gradually replaced by a sound that increasingly grew louder and louder, until it was like thunder.

Across the Martaban, thousands of torches and lanterns flickered as the armies of Great House Vadal and the Capitol manned their defensive positions. The river was a pitch-black divide between them. Jagdish had the workers create huge piles of wood all along the darkest patches of shore to be lit in case of emergency, and upon receiving Ashok's warning, the local workers had ignited their bonfires in order to illuminate potential targets for their Fortress rods.

Those piles of wood and trash burned all along the shore bright enough that the Sons didn't need Ashok's magical eyes to see that the river was draining.

For hundreds of yards in either direction the water level was falling rapidly, as if a great fissure had been torn in the riverbed beneath. The thunderous sound they were hearing now was from the great and growing waterfalls that had formed on each end of the gap, as millions of gallons of water cascaded into the unseen caverns below.

Then the world vomited up a horde of demons.

They erupted from the water, glistening black, crooked limbs twitching as they scrambled their way up the muddy banks. The demons were in many different shapes and sizes, but each one was unmistakably deadly. There were the gigantic titans, spidery-thin beasts, and hulking destroyers, but then there were unfamiliar breeds that even Ashok had never seen before, smaller darting creatures the size of monkeys or dogs, and big ponderous things that resembled beasts of burden. They seemed not built for killing, but for labor. Had the demons even brought their worker caste?

This army of hell clambering out of the draining river already seemed greater in number than what he'd seen in the Capitol, and *more were still coming.* His prediction had been right. Every demon alive would be attending this battle. Their number uncountable. Their hunger insatiable.

Despite the horrors moving in the dim light below, the Sons didn't quail. His officers shouted their commands. The paltans had already taken their positions along the high ground above the casteless quarter. The terrain enabled the gunners to remain up the slope where they could fire over the heads of the infantry.

Ashok glanced back the way they'd come from, toward where Thera was supposed to be observing the battle from the highest tower in the Lantern District. Even his keen eyes could not pick her out from here, but he knew she was there. He would not fail her.

The rift in the river was a few hundred yards away, but such a large target was well within the range of their rods. Ashok glanced back toward where Gupta waited on one flank, then Praseeda on the other. The workers, casteless, and foreign fanatics appeared ready. "Tell the gunners to begin."

Orders were relayed. A moment later, the air filled with smoke and noise as Fortress rods discharged. More guns fired along the opposite bank. Then there was a terrible roar, loud as the falling river, as the first of Gutch's great cannons ignited. It was followed immediately by another, and then there was a cacophony of ear-rending booms as months of worker-caste effort was unleashed. Thousands of men, working around the clock, with all the resources of the richest House, backed by the wealth of the Capitol, had managed to flood this city with hasty alchemy.

Projectiles hit blackened hide. Most of the lead flattened and bounced off, but the great metal balls fired from the cannons had so much power behind them that even if the demon's skin was impenetrable, the creature it hit was still sent flying. There were so many demons packed into the riverbed that they couldn't miss.

The well-practiced gunners of Fortress had fired a second time before the gunners of Lok had finished reloading from their first volley. The foreigners seemed a flawless instrument of efficient movements. They had been preparing for this moment since they had been assigned to the Weapons Guild as children and they were clearly determined to not let Ram Ashok down. They thought he was their ultimate hero reincarnated. The gunners would fight accordingly.

From this point on his gunners wouldn't stop until they ran out of powder, lead, or life. The rapid industry of Vadal City had seen to it that every one of them was carrying pounds of lead and powder, but their lives would not be so easily replaced. When their weapons became dangerously hot, the plan was to drench the barrels in water, sizzle the dangerous heat into steam, then continue. The duty of the spearmen was to keep the demons back so the gunners could continue their deadly trade.

The Sons and many of the city's Sepoys were armed with rods, which took very little training to become basically proficient with. Meanwhile, the warrior caste—given such ample time to prepare—had turned to the most destructive weapons of their tradition, such as ballista and trebuchets. The finest of those had been built by the engineers of Kharsawan who had come to Vadal hoping for appointment to the Order of Defenders. As soon as those implements of destruction were wheeled into place, giant rocks and bolts began to hurtle through the sky, plummeting down into the horde.

The Vadal had poured thousands of gallons of oil into wagons that could be set on fire and sent rolling downhill into their demonic foes, and in the distance Ashok saw one of those fire wagons explode into a massive conflagration. Black shapes moved like shadows through the flames. One of those shadows was promptly flattened by a falling boulder.

All along the falling river the demons were climbing up both sides, directly toward their hated foes. Their wicked claws had no difficulty finding purchase in the slick mud. Not knowing from which direction they would come, Jagdish had worried that one of the three armies would be forced to take the brunt of the attack, but it seemed there were so many demons that all of them would get buried equally. There were forces scattered everywhere around this vast city, but thankfully the few hours of warning Ashok had bought them had enabled most of the combatants to arrive in time.

But Ashok could no longer concern himself with the fate of the other armies, because the horde was rapidly closing on his.

"*Warriors, prepare yourself!*" Ashok bellowed so all could hear him over the gunfire. "*Hold this line. Upon the signal, second rank up while the first reforms. Repeat until they're dead!*"

Ongud, Risalder of Cavalry, who would normally be atop a horse, bounced with nervous energy at Ashok's right hand. "I don't know how foot soldiers stand this."

"I know you want to ride out there and hit them, but being infantry's not so bad once you get used to it." Risalder Eklavya was at Ashok's left, heavy armor freshly painted in his native Kharsawani red, which he wore proudly since the Law had declared their kind were outcasts no more. "At least we're on solid ground this time."

"I yearn to be on the move, with the wind on my face. Not standing here waiting."

"They'll be here soon enough," Ashok growled, though he too would have preferred to be atop Horse, even if for nothing else than the slightly better view of the battlefield that extra height would grant him. But alas, animals could not abide the presence of demons. Though Horse was so belligerent that he might very well have proved the exception to that rule, Ashok had decided not to risk it.

"I assume that signal to change ranks will be mine to give, General?" Eklavya asked.

"Yes. Odds are I'll be too busy to notice." Though he'd been given the ancient title of a supreme commander, Ashok and his sword were too valuable to waste merely watching. He would need to range about, fighting wherever he was most needed. Plus, Ashok lacked a clear understanding of what it meant to be a normal soldier, so was not a good judge of when the men had reached their limits. Eklavya had a keen mind, and a leader's heart, with the instincts to someday maybe even equal the wisdom of Jagdish, should he live that long. "They are yours to command, Eklavya."

"I'll do right by you, Ashok. That I swear." The demons were nearly in bow range, so Eklavya shouted, "Toramana, send it!"

It was rare for an arrow to pierce a demon, even using a hardened steel point designed to punch armor, but launch enough of them and a lucky few might make it through. The fletchers of Vadal had been kept very busy over the last few months to the point that the archers' arms would probably give out long before they ran out of arrows. Each of his fearsome swamp men was carrying a bundle of the things.

Ashok didn't need to give instructions to his wizards, as he had already conferred with Laxmi. The former slaves of the House of Assassins would do as they saw fit. As Ashok had no idea about how best to utilize magic on the battlefield, he had simply turned them loose to use whatever patterns they knew as the opportunities presented themselves. They had a supply of demon bone beyond what most wizards ever dreamed of, and no need to save any of it because it was doubtful any of them would live to see tomorrow.

Tendrils of fire rose into the air and then fell upon the demons. Magic ripped rocks from the ground and sent them tumbling between the demons' feet. Transformed wizards in the shape of birds wheeled about over the river, dropping smoking Fortress bombs to explode among the demons, and then flying back to where Shekar's skirmishers waited to supply them with more munitions.

The Sons' ears were pounded as the gunners kept firing above them. The obscuring smoke temporarily hid the churning demons from view, which probably helped keep the less stalwart men from breaking ranks and running away. But when the smoke parted for a moment, Ashok saw that the blue waters of the Martaban had been almost entirely replaced with demonic black. Even pessimistic Ashok had never dreamed the army of hell would be so great.

On the opposite bank, cannon balls struck the ground and careened through the demons. Smaller creatures were swept off their feet. Limbs were torn off. Greater demons took the hits, stumbled, then continued stomping toward their prey. The ground was shaking again, not from the sharp cascading of tons of bedrock into the depths, but from the stampede of demons.

The smaller, faster creatures were nearly upon them. Behind them were a multitude more. The strange beings showed no emotion, no hesitation. Their relentless approach never slowed, even as they were struck with bullet, bolt, arrow, and magic. For each demon that fell, another immediately took its place.

Helms were closed. Grips were adjusted on weapons.

Ashok drew Angruvadal. The shard in his chest burned hot as coals yet did not sear his flesh. It was for this moment he had been kept alive. It was for this moment he had been chosen. In this moment he would fight like no man had ever fought before.

As the sun began to rise over the horizon, the battle was joined.

Two thousand spears collided with the first fifty demons. Dozens of men died immediately as the monsters hurled themselves over the shafts, ripping and tearing on the other side. Behind the spears were men with swords, axes, and maces, and they immediately rushed to plug the gaps.

A smaller demon bounded back and forth before Ashok, weaving between the spear thrusts. It jumped, but Ashok had already surged forward to slash the beast from the air. Hide split effortlessly and white blood sprayed. It rolled down the hill, limbs flopping.

The nearest demons seemed to take note of that effortless killing. They must have recognized what Angruvadal was and then focused their attention on Ashok.

Good. Better for him to draw their wrath than a less capable warrior.

"I warned you demons the cost of trespass. Come and meet your fate!"

They did.

Ashok rushed ahead of the spears. A dog demon leapt at

him, jaws opening, but Ashok darted past, opening its belly as he went. The worker-caste demons didn't seem to have nearly as thick a hide. Right behind it, though, was one of the fearsome spiders, suspended on four spindly limbs. It lifted itself upright at the last moment to swing at Ashok with one of its long multi-jointed arms. Angruvadal caught its wrist and sent that hand spinning away, then turned and inflicted a brutal draw cut across the monster's chest, splitting ribs and spewing white organs. Even the tougher-skinned beasts were nothing compared to Ashok's righteous anger and Angruvadal's hungry edge.

Sword swinging, Ashok pushed farther into the horde until he was surrounded. That simply gave him more targets.

A hulking brute clawed for his helm. Ashok lopped off its fingers, swept under that arm, and sliced it from hip to knee. He caught the demon behind it through the chest with a thrust, twisted Angruvadal, and then ripped the blade out its side. White blood sprayed hot.

Angruvadal warned him of a multitude of incoming dangers, and he reacted to each in turn. He parried claws. He dodged fists and bites. Demon after demon was cleaved by black steel.

The sun climbed higher.

Upon that blood-drenched hill Ashok reached a state of being which even he, the greatest swordsman in the world, had never experienced before. His anger remained, but it did not drive him. Both anger and the river were a distant roar. He fought with a calm beyond meditation, in a state of complete awareness, outside the flow of time. His actions were not cruel, they were punitive. Since the shard had done its work in the starving pit of Xhon-ura, the most skilled warriors had seemed slow to Ashok. Now, in this great and terrible instant, even fearsome demons seemed inferior to him. Though still incredibly deadly, they were simply malignant things to be dispatched as efficiently as possible.

Behind him, a demon, nearly nine feet tall, was pushing its way through the teeming masses toward the Sons. Their spears glanced harmlessly off its incredibly resilient hide. Dozens of arrows and bullets had done nothing to it. Ashok flung himself after the beast, rolled beneath another monster's attack, and sliced the legs out from under the big one. It toppled through the forest of spear shafts, landing before Ongud, who laid into its head with a polearm and Defender might. Ashok left him to it and kept going.

It appeared the rest of the Sons' line was wavering. They didn't have his magical gifts. Mortal men, no matter how brave they were, couldn't withstand such an onslaught. Many Sons were dying, but they did not break. They did not flee. Every last one would die rather than yield. Their courage inspired the man bereft of fear to somehow fight even harder.

Ashok rushed down the line, darting effortlessly between his own men's spears, hacking demons along the way. The shard whispered secret knowledge to him—as it had when he fought the Dvarapala—and his eyes no longer saw demons as living beings, but as anatomical structures, with vulnerable points for him to exploit.

One of the barrel-chested beasts was about to ram its way through the Sons' right flank, but Ashok lowered his shoulder and collided with it. The demon outweighed Ashok by a quarter of a ton, but he was moving so fast he still knocked it aside, sending it crashing through the ranks of smaller demons. He followed through the chaos, launching two or three lethal strikes for every measured heartbeat, until he was standing over the fallen monster. It desperately lifted one hand, almost as if pleading for mercy, but Ashok had none. He stabbed Angruvadal down through its palm, straight through its eyeless skull, and then twisted brutally, the crunch of bone so loud it was audible even over waterfall and gunfire.

Despite being overwhelmed by the armies of hell, the Sons of the Black Sword who saw that feat roared. Even those who weren't true fanatics had to believe that the Forgotten had sent Ashok, because he fought with a merciless skill so far beyond theirs that it could only be a gift from the gods.

Demon after demon fell, but men died by the hundreds. Bullets and arrows continually rained into the horde. Clay pots full of Fortress powder were set ablaze and hurled out between the demons to explode as their wizards whipped flame and stone through the demonic ranks. The Sons kept fighting as Eklavya bellowed commands with a voice strengthened by the Heart. And through all that, Ashok tirelessly ranged back and forth to wherever instinct told him the men were about to give, to slaughter the demons there. He bought them a respite to trade in fresh arms, and by the time he returned the first men had caught their breath and the process could repeat.

No warriors had ever fought harder than the Sons of the Black Sword did on this bloody morning.

The plan had been to fall back into the city and regroup as necessary.

The Sons didn't give an inch.

He didn't know how much time had passed since the battle had joined. Perhaps an hour. Perhaps a million years. The pale disk of the sun had just risen over the tall buildings to the east, so closer to the former, but his arms ached like the latter.

Black-steel ghosts whispered that he had to stand and fight like never before. The fate of man was balanced on the edge of his sword. Instinct warned him that he had to hold until every last demon had been drawn into the light of the sun, and only then would the gods' terrible wrath be unleashed. Ashok didn't understand those strange whispers, but he continued anyway. Even with the Heart of the Mountain lending him superhuman might, Ashok's breath was ragged. Beneath his lamellar plate, his body was drenched in sweat. He reached levels of exhaustion that would have killed a normal man, and then crossed thresholds that would have felled even ancient Ramrowan himself.

On that day, Ashok Vadal became the greatest killer the world had ever known, the living weapon of the Forgotten.

All his efforts were not in vain, because it slowly dawned upon him that the entire slope of this district, from the Sons' line to the shattered casteless quarter below, had been soaked in milk-white blood, and scattered across it were the blackened lumps of dead and dying demons. He couldn't even remember wounding so many. He had trained himself to recall every man he had ever killed in battle, but demons were unworthy of such a courtesy.

"If man prevails, what we have accomplished here will become legend," Ashok told the demons. One tilted its lump of a head and hissed back, because they did not understand human words. Only then did Ashok note that through the sea of white ran veritable rivers of red blood, as thousands of his men bled out on the slopes above.

The Sons of the Black Sword were good men, noble and brave. Many of them had wives and children, and no legend, no glory or honor, would ever be enough to fill the void left by that father's or husband's passing. Ashok's pride for his warriors' lives was replaced with a cold and vengeful fury for their deaths. The eerie calm he had experienced before was pushed aside by something far more terrifying.

"Now I will show your kind what it means to truly hate."

Ashok cleaved that demon in half.

All the demons concentrated on Ashok now. Before they had been uncoordinated, and he had been able to move through their unruly pack, picking them off one at a time. Now they grasped that he was the keystone, without which this seemingly impenetrable fortress of flesh and bone would fall. While the weaker masses continued to harry the Sons, the fiercest warriors of hell assembled to challenge the Black Heart.

Ashok found himself surrounded by silent seething evil again, only this time that positioning wasn't his doing. These particular demons were organized, as if they had suddenly fallen under the command of some wiser power. Instinct told him they would fight as a unit. There were half a dozen of these greater beasts, each champions of their kind, all far bigger and stronger than Ashok was, and their obvious purpose was to put an end to Angruvadal's threshing of their kind like wheat.

While the Sons continued to battle the rest of the horde that had attacked this bank, Ashok and hell's elite paused before their duel. It was a mystery why these greater demons hesitated, but he was glad to use that time to let the Heart repair his torn and strained muscles. Ashok slowly turned in a circle, carefully studying his foes as the shard placed images into his mind of where best to target each type for maximum lethality.

"What are you waiting for, demons?"

The demons said nothing, but Angruvadal revealed the answer. *They await the orders of their king.*

"Then I'd best kill you all before he arrives."

He struck. The first demon caught Angruvadal with its forearm. Green sparks flew, but there was no white blood cut. The shard had not encountered such a thing before, but it appeared with this peculiar warrior breed the hide of their arms had been thickened and calloused by thousands of repetitive scarring cuts, making their limbs harder than any shield.

Ashok attacked ten more times, faster than the wind, but the elite demon parried each. Never before had a demon shown him such actual skill. Their danger came from their incredible strength, durability, and sheer unrelenting viciousness. This one fought like a swordsman rather than a ravening beast.

Then the six attacked as one and it took everything Ashok had not to die. Claws ripped across his armor. A mighty fist dented his helmet, and he was thrown, not from the circle, but into another demon's embrace. It immediately hoisted him from the ground and tried to squeeze the life from him. Steel groaned and bent. Ashok's ribs popped. He reversed Angruvadal and stabbed at a demon behind him. Black steel sliced across its knuckles and averted the blow meant to break his spine. He slammed his helmet down into the blank face of the beast that was restraining him. It reflexively bit back, and black fangs ripped through mail and sliced into his cheek. Unable to get an angle to strike the beast, Ashok followed the instinctual instructions of his sword and *dropped* Angruvadal.

The tip of the sword fell straight through the demon's foot. It was enough distraction that with a mighty draw from the Heart, Ashok was able to break free of its grasp. With magically fueled intensity, he kicked that demon in the chest so hard that it fell away and ripped stuck Angruvadal right through its foot.

Ashok snatched up his sword and dove out of the way, inches below a wild swipe from another demon that would've broken half the bones in his body. He rolled and slid down the wet hill, then immediately got back up as the six warrior demons pursued. Parrying an incoming arm, Ashok managed to cut that demon across the side, but it was too shallow to drop it. Then the attacks were coming so fast and from so many different directions that even Ashok couldn't keep up.

He was struck in the arm, in the leg, across the hip. Bones splintered. Then he was kicked brutally hard and stumbled to the side. He sliced a chunk from that demon's leg and then stabbed the next through the guts. That one hit him in the helmet with a thickly calloused elbow hard enough that the steel of his helm deformed, leaving him blind.

Even without eyes to see, the ghosts of black steel saved him. He parried two more strikes and then leapt over a kick he knew was coming only by the sound of it moving through the air so fast.

Instinct screamed to make distance or die, so Ashok dove farther down the hill. He hit the ground and slid even closer to the draining river. Knowing the six were following, quick as he could he rolled onto his back, leaving Angruvadal to rest across his breastplate, tore off his damaged helmet, and tossed it away. By the time he got up, the demons were nearly upon him. One of them even swatted aside a lesser demon that was getting in its way, nearly breaking the smaller thing in two.

Ashok met them with flashing black steel. The demon lifted one heavy arm to block his downward strike, but he only gave that a glancing blow, as he drew Angruvadal swiftly downward to thrust it directly into the demon's heart. He ripped his sword free as momentum kept the monster running downhill, dead before it even knew it.

Now there were five. He watched them as they watched their mortally wounded compatriot flop onto its nonexistent face.

With cracked bones, torn muscles, and some internal bleeding, Ashok had no choice but to turn the Heart from giving him strength toward tending his wounds. Suddenly he felt all the weight of his armor. Blood stung his eyes, dripping from a cut he didn't even know he'd received. Of the remaining warrior demons, one had a wounded foot, the other had white guts bulging through a gaping hole in its belly, but demons did not show pain. The remaining three were circling around behind him. They did not intend to let him escape their clutches again.

The demons closed. Ashok fought. Bounding back and forth between them, each time a demon drew near, Angruvadal raised sparks from their hide or wrung blood from their flesh. Except these were the fastest creatures Ashok had ever seen, each of them nearly his equal, and though Ashok had generations of ghosts to lend him aid, it seemed demons never forgot either, and each one of these had killed many men. It was a mystery how long demons lived, but from the scars, these had faced black steel before, perhaps even from a sword wielded by Ramrowan himself.

Ashok was struck from behind, and his shoulder blade cracked. A claw pierced the armor on his left side. That puncture went deep. He promptly slashed that demon's wrist open, but the damage was already done. The Heart compensated for the wound and slowed the flow of blood out the hole. A demon charged him and Ashok was unable to get out of the way. As he was knocked down and trampled, another of his ribs broke.

As that demon went past, he swung from the ground and Angruvadal opened the back of its leg, cutting to the bone. He didn't have time to watch that demon fall because the others were already upon him. Blade flashing, Ashok kept them at bay until he rose. One grasping demon left a few fingers behind.

They were near the outskirts of the casteless quarter, at the sandy border between untouchable squalor and worker prosperity. A cooling mist from the new waterfalls fell upon them here. Ashok stood at the ready, shaking, muscles quivering, blood running down his armor, as the demons advanced once more. The Heart seemed more efficient for him now, or perhaps it was from the magic of the shard, but whatever the cause his wounds were healing fast.

Just not fast enough.

The warrior demons swarmed. Ashok intercepted one and inflicted a deep laceration across its chest. A claw ripped through his bracer and left a long bloody track down his wrist. Instinct saved him from having his head swatted off by a giant fist. He ducked beneath the blow and sliced that demon through the ribs. Its heart burst open, but another kicked him, which sent him lurching back with a gigantic muddy footprint on his chest.

Four remained. He only saw three.

It was the demon with the crippled leg that he didn't see coming, for it had slithered in low to the ground behind him. Instinct came too late, as his legs were struck out from under him. Steel sabatons saved his flesh from the rending claws, but he was still sent flipping through the air, to land hard on his side.

He'd barely gotten to his knees when a demon barreled directly into him. Angruvdal pierced its guts, and Ashok lifted with all his might as he rose upright, splitting the demon's torso wide open.

But this demon had been on a suicide mission, and with Angruvadal still burning its way through demonic vitals, it wrapped its gigantic hands around Ashok's gauntlets and locked them around Anguvadal's grip, trapping him there. Ashok roared and pulled, but the dying beast wouldn't let go. Its jaws snapped for his face, and he had to lean back, narrowly avoiding death, and still left some of the skin of his neck upon its razor teeth.

With Angruvadal trapped, the remaining demons attacked. Blows rained down. His skull cracked. Blood flooded one of his eye sockets. All he could hear was the pounding of his pulse in his ears, far too fast. His flesh was torn open by obsidian claws. If he abandoned his sword he would die. If he did not abandon his sword he would die.

Ashok drove his body forward, calling on the Heart like never before, and he shoved the mighty demon back across the sand, then hoisted that vast weight into the air. Angruvadal and gravity cut the monster nearly in half, and by the time the black steel erupted from its shoulder, the claws fell lifeless from his gauntlets.

A claw slashed his throat.

He cleaved that beast across the skull hard enough to send chunks flying, but then was forced to stumble away as far too much blood suddenly flowed from his neck. Ashok pressed his hand against the gash as the severed artery sprayed. The leather glove within his steel fist was quickly soaked, and it was far too clumsy to find the artery to pinch it off. Forced to turn the Heart toward controlling that one mortal wound, the rest of his unnatural strength fled, and he immediately went to his knees. Dizzy and desperate, he threw off one gauntlet, and with fingers slick with blood he probed the hole in his neck until he found the severed tube, squeezed it shut, and dragged it back into what he thought was the approximate place it should go.

A demon put one massive foot on his shoulder pauldron and shoved him over. When Ashok's responding swing was easily avoided, the remaining demons knew they had him. Upon his next clumsy thrust, Angruvadal was knocked aside with an armored forearm. For one of the only times in his life, Ashok lost hold of his sword, and Angruvadal went skidding across the sand.

The last two converged for the kill.

Kule had stolen his fear, but not his regret. As his vision darkened, in the distance he could see the opposite bank and upon it the army of hell was ripping the warriors of Vadal apart. Demons were swarming across the Martaban bridges. Though the Sons had held their bank, the others had fallen, and soon the Great City of Man would fall with it. He had failed those who had trusted him, and most of all he had failed Thera.

The demon with the hole in its guts loomed over him. It raised one giant foot to stomp his brains out.

"For the Forgotten!"

The demon looked up just in time to get shot in the head. The bullet careened off, leaving a gray lead smear, but the distraction gave Ashok enough time to roll out of the way before the foot came crashing down where his skull had been.

All the Sons of the Black Sword came charging down the

hill. The remaining horde were retreating before them! His officers who'd touched the second Heart were in the lead, heading
straight for where Ashok was encircled by the last of the demonic
champions.

He had fought to save them. Now they would fight to save him.

Eklavya drove his spear into an elite demon's chest. The shaft
flexed as he pushed the beast away from Ashok with superhuman might. When the spear snapped, he drew his sword and
kept swinging. Ongud rushed past his comrade and struck the
demon's armored forearm with his polearm. Green sparks flew
from the chipped hide.

Toramana was behind them, wielding a mighty bow so powerful that a normal warrior wouldn't even be able to draw it all
the way back. The arrow struck the demon nearest Ashok in the
head so hard that though the steel point didn't penetrate, the
shaft shattered from the energy. It jerked away, giving Ashok the
chance to scramble after his sword.

Shekar ran by, screaming the battle cry of his raider house.
He rolled beneath the eviscerated demon's clutching hands and
came up on the other side to stab it in the back. With Defender
might, the demon had no choice but pay attention to this lesser foe.

With one hand falling upon Angruvadal's hilt and the other
pressed against his weeping neck, Ashok struggled back to his
feet and returned to the fight.

The spilled-gut demon struck Shekar hard enough to fling him
back against a casteless shack several yards away. Such a blow
would surely cripple him, but hopefully the Somsak madman had
paid attention to what Karno and Ashok had taught him about
the workings of the Heart. As soon as the demon turned back,
Ashok was ready. Angruvadal bounced off the hardened raised
arm, again and again as it desperately tried to block the black-
steel edge. Mercilessly hounding the creature, he drove it back.
The instant it stumbled over a discarded casteless net, Ashok
kicked it in the wounded belly, splitting it even further open.

Eklavya rushed past him and buried his pole arm in the
wound, driving it so deep that the skin of the demon's back
bulged outward. Even as it repeatedly clawed and slashed him, the
young officer kept shoving the beast across the sand. The demon
struck Eklavya's helm with a mighty overhand blow, knocking
him flat, but Ashok swept in and promptly buried Angruvadal

in its head, sending bits of brain flying like wood chips when a worker hit a log with an axe.

Only one of the elite remained. Ashok turned back to see that with his polearm broken, Ongud had thrown himself onto the back of the demon with the crippled leg as it crawled. The demon managed to lurch upright, trying to throw the warrior off, but in an incredible display of courage Ongud wrapped his arms around the monster's head and wrenched its jaws open wide. Toramana promptly launched an arrow straight through the roof of the demon's mouth and into its brain. The monster fell over backward on top of Ongud, crushing him beneath.

The lesser demons were rushing through the casteless quarter and down the now empty shores to leap back into the fissure where the Martaban had been. The Sons chased them all the way to the usual edge, but then stopped there, for following them down the slick mud- and slime-coated stones would be madness. Only a suicidal fool would risk sliding into that hole.

When the Sons saw that all the demons who'd invaded the district they'd been assigned to protect were either dead or running, they let up a cheer. Still holding his lacerated neck together with one hand, Ashok was so delirious from the loss of blood that it took him a moment to realize his entire army were all chanting his name.

"Ashok. Ashok. Ashok."

Leaving the Heart to do its healing work, Ashok could do nothing else but stand there, pulse pounding, damaged lungs struggling for air, trying to understand how so many of them had survived. The expected trade was the lives of fifty warriors for a single demon's, but from the look of things it cost a whole demon to kill but a few Sons of the Black Sword. The men must have believed that it was because their gods were watching over them, but when he looked toward the eastern bank Ashok knew why the enemy had retreated. The demons weren't afraid. They'd broken through somewhere else. Why fight the indomitable Sons when there was easier prey elsewhere?

The battle for the city of man had just begun.

The Sons were lifting their weapons skyward in time with his name, but his throat was still too damaged to address them. Toramana pulled on the dead demon's arm so that Ongud could free himself from the weight of the corpse. Gradually his officers assembled around him, each of them seeming astounded to still be alive.

Except, Ashok realized that the man who had led the charge that had saved his life wasn't by his side. Eklavya lay there in his red armor, unmoving.

"No time for napping, Ek. There's still glory for us to claim." Shekar limped over, knelt, and pulled off Eklavya's helm. "Oceans!" Shekar exclaimed as Eklavya coughed up a huge gout of blood.

There was a wide gash through the side of his breastplate, with the wound slicing through liver and lung. Blood poured out. It would've instantly killed a normal warrior, and perhaps still might kill even a mighty Defender, but rather than stop and give the Heart a chance to heal him, and let the men see him falter and perhaps lose hope, Eklavya had led them all the way down the bloody shore to victory first.

Shekar grabbed Eklavya by the armor and shook him. "Come on, lad. Hang on."

Ashok knelt next to his risalder, whose eyes were wide with fear, surely gazing into the great nothing that waited to consume him.

No, Ashok told himself. There was no such thing as *nothing*. Keta had told him there was something more as he had bled to death in Ashok's arms. The Law said there was no life after death, but to the ocean with the Law. In honor of their courage, Ashok would no longer believe that particular decree ever again. If Eklavya were to perish here, he was going wherever the gods sent the bravest heroes when they died, but in the meantime Ashok would do his best to prevent that.

"Listen to me, Eklavya. You must let the Heart do its work. Calm yourself and focus upon the injury. Do not give into the pain. Your will to live must pull stronger than death itself. To do so you must forsake your fear."

Eklavya looked to Ashok, blinking rapidly. It was easy for a man without fear to tell a warrior to mock death, but such defiance was necessary, for Ashok had seen even experienced Senior Protectors succumb to wounds less than this. Even the potent Heart of the Mountain could only do so much. But then Eklavya looked past Ashok, seeing something over his shoulder, and his expression seemed to change, from one of terror to a look of pure determination.

Ashok glanced back to see the wizard girl Laxmi running toward them. It appeared Eklavya had found his motivator after all.

"That's right, Risalder. You've done your part in this fight, but you must live so you can live for others. Do not disappoint her." Then he shouted at some of Eklavya's infantry. "Keep him still until he is coherent, then carry him to the nearest fort."

The Sons continued their cheering and shouting. He would let them have this moment of triumph. Soon the overwhelming number of casualties they'd taken would sink in, and the nature of the insurmountable task that still lay before them might cause even the most devout among them to fall into despair, but for now, on this beach at least, they were victorious.

There was a dark flash above as a great bird circled. The eye-searing dark light faded as it swooped toward the ground, and then vanished entirely as a Vadal wizard appeared running across the sand.

"Ashok Vadal, Phontho Jagdish needs your help!"

Before the wizard could even deliver his message, Ashok received another warning from his sword. Man's stubborn resistance here had finally forced the greatest danger of all to reveal itself. Having not set foot on dry ground since the Age of Kings, this trespasser was ruler, controller, and both god and king to all the armies of hell.

It is here.

Chapter 26

Desperate, Jagdish tried to save Great House Vadal.

He had claimed a workers' factory as his command post because it was the tallest structure near the fissure. From that wide flat roof, he had watched in horror as the demons had ripped through the armies of man. The air was filled with smoke, first from the endless firing of guns and cannon, and then from the fires that had broken out along the riverfront. Those now raged out of control, unable to be fought by the workers' fire brigades because demons danced between the flames. With Heart-augmented eyes he no longer required a spyglass to see distant things, but the situation was so dire that he'd rather be blind.

It appeared that one of Vadal's armies on the west side of the river had been routed, leaving an entire district of the city cut off. His scouts reported that an organized force consisting of hundreds of demons were advancing inland there, including several of the giants. The surviving warriors had retreated to prepared fortifications to withstand a siege. The fate of every Vadal citizen who had not evacuated yet would be left to hell's nonexistent mercy.

Worse, the reports said that a particular group of demons was being led by an especially deadly creature with a physical appearance different from all the others, and every wizard and Protector who had tried to stop it had been effortlessly eradicated by the thing.

Yet why were the demons concentrating their wrath against that one particular district? It held nothing of strategic note. Jagdish had already sent word to the only force near enough to try and intervene, but he didn't even know if the Sons of the Black Sword were in any shape to respond, or if they would be able to catch the odd demon in time. All Jagdish could do now was try to manage the rest of the chaos as best as he could.

From up here he had a fine view of the end of the world.

"I require another flyer!"

"Here, sir!" A young wizard rushed forward.

"Go to Phontho Gotama and tell him the demons have broken into the eastern market district. He must send a few paltans to reinforce Girish along the jade avenue immediately."

"Yes, sir!" That wizard immediately went to the edge of the roof and leapt off like a lunatic. A moment later, a great black bird flew away. Such a transformation was unnerving no matter how many times Jagdish had seen it, and since nearly half the wizards in Lok had converged on this place and been granted more bone and hide than they could imagine, it had become a relatively common sight. Wizards were more likely to get past demons than runners. They were even more reliable if he knew there was another wizard waiting on the other end capable of receiving words sent through the air itself.

"I need someone who can do a message spell."

Another wizard ran to him, this one wearing the colors of Great House Vokkan. War against demons made for strange allies amongst man. "I know that pattern, Phontho."

"Good. Send to your counterpart among the Maharaja's wizards that he's got demons moving south of his position swimming up Cold Stream. Phontho Luthra saw at least ten of them. Warn the Maharaja he needs to strengthen his left flank or risk being cut off."

"It'll be done."

After that wizard left to weave his magic, Jagdish took a deep breath to steady his nerves. Those were all the orders he could give for right now. So he went back to pacing along the edge of the roof, watching the destruction unfold below him.

His fanatical bodyguard was standing by, watching him in silent judgment.

"What're you looking at, Najmul?"

"I see a tiger stalking about in a cage. You are a warrior who yearns to be in the fight."

"Of course I want to fight. This is my home. Those are my people!" From up here Jagdish could hear thousands screaming in terror. He'd had the evacuation bells rung as soon as the warriors were in position, but over a million people lived here. Ashok's warning had surely saved many lives, but an untold number remained trapped while demons spread like wildfire. "Every drop of Vadal blood that gets shed is my responsibility. Yet even though I'm stronger than I've ever been before, here I sit in relative safety above the fray, while men I trained and have fought beside lay down their lives."

"You've been called to fight with your mind, rather than your sword. There's a time for both. No offense intended, Jagdish, but I've fought you. Your mind is worth more than your arm."

Unsure if that was a compliment, an insult, or both, Jagdish snorted. "Don't worry. I will fulfill my obligation."

Najmul nodded. "Good. Because only fools let their passion trample sense. The gods have chosen wisely."

"Look at my city burning, Najmul. If your gods are real, then they've clearly forsaken us."

"We forsook them first. They were forgotten. Remembering is a painful process."

"I'd throw your idols in the sea right now if I could," Jagdish snarled. "If your so-called gods expect us to prevail, they'd best send help soon."

"I trust they will when the time is right. If they don't, then I will die assuming they withheld their aid because we displeased them somehow."

"Well, they're a petty, spiteful bunch, then."

Najmul shrugged, as if to say such was life.

There was a flapping of wings as a great black bird descended upon them. It rapidly melted into the form of a Vadal battle wizard who landed gracefully on the roof a few yards away. Jagdish saw that it was Mukunda, whom he trusted more than any other wizard. That was why he had been the one Jagdish had dispatched to warn Ashok of the western breakthrough.

"What's the word, Mukunda?"

"The Black Heart says his army will march toward the incursion immediately."

Jagdish breathed a sigh of relief at that. With unstoppable Ashok

harrying them, the demons wouldn't be able to feast on the innocents quite so easily. "How did the Sons of the Black Sword fare?"

Wizards tended to be a canny lot, but Mukunda had spent far
too much time among the warrior caste, so he was unable to hide
his genuine emotion. "It is like nothing I could imagine. They lost
probably a quarter of their number, but Jagdish, the shore was
filled with dead demons! From the bluff to the casteless quarter
are strewn carcasses. No one has ever seen such a thing. Demon
corpses litter the ground there. They told me Ashok killed half of
them by himself, but I think those fanatics slew nearly as many of
the beasts as the rest of our armies put together. The Sons didn't
just hold, they killed them by the score, then chased all the demons
who dared challenge them back beneath the ground."

Everyone on his command staff roared approvingly as they heard
that report. It was the only good news they'd received over hours of
unrelenting awfulness and endless defeats. Most of the other warriors
had been unable to hold the riverbanks for long at all and been forced
back to their designated fortifications to withstand a siege. But the
Sons had prevailed! Who would have ever imagined that Law-abiding
officers of the warrior caste would cheer for religious fanatics?

Jagdish couldn't help but grin, for the tiny gang of criminals
he'd helped lead and organized had turned into an army, thousands strong, and able to beat demons! What warrior wouldn't feel
pride at hearing that his old unit had done so well against such
impossible odds?

"That's my boys. Make sure news of this great victory is sent
to every other phontho of every house. They could use some
inspiration."

"Can't have criminals outfighting them, now can they?"
Mukunda said. "I'll see to it, Phontho."

As his men returned to their duties, Jagdish saw that his
bodyguard was smirking. "What?"

"Don't throw my idols in the sea just yet, Jagdish. The gods
may have already sent us all the help we need. What's the army
of hell when compared to the might of the Forgotten's Warrior?"

Having fought with and against Ashok, Jagdish couldn't argue
with that assessment. From the reports he'd received, the other
bearers had fought well, but nothing like that. "As long as most
of the bridges are under demon control, that whole section of
the city is in Ashok's hands now."

"It appears Ashok has gone from your house's greatest enemy to their only hope."

That was doubtlessly true. There had been a few other mighty ancestor blades and some skilled Protectors on that side of the Martaban, but Jagdish hadn't received any word from them yet. Those heroes were probably either dead or besieged. Yet somehow dishonored Ashok Sword Breaker still fought to save Vadal. Jagdish was honored to be called brother by such a man.

"I will see to it that Thakoor Bhadramunda is told of this," Jagdish vowed. "Even if we all die, Ashok deserves to have his name restored for what he has done for us today."

The phontho returned to studying his battleground. Yet his eyes kept being drawn toward the plumes of smoke rising to the west.

The demons were lashing out everywhere, but this particular incursion was especially troubling, because he could not understand *why?* Why was the army of hell concentrating on a part of the city that held nothing of strategic value? The Thakoor's holdings were to the east. The Defender's Heart had been moved to their strongest-walled fort, also to the east. Everywhere else the demons had broken through they had immediately split up to range about and cause the most carnage possible, while his scouts told him these particular demons were remaining in a cohesive force, organized and hundreds strong. That force was pushing toward an old worker district, home to metallurgists, foundries, and refineries. Even if they didn't understand humanity, wouldn't demons be more inclined to destroy their imposing buildings rather than the humble ones?

"Bring me a map of the Lantern District."

"What're you thinking?" Najmul asked.

"Demons are savage, but they're not without logic. While the rest of them spread out and distract us everywhere, these demons push toward a mysterious goal." Jagdish took the offered map from one of his aides and unrolled it. He studied the detailed drawing, but nothing there leapt out at him of having any particular value. It had always been easy for Jagdish to put himself in his enemy's shoes, to understand their perspective so that he could anticipate their moves, but how could a rational man think like a demon?

The terrain was mostly flat and on the other side of that district was humble farmland, so unnoteworthy that it was specifically where he'd sent the Sons of the Black Sword to set up their camp, to try and avoid drawing the ire of the city's more respectable residents...

"What if their target isn't a place, but a person?"

"Who?" Najmul asked.

Jagdish had ridden with the Sons long enough to know they truly believed with all their hearts that Thera Vane was the prophet of the ancient gods. He himself had heard the Voice roar like a thousand lions in his mind so he knew she was *something*. Jagdish had seen Thera's badly burned palms after she'd formed a molten spear in order to slay a powerful demonic entity, so he knew her magic was powerful. The deadly House of Assassins had believed her form of magic to be unique, and so had the Inquisition...

Maybe the demons did too.

"I think you fanatics might not be the only ones who believe in prophecy, Najmul."

Just as Jagdish had sent Shakti and Pari to his distant estate so he could concentrate on his duties, Ashok wouldn't want the only woman he had ever loved standing on the shore a few hundred yards from a demon invasion. He'd have sent her someplace safe. Only, Thera Vane was warrior caste and proud, and the Sons had sworn their allegiance to her. She wouldn't abandon them. Just as Jagdish had claimed the high ground here to watch over his responsibilities, she would want to be somewhere she could see her army fight. There was only one great tower in that district, an ancient structure that now served as a school for skilled artisans. He checked the map again, and sure enough that had to be where these demons were headed.

Were they after Thera for revenge? Jagdish had threatened to throw his fanatic's idols in the water, but Thera had actually melted the only demon idol anyone had ever seen. Or were they trying to claim her curious magic for themselves? Jagdish didn't know, but if the demons wanted something so badly, all his instincts told him they could not be allowed to have it. The Sons might not be a match for a force of that size, and they couldn't be reinforced as long as demons held the river.

Jagdish's army was being held here in reserve to respond to any breakthroughs. There was no one else available. To reach the west he would have to reclaim one of the bridges.

In less time than it took the needle of the tiny pocket watch to click off a minute, Jagdish adjusted all his plans.

"Ready the men. We must cross the Martaban."

Chapter 27

The Sons of the Black Sword moved quickly up a wide avenue. It was the only path available to them not totally consumed by fire. The demons' trail was easy to follow because of all the corpses and body parts left behind. Flaming buildings crumpled and fell around them. The heat was overwhelming. The gutters ran with blood, which boiled and sizzled as burning debris fell into the red rivers. The air was choked with smoke.

Through this hell of fire, Ashok led them toward the final battle against the hell of water.

Broken glass crunched beneath their boots. The Fortress gunners kept their sacks of powder close to their bodies, shielded beneath their leather aprons so one of the many sparks that rained down upon them wouldn't cause an inadvertent detonation. Innocents were trapped in the flaming rubble, but they could spare no time to aid them. Their pleas would haunt the survivors for the rest of their lives.

Warriors of Vadal and other houses, Protectors, Defenders, wizards, and even other bearers who had been scattered by the demonic assault had seen the Sons marching past and rushed to join their ranks. In this final hour there was no longer division between criminal or caste, of fanatic or Law-abiding, but only man united against demon. They abandoned the relative safety of their forts to follow Ashok into battle, not because they were ordered to, but because honor demanded it.

Through that chaos, Ashok moved as if in a haze, existing both in the present and a millennium ago simultaneously, for the memories buried in Angruvadal had never been more clear. The images rushed over him like being submerged in a rushing river, and these memories were so old that they could only have belonged to Angruvdal's first master, Ramrowan himself.

As Vadal City burned now, so too had it burned a thousand years before. But those towering cubes of steel and glass had been far greater than the comparatively humble ones made of wood, brick, and carved stone that they marched past now. While the Sons faced hundreds of demons today, the ancients had fought millions, and both sides had been armed with weapons made of scalding light capable of slicing bodies to pieces. Above them today remained nothing but empty Upagraha, but for Ramrowan there had been many flying castles that had hurled down flaming bolts to split wide the sky. One by one those castles had fallen, burning through the air, and when the charred remains had struck the ground, they'd blown apart the world.

Yet in both times, at the end, all that remained to decide the fate of mankind was a small band of heroes who simply refused to quit.

They were but a thin shadow of the glory that had come before. Except Ashok, who had become something more. Blood of the gods, hybrid of black steel and man, defier of death, he was a weapon refined, prepared for this time over generations.

The sword's memories faded as the enemy came into view once more. Ashok raised one fist.

Thousands of men stopped in the street, awaiting his orders.

Ahead of them were two of the giants, each as big as an elephant, blacker than night. That was the enemy's rear guard. They turned toward Ashok when they sensed their doom approaching. In the distance, behind the giants was the lone tower, atop which was likely still the woman he loved.

Thera should have left as soon as the demons broke through. In his heart, he knew she hadn't.

With Eklavya wounded, the real leadership of the Sons now fell to Ongud. "Your command, General?"

Ashok had been carrying his battered helm. He reached down and pried the bent steel of his visor back into place. Then he put his helmet on and, satisfied he could see sufficiently, drew Angruvadal.

"Follow as best as you can."

Chapter 28

All about Devedas, his men were dying.

They'd been driven from the high ground and hounded across the workers' district. He was trading dozens of lives for each demon they managed to kill, and for each demon slain, two more had taken its place. The Army of Many Houses had been forced to retreat from the evil water back into the city, and hell had hungrily followed.

Beneath the pounding cannons the Maharaja and his Army of Many Houses fought a desperate, losing battle. Twenty yards from Devedas, a demon got its skull splattered open by a giant metal ball. The projectile sped through the rest of the demons, rebounding off bodies, and knocking several of the smaller ones down. The gun man Gutch had certainly earned his bank notes today.

They stood in a rain of sparks and swirling white smoke. Through that smoke came death, as more and more demons poured into the district. There were worker-caste gunners atop every building, but the demons simply clambered up the walls to throw those annoyances to their deaths.

"Light the trenches!" Devedas shouted.

The Vadal were a wily bunch, and Jagdish had proven to be by far the cleverest of them all. His defensive preparations had including setting up a series of traps all across the city. Lantern oil and a volatile alchemical sludge had been dumped into trenches the workers had dug in strategic places. A moment later, a blazing wall of fire rose up between the forces of land and sea.

Devedas had seen demons get set on fire. They seemed fairly resistant to it, yet it must have been uncomfortable enough that most of them still tried to avoid being burned. The army of hell waited on the other side while the trench burned. It appeared filling the intersections with fire would give them some time to regroup.

"They'll cross soon as it dies down a bit," Broker Harban warned as he approached. His mace had white chunks dripping from it.

"How fare the Protectors?"

"Of the five I had with me, two died at the river. Everywhere else, who knows? We can't hold here in the open for long."

"This district is lost." Admitting that fact galled him, but he had no choice. Even his worst estimates of the demons' numbers had been far less than this. He shouted for his subordinate. "Rane, send a runner to worker Gutch to move his cannons back. Those weapons have proven too useful to abandon here." The heavy things were on wheels. Hopefully the workers would be strong enough to move them deprived of their oxen, because every animal in Vadal, down to the rats and roaches, was instinctively trying to escape from the demons. Only man was stubborn enough to fight against the army of hell.

Devedas turned back to Broker. "We'll buy those workers some time before we sound the horn to retreat to the fortifications farther into the city."

"Maharaja!" someone cried. "Our right flank collapses!"

"Damn it." Devedas looked that way. A few hundred yards away, several demons had crawled over one of the workers' foundries to leap down on the men below. The red warriors of Kharsawan had been holding that point, led by their house's bearer, but it appeared they had been taken by surprise. Without hesitation, Devedas said, "Broker, take command here and prepare the retreat." Then he shouted, *"Garo, to me!"* He ran toward the demons without even giving his bodyguards a chance to keep up.

The demons had dropped directly into the Kharsawani ranks and immediately gone to killing. The eastern house's armor was of such legendary quality that even demon fangs often failed to pierce it, but the men inside could still be picked up and hurled against the nearby walls. Or the demon would simply grab hold of a warrior's body and some limb and pull until the one was torn from the other.

The bearer, Tejeshwar, was recognizable only because of the black-steel blade in his hand. He slashed a demon's chest wide open, but the soldiers of hell must have recognized that he was their most dangerous opponent, because three others pounced on him from above. Even with the ancestors' warning, there was nothing the proud bearer could do about it, and Devedas lost sight of him beneath a frenzy of tearing claws.

A bearer was worth fifty regular troops or more. They could not afford such a loss.

Devedas rushed into the fray. It was pure chaos. His gold armor passed between flailing red, and each time he saw pitch-black hide, he swung at it. Kharsawan's strength in battle was their warriors' discipline. Their weakness was anything that broke that organization. Nothing was more disruptive than demons suddenly appearing in your midst. When their bearer went down, even the bravest of warriors lost heart. Some of them began running away.

"Men of Kharsawan, your Maharaja commands you to fight! Die a hero or live a coward!" Devedas' roar seemed to break through the cloud of fear. Even those who'd began to run away reluctantly turned back, because to the warrior caste, shame was far worse than death. *"I see no cowards here! Follow me to glory!"*

Devedas pushed toward where he'd last seen the bearer.

A few feet ahead, a demon was trying to wrench a fallen Kharsawani soldier's head off, but all it pulled free was the helmet. The demon held up the steel bucket and shook it, seemingly confused why there wasn't a tasty human head inside to eat.

Using the Heart of the Mountain to give him strength, Devedas slammed his shield against that demon's chest and shoved, pushing it back until it crashed through the glass window of a workers' shop. Before the creature could spring back up, four burly Garo had leapt through the window after it and began beating it with axes and war hammers.

Devedas kept running toward the pile of demons that buried bearer Tejeshwar.

A point of black steel erupted through the top demon's back.

When that one lurched away from the devouring sword, Devedas' shield-slammed it in the teeth, knocking it aside. But

another demon kicked him in the legs so hard that it sent Devedas spinning through the air. He landed rolling, and immediately
sprang back up. A perfect chop from his southern blade took a
chunk of meat from that demon's shoulder.

The black steel of Khartalvar ripped through another demon's
ribs, and when it rolled off spasming and gushing, Tejeshwar
Kharsawan was revealed beneath. His armor had been torn open,
and many terrible wounds inflicted upon his flesh. He lay in a
puddle of his own blood, and when he rose, red drizzled down
broken leather straps. Despite the mortal injuries, he fought on,
slashing at the monster Devedas had wounded.

Until a huge demon grabbed Tejeshwar from behind by neck
and hip, lifting the dying bearer high overhead.

Tejeshwar desperately reversed his grip and tried to stab
downward to pierce the demon's skull, but he was too late. And
the demon hurled him down into the oil fire gutter. He struck
the ground with bone shattering force. Droplets of flaming oil
were thrown in every direction. Tejeshwar did not so much as
scream as he burned to death. Devedas chose to believe that was
because a bearer would never give the enemy the satisfaction or
risk damaging the morale of his men.

Devedas kicked that demon in the back. It stumbled toward
the fire. When it turned around, he struck a mighty overhand
blow against the dome of its head. Once, twice. He ducked beneath
a swing and drove his shoulder into the beast. Going against
the grain of its hide stripped the gold from his steel armor, but
Devedas came up and hit it over the head a third time. Claws
rent a hole in his shield, but the fourth blow across its face sent
the demon spiraling into the fire.

There was no way Tejeshwar survived within that inferno,
but somehow, by magic or incredible will, his final defiant act
was to throw Khartalvar out of the flames.

The ancestor blade landed near Devedas.

Satisfied his sword was safe, Tejeshwar sank into the fire, flesh
turning to ash, leaving nothing but a steel shell behind.

Devedas stared at the ancestor blade. His own family's sword
had denied him. That denial had forged him into a king. As
Ashok was the Son of the Black Sword, Devedas was its orphan.
Losing his birthright had made him bitter, but bitterness had
turned to ambition, and Devedas had used that to accomplish

what no one else alive could have. Ashok believed it was because the gods required there be a king who would give the fanatics their freedom when no one else would have dared. If that was what the ancients had needed him for, then his purpose was done, and the black steel would punish him for his hubris...

But if not, and he were to take up Khartalvar, then he would be a warrior king, who would drown this city in demon blood.

He sheathed his sword and reached for the ancestor blade, but then he hesitated, for he'd done many terrible things since Angruvadal had rejected him. If it had scarred the face of an honorable boy with noble intent, what would it do to a dishonorable man who'd overthrown the Law itself? Worse than death, if black steel rejected the Maharaja, his legacy would be saltwater. His rule over. Rada would be exiled in shame. His unborn son would inherit nothing and, like his father before him, would be claimed by no house.

All his effort, the crimes, the betrayals, the sacrifice and pain and lies... all that would have been for nothing.

So be it.

"Hear me ancestors of Kharsawan, I'm not of your house but I would use you to slay many demons. If you find me unworthy, then cut me, but I beg you, keep it shallow enough I can keep fighting, because there are a whole lot of these bastards still to kill!"

He took up the sword. It promptly stung his palm and weighed his sins.

Wreathed in fire, the demon leapt up from the gutter. Devedas cleaved it from shoulder to belly.

As the monster tumbled back into the flames in two pieces, the Maharaja turned back to his Army of Many Houses and lifted the black-steel blade high for all to see.

"Rally to me, brothers! Today we fight for Lok!"

Chapter 29

High atop the artisans' tower, Thera watched the demon army approach.

Oddly enough, she wasn't afraid. She was more resigned than anything.

As her father, the great Andaman Vane, had observed his daughter play at dirt war so long ago, Thera had watched the Sons of the Black Sword the same way. She'd never been able to have children of her own, but somehow she'd wound up with several thousand Sons, and she was proud of every last one of them. Where the greatest warriors in Lok had turned and run, her army of criminals had stood firm.

But another part of the defenses had fallen, demons had flanked the Sons of the Black Sword, and a different force was slaughtering their way through this district and there was no way Ashok would reach her in time.

"We must run now, Prophet, while we still can."

Thera looked back toward her bodyguards. "Save yourselves. I'm staying."

Except they were faithful of the Forgotten, and she was their Voice, so they didn't move, nor did they question her will. If the Voice said this was where they were supposed to die, then this was where they'd proudly die.

"You honor me, but your obligations are fulfilled. My journey ends here. Yours doesn't have to."

None of them left.

Their dedication was humbling. "Alright, then." Thera turned back to face the demons.

In the lead were several of the giants, so heavy that each of their ponderous footsteps made the tower vibrate. Behind those were rank upon rank of sleek demonic killers. This district was one of the places the casteless who lived near the river had been sent to shelter. Those who had not escaped ahead of the spreading fires had been trapped in the courtyard and gardens below. Demons effortlessly ran them down or dragged them screaming from their hiding places to tear them to pieces. She watched in horror as hundreds of casteless died.

These were the people she'd supposedly been sent by the gods to save. They'd heeded the Voice, they'd gone where her priest had told them to go, and this was their reward for it?

"Where are you?" Thera screamed at the sky. "You claimed them! Why won't you protect them?"

As usual, the gods did not deign to answer.

The opportunity to feast on the casteless had distracted most of the demons, but a lone figure continued toward the tower. This demon was only a few feet taller than a man, and lean, but something about it struck her as being far more dangerous than any of the imposing giants. It walked upon two legs like the others, but had multiple arms, like a sick parody of some of the forbidden statues of old gods the Inquisition had failed to destroy. While all the other demons she'd seen had hides that were sleek as cursed fish, this one was covered in cryptic markings, and several horns grew from its head and neck. Demons never wore clothing, but this one had some manner of rough belt around its waist, from which hung several skulls, human and demon both.

There was something about this one's demeanor, and the way that even in their bloodthirst frenzy the other demons deferred to it or scurried to get out of its way, that warned her this one was far greater than all its peers.

The strange demon paused for a moment, to raise its horned head to look directly at her, as if it recognized that she too was an oddity. With relentless purpose, it began walking toward the tower once more.

The King of Hell was coming for her.

"I understand the ancients' plan now."

Thera turned around to see who had spoken, and gasped when she saw that her bodyguards had been silently struck down. Standing over their bloody, lifeless bodies was a robed figure wearing a golden mask. His murders hadn't made so much as a sound.

"We finally meet, Thera Vane. I am Grand Inquisitor Omand."

Thera reflexively drew a knife from her sash and flicked it at Omand's chest. It stuck there, deep, right below his heart. Omand casually plucked it out and held it up to show her that the shining blade was clean of blood.

"An impressive throw for someone with mangled hands." He tossed the knife over one shoulder. It landed with a clatter. "Except a mortal cannot harm a god. Only a god can wound a god. Do not waste what little time we have together trying."

Quivering with fury, Thera awaited Omand's next move. Having accepted she was going to die today no matter what, even in the face of pure evil, she still felt no fear. Perhaps this was what it was like to be Ashok, and that thought made her laugh aloud.

The mask tilted quizzically, for Omand hadn't expected that particular reaction from her. "Do you mock me?"

"I spit on you, filth." With one monster before her and another monster below her, Thera remained a warrior daughter of Vane, bold to the end. "I'm not afraid of you."

He gave her a respectful nod. "Very few could say such a thing and not be a liar. I can tell you are not a liar. You outwitted Sikasso and corrupted my finest witch hunter. I see why the predictors chose you to carry their precious Voice."

"They punched a hole in my skull and left it there. Are you here to try and steal it again?"

"No. My wanting to dissect you was before I became more familiar with the details of the ancients' plot. Now, with all the pieces in place, the true nature of the game has become apparent to me. Even I stand in awe of their patient manipulations."

Omand walked up to her, put one gloved hand against her cheek, and when Thera didn't flinch away, roughly shoved her so that she was looking at the demons again.

The leader of hell's army was once again staring up at her, as Omand whispered in her ear. "Do you understand what, or rather I should say, who, that is?"

"Some manner of demon master, I suppose."

"Like us, he is a child of prophecy. In fact, he is the last piece of the prophecy. The sixth and final force required to bring about the end of this age. The Forgotten's Voice, Priest, and Warrior, and their refining opposition, the King, the Mask"—Omand reached up to tap two fingers against his metal cheek, before pointing them toward the ground—"and the Demon. The direction of the next age will be determined by whichever one of us carries this day."

"Then you should go duel him for it."

Omand chuckled. "I do not think so. For this demon is far stronger than I expected. He is the last of his kind. I am afraid the armies of hell would certainly prevail, if not for the careful planning of the gods. It is good that I did not kill you earlier, because now I can see their true purpose for you."

There was a keening noise from below, so piercing that it stole Thera's attention from the freakishly powerful wizard and demon lord, to one of the lesser members of his horde.

A smaller demon lifted its bloody jaws from out of a casteless torso to let out a terrible sound of alarm. Demons were usually completely silent, so this wail was so out of place to be unnerving. Suddenly, another of that same breed of demon let out a similar noise. It too had been feasting on a casteless body and tasted something not to its liking.

The demonic leader turned back toward the river, as similar screams echoed throughout the city.

"They have just found that which they dread most, the blood of holy Ramrowan. The demons believed I had eradicated most of the untouchables for them. They tested this first in Kanok, where the Makao in their malicious obedience had exterminated all their fish-eaters, and though the demons searched, they found no one with the blood of Ramrowan there. Then their underground path took them to the Capitol, but how were demons to understand our ways enough to grasp that there had never been very many casteless there to begin with? If they discovered any casteless blood in those places, it ran too thin for them to worry about. These cry out in fear now, for they have found that in Vadal the blood of Ramrowan still runs thick. Even among the casteless it is a rare trait, that only one in a hundred non-people might inherit, yet in this place that still represents a dangerous multitude."

The demons seemed to be . . . panicking.

Thera muttered back the words Javed had revealed to her. "'*In their blood hides my avenging fire, and in that city is buried the fuel. Draw forth my eternal enemy. In his moment of triumph he will know he has been deceived . . . then shall he be consumed.*'"

"Javed refused to reveal that to me. He died trying to protect you. In the end he was a better priest than an Inquisitor, but no matter. I did not come to kill you, Thera Vane. I came to watch you fulfill your destiny. The gods set the trap. The demons have taken the bait."

The great demon stood perfectly still as the warning wails tapered off. He had believed he was victorious and was coming to seize his prize. The Voice would have been his trophy. Now the entire army of hell was surrounded by an invisible enemy, a thousand years in the making.

A magical pattern began to unfurl in Thera's mind, far beyond anything she'd ever seen before. It was a thousand glowing lines awakening terrible powers. She had no black steel or demon upon her, but this spell would not be drawing upon those magical forces to guide it. It was drawing upon *her life.* There was only one way to unleash this pattern upon the world.

This was the end for her.

So be it.

Soundlessly, the demons began to retreat back the way they'd come. They would try to escape into the safety of the depths, where in the darkness they might hide from the wrath of the gods.

Then on the other side of the courtyard a man in black armor appeared, walking between the flames. He stopped there, blocking the demons' escape.

Ashok.

He looked up at her and could not possibly have missed the leering golden mask of the Law over her shoulder.

"I must admit, Omand, you've done me two great favors in my life, and for that you have my thanks."

Even a dark god could be surprised. "I have granted you nothing, criminal."

"No, you gave me *everything.* When you tore Ashok from the Law, and sent him to me, I despised him at first, then I respected him. Finally, I loved him, and he has loved me back, and given me happiness more than I ever dared dream I'd have in my miserable life. With Ashok, I knew joy. Real joy. Do you understand what that's like?"

After a moment, Omand admitted, "I cannot."

"It's wonderful. For giving me that opportunity, I'll always be grateful to you."

"Very well. And the second favor?"

The magical pattern had revealed itself in its entirety for her. Now it simply waited for her to do what had to be done.

"I knew the gods intended me to die today. I came here anyway. But I had to hide that from Ashok. I lied to the man I love. I promised him I'd retreat. My greatest regret was that he'd take my sacrifice as some kind of betrayal, as if somehow I could love the gods more than him, or that I doubted he could protect me and gave up. He'd hate himself for that, but now, he can hate you instead. Thank you, Omand. Thank you so much."

"For what?"

With tears in her eyes, Thera raised one hand toward her distant husband and waved goodbye.

"Instead of thinking I jumped, Ashok will think you pushed me."

Thera stepped over the edge.

Chapter 30

⟨≈≈⟩

Ashok watched Thera fall.

"NO!"

He ran toward where she'd disappeared from sight behind the horde of demons.

They rushed him. Angruvadal sliced them into pieces. Claws caught hold of his shoulder and one demon tried to pull him down. He grabbed that demon's mighty arm, and with a strength born of desperation twisted it until iron-dense bone snapped. Ashok cleaved it from neck to pelvis and barely slowed. He collided with demons and hurled them away. A giant crashed toward him, but Ashok slid beneath it on his knees, opened its belly with Angruvadal, then on the other side leapt back up and kept running.

"Thera!"

Behind him guns roared as his Fortress gunners opened fire. Ashok kept pushing forward, ripping through demons as if they were made of paper. Limbs and heads were sent flying. He kicked a thousand-pound demon in the chest hard enough to launch it back through a brick wall.

The base of the tower came into sight and upon the stones there ... Thera lay broken.

Ashok stopped. Amid a garden of dead casteless, the woman he loved was sprawled, bones shattered, blood pooling.

He'd killed well over a thousand men in battle and hundreds more as their executioner. Ashok understood death far too well for it to ever deceive him. He knew death, because he had been death's greatest servant, and death's truth stabbed him in the eyes.

She was gone.

Ashok stood there. Numb. Trembling. Blinking. Uncomprehending.

Kule had stolen his fear, but he'd left behind everything else. His guilt. His grief. Ashok had thought he'd known what pain was, but that had been a lie. That had been a shadow of real pain. A hook through the heart had been a sliver in comparison to what he experienced in that horrible moment. Dying hurt so much less than this.

Thera is dead.

The ultimate Protector had failed to protect the most important thing of all.

Atop the tower, a dark god waited, aloof.

Ashok looked toward the Grand Inquisitor, then back at Thera's body, then back up at the twisted Law-faced *thing* who had murdered her. His grip tightened around Angruvadal, so hard that even black steel creaked.

Kule had taken his fear, but Omand had just filled that void with something far more dangerous. Beyond suffering, beyond loss, beyond even hate . . . there lived *rage*. Not of fire, but cold, crueler and more unforgiving than the glacier ice that concealed the Heart of the Mountain.

With the shard in his chest burning with such intensity that the black light bled through his skin and shone through the gaps in his armor, Ashok started toward the tower's stairs.

Four demons attacked at once. Ashok barely even noticed them. Four demons promptly died.

But before he could ascend the stairway to vengeance, the king of demons hit Ashok with the entire world.

It came from nowhere, fast as lighting, to strike him across the chest. Ashok tumbled and skidded across the ground, rolling through the spilled blood of many casteless, to crash against a great foundation stone hard enough to crack it in two.

Angruvadal had not predicted that attack, for even mighty Ramrowan had never fought this thing in person. But encoded in the black steel was a warning about this particular demon, for the gods had known of its existence even before the swords had been forged.

During the great war that had raged across the world and sky this beast had hidden itself beneath the sea to avoid the fiery arrows of Upagraha and her sisters. Just as Ashok's ancient ancestor, Ramrowan, had the blood of the gods pumping through his veins, this demon had a touch of its creator, the gods' eternal enemy, seared into its makeup. That dark empire had created the demons to challenge gods and man, but this one in particular they had fashioned in their own image to lead the others. It had been designed as the dark counterpart to Ramrowan's light and imbued with some of the power of its masters. If this beast had been free to stalk the land back then, even man's greatest hero would have likely fallen before it, and mankind would have been eradicated, for this being was the living embodiment of demonic malice.

The ancients had given it a name, called after a legend that haunted their nightmares...*Rakshasa*...and the shard warned him that this was the most dangerous creature that had ever been, or ever would be.

But it was standing between Ashok and avenging Thera, so none of that mattered.

Calling upon a connection to the Heart of the Mountain that was stronger than ever before, Ashok's many broken bones knitted back together rapidly, and he stood.

The master demon waited.

"Offense has been taken." Ashok pointed Angruvadal toward the top of the tower. "Against *him*. But your existence has offended the entire world, so I will have to kill you first."

The Rakshasa's answer was to bend down and pick up an arm that Ashok had sliced from one of its soldiers. That limb glowed, then seemed to melt and flow into a new form as the demon worked some perverse spell upon it. Ashok had not been aware that demons had wizards. Nor had he ever seen a demon wield a weapon before, but when the spell was complete the limb had reformed into a spear made of flowing green fire. Bits of liquid slid off, dripping like molten metal in a workers' foundry, and when those globs hit the stones they immediately began to burn through.

It charged.

So did Ashok.

It was two whirlwinds clashing as demon spear met black steel. Fire scorched the metal of Ashok's armor as Angruvadal crossed a weapon that burned with the heat of the sun. Angruvadal absorbed enough of the intensity to keep Ashok from combusting, but cloth charred and the casteless blood he was coated in bubbled and blackened.

The demon pushed him back, spear spinning too fast for the eye to track. The strikes flew at him, but Ashok kept parrying them or narrowly dodging aside. Each time he countered, the Rakshasa did the same. It was too strong, too incomprehensibly fast. Yet somehow, in a holy combination of magic and fury, Ashok matched that intensity, and gave back even more.

Other demons fought with might and savagery. This one had those traits in greater quantity than any demon Ashok had met before, plus a martial skill that would make a Protector jealous. Just as black steel contained generations of instinct about how to fight, the Rakshasa had similar information coded to its bones about how best to defeat humans.

The two combatants moved back and forth, constantly attacking and weaving. Around them the plants of the garden wilted and caught fire. Their weapons were moving so fast that the wind of their passing tore all the leaves from the trees, swirling gold and red, the colors of Fall, as the casteless had named him.

The spear never stopped flashing, each end a deadly point, as the demon effortlessly shifted it between four different hands. Ashok met each, as Angruvadal was a seamless extension of his will. When either weapon clipped stone, it sliced through clean.

The Rakshasa drew first blood, as the tip of the spear burned across Ashok's chest, ripping a jagged line through the steel of his breastplate, but it took no triumph from that, as Angruvadal promptly caught one of its arms and opened a milk-white gash. As it drew back, he clipped it again, shallow, across the hip, cutting through the hide that held its belt of trophy skulls, scattering yellowed bones across the ground.

Ashok did not know whose heads this demon had seen fit to collect, but he would avenge them too. The human ones, at least.

They parted, circling. The ragged tear across Ashok's armor glowed red from the heat. The skin beneath charred and split. The smell of his own flesh roasting assaulted Ashok's nostrils. Boiling blood and burning hair. The pain was unbearable.

Until he caught another glimpse of Thera, and then it was *nothing*.

The Rakshasa stepped aside to make room for one of the titanic demons to try and run Ashok down. The garden shook as the giant rushed him. From the way it left a trail of white behind it, this was the one whose bowels Ashok had split open.

But before Ashok had to dive out of the big one's way, he saw Shekar Somsak sprinting alongside it, unnoticed by the giant. The wick was almost burned down on the Fortress bomb in Shekar's hand. With an incredible burst of speed, Shekar got in front of it and drove the clay jug deep into the giant's guts, but he paid for that audacity by being smashed beneath a massive foot.

The giant exploded.

White blood and demon meat were flung in every direction.

The giant toppled, skidding forward, plowing up plumes of dirt, until its head stopped inches from Ashok's boot. Fortress smoke spilled from its burst-asunder side and out its open mouth.

The lord of demons fell through the plume of smoke, slashing.

Angruvadal turned aside the flaming spear at the last instant, and then the two of them went rolling across the ground, through puddles of casteless blood. Ashok leapt back to his feet as the Rakshasa used its extra arms to launch itself back upright. They traded a dozen blows in the span of two heartbeats, and this time black steel bit deep.

They broke away, and the demon raised one of its hands to probe the deep laceration across its blank face. It was as expressionless as every other spawn of the sea, but surely that cut had surprised it. Just as Ashok possessed no instinct about how to fight such an unknown threat, it too had no knowledge sufficient to predict his actions, for no man had ever been as dangerous as this one. Even Ramrowan had not been devoted enough to become a hybrid of black steel and flesh.

However, the Rakshasa still remained far stronger than even the Heart and shard could make him, so it went at him, relentless.

Each impact of the spear hit with a crack of thunder, louder than a Fortress cannon. When it struck the ground where Ashok had just been, it threw up clouds of dirt and left behind craters. Ashok moved through those clouds to strike at the demon's legs, but demons had no eyes to blind, so it anticipated and jumped over his swings, striking at him from above.

Ashok blocked, but green fire spilled across his helmet. Steel melted and seared the side of his face. The demon landed, spun the staff overhead, and brought it down hard. He managed to intercept it with Angruvadal's guard, but that left the demon with two other hands free, which it used to pummel his torso. Each fist hit like Karno's war hammer. Ribs broke. Organs ruptured. Ashok threw his weight forward and kicked the Rakshasa in the leg with all his might. He might as well have been kicking a steel rod for all the good that did.

Its free hands grabbed hold of Ashok's armor, spun him hard, and sent him flying back through the garden and across the courtyard, to slam against the artisans' tower hard enough to break his spine.

He landed on his back, next to Thera's body.

Ashok lay there, crippled, commanding the Heart of the Mountain to perform its healing work. Even as a twenty-year Senior Protector, such an injury would probably have killed him immediately, and if it hadn't, it would have taken him days, if not weeks to recover. This time the ancient magic mended his shattered spine back together in a matter of seconds.

This draw was not without cost. He could not see it, but somehow he knew that in distant Devakula, a crack appeared through the Heart of the Mountain.

Even with that incredible expenditure of ancient magic, the Rakshasa was on its way to finish him, and then everyone would die.

Directly above, the golden mask of the Law glared down upon him in judgment. Thera was beside him, one bloody hand extended as if reaching out to him. Ashok placed his shaking hand atop her still one, which had been forever scarred from once holding the fiery might of the gods in her mortal hands.

"Forgive me, Thera."

The Rakshasa arrived expecting a dead man, but Ashok rose before it, took up the fighting stance taught to him by sword master Ratul, and raised Angruvadal high.

If a demon could speak, it would have asked *How?*

They clashed there for the final time, with his dead wife, a dark god, a band of warriors, and a horde of demons as their witnesses.

The spear came sweeping around in a flashing arc, Angruvadal met it. The shock of the impact shook centuries of dust from the tower. Again and again, the Rakshasa struck. It went high. Ashok went low. When it tried to entangle him with its extra hands, Ashok smote one off at the wrist.

It stopped to look at the stump, as if puzzled. The Rakshasa knew it should have killed him by now, but somehow this adversary refused to die. Ashok knew the Heart of the Mountain neared destruction as every Protector assembled here today used it to fight past the limits of human capability, and Ashok by himself drew might sufficient from that dying artifact to challenge gods.

But more than that, it felt as if Thera was aiding him from beyond.

A strange light began to shine around the base of the artisans' tower. An eerie stillness descended over the courtyard as a glowing mist rose from the ground about them.

The Voice was here.

But this was not like before. The Voice had not come to dispense some prophecy to guide its servants. This was a wrathful god freed, come to collect retribution.

As the fog thickened, the puddles of spilled blood began to shake, and then flew *upward*, as droplets broke free and floated up into the air, like a reverse rain. The fog gradually turned the color of congealed blood. Lines of stark golden light pierced the mist and lingered there to sear the eye as an ancient magical pattern was revealed, words and images, expanding in size and complexity, unfurling, a fractal growth, a mandala of retribution. As the whole world began to tremble, every dead body, human and demon both, levitated from the ground, lifted up by whatever blood remained inside.

Unleashed from the body that had carried it for so long, the Voice was seeking out the blood of Ramrowan and the secret weapon hidden within.

The Rakshasa realized it was too late, and as one, the demon army began to run back toward the river, wading through the bloody fog.

The pattern was complete. The spell was cast. Reality itself jolted as a tiny bit of the world was unmade.

Millions of the suspended blood droplets ruptured.

No one living had ever heard a demon scream in pain before. Until now.

Chapter 31

Karno smashed a small demon over the head with his war hammer, then kicked it over the battlement's edge. There were several more demons climbing up behind it, and these were the more fearsome breed, so resilient that they even resisted many of Karno's hammer blows. As the demons climbed, they shrugged off hundreds of warrior arrows and worker bullets, and even the boiling oil that was dumped on them from cauldrons. Despite their best efforts, those demons would soon reach the top of the fort.

"Rally to me, Defenders!" Karno bellowed.

Several warriors rushed to aid him. They were men from many different houses, but they shared a code, distilled from what Karno believed to be the Protectors' most important philosophies, except without the traps of customs and politics that had burdened his beloved Protector Order for so long. And on this bloody day his new Defenders had fought with courage and honor, willingly putting their lives at risk, not to protect Law, but to protect humanity itself.

As the demons clambered over the top, his men laid into them with the incredible strength bestowed by the second Heart. Swords shattered and spears broke, but Defender arms did not tire. Weapons could be replaced. Lives could not. They fought accordingly. Even the mighty soldiers of hell had not expected such an onslaught, and they were hurled back down the wall.

He did not know how long this lull would last.

"Master Karno! Master Karno! Come quick!"

Since there were still demons circling below, Karno couldn't even spare the time to look toward the desperate messenger as he stated the obvious. "I am busy."

"Please, Master, it's Order business."

That could mean only one thing. "Carry on without me for now," he told the other Defenders atop the wall. Karno waited for someone to take his place before stepping away. The messenger was Defender Indhrakaran Gujara. "What is it?"

Indhrakaran leaned in close so none of the regular warriors would hear. "It's the Heart. There's something wrong with it."

"Oceans." Did they not have enough crises to deal with already?

Karno followed the swift messenger down the stairs and through the Vadal fortification. The already narrow passages were even tighter because of all the supplies that had been piled up everywhere. Karno was so massive, especially in armor, that he had to turn sideways to fit between the stacks. The preponderance of supplies was because no expense had been spared in preparing this particular fort to withstand a long siege, for this was where the second Heart had been moved to. But not even Karno's men knew it was the second, for the first remained a Protector secret. To his Defenders theirs was just *the* Heart.

The artifact had been placed in a vault in the central keep of the old fortress. If demons could smell magic, then surely it would draw them here like moths to the flame, which suited Karno just fine because he had turned this place into a killing ground, designed to bleed as many demons for as long as possible.

When they reached the vault, Karno could tell immediately that something was very wrong, for even though the black-steel device still beat, that pace was *far* faster than before. This wasn't the steady cadence, like unto that of a healthy warrior resting, as before, but the rapid thrum of a hummingbird. It appeared it was about to burst.

"Is it because so many of us are using it to fight at once?" Indhrakaran asked.

"Perhaps." Karno was unsure, for even though he had no gift for detecting the presence of magic like his old sword master Ratul, the sensation here so strong that the blind would be able to see it and the deaf hear it... Magic was spiraling around this room, dense as the grit blown about in a Zarger sandstorm. The Heart was a reservoir of magical power, and *something* was rapidly draining it, as fast as the mighty Martaban had been stolen when the demons had broken open the world beneath.

A great and terrible magic was being fueled.

Rada's mirror had referred to this buried Heart as a weapon, left behind by the ancients to be unleashed in the last days. Karno had believed his Protector predecessors had left it in that tomb to be used in the same fashion that the first Heart of the Mountain had been, to create superior warriors, but it appeared they may have had a much different purpose in mind for it.

And whatever that spell that magic had been intended to fuel, its time was now.

"It's dying! Can you stop it?"

"Even if I could, I doubt I should." Karno was wise enough to not try and meddle with magic beyond his comprehension. He didn't believe in the gods of Ashok or Lady Vane, but he had faith in the Protectors, including those who had died centuries before he had been born. "It must fulfill its purpose."

The Heart shattered.

Chapter 32

The gods unleashed their plague.

Wherever the blood mist touched demon hide, it sizzled and smoked. Blisters formed across the demons' bodies, growing larger, and larger, until they burst and sprayed. Demons who had feasted upon the casteless vomited up their own stomachs and then fell over and spasmed as the blood curse rapidly tore its way through their bodies. The soldiers of hell flailed and clawed at themselves, desperate to peel off their own infected skin, but that just exposed the vulnerable meat beneath to the caustic death that was now floating unseen through the air.

All the demons ran, even the fearsome Rakshasa.

Ashok roared, *"Let none escape!"*

He intercepted the demon king. Angruvadal flashed. The spear caught it, but the Rakshasa faltered as patches of its body began to hiss and bubble from the curse. All around them, mighty demons were crumbling into pieces.

Ashok got ahead of the monster. He blocked its thrust, slid Angruvadal up the spear, and cut it deep across the arm. As it stumbled back, Ashok kept on it. Weapons crossed, it grabbed hold of Ashok with its extra hand again, but this time he was ready, and Ashok slammed his palm against the Rakshasa's head. The leather glove inside his gauntlet had been soaked in casteless blood, and it burned a handprint into the demon's face, hot as when its molten spear had scorched Ashok's chest.

Disoriented, overwhelmed, the demonic king staggered away.

Ashok struck it down across the torso, immediately recovered, and then slashed it upward, twin cuts, perfectly parallel. White blood spurted, but sparked in the air as it met the gods' curse and ignited. The edges of the cuts immediately began to foam and gurgle as the plague devoured flesh.

Ashok hit it again, and again, and again.

Desperate—dying—the Rakshasa raised the flaming spear high. All the dead demons near them were instantly consumed in a flash, as terrible magic was ripped from those bodies and gathered into the tip of the spear.

Ashok didn't need instinct to tell him the Rakshasa's final spiteful act would be to obliterate them all. It was what a creature designed for malice would do.

The demon thrust its flaming spear toward the ground.

Ashok caught it.

The point stopped inches from impact. The collected energy immediately burned through Ashok's glove, but Angruvadal was already descending toward the demon's arms.

The Rakshasa lurched back. It didn't have time to be shaken at having now lost three hands, because Ashok immediately drove the spear—and all its destructive magic—straight into the monster's heart.

The energy that had been meant to take Ashok to the grave with it was instead directed into the demon who'd called it forth. A ball of scalding light engulfed the Rakshasa, so bright its bones could be seen through its hide before all of it was wiped away in a wave of destructive force. Walls came apart. Trees were uprooted. A vast chunk of the artisans' tower was pulverized into dust.

The lord of hell was gone.

Ashok remained.

The demon spear turned into ash and crumbled into bits. Ashok threw down his burning gauntlet before it could melt the flesh of his hand.

The glowing lines of the gods' pattern slowly dissipated. The clouds of blood fell in a great splash, drenching Ashok in red. The gods' vengeance spell was unleashed. Their curse was already on the wind.

There was a groan as the high tower began to lean to the side. Cracks spread up the walls. Rocks broke free and tumbled down.

Ashok looked toward the top and saw that haughty Omand still remained there, but a wizard of such power would never allow himself to die in a manner so ignominious as riding a collapsing tower to the ground to be buried in the rubble.

"I am coming for you, Omand! Fight me!"

Omand made it so his voice could be heard easily over all the noise. "The demands of your honor mean nothing to me, but in his fury would the unkillable Ashok pursue me, thus allowing some demons to escape, to render his woman's death meaningless? Will Ashok finish what the gods have started, or will he let victory slip away?"

The surviving demons were running, desperately trying to reach the safety of their watery tunnels as the plague spread between them. The Sons of the Black Sword continued to fight them, and every beast they managed to delay was quickly devoured by a retribution a thousand years in the making, but many more were going to get away.

Even now foul Omand manipulated him by his sense of honor, but worst of all, he was right. *"We are not done, Omand!"*

Ashok sheathed Angruvadal, then went to Thera and gently picked her up. Her body was empty, the fire gone out, but he would not leave her here to be crushed.

"Of course, Ashok. We are not finished, for three of the six remain," Omand shouted as Ashok walked away. "Only one of us can rule the next age."

The Grand Inquisitor vanished as the tower toppled.

Ashok set Thera's body down gently in the garden, among the fallen leaves. He wanted nothing more than to remain here with her, but to do so would be to leave her obligation incomplete. She would not want that.

Some of the Sons were nearby and they began to wail when they saw the fate of their beloved prophet.

"Watch over her."

Drenched in casteless blood, Ashok left to carry the plague to the river.

Chapter 33

Never before had Jagdish felt so mighty. He fought with the strength of ten of as he fearlessly led his army across the Nurabad Bridge. Demons fell before his sword. The Defenders' Heart gave him might, but his own warrior heart gave him courage.

"Keep going! We're almost there!"

Around and behind him, hundreds of warriors roared as one. *"VADAL! VADAL!"*

He'd picked the narrowest stone bridge to fight their way across. The Nurabad was barely wide enough to fit a single wagon, which had caused a lot of fights over the years as westbound carriages had met eastbound wagons somewhere in the middle, with no place for either to turn around. But that narrowness created a natural chokepoint, which made it so his men only had to fight one or two demons at a time.

As men died or became too tired to fight effectively, Jagdish brought up the next rank, and the next, and the next. Yards were steadily crossed, and the western shore grew closer, and more and more demons were killed or forced over the side to tumble into the roaring waterfall beneath them. Jagdish had rotated through paltan after paltan of exhausted warriors that way over the last few hours of brutal combat...yet he had never once left the front line himself.

Jagdish had no gods, but he believed in fate. And his fate

was to be the kind of commander who never faltered, who never gave up, and who always, always led from the front. Fate was cruel, but she had must have decided Jagdish was to be the kind of warrior who they'd sing songs about for generations. For the first time in his life, with incredible Defender magic in his blood, his body was able to keep up with his warrior spirit.

Battle was terrible but magnificent. Awful but exhilarating. Jagdish was too excited to be scared. Too worried about his boys to worry about himself. *This*, this glorious instant, was what it meant to be warrior caste.

Until all of a sudden, fate—that fickle bitch—stabbed him in the back one more time.

A big demon was coming at them, seven and a half feet of angry saltwater-hell-spawned muscle and snapping teeth. Fifth Paltan was up, shoulder to shoulder, row of spears unwavering. Jagdish was among them shouting advice and encouragement. His loyal bodyguard, the Sarnobat fanatic Najmul, had never left Jagdish's side, for he too had touched the Heart.

"Oceans, how many of these bastards do we have to kill?"

"I lost count," Jagdish responded, before roaring at the Fifth with a voice powered by magic sufficient to be heard over the unnatural waterfall. "Keep those spears up! Don't let it jump the line. Stick the chest and arms. When it's entangled, second rank, hammers and axes against the legs. Let's throw this salty son of a whore over the side! Let's—"

Jagdish's voice suddenly broke, and his throat felt torn and raw, as if he'd been shouting for an entire day, which he had. His armor had felt light as a feather, and now it threatened to smother him. Then the pain of every ache, bruise, strain, and scratch washed over him, followed by a weariness so profound that it staggered him. Hours of stored-up fatigue hit all at once and it took everything Jagdish had to not curl up in a ball of misery and die right there.

Najmul was staring at him, blinking in confusion, as if he too had suddenly been overcome by weakness. The best swordsman in Sarnobat stumbled, like an old man who'd had his cane stolen, until he grabbed hold of the bridge support to steady himself. "Karno's magic...It's gone."

"Well, that's bloody unfortunate," Jagdish muttered as the demon charged.

It crashed against the line. A dozen spears stuck it. Not a single one pierced the hide, but between all the warriors shoving, they held it back. Claws tore, but for each shaft splintered, another took its place. Despite the demon's ferocity, not a single man ran. They had nowhere to run. There were demons behind them and demons below them too.

Jagdish ducked between the spears and hacked at the demon's arm. The fine steel bounced off uselessly. He nearly lost his grip from the impact. Fate had picked a fine time to screw him once more.

Spear shafts flexed and snapped, then suddenly the demon was among him.

Jagdish landed flat on his back, having never even seen the fist that had left a big dent in the side of his helmet. Through the blood running into his eyes, he saw the demon lift one foot to stomp him through the bridge. He rolled aside an instant before the impact.

Najmul grabbed hold of Jagdish's sash and pulled him back through the line, as the demon was pushed back by more bending spears.

Jagdish called upon the healing power to find that it was no longer there, so instead of lying there useless he ordered, "Help me up, Najmul," because he could not let the men see their leader lie down on the job. And once he was back on his feet, he used his bodyguard's arm to stay upright, which was difficult since the entire world wouldn't stop spinning. But as long as the men saw the colorful plume of his helmet, they'd know their phontho hadn't abandoned them.

The demon got ahold of a warrior and ripped his head from his body. It smashed another two more over the side of bridge to drown in the raging Martaban. Fifth Paltan started to falter. If they lost their nerve, all was lost.

"Sixth Paltan up!" Jagdish bellowed, but his ragged voice was that of a mere human, not a roar of commanding thunder anymore. They couldn't hear him over millions of gallons of plunging waterfall.

At the edge of a breakthrough, the demon stopped.

It froze in place, then slowly turned toward the west, where one of the great towers of the Vadal skyline was collapsing into an expanding cloud of dust. Even as warriors thrust spears into its back, the demon seemed too preoccupied to notice. Then it turned its blank head toward one of the mutilated human bodies that was dangling partially over the edge of the bridge. From the rags that had been some poor casteless, probably caught here and trampled during the initial chaos of the evacuation.

The demon flinched away from that corpse, seemingly more afraid of it than the hundreds of warriors it had been throwing itself against.

The entire bridge was covered in a cold mist from the waterfall, but there seemed to be a different, heavier kind of fog gathered around that dead casteless. Perhaps it was Jagdish's blood getting in his eyes, but the fog seemed red.

Suddenly, the demon began thrashing madly about and clawing at its own face.

Jagdish had no idea what was happening, but he could tell this was their chance. "Push! Attack! *Attack!*"

Enough of the warriors heard him and acted that the rest saw them and followed, but before they could reach it the beast opened its mouth and shrieked. Warriors flinched. Even muffled by the steel and padding of their helmets, the noise was still deafening.

The demon seemed to be *melting.*

Chunks of black hide began sloughing off. Milky blood bubbled from the rapidly multiplying wounds.

There were other soldiers of hell on the bridge. When they saw what was happening to their brother, they promptly abandoned it, vaulting over the side of the bridge and dropping a hundred feet to disappear into the great frothing chasm that had opened in the Martaban.

The dying demon didn't even try to escape. It staggered a few feet, went to its knees, and then sank down, head lolling forward, until its face slid off to splatter on the bridge stones. Steam hissed from its now visible skull as its body seemed to crumble to pieces. It lifted one arm toward the east, plaintively, until the limb snapped off under its own weight at the elbow.

"Forgotten save us!" Najmul cried. "What in the fish-ridden hell was that?"

"Halt!" Jagdish shouted, raising his fist high. He didn't know if the men heard him, or they simply didn't need encouragement to know not to interfere with whatever horror was happening here. "It's got to be some kind of wizard's curse. Don't get it on you!"

They watched, awestruck at the gruesome death. In less time than it took his little pocket watch to click a single minute, one of the fiercest servants of the sea had been rendered into an oozing puddle with a skeleton lying in the middle of it.

Across the Nurabad Bridge all the other demons were either dying in a similar excruciating fashion or leaping into the river. In fact, as far as Jagdish could see in every direction, it was the same. He could no longer sharpen his vision like a hawk's, but even mortal eyes could see the cursed demons were dying in agony, while the rest were trying to flee back into the water.

"They're retreating!" a warrior cried.

The bridge was clear of demons. Fate had spared their lives.

The men began to cheer.

Hordes of demons were tumbling down the waterfall to vanish into the shelter of the hole they'd torn in the middle of Jagdish's city. None of those demons appeared to be falling to pieces yet. The water must be able to shield them from the affliction that had frightened them away. He limped to the edge and looked over. Below could be seen a multitude of shadowy figures climbing down the side and swimming through the water.

Jagdish should have felt triumph, but instead there was only bitterness as he watched the demons get away.

Najmul walked up next to him. "Time to eat your words, Vadal. The Forgotten sent us a miracle after all!"

"As long as demons live to torment us again, it's not enough."

Najmul grew solemn. "Take this victory, Jagdish. It's a miracle any of us are alive."

"No!" Jagdish turned and shouted at him. "You fanatics promised us a *final* battle. Mark my words, should they live, they will return! If this is a victory, it'll be a temporary one."

"We can't fight them beneath the waves, brother."

Then Jagdish noticed movement on the eastern shore. A single figure in armor was sprinting with seemingly impossible speed up one of the riverside cliffs.

"We can't...but he will."

They watched as Ashok Vadal dove into the chasm.

Chapter 34

Down into the darkness, Ashok went. Bounding from rock to rock, falling through the torrents of water.

Around him demons climbed. The mere act of brushing past them in his blood-drenched armor was enough to doom them. The climbers slipped and fell as their skin began to peel off.

Initially, Ashok tried to control his descent, but that wasn't fast enough. Too many demons might reach the safety of the underworld. So he let go.

Ashok broke his collar bone smashing his body against a jagged boulder, and then he was in free fall, spinning into the depths. He dropped past hundreds of demons clinging to the walls, condemning them all.

The impact against the surface nearly snuffed out his consciousness. The cold waters of the Martaban washed away the blood, but even diluted the curse continued to spread. It was relentless in its pursuit of demon flesh, because the gods had been waiting a very long time for this.

All around him swam sleek black shapes. Rather than attack, they recoiled in fear. They thrashed and floundered, trying in vain to evade death. Raised as a whole man, Ashok did not know how to swim, but he didn't need to swim to reach the bottom. The weight of his armor would do that for him.

The water was a powerful whirlpool, draining into the underworld. Nearly blind, Ashok was hurled about the depths, colliding with rocks and demons.

With their king dead, the demons had lost their direction, but some of their warriors must have realized Ashok was trying to reach the ancients' tunnels, and in doing so would slay every last one of their kind still beneath the world. They tried in vain to stop him, but despite the many impacts, loyal Angruvadal had never left his hand. Each desperate demon that tried to intercept him, Ashok turned and stabbed by instinct. Evil water slowed the speed of his arm, but every thrust still split hide. Any demon that managed to hook its claws into him, did so for only a moment before the spreading pink cloud caused it to flinch away, hands rapidly dissolving.

Blood. Blood in the water.

Ashok held his breath, not for any hope of returning to the surface alive, but to ensure he was conscious enough to reach the bottom. To the Vadal he was Ashok Sword Breaker, to the demons he would be Ashok Plague Bringer.

His journey was not straight down, but in a violent spiral, carried by a powerful current that smashed him against rock and demon. Eventually the chaos subsided.

When he hit the bottom, it was so dark even his eyes could not see, but the shard told him this rubble-strewn hole was the breach. On the other side was the underworld.

The Heart had already sealed the burned flesh of his left hand, so he used Angruvadal to slice it open once again. That black-steel cut hurt worse than the demon fire, but all that mattered was that it spilled casteless blood over the entrance to the underworld. The current would carry the vengeance of the gods into the world below, and in those narrow, flooded corridors, there would be nowhere for the demons to hide.

Now there would be no escape for any of the soldiers of hell.

Such was the price of trespass.

As water began to fill his lungs, Ashok understood that this graveyard of demons was where his journey would end.

The first time he had drowned had been the closest he'd ever come to understanding fear. Now, there was nothing but weary acknowledgment, for being the final instrument in destroying hell itself was a far more honorable death than he had deserved.

Out of air, out of blood, nearly out of consciousness... at last he could rest.

Except if he stopped now, Angruvadal would be lost forever beneath the river. That violated his oath as a bearer.

And though he had just finished what Thera had started, her killer would go unpunished. That would violate his oath as a husband.

The first time he had drowned, it had been Thera who had breathed the life back into him. She would not want him to die here.

Ashok began cutting off his armor.

Chapter 35

~~~◊◊◊◊~◊◊◊◊~~~

Spitting up water, Javed coughed himself back to consciousness. Clothing soaked and body brutalized, the Keeper of Names found himself lying on a narrow shelf of rock, somewhere deep beneath the ground. The sun was obscured by a vast waterfall above, so very little light made it down this far. The air was filled with mist as torrents of water fell down the chasm around him. He was in part of the river...or what had been the river but was now an emptied basin.

How am I alive?

"You live because I'm not done with you yet."

With bleary eyes he saw the shape of Mother Dawn perched on the ledge next to him, her form perfectly still. While he had been tossed about by the river, his shirt had been caught by one of her many hands, and she'd held him safe in her four arms as the Martaban had drained around them.

"I was told you died," he croaked.

"I *am* dead, so heed my ghost, Javed."

This wasn't the terrifying giant who'd condemned him in the desert, but something small and unimposing and still. Her skin was not eye-scalding silver but rather a covering of soft green moss, which made her dangerous lines seem far gentler than before. Slowly he realized that this was no mighty avatar he was talking to, but merely a humble statue that had been submerged beneath the river for an unknown amount of time. Probably thrown into the river by Inquisitors long ago to dispose of it, where it had come to rest on this shelf.

Groaning, he tried to sit up, but everything hurt far too much for that. The last thing he could remember was trying to kill himself before Omand could tear the truth from his mind. He'd been surrounded by demons, cutting himself against their abrasive skin as water had choked him and smothered all thought. He had thrashed against the pain, but then gone still and drifted through the darkness. In that final moment he had known peace.

"How am I not done? How was I not eaten by demons? I gave my life to protect the Voice! Was that not enough for the gods?"

The stone lips didn't move, but Javed could still hear the gods' loyal servant clear as the fateful day he'd met her. "You survive because, to the demons, you were naught but debris. They had a million living beings above to exercise their hate against. As for the gods, they were satisfied by your labors. You did well. Your purpose to them had been fulfilled. You helped the Voice to accept what she needed to do. The gods would be content if you died here, just as they were content when Omand murdered me. We were both humble servants who had fulfilled our part in their great calculation. At last, the gods have had their revenge. Now that their eternal foe has been defeated and will never be able to rise again, the gods truly don't care what happens to any of you next."

"I don't understand."

"Look down."

Javed peered over the side of the ledge.

Hundreds of yards of riverbed had collapsed into a hole. It was a maze of boulders with rapids in-between. The river was falling on them, but the Martaban flowed so swiftly that already this newly revealed underground world was filling up. There must have been gigantic empty spaces below, which were now flooded. Soon this chasm would be refilled entirely, and the river above would be reunited, but for now it was a great underground lake, and the water was steadily rising.

Upon the top of that lake floated bodies. Hundreds upon hundreds of demon bodies.

"Behold, a slaughter incomprehensible," Mother Dawn said. "Upon these bones will be built a new age."

"Are they all dead, then?"

"Those that came against us? Yes. To the very last demon, slain. As for the rest of the world, not even I can guess what is still out there lurking, but the Martaban will carry many of these plague-ridden bodies out to the sea. The gods' revenge is most thorough."

Much had happened while he had been unconscious. "How did the gods smite them?"

"This is a death toll far greater than could be inflicted by sword, rod, or even the mighty flaming arrows drawn from Upagraha or the quivers of her long-lost sisters. These demons were struck down by a devouring sickness. A most virulent plague, a thousand years in the making."

"The gods cursed them." Javed spat over the edge. "Good."

"Sadly for the gods, this particular curse was not ready in time to use it to save themselves. Some of the gods fashioned this plague to send against the demons during their great war, but demons are hardy, and their bodies complex, so what they had was insufficient, and the demons were immune."

Javed, being a master of poisons, knew how such things worked. "If a poison proves ineffective against a specific target, you change the alchemist's recipe and try again."

"Were it so easy. Demons are not beings of flesh and blood and spirit. They are not like us. They are constructions, like the most difficult of spells, complex patterns brought to life, designed to adapt, survive, and kill. But some of the gods were clever. Knowing their plague would not affect humans, the gods hid it in the blood of their chosen warrior Ramrowan. With each child the plague changed, taking on a slightly different form. This way the gods would not have one alchemist experimenting, but rather millions unwitting. This secret plague was passed down through the generations. Whenever the blood grew thin, the Keepers thickened it. Choosing mother and father, in endless combinations, this inheritance went down through the generations, for the wisest gods had peered into the future and their calculations had shown that eventually, inevitably, there would rise a strain that even the hardiest demons could not withstand."

All this time he had thought the Keepers' purposes had been altruistic. "The book...the genealogy. It was for this?"

"Every Keeper of Names did his sacred duty to safeguard the

bloodline of Ramrowan, to shepherd the casteless. You did. As did Keta did before you and Ratul before him. And Chandradatt, and Bull of Vahin, and Kashi, and a hundred others before them, wandering the land, recording the names, guiding the line, all toward this great day."

It was difficult to tell in the darkness, but the bodies seemed as packed atop the water as tightly as the lily pads covering a Gujaran swamp. "I ... I didn't know. I thought what the Keepers did was to build, not to destroy."

"Oh, Javed, you can't have one without the other."

He was quiet for a long time as he watched the corpses bob atop the water. They seemed twisted and distorted, half dissolved, with bones showing. The gods' wrath was tremendous. "Then it is over?"

"This particular war is over. The Age of Law is over. Now begins the next, but what it shall be is not yet determined. We shall see what man can accomplish freed from the shackles of hell. Do demons still live? Out there somewhere, maybe. There are other continents beyond my sight. In fact, there are whole other worlds which are out of man's reach for now. But this one, you can still do something about the fate of."

"But you said the gods don't care anymore."

"That is unfair of me." Mother Dawn sighed. "It is more that they could only predict so far, and then things grow beyond even their ability to influence. Why concern themselves over something they had no control over? However, *I* still care. As did Ramrowan, which is why he left a buried city full of hidden treasure for the people of his workshop to guide them into the future. I could never see as well or as far as my old masters could see, but I know that of the forces which remain capable of seizing this age, each of them is flawed somehow. Yet there is one among you who would rule over this world with a terrible cruelty."

Mother Dawn spoke of Omand. "The Night Father."

"Should he triumph, man will have traded demons of the sea for a devil of the land. The Age of Law would become the Age of Slaves, to be toyed with for his eternal amusement."

"He was far too strong a wizard for me to defeat even when I had both hands, and that was before he turned into whatever evil thing he is now. What do you expect me to do, Mother Dawn?"

"I expect you to do your sacred duty, Keeper."

Confused, he turned back to the ancient statue, and this time he saw clearly that it was just a pile of green-covered rocks, that was only vaguely in the shape of a woman. He had been saved by his clothing getting caught on a random stone. The ghost was gone.

How was he supposed to do his duty down in this hole? Had he not done enough?

As the water continued to fall and the lake of the dead continued to rise, Javed noticed something else below. One of the giant demons floated on its back, and lying atop its chest as if the vast corpse was a raft...was a man.

A man with a black-steel sword.

Far below, Ashok Vadal stirred, somehow still alive.

The Keeper of Names' sacred duty is to safeguard the bloodline of Ramrowan and shepherd the casteless.

That casteless in particular would do.

Chapter 36

~~~~~~~~~~~~~

Devedas shoved the dying demon off the end of his new sword.

Raising Khartalvar, he turned in search of his next challenge . . . and found nothing.

He had been fighting for so long without pause that he couldn't comprehend there being an end to this battle. There were still demons as far as the eye could see, but they were unmoving, torn apart not by blade or cannonball, but by some unseen power far more violent. It was as if these demons had been turned inside out.

"Who will fight me? Who is next?" the Maharaja roared, but the streets were quiet. He turned back to his men. "Where is our enemy?" But what remained of the Army of Many Houses had no response to give him. They were just as confused as their commander.

He spotted Broker Harban, standing over the body of a spider demon that appeared to have reached into its torso to pull its own stomach out before expiring. The Protector was soaked in blood, badly injured, and just as baffled as Devedas. "I don't know. They just . . . died."

"Broker, take command here while I figure out what's going on."

Devedas ran to the nearest tall factory building, past the exhausted workers covered in soot and filth, up many flights of stairs, to reach the roof, upon which the cannons had fallen silent for the first time in hours. As the warriors had held the demons back, the workers had hauled the incredibly heavy weapons all the way up here with ropes and pulleys, and immediately gone back to shooting. Never again would Devedas doubt the capability of the worker caste.

Sprawled below him was Vadal City. He sharpened his vision and searched in every direction. Vast swaths of the city had been destroyed. Fires raged out of control. But...it seemed the demons were all dead. Their bodies were splayed across rooftops or lying in the streets. Not a single one was moving. Not so much as a shiver.

The army of hell had been defeated.

He couldn't believe his eyes. Victory had seemed so impossible that Devedas was overcome and began to laugh. He laughed until tears came out of his eyes.

The worker Gutch approached him, shouting, "We're out of targets. Did we win?"

"We've won."

"What?"

The poor worker had been around the loudest things in the world all day. Of course his ears were ringing. So Devedas used the Heart of the Mountain to shout loud enough for the entire city to hear, *"We are victorious!"*

As that shout echoed through the streets, the surviving warriors began to cheer. The workers hugged each other and leapt up and down.

Gutch cackled with glee. "Piss on you, demons!"

They had paid greatly for it, but they had done the impossible.

Devedas may have failed the Capitol, but he had helped save Vadal and hopefully the rest of Lok as well. Their accomplishment was so great that in the moment even a man of Devedas' vision couldn't grasp the implications.

But ever the commander, he knew there was no time for celebration when there was still work to be done. There were wounded to tend, citizens to rescue, and fires to fight. And just because he couldn't see them didn't mean there weren't more demons hiding somewhere. These men had fought like legends, but he had far more to ask of them before they could rest.

He grabbed Gutch by the arm and shouted into his ear. "Gather your runners to find Jagdish and your leaders. I will send wizards to tell Thakoor Bhadramunda to send in those obligated to fight fires and aid the injured."

"I'll be damned."

"What?"

"You actually care. You might make a good king after all." Then Gutch realized he probably shouldn't have said something so brazen. "I mean no offense—"

Devedas roared with laughter and slapped him on the back. "You can offend me tomorrow, gun man! Today I love you and your criminal scum as if they were my Protectors. Now go! Our people need us."

As Gutch hurried off, Devedas turned back to the city he'd helped save, still struggling to believe that they really might have prevailed. He should have died a hundred times over today, and would have if he hadn't taken up an ancestor blade.

At that thought, Devedas reached for Khartalvar, sheathed at his side in a scabbard he'd taken from a dead Kharsawani warrior, but he hesitated, hand inches from the grip. For it had allowed him to wield it during a desperate battle with the fate of mankind hanging in the balance. Surely, it would recognize his crimes and find him unworthy now.

He drew it anyway.

Khartalvar spared his life.

Perhaps Gutch was right. Maybe he wouldn't be a bad king after all.

Suddenly, the sword's instincts warned him of a deadly threat, worse than any of one of the demons they'd fought together so far, more dangerous than anything any bearer had faced, going back to the forging of the swords. He turned around to find himself face-to-face with the golden mask of Grand Inquisitor Omand.

"Did you think it would so easy, Devedas?"

Before Devedas could strike, Omand grabbed hold of his wrist with bone-crushing force. He was in the shape of a man but possessed the strength of a demon.

"Easy?" Devedas snarled. "There are so many dead it'll take days to count them! There was no *easy* here, except for the coward who sat out the battle, letting everyone else bleed, so he could come out of hiding to claim the glory for himself at the end!"

A low growl came from behind that golden mask. "That's where we are different, Devedas. Glory is something you yearned for. Adulation means nothing to me. I care only about power. With the Voice and her priest dead, and the Forgotten's Warrior having thrown himself into the abyss to destroy the last of the demons, all that remain in competition for that power are the king and the mask."

Devedas put both hands on Khatalvar and tried to lever it toward Omand's body. The workers saw the struggle and began shouting for help.

"Even the mightiest weapon will do you no good. I am the appointed custodian of black steel now." Omand let go.

Devedas slashed. Omand's flesh parted like smoke.

That blow should have removed his head, but Omand reformed, unharmed. "Fool. You lack the status to harm me."

Then a wave of unseen force shattered the stones around Devedas, flinging him over the edge. The distant ground rushed up to meet him. A dozen bones broke on impact.

Omand landed softly a few feet away.

There was only pain. Devedas tried to move, but he was too broken. The Heart of the Mountain managed to keep him alive, but just barely. All he could do was lie there in agony as his enemy approached.

"You should never have betrayed me, Devedas."

Warriors saw their golden Maharaja's impact and ran to his aid. With a casual wave of Omand's hand, an invisible force hurled them all away.

"I would have been content to let you manage the herds in my name. Wear your little crown, sit upon the throne I gave you, and play at being the Law. I would have allowed that because a god should not waste his time on the menial."

Omand could have killed him easily right then, but he was, by both obligation and nature, a torturer. He kicked a dent in Deveda's breastplate, driving broken ribs into his lungs.

Khartalvar flashed through Omand's body, but met no resistance.

"Every man has his place. You forgot yours." Omand took him by the neck, effortlessly lifted Devedas, and threw him against a nearby wall hard enough to crack the bricks. More bones broke, including his arm.

He bent down to whisper in Devedas' ear. "It's a rare treat to be able to play with a Protector, because your kind can be cut on for days before they die. You do not have that much time, but I will enjoy every moment of this."

More warriors were approaching, and now that they realized there was an all-new form of demon in their midst, they were ready to fight. Omand saw them forming up against him and laughed. "Pathetic."

"Leave them be," Devedas managed to gasp. "They're honorable men fulfilling their obligations."

"They are naught but insects to me."

With those words, Omand confirmed the mad tyranny he had unleashed in the Capitol was but a tiny glimpse of the terror he would inflict upon Lok. These men had crossed a continent to shed their blood on behalf of a foreign house and stood firm against the army of hell. If Omand could treat such heroes with such disdain, what hope would anyone have under his terrible reign?

Devedas concentrated on a few specific injuries. Not the failing organs, but on the bones and muscles of his sword arm, so that he might launch one last desperate attack.

"Behold your Maharaja!" Omand shouted, before kicking Devedas again, hard enough to flip him over and slide him across the bloody street into an ashen gutter. "He does not rule you. *I* rule you!"

"Kill the Inquisitor!" Broker Harban roared back.

A hundred warriors charged. With the sweep of one hand, Omand sent a hurricane through them. Men were thrown in every direction and slammed against the stones. The ground split open and warriors fell through the cracks. The few Protectors stumbled, but continued pushing onward through the magical onslaught, until each of those was lashed by waves of fire and force until they too were hurled down and sent rolling away.

Not a single man was left standing except for Omand. There was no doubt that he could have killed them all if he'd felt like it.

The sky blackened. Faster than a Vadal monsoon, rumbling storm clouds formed out of the clear blue, as the Grand Inquisitor bellowed, *Do you fools understand what I am now? I am the god of this world!*

"The Law-abiding have no gods!" a fallen Protector shouted.

"The Law is your collar, dogs, and I hold your chains. I have *always* held the chains. You will do as you are commanded or pay with your lives! And your families' lives! And your houses' lives! Every man has his place and yours is beneath my boot."

Devedas had only known Omand to be devious and calculating, his manner cold. He had never before seen him ranting
with the fury of a madman before. The ancient magic Omand
had found must have further corrupted a thing that had already
been rotten to the core.

Lightning flashed above. "I was already your master, for as
you obeyed the Law, the Law obeyed me. Now I am your god
and the Law will be my scripture, the Inquisition my priesthood.
Any man who fails to serve me will perish."

Slowly, what remained of the Army of Many Houses got back
to their unsteady feet.

Omand's fury seemed to calm a bit, though the unnatural
clouds continued to flash and rumble. "Your courage wavers,
because you know what I say is true. Those who resist will be
punished, but those who obey will be rewarded. I will make you
an offer to demonstrate this, so that you can return to your houses
to preach of my wisdom and mercy. Whichever one among you
who would come forth and cut the throat of Devedas, I offer you
his crown. Whoever steps forward and kills Devedas right now
will become Maharaja of Lok."

The cruelty was masterful. Devedas, to atone for being denied
his birthright by black steel, had spent his life in pursuit of a
seemingly impossible goal. Risking everything, sacrificing honor
and friendship, betraying the Law he'd been raised to serve,
and even endangering those he loved, all so Omand could give
the title he'd earned to the first soldier hungry enough to put a
broken man out of his misery.

Omand walked a slow circle around Devedas as he beckoned
the crowd to draw near. "Hear me, Army of Many Houses. Come
and test the generosity of your new god. The Capitol will be
yours to rule as you see fit. Lift your house up or cast down the
others you hate. Claim your riches. Take your revenge. I do not
care what you do with your reward. I simply ask, who among you
would be king?"

Through the haze of pain, Devedas watched his men, unsure
and afraid. Here was the face of the Law, wielding magic beyond
comprehension, defeating Protectors as if they were nothing,
promising them power undreamed to them and their houses,
and all they had to do was turn their sword against the usurper.

He saw his bodyguard, Rane, who had been forced to look

the other way while Vassal House Garo had made a dishonorable pact with Devedas and thrown Ashok into the sea. Ashok, who'd shown Rane mercy and saved his life on the plains. His people barely survived on the ragged edge of the world. What was the life of one master against ensuring the eternal safety of his house?

But neither Rane nor any of the other Garo faltered.

He saw Broker and the other Protectors, who had kept enforcing the Law even as Devedas had twisted it and used it for his own ambitions. He had been their brother, then their Lord Protector. Yet his actions had put them all in danger and allowed a tyrant to seize control of the Capitol. Good men had died atop the Tower of Silence because of Devedas' actions. Would one of them be tempted to punish him and then use his authority to set things right?

No... The Protectors remained where they were. They too were drawing upon the dying Heart, summoning strength for one last desperate attack against Omand, who was a vile blasphemy against the Law.

Warriors of every house were present. He'd been friend to some, foe to others. Omand's offer was surely tempting, but if there had been a dishonorable one among them, the demons must have culled them today, for not a single warrior moved. They had followed Devedas into battle, and his courage had shown them what it meant to be the Maharaja. They would not forsake him now.

But then there was Gutch.

"Hey, Grand Inquisitor!" The shout came from high atop the damaged factory, where the big worker stuck his head over the edge. "Do workers count in this here Maharaja offer of yours?"

All eyes turned upward, including the black holes of the golden mask. "You are all equally nothing beneath my contempt. If a lesser caste is who would serve as an example of my generosity to those who would be loyal to me, then so be it. Come and take your prize."

"Well, I am exceedingly interested in this opportunity, as I think I would make a fine ruler, but it's going to take me a minute to climb down there, because as you can see that's a great many stories I must traverse before I can proceed with the ceremonial throat slitting..." As warriors began to hurl curses at Gutch for his treachery, the big man looked toward the other side of the roof, where the bronze endcap of one of his cannons had just appeared, sticking over the edge. "Ready, boys?" He waited but a moment for their unseen affirmation. "Close enough. *Fire!*"

The cannon went off.

The great weapons were not particularly accurate, but these workers must have been very lucky, because their projectile struck the Grand Inquisitor, dead center.

As the smoke cleared it revealed Omand, not just still standing, but holding the cast-iron cannonball overhead for all to see that he had caught it. The impact had deformed the projectile, leaving imprints of his fingers in the metal. Omand dropped the cannonball. As it rolled away, the workers ran for their lives.

Lightning struck the rooftops. There was an ear-splitting crack of thunder, followed by even more noise as the Fortress powder stored there detonated. Chunks of building and worker rained down on the street.

"You have spit on my benevolence. Your labors have been for nothing. This entire city will die for this insult."

Omand's cloaked form seemed to grow in size as magical energy gathered about him, coalescing into a halo of darkness. As the Grand Inquisitor reached out and took hold of that magic, the power curled around his arms like snakes. That magic unfurled into two deadly whips that immediately began to burn their way through the road.

"*Look upon your god and know fear!*"

The shadow whip descended to take Devedas' life.

It was blocked by a black-steel blade.

"I fear nothing." Ashok Vadal flicked the whip away. "Look upon your executioner, Omand, and see death."

Chapter 37

Having been carried back to the surface by the witch-hunter priest, Ashok stepped from the space between worlds to fight the monster who had murdered Thera. He arrived just in time to save the life of his fallen brother.

"You should have stayed and died in the water where you belong, Black Heart, for I shall—"

Ashok slashed Angruvadal across the mask. The golden jaw flew off, but the face behind it was somehow unharmed.

Omand reacted with demonlike speed, leaping back twenty feet. Both whips lashed toward Ashok, moving as if they had minds of their own. He caught one with Angruvadal, but the other struck him in the side, and his armor had been left at the bottom of the river. Shadow burned like fire. He grimaced as it cut deep.

The Grand Inquisitor pulled off his damaged mask, revealing his true face to the world.

He was just a man.

Omand was wizard and manipulator, conspirator and tyrant, who had punished Ashok with life, and somehow stolen for himself the power of the ancients... but despite all that he was only a man. As Ashok and Javed had swum up through the rocks in the darkness outside of reality, he had heard Omand's mad boasting, but this was no god. This was a liar and a thief.

The mask was discarded. There wasn't so much as a mark where Angruvadal had split his mouth. No matter. Ashok would find a way to kill him anyway.

Running toward his enemy, he leapt over one flashing whip, and dove beneath the next. Ashok rose, striking upward, through Omand's side and out his neck. He even felt resistance to the cut as black steel hewed through flesh and bone, but when he stepped away, Omand was already whole.

The air itself coalesced into an invisible hammer, smashing Ashok over the shoulder, driving him to one knee. It hit him again, across the face, throwing him down. The whip struck, but Ashok had already rolled out of the way. It split a divot in the stones.

The Protectors ran to help, but they collided with an invisible barrier and bounced off. Warriors struck at that shield, but their weapons did nothing. He had seen the Voice use a similar pattern in the Graveyard of Demons, and even Ashok's desperate actions had been futile to break through.

Only Omand, Ashok, and the gravely wounded Devedas remained inside that unbreakable dome. It seemed the Grand Inquisitor wanted to keep this duel personal, or perhaps he just wanted more time to toy with them without further interruption.

Ashok launched himself back to his feet and attacked. Omand possessed incredible speed, and he must have been a passable swordsman as a mortal man, but he was no Protector. Sword spinning, Ashok moved between the snapping whips. Instinct helped him dodge the hammers of air. He hit Omand again, with a slash that should have left both of his legs bloody stumps, but it was as useless as striking through sand.

Angruvadal had no suggestions to guide him, for black steel had been designed with safeguards, so as to never be turned against its creators, and Omand had stolen that mantle of their authority.

The lightning had set the roofs ablaze, and that fire spread to more stores of the workers' Fortress powder. Explosions shook the district. Sparks and fiery debris rained down on the top of the invisible barrier as they fought on inside.

Omand knew many magical patterns, and he struck Ashok with several different kinds, one after the other. He was stabbed with beams of piercing light. The shard sealed those lacerations. He was blasted with a cold so intense it caused his skin to crack and ice crystals to form in his veins, but the Heart of the Mountain warmed his blood and kept it moving. Even his mind was tormented with visions of Thera falling to her death, over and over again. Ashok didn't know if that last one was truly an attack, or rather his guilt motivating him to continue fighting through the pain.

Ashok should have died ten times over, but he refused.

He fought until the Heart of the Mountain had nothing left to give...and when even that ancient artifact reached its breaking point, Ashok *almost* managed to hit Omand one more time.

Omand floated away. Amused. "It appears your Protector tricks have finally reached their limit."

Exhausted, Ashok collapsed to his hands and knees, blood drizzling from his mouth. Next to him lay Devedas, who wore the pallor of death, and had broken bones sticking through his skin. Only a few feet away, Protectors and warriors uselessly struck their weapons against the invisible barrier, screaming for their champions to rise and fight. Javed tried to work some magic with the demon flesh he'd taken from the river, but the pattern he'd used to save Ashok there was powerless against Omand's shield. The Keeper of Names gave Ashok a stricken look as his former master strolled over to kill the Forgotten's holy warrior.

When Devedas wheezed, blood bubbled from his chest. "Today was still a great victory."

"That it was, brother."

"Did you see I got a sword?"

It was true, because Devedas clutched an ancestor blade in his bloody hand. "I never doubted you were worthy."

"I doubted enough for both of us. Help me up, Ashok."

Together, the two of them staggered back to their feet and prepared for battle, just like when they were boys, fighting for their lives on a frozen mountaintop.

Omand approached, whips devouring parallel lines in the stones behind him.

The Heart of the Mountain was not broken, but it was drained for now. Their arms were weak, their injuries great. They could barely move at all. All they had was each other.

"I have an idea..." Ashok said. "Just like old times."

"Just like old times," Devedas agreed, even though that meant sacrificing himself.

As they'd done against many foes before, Devedas would

distract and divert the limbs, while Angruvadal delivered the killing blow.

"Ashok and Devedas..." Omand gave them a cruel smile. "As you die, I need you both to know that I could never have ascended without your help. That knowledge, I think, is the best torture of all."

Omand swung a whip at each of them. Devedas lunged forward to intercept both. With the path cleared, Ashok swept past him and thrust Angruvadal deep into Omand's guts, driving it clear to the hilt, shoving him back. They ended up face to battered face. Omand sneered as three feet of black steel through the belly did absolutely nothing to him.

"You lack the authority to wound me, Ashok. *Only a god can kill a god!*"

"Then hold this for me."

Ashok let go of Angruvadal.

Realizing what had been done, Omand looked down in terror at the deadly weapon buried in his torso and shrieked, "No! I do not try to claim this blade! I don't want to be its bearer!"

Angruvadal judged him regardless.

The ancients had designed their ultimate creation to not harm them, but they had also commanded the ancestor blades to weigh and measure the worth of whoever tried to take one up. In that moment, Omand alone was touching the deadly material. Angruvadal must have deemed that sufficient, for it began to *cut.*

Omand screamed, for now he felt the wrath of black steel. Panicking, he grabbed hold of the hilt with both hands and tried to pull Angruvadal free. The black steel immediately bit into his palms, securing them in place.

The sword found him *unworthy.*

Angruvadal forced Omand to *saw.* Back and forth. Now there was blood. *So much blood.*

Even a false god could still feel pain, for Omand's wails echoed through the city. Ashok had seen Angruvadal angry before, but never like this, for the black steel burned and spit as it cut. Flesh charred as if put to the torch. Blood boiled. Organs expanded until they popped. Omand's limbs were forced to drag the blade down through his bowels, shearing through the bones of his pelvis, and out through his groin, obliterating everything along the way.

But Angruvadal was not through, and immediately sliced one of Omand's legs off at the knee. Then it took the other at the thigh.

The Grand Inquisitor fell on his back, but Angruvadal was not sated, and it cut off one of his arms at the shoulder. That hand remained welded to the grip, and the severed limb dangled, drizzling blood, as Angruvadal forced Omand to lever the sword back into his chest.

Omand must have called upon the pattern to escape into the space between, as the air around him darkened briefly, but Angruvadal was far too vengeful for that, and the ancestor blade dragged him back into reality. There would be no reprieve from this sentence.

The invisible barrier failed along with the rest of the Grand Inquisitor's protections, and warriors spilled into the circle. Together they watched in silent awe as Omand lacerated his own lungs, before pulling the sword free and placing the edge atop his throat. Angruvadal could have sliced his head off instantly, but that was far too kind for Omand, and instead it let gravity *slowly* do the work.

Omand screamed until he couldn't, then he silently cursed Ashok with his dying glare.

It had been Omand's curse that had given him to Thera, and with another curse Ashok avenged her. "To the ocean with you, demon."

With a sick crack, Omand's spine was severed from his skull, and a moment later the head rolled free. Omand's face continued to make incomprehensible expressions for several seconds, and when Ashok was certain the life had fully gone out of it, and this was nothing but the spasming of muscles, he kicked Omand's head into the blood-filled gutter.

Ashok bent down and retrieved his sword from the mess. "Apologies, Angruvadal. I saw no other way."

The sword did not mind.

He went to Devedas, who was lying still upon the ground, surrounded by Protectors and loyal bodyguards. They parted to let Ashok through. It was bad. Devedas was clearly not long for this world and the Heart of the Mountain was too depleted to do anything beyond dull his agony.

Kneeling beside his brother, Ashok took him by the hand.

"Omand's dead?"

"He's dead," Ashok assured Devedas.

"Good." Weary, Devedas closed his eyes. "Bury me in the south. Put on my grave I did my best."

"I'll see to it," a young Garo with tears streaming down his cheeks swore.

"Tell Rada...I love..." Devedas trailed off, and the Maharaja of Lok was no more.

Ashok wept.

Chapter 38

The Asura's Mirror informed Rada that the great enemy had
been neutralized when the image that represented the demonic
menace, which had appeared upon the map of northern Lok
stopped flashing an angry red and went away.

As the tiny glowing demon faded away, Rada knew that they
were victorious.

The alert had come early that morning while she had been
holding court in the Astronomers' hold, hearing the petitions of
the arbiters and deciding matters of Law. She alone had heard
the whispered warning, had stopped mid-sentence, and abruptly
walked away from the men of status without another word. Rada
had then spent the remainder of the day watching symbols she did
not fully understand move about on a map made of black steel.

One of the symbols the Mirror had assigned to the forces
assembled in Vadal was a crown. When that crown winked from
existence, Rada began to cry, because she knew it meant her
husband was gone.

A moment later, the symbol of the mask also disappeared,
and she knew that Devedas had not died in vain.

Rada dried her eyes, composed herself, decided what had to
be done, and returned to the court.

The judges had continued their debates in her absence. By this
point her pregnancy could no longer be hidden, yet it remained

politely unrecognized in her court, for should it become widely
known among the rest of the first caste the detractors of Devedas
might use her condition against her. It had angered her that a
thing which should have been celebrated was instead hidden. She
had become far too used to the snide insinuations and clever
games of the political animals. They would claim that surely a
mother-to-be's attention would be divided, that the chief administrator of the Law could not afford to be distracted or physically
weakened, and that she would need to concentrate on giving their
beloved Maharaja a healthy heir. Then they would use all that
as an excuse to shove her aside and take power for themselves.
Once the baby was born there would surely be some new excuse
to remove her entirely. A new nest of vipers would be installed,
bearing all the same petty corruptions of the old next, and all
of Devedas' efforts to reform the government would have been
for nothing.

That, Rada would not allow.

There were fifty men of great status assembled in the temporary chamber. Between them they represented most of the Orders
and every great house. They would be her witnesses.

Curious, they watched Rada walk with intense purpose to the
front of the humble room that had replaced their opulent Chamber of Argument of the Capitol. The judge who stood behind the
lectern stopped his speech, bowed his head deferentially, and then
offered her the speaker's staff. Her tireless work in supporting
the war effort and keeping the Law had earned the respect of
many, that one included.

Rada did not bother taking the staff, for she required no
symbol declaring who was in charge here. Instead, she lifted the
Asura's Mirror for all to see. There were gasps as it was recognized
for what it was, because their Maharani bearing her own black
steel artifact had been a matter of rumor and speculation, and
such a dangerous implement was not the sort of thing casually
bandied about in a polite court.

"The demons are defeated. Devedas has won."

At first they were incredulous, for such a dream seemed
impossible. They were too used to bad news to easily accept any
good. These men had been here, despondent, yet carrying on
ever since the Capitol had fallen. Having seen what the demons
could do, they had all but given up hope. But then her husband's

supporters began to smile, for they knew Rada would never lie to them. Even Devedas' enemies despised demons far more than their political foes, so they too wanted to believe.

"Send for your wizards and they'll confirm it soon enough. Your Maharaja is victorious. The demons are no more. Grand Inquisitor Omand, who shed the blood of noble warriors and threatened my life in this very building, is *no more.*"

They shared nervous glances, for since the night Omand had demonstrated he could take his revenge against any of them with impunity, everyone who had not bent the knee to his tyranny had lived in fear.

"The demons are gone. The tyrant is dead. Long live the Maharaja."

"Long live the Maharaja!" many of the judges shouted in response.

It took everything Rada had to hold back the tears, but she could be human later. Now she had to be strong to ensure the legacy of Devedas lived on. Just as Harta Vadal had taught her, a leader did whatever was necessary for the good of their house, and her house now was all of Lok. She was certain those messages sent by magic would confirm their victory, but it would also let them know their king was dead. Rada refused to let his house fall apart without him.

"We will return to the Capitol *immediately.*"

The important men hesitated. "Immediately, Maharani?" one of them squeaked.

"As soon as I have finished speaking and leave this room, I will gather my cloak and ride to the Capitol myself. Whoever among you is honorable will follow me. We will ride through the darkness and tomorrow we will watch the sun rise over the Capitol renewed. We have hidden here too long. I will not hide a moment more. Our obligations need us. Our Orders need us. Our people need us."

Rada counted the nods of determination. Hopefully those would be enough.

"That dawn will represent the beginning of a new era for the Capitol. For too many generations, too many of members of our caste have sat in aloof comfort, lording our wealth and status over the masses we were supposed to have been serving. The Law was created to bring order and prosperity, but our caste let it turn into a weapon to be exploited by the vilest among us. Our responsibilities were forgotten as the Capitol grew out of control. There were far too many branches to this tree and most of them have been barren of fruit. Demons trimmed the tree. Now we have the opportunity to start anew, free of wickedness, corruption, and lies. You who have remained fulfilling your obligations in exile have proven that you are the select of our caste. You are the honorable few who put duty over safety. You will become the respected foundation of the Maharaja's new government."

More of them were nodding along now. She was no orator, but they knew Rada had wisdom, passion, and her belief was sincere, all things that had become a rarity among their jaded caste.

"Together we will reform this system. Our Law will be just, and administered not just for our benefit, but so that all may prosper, every house, every caste, just as my husband has commanded. Let us go and prepare his great city for his triumphant return."

One of the judges stood. "We will follow you to the Capitol, Maharani."

"Excellent. Long live the Maharaja!"

"Long live the Maharaja!" shouted the rest.

After the men of status had rushed off to gather their households, as Rada returned to her quarters to tell her servants to pack her things, she found Vikram Akershan there waiting for her. With the wave of her hand, her Garo bodyguards knew to stop a polite distance away so that she could converse privately with the Historian.

"With this news from the north, does the Asura speak freely now?"

"The direct whispers are seldom, but the paths that were locked before all appear to be open to me now." Rada held out the mirror to show him that with the flick of a finger, hundreds of pages could be revealed. "It appears the access which has long been denied us all has been granted to me alone, but I can read whatever I want."

The mirror's prior custodian was stunned by this revelation. "That might contain all the collected knowledge of the ancients!"

"Maybe. Who knows what was lost? If it isn't all of it, there's still an incredible amount of information contained within the mirror, possibly greater than every book in my beloved Capitol Library combined. So far I've seen works of mathematics, engineering, medicine, and sciences I don't even know if we have the words for today." Despite her grief, she was too much the scholar to not be nearly overcome with excitement at that. This was truly a treasure beyond comprehension.

"The revelations contained within could change everything," Vikram whispered reverently, and he seemed tempted to reach out and try to touch the mirror, but thankfully did not, because whether sword or mirror, black-steel artifacts were very particular about who was allowed to use them, and she'd hate for Vikram to lose his fingers.

"I'll find a way to record it all, even if I have to read the entire thing aloud to a room full of scribes until my voice fails or the Capitol runs out of ink."

He was a Historian. She was an Archivist. They understood the enormity of what this meant. It would take the rest of the world a while to catch up. "So many *ideas*. What will you do with all that?"

"Whatever I can to ensure our future. My obligation was to facilitate the spread of knowledge. Once before in my life I failed in that obligation. I was afraid, and untold multitudes of caste-less died for it. Politics are just an obstacle. Ignorance and lies are my sworn enemies now, Vikram. I'm going to do everything in my power as Maharani to make sure our people don't make those same mistakes again. The Capitol will become a place of learning. I will rule it as best I can and raise Devedas' heir to do the same after I am gone."

"*You* will rule?"

"Only because I suspect Devedas didn't survive the battle." She did not suspect. She knew, but she could not yet say that out loud, for to do so hurt too much.

The Historian grimaced. "My condolences. By all accounts Devedas was a good man."

"He was a *great* man, for good or ill, and all that entails. I'll try to rule as I think Devedas would have." Except even as Rada said that she knew it was untrue, because Devedas' harsh upbringing had made compassion a difficult thing for him. Hopefully, her comparative gentleness would not leave the Capitol vulnerable. "Or I'll try to, anyway."

"You didn't reveal any of this to the judges... Is this mad dash to the Capitol some kind of ploy?"

"In a way. We both know our history. Whenever a great man dies, the opportunistic always rush to fill the void. I'll be in the Capitol ready to meet them when the get there. If they wish to challenge me, they will do it in *my* city, on my terms."

Vikram nodded. "I'm glad to see that the mirror has been left in capable hands...but if you'll excuse me, Maharani, I've no stomach for politics anymore. I think I'd prefer to stay here and watch the sky."

"Do that, and should the heavens awake, I'll make sure the forces of the Law are prepared to meet that challenge as well."

The Historian bowed and took his leave.

Rada left her guards at the door, went into her chambers, and placed the mirror upon her bed. It was tempting to collapse with grief, but there was no time for that. There was work to do and a throne to claim. She could cry on the ride and let the desert have her tears.

It was then that Rada noticed something had changed upon the surface of the mirror. It still showed a map of the continent, but the symbol of the crown had reappeared.

For a moment her hopes soared, as she thought Devedas had been found alive...Only, the crown was not in Vadal, but farther south, upon the slopes of Mount Metoro where the Astronomers dwelled.

And Rada knew that when she returned to the Capitol, that crown would follow her.

Chapter 39

Omand's unnatural storm had brought with it a rain that had helped quell the many fires that had broken out across the city. After a life of so much evil, at least his death had granted that inadvertent blessing.

Ashok had returned to the fallen tower to find that the Sons of the Black Sword were still guarding the body of their beloved prophet. They had wrapped Thera in a sheet and moved her beneath a stable's roof to keep her out of the rain. He had commanded them to leave him be and they had reluctantly obeyed. Then he had remained there next to her waiting for the rain to stop.

It was a foolish, naïve hope, but when the others were gone, he had uncovered her face to be sure it was really her. It was truly Thera. There had been no mistake. The gods had not pulled some elaborate trick on him. They had only tricked the demons.

His body ached and the Heart of the Mountain was too spent to answer, but the shard remained, and it saw to it that he would live and heal. But the hurt he felt went far deeper than cracked bone and torn tissues. There was no magic that could salve this pain. Perhaps a wizard could take his memories away, like Kule had stolen his childhood, but Ashok would rather die than forget Thera.

He slept by her side.

After a time, the rain had stopped, and Ashok began to gather wood.

Throughout the morning, he built the funeral pyre. Each time one of the faithful approached to offer their assistance, he commanded them to go away. He wasn't cruel to them, but this was his duty. Alone. As his father had been a cremator in this city, so would his son.

He wore two swords as he worked, for he had taken Khartalvar from Devedas. He didn't know why he'd been compelled to do so, but no one had tried to stop him.

By the afternoon the pile of wood in the middle of the garden was of sufficient size. Most of the lumber he'd dragged from inside the ruins had still been dry, so it should burn well, and to be certain he drenched it all in oil he'd taken from a barrel that had never gotten poured into a defensive trench.

Then Ashok went back into the stable to speak with Thera one last time.

He did not know what to say.

The Law said there was no beyond, no ghosts, but to hell with the Law. Its words were dust to him now. Keta had sworn to him that there was a land for the honored dead. That had to be true, because he could not bear it to be otherwise.

So Ashok challenged the gods. "Forgotten, if there is any justice in you at all, you will reward this woman for all that she has done for you. She carried the weight of your Voice. She always did what she thought was right, no matter how much it hurt her. In return you burned her hands and let her die." His voice cracked. "You must make this right in the next life, or else you are no better than the Law. I beg you, let Thera know peace. Then when the shard finally lets me die, I can be reunited with her in the land of the dead. Until then, I will try to live as she would have me live, so that I may be worthy. If you deny her from me, I will find a way to overthrow the heavens, and find her myself."

After delivering his ultimatum, a cold autumn wind blew golden leaves through the stable. The leaves circled about, before settling atop Thera's sheet. He would take that as a sign that the Forgotten had agreed to their pact. "Thank you."

After a time, the man without fear summoned the courage to speak to his wife for the last time in this world.

"Thera, it was my duty to protect you. I tried... I failed... but I never believed we'd make it so far. You accomplished so much. The demons are all gone. Your people... our people... safe. You bought freedom for the believers. You turned non-people into whole men. Where they'll go without you, I don't know. Where I'll go without you... I don't know that either. But I think I will live as you had me live before, protecting those who can't protect themselves. You gave me purpose when all I wanted was to walk into the sea. You sent me to war. You collected those without hope. Out there somewhere are more people you would have helped... if only you'd had more time. I couldn't protect you, but I will protect your dream."

Ashok did not make promises lightly. For a man of honor, saying a thing would be done should be sufficient, but for this he would make a new vow.

"I will always love you. I will find you again. This I swear."

Gently, he picked up her body and carried her outside.

A great crowd had gathered in the garden, waiting.

They were of every caste and none at all. Of every status, from the lowliest fish-eater to even the Thakoor of Great House Vadal himself, come to pay respects to the prophet who'd died protecting his city.

Ashok carried Thera past the Sons of the Black Sword, who'd followed her across the entire continent and fought in her name. They loved her as much as Ashok had, only he'd known the woman, while they'd only known the idea. He carried her past the foreigners of Fortress, past representatives of every great house, and the Capitol, past workers and warriors, and many silently crying casteless—who, because of Thera and Devedas' bargain, actually had the right to be here. Ashok saw Jagdish at the head of a delegation of Vadal warriors, and at his command, they all saluted in unison. Behind the Vadal was a palanquin, from which Bhadramunda, son of Harta, nodded his respect, because if not for these outsiders, his house would have fallen. Even mighty Protectors were present to pay their respects to someone they'd considered a criminal. And in their shadow stood a humble casteless girl holding a baby, whom she had named after her hero.

He carried Thera to the top of the pyre and carefully set her down. Then he sparked the oil-soaked kindling with the fire starter given to him by another dead friend and walked away as the fire ignited.

As the blaze spread, Ashok looked out over the solemn crowd and recalled something that Master Mindarin had once told him after a battle as they'd watched the corpse fires burn.

We honor the dead so the survivors remember to live.

Chapter 40

Days later, after the ashes were cold, Ashok summoned the leadership of the Sons of the Black Sword to meet on a hilltop overlooking their camp. It was time to move on.

Over half the Sons had perished in the battle, but, having been temporarily gifted with Defender might, some of his officers had survived. Shekar Somsak had been crushed to death beneath the feet of a giant but had blown it to pieces with a Fortress bomb. The remaining Somsak raiders were already planning their tattoos to commemorate being witnesses to that incredible act of valor. Shekar had died as he had lived, a malicious, loyal, clever maniac.

No one would have mourned the loss of Shekar more than Gupta, for even though the workers of Jharlang had long been terrorized by the vicious Somsak, the two had joined the Sons at the same time and become brothers, united by their faith. But Gupta had been killed during the demons' final, desperate attempt to escape. He had fired until his weapons were too hot, and then he'd used that rod as a club, fighting with as much courage as any warrior of legend.

The faithful would tell stories of their bravery for generations.

Toramana, Ongud, and Eklavya were all who remained of his commanders, and Eklavya had nearly succumbed to his injuries. The second Heart had barely had enough time to mend the worst of his wounds before it had been consumed to fuel and spread the Voice's plague. The young warrior was still in a great deal of pain as he was helped up the hill, but the wizard Laxmi refused to leave Eklavya's side. The devotion the two had for each other was plain for all to see, and that small thing made Ashok happy.

Though Javed was their Keeper of Names, Ashok had requested that the priest not be among them for this meeting, but to remain nearby to be summoned. Despite Toramana being present and knowing that his purpose had been fulfilled, and that he would most likely not leave this meeting alive, the priest had still come as ordered. Javed waited a short way down the hill, praying.

To represent Fortress, Ashok had asked for Envoy Praseeda Jaehnig, the monk Lama Taksha, and Collector Yajic Kapoor. Though their alchemy had not been nearly as effective against demons as it had been against the Capitol's soldiers, the foreigners had fought with honor, and earned the respect of all the Sons.

Last of all, his council had been joined by Jagdish and Gutch, whom Ashok had not called for, but if anyone had earned a place among the Sons, it was their first risalder and the smuggler who had proven to be their most loyal friend.

"How did you hear about this?" Ashok asked as those two came strolling up the hill.

Jagdish had left behind his extravagant phontho's uniform, probably the better to pass through the city without being slowed down by the fawning adoration of the people he had saved, and was instead dressed as a humble border scout. "Word in the court is the Sons are pulling up stakes and moving out. I couldn't hardly let you go without saying goodbye, now could I?"

Ashok bowed respectfully. "I would have sought you out. We have been through too much together to not do so."

Jagdish returned the bow. "You honor me, Ashok."

In contrast to Jagdish's humility, Gutch wore the most opulent robes Ashok had ever seen outside of the Capitol, and also had a shiny new chain about his neck with a bronze medal that marked him as a hero of Vadal. "I myself took a break from the organized harvesting of ten thousand tons of demon bone to see you off, General."

"Sounds like rigorous labor."

Gutch grinned. "Oh, I'm too important to use a saw! Due to my expertise in demonic anatomy and the shipment thereof, I have managed to get myself appointed to a position in the management of this great endeavor...and I've come to inform you that the bounty will be shared with every house in direct proportion to how many men they sent to the fight."

Ashok nodded, for it was wise of Vadal to share such incredible wealth with those who'd had the courage to come here and defend their city. "It is not often the Vadal are so generous."

"It was my idea," Jagdish said. "Sold as an attempt to avoid future conflicts, but Harta's son is no fool. We've had enough wars caused by envy lately that even my caste yearns for a time of peace. This reward includes the Sons. You've got your own wizards and are a house in all but name."

"This gratitude is appreciated."

"I insisted on it. Just let me know where to send the caravan once it is all done being counted and allocated."

"Send it to the Cove," Ashok said, which answered the question that everyone present must have had concerning where they would be going next.

"We're going home!" Ongud couldn't hide the relief in his voice, for he had a young family waiting for him there. "Thank the gods, we're finally going home."

"Some of us are," Ashok replied. "Everyone, sit. I must speak."

They rested in a circle upon the yellow grass. The view was such that the vastness of Vadal City was laid out below them. Portions of it had burned, but the Vadal were industrious, and would surely rebuild, better than before. Even the Martaban was whole once more.

"I am not one for moving speeches. That was Keta's specialty." When Ashok said that, everyone who had known Keta laughed. "I will keep it simple. It has been an honor to serve with you. You have made me very proud."

Such praise, coming from legendary Ashok, humbled them all.

"Thera dreamed of making for ourselves an independent house, a place for the unwanted. A place where those outside the existing Law could make their own rules and live by those rules in peace. A place without castes. A place where the faithful could worship openly, without fear. Devedas gave us an opportunity no other ruler would have. The courage shown by the Sons has made the great houses respect us. Now is the time to see Thera's dream fulfilled."

"Hear, hear!" Ongud shouted. "The Cove lies within Akershan.

As long as Ashok bears their sword, my old masters won't dare to move against us."

"I am not going with you. My obligation is not done."

The Sons grew restless at that. "What do you mean?" Toramana asked. "You did all the Voice has asked of you."

Ashok was not doing this for the Voice, but for the woman who had carried it. "The leadership of the Sons falls to this council to decide, as it truly already has for a very long time. You do not need me. I am barely a leader in war. I was not made for peace. But you are correct, Ongud. I told the army of Akershan if they wanted their sword back, they would leave our lands alone, and allow safe passage for the casteless to get there. It seems they have honored this bargain. So I will return this sword to Great House Akershan."

Giving up the ancestor blade was inconceivable to them. "No, General. Please. The threat of losing their sword is the only thing ensuring our safety."

"You are astute, Ongud. You have always been the Sons' finest tactician."

"Thank you, but it doesn't take a prophet to see into the future. Our lands are surrounded by Akershan's mountains. They might tolerate our presence for now, but what about their next Thakoor? Or the one after that? What happens when they forget the kindness of your giving their sword back, and decide the faithful have no place in their lands?"

"Then earn that place. I fought Bharatas for this ancestor blade. Outside of duels, when a sword chooses a new bearer, it is usually from the same house, but sometimes it goes to a vassal." Ashok unbuckled his sword belt and held out sheathed Angruvadal, that had once been Akerselem. "Ongud Khedekar dar Akershan, I offer this to you."

Ongud stared at the deadly weapon. "I'm not worthy."

"That is for the sword to decide. If it allows you to wield it, then you will be in a position to ensure the future of the Cove. Akershan would get their sword back, only it would be in the hands of one of the faithful. Bearers command respect. Show Akershan the faithful make for better allies than occupiers, and secure the future Thera's house."

It was a lot for the young warrior to take in. "And if the sword disagrees?"

"Then it will hurt you." Ashok placed Angruvadal on the ground in front of Ongud, who stared at it like it was a viper about to strike. "Take your time. It will wait."

Losing an ancestor blade was like losing part of yourself, but Ashok had done it before, and this was no longer that. With the shard of Angruvadal in his heart, he had become his sword, and his sword had become him. Angruvadal had made him a weapon of the gods. Thera had taught him how to be human. He knew which loss hurt more.

The only hybrid of black steel and man to ever live looked toward Jagdish. "Unless you wish to try to claim a sword? You did before."

Jagdish mulled that temptation over for a time, as if carefully choosing his words. "A few years ago, I wanted nothing more in the world than to try for that honor. By the time we hunted you down, Angruvadal had broken. So I didn't get to find out if I was worthy. Then I went to war with Sarnobat, then Vokkan, trying to claim what belonged to another house, and still the opportunity never presented itself... Now?"

Ongud watched Jagdish closely, still reeling at the honor and danger he had just been offered, and seemingly unsure if they were about to duel over an ancestor blade or not.

However, Jagdish shrugged. "Eh. I don't think that's supposed to be my fate. My house is safe. I've claimed enough glory for myself to last ten lifetimes. All I desire now is to return to my estate, love my wife, and raise my daughter. I'd prefer not to be required to fight a duel against every warrior in Lok with a chip on his shoulder."

"It's a good thing you left Najmul home," Gutch said. "He'd have certainly dueled Ongud for it."

"Oh, absolutely, guaranteed," Jagdish agreed. "I'll be sure not to tell him until long after you have all left. Carry on, warrior. And if the sword lets you bear it, all I ask is that you treat the Sons as I did."

"I will, sir," Ongud promised. "A leader serves."

"Good, lad." Jagdish looked toward Ashok. "What are you moping about for? You've still got a spare."

"This is not mine." Ashok held out sheathed Khartalvar and turned it over in his hands, as if to study it, to truly feel the weight of such a thing. "Devedas showed the world who he really was when he took this up to fight for his people... but it belongs to Kharsawan, who has done us no harm. That house should not be robbed for their bearer heeding the call."

"If I may..." Eklavya grimaced as he spoke, for there were a great many stitches holding his wounds closed, and deprived of the Heart's magic, his recovery would take weeks. "That's my old house. I once served in the same infantry paltan as family members of bearer Tejeshwar. I can make sure that it's returned to them."

"They branded you a criminal for religion, and you would still help them despite that?" Envoy Praseeda was incredulous. "You mainlanders astound me."

"As Fortress has its guilds, our house and caste define us here, even long after we've forsaken them. But Ashok is right. That sword rightfully belongs to Great House Kharsawan. They condemned me and my friends for believing in the gods, because they believe in the Law. We are all governed by the codes we hold."

In Ashok's absence, Eklavya had been the one to keep the Sons organized and united. After Ongud had made the plans, Eklavya had been the one to execute them from the front. He'd commanded the Sons in many battles, never hesitating to risk his life for any of the others. Despite receiving what should have been mortal wounds he had still led the charge to drive the demons back into the river. And off the battlefield, his kindness had earned him the love of a gentle slave turned fearsome wizard. Ashok knew ancestor blades better than anyone, and if Khartalvar thought Eklavya wasn't worthy, then no one was.

"Return it..." Ashok set Khartalvar down in front of their red warrior. "Or bear it yourself, Eklavya, and claim as your reward for not overthrowing your Thakoor the unsettled lands around the Nansakar to get room for the house of Thera to grow. Protect both houses, and that will show your old house who the fanatics they once condemned really are."

Eklavya seemed nearly overcome by emotion at that suggestion. "Do you think this is the will of the gods?"

"I am the Forgotten's Warrior, not his Voice. I do not know. But that is what *I* want."

"You honor me, sir."

Jagdish let out a low whistle. "Oceans, Ashok. Two neighboring houses' bearers defending the faithful house locked between their borders... That's politics clever enough that Shakti would be impressed. I didn't know you had it in you."

Ongud addressed Eklavya. "That would be quite the thing, wouldn't it?"

"That it would, brother," Eklavya agreed. "Or this black steel might take our hands for asking."

"Shekar would call you both cowards if you didn't try," Laxmi declared in support of her man.

"Then we do this for him," Ongud said. "And Gupta, and every other Son of the Black Sword who laid down their lives on our quest for freedom."

"For our people, for our gods," Eklavya stated with grim determination. "Let's do this."

The two warriors prepared to take up the judgmental swords. If Ashok was right about the character of these men, then the vision of Thera and Keta would be safe for another generation. But the will of black steel was often inscrutable, and if he was wrong about them, then their blood would water the grass. This attempt would end in triumph or tragedy.

Just in case it helped, Ashok made a silent request to the swords. *I have given you much. Allow me this.*

"Step back, just in case there's flailing," Eklavya warned Laxmi, more worried about her safety than his own.

Two fearsome swords were grasped, drawn free, and then held out in trembling hands. Both warriors winced as the grips bit their palms and the black steel tasted their blood. Every observer except Ashok held their breath. He alone understood what they were going through, as their lives flashed before their eyes. Every flaw, mistake, failure, and desire was observed, calculated, and weighed against their current worth and their potential for both good and evil in the future.

Ashok noted that in the distance, Javed also watched, for he too understood this process. He and Ashok were the only bearers to ever willingly give up an ancestor blade. What did that make them? He did not know. Long ago, Ramrowan had set the swords working toward a purpose beyond mortal understanding, and they had done their duty without hesitation or remorse. Long after their first bearers had turned to dust, the swords remained. Ramrowan's mission was done. The swords' purpose now? A mystery.

A few terrifying moments passed, and when the swords didn't force them to cut themselves, the Sons began to smile, for it appeared that Ashok had chosen well.

Then an understanding came upon Ashok that securing the Cove was Angruvadal's way of paying its respects to Thera.

He pressed his fist to his chest and bowed his head. *Thank you, Angruvadal.*

Ongud and Eklavya were unharmed, but both appeared ready to topple over from the stress of the judgement. Sweat was pouring down their faces. Eklavya could barely move as it was.

"Well done, warriors. Sheath those blades before you hurt anyone. They're a bit sharper than what you are used to."

"Najmul would especially go after the crippled one before he could heal up," Gutch whispered to Jagdish. "Wolves do that, you know, targeting the sick and the weak."

"I'll be sure to send him off on some distant mission in the opposite direction," Jagdish responded.

Toramana spoke up. "I am overjoyed for my brothers, General, for I have no doubt they'll keep my people safe. I know there's no magic sword for me, but I have asked you for one small thing. Is this the time?"

"I have not forgotten, Chief. The two of us will deal with that at the end."

Toramana dipped his head in respect. "Very well."

Ashok turned to the Fortress folk, who seemed baffled by what had just happened, for they did not have ancestor blades on their island, and their customs were very different there. "Envoy, Lama, and Collector, your help was invaluable against first man then demon. Our battle is done, so I release you from your obligation. As agreed, you can take as much treasure back through the underworld as you can carry."

Collector Yajic rubbed his hands together with glee. "There are so many pretty things to choose from."

"The Weapons Guild was honored to serve you, Ram Ashok," Envoy Praseeda said. "I will return to the workshop and tell the council of our new friendship with the mainland. I'm sure we will both profit from future trade between our island and your Cove."

Gutch perked up at that. "Trade now, huh? I rather enjoy facilitating trade. Before you go, the two of us should talk."

"I am amenable to this, Forge Master Smith."

"You know, Envoy, steel and wood are heavy and I hear your underground paths are treacherous. If the demons are truly gone, we could maybe even build a *boat*, like they supposedly had back in the old days, like a great big barge, but instead of rivers, made to cross the sea."

Ashok could only wonder at what manner of terrible illegalities would result from that conversation, but that was no longer his concern. "Tell Guru Dondrub that the prophecy written in metal is fulfilled."

"But all is not yet decided, Ram Ashok!" the Fortress monk exclaimed. "Of the six opposing forces, only one can determine the direction of the next age. Prophet, priest, and king defeated the mask and demon, and the Forgotten's Warrior, clearly, is the victor. Yet two remain. Who shall I tell the Guru will decide?"

Ashok doubted very much that their priest would be around much longer, but that was up to Toramana. "I was made to protect. Not rule."

"But the will of the gods—"

"Is not mine," Ashok told the monk. "I would not be Omand, to rule with blood and fire. I am not even Devedas, thinking I am capable of deciding what is best for all. I hold no illusion that I am anything more than I am. What I did on behalf of the Law took *so many* lives. To ask Black-Hearted Ashok to judge the world would be to trade one tyrant for another, for eventually I might become just as cruel and unforgiving as I was created to be. So I will not rule. Let the people figure out how to rule themselves and I will leave them to it."

"And if left on their own, those leaders choose to do great evil?"

He had never cared for the Fortress monk's strange philosophical games. "Then I would correct them."

The monk gave him that peculiar hand-clasped bow his people used to indicate their subservience. "Then the decision is made. I will tell the Guru that is the path which has been chosen by the Avatara. The Workshop will abide by it."

Ashok scowled, for part of him wondered if he had stepped into some kind of trap. "Do as you will, but I will not be here to watch."

Chapter 41

Javed knelt between the trees upon a carpet of leaves, patiently awaiting his execution. It was a beautiful fall day. The air was crisp. The sun was bright. It was not the stark desert where he'd been born, and then reborn, but this was a fine place to die. Though he was unsure if that was what the gods intended for him or not. He would soon find out.

Ashok and Toramana approached, so Javed rose to greet them. "General." Javed bowed in greeting. "Chief."

"I have stepped down and do not command the Sons of the Black Sword anymore. The leaders have counseled. Toramana is no longer chief of the swamp folk. From here on he will be the Thakoor of Free House Thera and will rule the Cove and the lands around it."

So Toramana had gone from being headman of a lost village in the swamp to running a rebel kingdom that in all likelihood would someday grow to become a great house. "That is a significant change. Is the Law aware of this?"

"They will be soon enough." Ashok sat on a nearby log. "I will not draw out this affair. Your crimes are known. Your sentence passed. Make no appeals to me. Your life is in the hands of your Thakoor whom you have wronged."

"Very well." Javed turned to face Toramana.

In battle the swamp folk painted their faces in white and black ash to mimic skulls to better intimidate their enemies. Toramana wore no ash now, but the razor-sharp axe in his hand and the hatred in his eyes were enough. Death was all but certain, but Javed had one final request.

"I would ask for one thing."

"Why should I care?"

Javed had thought he was resigned to his fate, but that offended him, and he responded with anger. "Because I took up an ancestor blade and then willingly put it down. Because I converted thousands in a land notorious for how much it hates the faithful. Because I flooded the world with the words of the prophet and destroyed centuries of the Inquisition's work in only a few seasons. Because I have kept my word, returning to the Sons despite knowing I'd be punished for my crimes. After my fate was sealed, I could have run away at any time. I didn't. I could have slipped away after the battle, and you would've thought I'd died somewhere along the way and never been the wiser, but I stayed and tended the wounded instead."

"Even murderers can be brave."

"There was no bravery in what this murderer has done, Tha-koor Toramana. It was fear that kept me on this path. Fear of a punishment far beyond what any man, even you, can bestow upon me. It was fear of displeasing the gods that caused me to throw myself to the demons rather than risk the Voice. It was that same fear that compelled me to carry Ashok out of the depths and bring him back to the light to slay my old master, Omand."

Toramana glanced at Ashok, who nodded, affirming that to be the truth.

"Then that has earned you my ear for now. Speak your request."

"Let me live long enough to tell the story of what really happened here."

The Thakoor mocked him with laughter. "Pathetic! Everyone will tell this story around every campfire for the rest of their lives, for what we did here will become legend."

"Lok is far bigger than some village in the swamp. You know of the scriptures I wrote?"

"Of course. You think because you're a civilized man the men of the forest must be fools. We had no books in the Bhadjangal, but those who escaped the assassins knew their letters. I learned them because I was curious even when all I had to write them with was a stick in the dirt. I have learned more since and even managed to read these books of yours myself. In them I found some of the same stories Mother Dawn shared with my people long before we dug Ashok from the rubble."

"Then you recognize the power those words have to spread the teachings everywhere, to every great house and everything in-between, so that everyone can learn the truth and remember what has been forgotten. And unlike your campfire stories, the words of the book won't change with each teller."

"I tire of this, murderous priest. What do you really want?"

"Let me finish the books! Let me write about what really happened here. Let me tell the story of Thera's courage. Let me write of Ashok and Toramana and the Sons of the Black Sword and all that they have done! Let me write about how good king Devedas let the casteless become whole men! If I do not tell the truth, it will become corrupted. It will inevitably be replaced with lies!"

"No." Toramana shook his head. "You've had enough time."

"My time is not for me!" Javed shouted. "Can't you understand? Yesterday I went to where our prophet was cremated so I could pray, and do you know what I found there? The faithful, picking through the ashes to find fragments of her bones and teeth to keep as magic charms to pray to!"

Ashok scowled at that.

"They are devout but without understanding. They believe but don't know in what. They'd turn her into nothing more than the nameless idols the Inquisition used to smash. Without knowledge the people *will* be lost. They'll become corrupt. You know the stories of what happened to the children of Ramrowan the first time. They fell into ignorance and pride and destroyed themselves. We will do the exact same thing, only without the guidance of truth will fall even faster! Let me record that truth before you kill me. That is all I ask."

"You ask too much."

"I ask for seasons. In return I would provide your house decades, centuries, of knowing what really happened here. Of what was sacrificed and the cost of all that was lost to create this graveyard of demons. I do not ask this for myself, but rather for the good of all the faithful. They must know the truth, or it will be denied." Javed held up his remaining hand. "In your wisdom you left me one hand to write with. Allow me to use it."

Toramana's anger was apparent, but it was a calculating one. A good leader put the needs of his people over his own desires. Whether he lived a bit longer or died now, Javed suspected Toramana would make a worthy Thakoor.

"Having this scripture sounds like a fine thing, but why should I not pick someone else to write this truth?"

"Who else is there? One of the priests I set apart in Kanok? The one I sent to the Cove? They weren't here. Their words will be hollow. I have already demonstrated what my words can accomplish. I'll do the same as before, and then use the printer of Makao to send the truth everywhere, so all the faithful will be lifted up, and many more will convert, so many that the Law will never dare take religion away again. I would give you allies in every great house. But denied the truth, false prophets will surely rise, and within a generation they will be the ones taking the credit for what was accomplished here instead. Thera will be forgotten. The Sons will be forgotten."

"Never!"

"We forgot our own gods before, Toramana! What is our glory compared to them? Men who weren't even here will claim honors they did not earn. I beg you, let there be a true account for the faithful to hold onto."

Toramana looked to Ashok for wisdom. "What do you think?"

"I think it is entirely your decision to make, Thakoor."

Javed had made his case. There was nothing else to say. His plea was an earnest one, but even he didn't know if it was the right thing to do or not. His final instruction from Mother Dawn had been to do his duty for the bloodline of Ramrowan. This seemed the best way to accomplish that. Like Toramana, he could only try to do what he thought was best for those he was commanded to serve.

The Thakoor was silent for a *very* long time. It was cruel that his first act of judgment would be to weigh the value of his child's memory against the good of the faithful.

"I would not have those boys die for nothing...I have other children, and they will have children, and they will have children. Thera wanted us to make a future for *them*. Not just now, but forever. Is my anger worth more than their faith? Eklavya and Ongud will keep us safe for as long as they live, but after that, we must be strong on our own. Would Parth and Rawal curse me for being a coward or praise me for my foresight? That's the question you ask me to live with."

"I am sorry for what I have done," Javed said truthfully.

"I believe you. It does not make me hate you less." The new Thakoor stared at the great city of man that had stood for over a thousand years, surely asking himself how he could keep his people alive over the next few. "I must care for the living and those not yet born before I can satisfy myself and the dead... I'll allow you to finish your book and send it to the world. *Then* you will die. I have spoken."

Javed nodded at this wisdom, for they both wanted what was best for their people.

"Now I must go and apologize to the ghosts of children." Toramana began walking down the hill.

Ashok and Javed watched him go.

Toramana was a good leader and honorable man, but he was unwise to the ways of the courts. He was a simple hunter, who would be competing against the likes of Bhadramunda Vadal or Venketesh Makao, who had been trained since birth by philosophers and scholars how best to strive for the betterment of their house. For the faithful to survive as a cohesive people would take cunning. Every other house would either despise the faithful or try to manipulate them for their own advantage. The world had changed, but the fundamental nature of power had not. Toramana would need Javed's help for this ambitious new house to survive.

"I spoke the truth, Ashok."

"I know you did, but it was not my place to decide your fate."

"What would you have done with me?"

Ashok stood up. "I would have killed you."

"Do you still doubt my conviction, then?"

"Not at all... I would kill you because that conviction is what makes you so dangerous. Do not lead these people astray. Farewell, Keeper."

"Goodbye, Ashok."

Chapter 42

Ashok sat atop Horse, watching what remained of the Army of Many Houses march past. Most of the volunteers had already left to return to their homes, but a considerable honor guard had chosen to remain with their beloved Maharaja to escort his body. They were heading south, first to the Capitol and then on to Devedas' ancestral lands on the Ice Coast where he would be entombed. There were plans for a giant monument to be placed there to honor him. It was a somber procession, for though they had accomplished great things, great men had died to do it.

These were new and uncertain times.

All along the road, citizens of Vadal had turned out to see the carriage that held Devedas' casket pass by. To them Devedas had once been a hated invader, but now he was the hero who had saved them all from demons. Workers took off their hats and knelt as the carriage went past.

A rider spotted Ashok and broke away from the column, heading in his direction. Ashok did not call upon the Heart to sharpen his vision, for even having recovered a bit from the battle, it was but a faint shadow of what it had once been, and he would steal none of its remaining power from the last of the Protectors. And it seemed that the shard could now do for him everything the Heart once had, and more.

The rider was Jagdish and for this particular journey he was dressed in his phontho's regalia, with turban full of stars and chest covered in medals. Ashok doubted there was an award left in Vadal they'd not pinned on him yet, and the first caste would probably need to make up new ones to give him. Such was the glory of the warrior Jagdish.

"Well, if it isn't the most infamous criminal in the whole world," Jagdish called out as he rode closer.

"How did you know it was me?"

"A big straw hat is hardly a disguise when you sit upon the scariest stallion anyone has ever seen, that's white as a Devakulan mountain and nearly as big."

Horse snorted at the compliment. Jagdish's mount was wise enough to stay out of biting range.

"I didn't expect to see you here, Ashok."

"I did not expect to be here."

The two of them watched the carriage pass in silence.

Ashok would miss him.

"I'm accompanying them all the way to the border as a show of respect," Jagdish explained. "My association with Devedas was complicated."

"I could say the same."

That understatement made Jagdish laugh. "I imagine so... Devedas betrayed my house before helping save it. I'm here, not just out of respect for the man, but for his family. I'm only alive because his wife once out-politicked Harta Vadal on my behalf. Someday, I'd like to visit Rada again. Someone from Vadal needs to let her know just how brave her husband was at the end."

"I suspect she knows."

"Probably. She's very smart. What do you think will happen with the Capitol now that they've lost their king?"

Ashok shrugged. "That is unknown to me. The Capitol might never recover. Maybe someone else will be ambitious enough to claim that singular authority for themselves."

"The first caste duel as spitefully as us warriors, only they use speeches and letters instead of steel. I think they might be equally deadly, though our way is far more honest."

That observation caused Ashok a small smile. "True. Will the Law be all powerful again, or will the houses chafe against that authority? Will workers armed with alchemy be content to remain in their place? I do not know. Perhaps the great houses will simply send more judges and things will go back to the way they were before."

"Something tells me that things are never going back to the way they were before all this, Ashok."

Jagdish was astute, and he said that without knowing about the Protector Order's new weakness. The Heart of the Mountain still beat, but what power remained would have to be used sparingly. It was doubtful there would ever be more Protectors created. "Many Protectors gave their lives in Vadal. The Inquisition has been shamed and deprived of purpose, and the militant Order that Devedas created to replace it, to bring balance between the houses, castes, and Capitol, is no more."

"Eh . . . Sorta. We Defenders might be a bit more stubborn than you think."

That made Ashok curious. "What do you mean?"

"The ancient artifact broke itself to give life to the plague, but fragments remained. Karno's last act as the Order's master was to give each of his Defenders who'd survived the battle one of those fragments." Jagdish reached into the neck of his uniform and pulled out a chain. Hanging from the end of it was a small piece of black steel. "I've tested it. We're no wizards, capable of learning new patterns or anything like that, but a connection remains. Everything I could do before, it seems that I can still draw upon this piece in the same fashion. Perhaps not as strongly as before, but it is something. I doubt there will be any more of us ever, but what remains, remains."

"But the Order itself is done?"

"Returned to our houses and left to our own devices. We still took an oath to defend the people, though. I never forsook that."

"It is a great power. Respect it."

"I intend to."

Ashok would expect nothing less from such an honorable man. "And Karno?"

"After he handed out the fragments, he told me he's going home to Uttara to be a farmer, then he rode off into the western sunset."

His old friend deserved a peaceful retirement. "Good for Karno."

The column had moved past, but Jagdish remained, clearly not wanting to say goodbye. "Karno's not the only one who has earned his rest. You know I have a fine estate in the east now. You're welcome there. You can stay as long as you wish."

"You are offering me a place to mourn."

Jagdish gave him a sad smile. "I didn't say that. You said that...but you've earned the right. When I lost Pakpa I went mad with grief. But I had an army to build and a daughter to raise, so I had other things to distract my uncalm mind. Until I found Shakti...well, she found me, but you know what I mean. She makes me happy. Thera wouldn't want you to be miserable any more than Pakpa would have wished that on me. It's not good for a warrior to be alone."

"The offer is appreciated, brother. But it seems strife follows wherever I go, so I will make nowhere my home. I've been Ashok the Black Heart long enough. I think now I will be Ashok the Wanderer for a time."

"I understand..." The two of them both knew that this was probably the last time they would ever speak. "Where will you go?"

Ashok had been pondering upon that question a great deal since Thera's funeral, and whenever he did, his thoughts had irresistibly been drawn back to the ancient map of the entire world carved within the secret chamber that held the Heart of the Mountain. There were eight other continents and thousands of islands between them, and Ratul had told him that all of those had been inhabited long before the demons had fallen to the world.

Were there survivors as there had been in Lok? Did demons still trespass in those mysterious lands?

As long as the shard of Angruvadal lived, Ashok suspected he could not die, and thus he could not be reunited with Thera. Until then, he remained a living weapon, predicted by gods, forged by justice, sharpened by black steel, tested in icy sea and starving darkness, who carried in his blood a curse fatal to all the wicked soldiers of hell who might still infest the world. He would not waste what time he had.

"I will go wherever I am needed."

Chapter 43

One Year Later

"Have you written it all down?"

"The book is complete," Javed told Thakoor Toramana.

"Have these books been sent out into the world?"

"It has been arranged."

The two of them stood within the stone room that had served as Thera's command post at the Cove. Still drawn upon the wall with chalk was the map of Lok, as created from memory by the Sons. Javed had drawn much of it himself, because he had been well traveled compared to the rest. They had thought it was because he was a merchant. He had been a child of the caravans, but in truth it was the Inquisition that had sent him wherever there had been secret heretics in need of rooting out. Now he was a leader of a heretics, and had just returned from Makao, having overseen the printing and distribution of the scriptures. Thakoor Venketesh—who remained converted to the Forgotten—had begged Javed to stay and be their priest, but knowing that was not his place, Javed had returned to the Cove instead.

Most of the faithful still did not know about Javed's treachery yet, so they had welcomed him back as a hero. He had walked up the drained tunnel, past the rough statue of Keta that had been placed in the spot where he had been slain by bearer Bharatas, and every step of the way the people had cheered for their priest.

They had chanted his name. They had begged him to bless their children and their crops. He was loved.

"Has the sacred Book of Names been passed on?"

"Yes. A new Keeper of Names has been chosen. The priesthood is secure."

"That's good."

Toramana had proven himself to be a fine leader. The faithful had thrived under his watch. Their holdings had expanded into the wilderness and new settlements were being built. Tens of thousands of casteless and converts had joined them, and a hundred of the Fortress folk had decided to stay rather than return to their gray and dreary island. Their merchants traded with Akershan, Devakula, and Thao. They had even built a small church in Neeramphorn, where the Law reluctantly allowed one of their priests to preach.

And no matter how much the faithful were still despised by many, none of those dared move against them as long as Ongud and Eklavya lived. Those bearers dwelled once more in their ancestral lands, as required by their obligation, but their estates had become havens for the faithful. And it was known that anyone who trespassed against the Cove, also trespassed against two bearers.

Yet Javed knew that was not enough.

Toramana seemed remarkably calm for a man denied justice for so very long. "Is there anything else you must do before I finally have my revenge?"

Javed had struggled with this decision for months. Toramana's desire for retribution was a righteous one. He knew he deserved to die for his crimes. Tormented by guilt, Javed yearned for the release of death. But the faithful were not yet truly secure. They remained surrounded by enemies, who were soaked in ancestral hate. Maharani Rada had continued Maharaja Devedas' policies toward them, so the Law granted them leniency for now, but how long would that last? The faithful were a tiny minority in Lok. Javed knew their only hope for long-term survival was to convert so many to the faith that the Law could never threaten them again. Or better, convert the entire continent, and then the gods' holy commandments would be the only Law.

Javed knew his audacious plan would surely end in war, but this blood would be shed in self-defense, for all who were not converted were enemies. If the faithful did not control the world, then that world would eventually, inevitably turn against them. Two ancestor blades had bought them respect for now. Javed would use that time to convince the undecided and sway them to his cause, and once he had a big enough army, Javed would convert the rest of the world by the sword. They would have to obey the Forgotten or taste his wrath.

The gods had not commanded him to do this. He had no Voice to guide him. But he could see no other way out. The faithful were his responsibility now, and they had to be protected at all costs. Javed the Witch Hunter had contaminated the believers' water and murdered their children to fulfill his obligation to the Law. Javed the priest would kill millions for his gods if he had to.

"I said, is there anything else, priest?"

Javed returned to the present. "No, my Thakoor. That's all. I am sorry the time has come." Then he jabbed the poisoned needle into Toramana's neck.

The Thakoor of Free House Thera stumbled back with a look of surprise on his face. He tried to shout but no sound came out, for the muscles of his throat were already constricting. He reached for his axe, but his hands were suddenly too numb to grasp it.

"Rest, Thakoor. This is a powerful toxin. Death will be swift and painless. Go to your reward knowing your people will be saved by me. The deaths of Parth and Rawal will not have been for nothing. The faithful will sing of them as heroes for generations, as they will you. I will make sure of it."

Toramana's face had gone as white as the ashen masks of the swamp folk. He crashed against the wall, clumsy hand pressed against the tiny puncture wound. Such a murder was an old witch hunter trick. No one would notice such a small, innocuous injury. It would look like his heart had given out, a not uncommon death for such a large man who worked so hard and lived under so much stress. It would be a tragic death, but Javed would help the people cope with their loss.

"I will not ask for forgiveness. I know I'm condemned. But when you get to the other side you will understand, I do this not for me, but for the future of the faithf—"

The point of a sword erupted out Javed's chest.

He stared at the red steel in disbelief as blood gushed down his robes.

The blade was wrenched out from between his shoulder blades, and Javed dropped helpless to his knees.

The wizard Laxmi stepped out from the darkness of the space between worlds right behind him. "Are you alright, Toramana?"

The Thakoor held up one hand to show her he was wearing a silver ring, and embedded in it was a fragment of black steel. Then he gasped, unexpectedly able to breathe again. Slowly, the color returned to his skin.

"I will be, Laxmi. Inquisition poisons are nothing compared to Defender might."

"That was a stupid gamble. I warned you not to trust this bastard. I knew far too many just like him at the House of Assassins."

"I was foolish enough to hope he might die with dignity." Toramana drew his axe from his belt and approached the mortally wounded priest. He grabbed a handful of Javed's hair and pulled his head back, better to expose the neck.

In the desert, Javed had met a god. In the Cove, he would meet his death.

"This...is not...what...I wanted."

"Tell it to the gods in person. This is for my son and everyone one else ever hurt by your lies."

Toramana began hacking.

Chapter 44

Five Years Later

The farmer toiled in his field, hoping this year would give him a good crop.

Well, unless the bugs kept eating his leaves. Or they went too many days without sunshine. Or too many days with too much sunshine. Or animals burrowed holes in his ditches and stole his irrigation water again. Or one of the hundred other things that could happen to make a farmer's life miserable.

It turned out farming was a lot more complicated and far less relaxing than he had imagined it to be...but it was far more peaceful than tracking down lawbreakers and killing them with a hammer.

As it grew too hot to continue laboring beneath the Uttaran sun, Karno put his shovel over one broad shoulder and began walking back toward his humble cabin. When he saw that there was a group of warriors on horseback approaching, he scowled, for it was rare to have visitors in this isolated place.

The warriors were fellow Uttarans, but they were escorting a young arbiter. That was probably because this area was notorious for being menaced by bandit gangs. Except, he had dealt with those already, no different from the other pests who damaged his crops.

They stopped their horses in the dusty lane and the arbiter

addressed him. "Hello, worker. We seek retired Protector of the Law, Karno Uttara. Which way must we go to reach his estate?"

Karno pointed at the nearby cabin. "It's right there."

The arbiter frowned at what he assumed to be a joke. "That's a hovel, unfit to hold fish-eaters or pigs."

There was some offense to be taken at that, since he had constructed it himself. It was no mansion, but it had a solid roof and four sturdy walls which kept out the wind and rain. What more could a man ask for?

"The mighty Karno Uttara was friend to Maharaja Devedas himself and was once master of the disbanded Defender Order. Maharani Radamantha the Wise has named him a hero of Lok for his service at the Battle of the Capitol *and* the Rakshasa's Reckoning."

He grunted at that, because he'd not known they'd come up with an official name for that momentous yet terrible day. "I am Karno Uttara."

Covered in mud, he hardly looked a hero of Lok, but even the dumbest warriors had to realize that men of such physical stature were exceedingly rare, and this farmer was a head taller than the biggest among them. They immediately saluted. The arbiter quickly realized his mistake and began to stammer his apologies.

Karno was not offended. If he had wanted to be recognized he wouldn't have asked his Thakoor to grant him land in the middle of unsettled nowhere. He'd requested no bank notes or slaves. Everything here had been built by his own two hands. He had chopped down the trees and made fence posts to put in the holes he'd dug in the ground. He had carried off the rocks so his oxen could plow. It was humble, but it was honest, and it gave him plenty of time to think without people constantly yammering at him. Even the workers in the nearest village thought he was just some manner of hermit.

"Have you come about my application?"

"Your application, Master Karno?"

"I sent a letter to the Thakoor requesting a marriage be arranged for me several months ago."

"An arranged marriage?"

Would this annoying little man repeat everything he said? "Yes, an arranged marriage." It had been a simple request. Karno had not asked for much. Though he was technically a man of status, a worker-caste farm wife would do. In fact, that would be preferable, because at least she'd already know how to milk the cow and cut the hay. He didn't care about her family name, or if she was a widow, or even if she was ugly. His only request to his Thakoor was that she be kind natured and smart enough to have a good conversation with, because he had grown lonely.

The arbiter swallowed nervously. "I am sorry, Master Karno. I was unaware of this letter and was not sent by your Thakoor. It is the Capitol that has summoned you."

"What for now?"

"I don't know the purpose. I am to deliver this." The arbiter pulled out a letter with a wax seal. "And then we are to escort you directly there."

There was no question that he would serve as expected, because that was what a man of honor did when called. The Capitol was a long way from Uttara. His crops would surely wither and die while he was gone. His animals would starve, so he would give them as gifts to the local workers instead. And when the Law was done using him again, he'd return to fields overgrown with weeds to start all over again.

Karno sighed. "I will fetch my war hammer." Because obviously, if the Capitol called for him, someone or something was in need of killing.

Once inside his home—which despite the arbiter's offensive description was perfectly acceptable—Karno studied the letter. It bore an unfamiliar seal with an ornate crown upon it. He broke it open and read.

"Hmmmm..."

It appeared his request for an arranged marriage had been answered after all.

Chapter 45

All the people of Lok called her Radamantha the Wise. That name had been earned.

Her rule thus far had been one of peace and prosperity. The regular pronouncements of the scholarly Orders were eagerly anticipated by every house and caste, as ancient knowledge was continually sent out into the world. She had no tolerance for sloth or corruption within her government, and the Law was administered in a manner that was just and fair for all.

But it took a mighty amount of effort to keep it that way.

It was a cool day by Capitol standards, as Rada sat in the shade upon one of the many balconies of her palace with her recently arrived honored guest, while their children played together in the gardens below.

"Pari is turning into a lovely young lady."

"That she is," Phontho Jagdish agreed as only the proudest of fathers could. When his daughter violently tackled the next Maharaja and they both went crashing into the carefully trimmed flowers, he winced. "Ah, that's the warrior caste side. She gets that from me, I'm afraid. She's a champion at dirt war."

"Oh, he'll be fine," Rada said, and that was confirmed as both children promptly got up and continued giggling and chasing each other.

"Young Devedas is the spitting image of his father."

She smiled at that compliment, because it was obviously true. He would certainly be as handsome as his father, though this Devedas wasn't being raised in a land of ice and cruelty after being manipulated by black steel. This Devedas was disciplined, educated, and loved. Her husband's birthright had been taken from him. She would do everything in her power to secure her son's.

"So how many children do you and Lady Shakti have now?"

"With the twins now, five. We keep going at this rate and I'll able to obligate an infantry paltan off just my sons. My apologies Shakti couldn't make the journey."

From what her spies told her, Shakti basically ran the entire court of Bhadramunda Vadal, while Jagdish remained the beloved and respected supreme commander of the most powerful warrior caste in the world. Despite being the only great house lacking an ancestor blade, under their leadership Vadal had grown stronger than ever.

"I understand. The two of you have been rather busy."

"It was the babies that kept her home, not the politics. I assure you Shakti would much rather be here, and only relented after I promised I'd make it to the Capitol in time to represent our family at your celebration."

"You honor me, Jagdish."

"It's only fair. You came to my wedding."

"Your wedding night was interrupted by assassins and then my husband declared war on your house the next day."

Jagdish snorted. "Then here's to hoping yours is a bit less eventful!"

Vadal had been an ally to her rule, but more important than that, Jagdish had been a true friend, and one of the only people in the world she could confide in.

Rada grew somber as she spoke. "We live in tumultuous times. Everything is in a constant state of change. I've tried to dole out the ancient's wisdom in a way that would make this an Age of Reason. New houses rise. Old traditions die. The Law evolves. But that offends many. Sometimes I'm jealous of Thera Vane, because I wish I knew what the future holds."

"Don't be jealous. I saw that cruel Voice in action. It didn't deserve someone as good as her. I think it's better to work toward the fate you desire, than to be imprisoned by a fate imposed on you. Even her gods couldn't know everything. They made their bets and cast their die."

"You talk as if an intricate plan a thousand years in the making is no different than a soldier's gambling."

"Isn't it, though?" Jagdish pulled out his little pocket watch, examined it, and sighed. "Sadly, Your Highness, I must go. My Thakoor has commanded that while I'm here I might as well give a speech to the Vadal contingent of your Army of Many Houses today. Apparently, my war stories are good for their morale."

"You'll do fine," she assured him, for Jagdish told the best stories. "I'll see you at tomorrow's feast, then?"

"Of course, Maharani. I wouldn't miss it."

As Jagdish got up and went to collect his daughter, Rada called out after him. "Speaking of the future, when you see Lady Shakti again, remind her that it's still several years away but it's never too early to start thinking about offers arranging the heir's marriage." Rada nodded pointedly toward where Pari was shrieking as Devedas splashed water from a fountain on her.

"Oh..." It was a good thing Jagdish didn't lock up in combat like he did in politics, because he would've gotten himself killed a long time ago. For a moment, it was as if he couldn't even comprehend what that offer meant to his family. "That's... You remember Pari is half caste, right?"

"Of course. What better way to tell both warrior and worker that the Capitol respects them as well? Even the fanatics in their mountain cove would be pleased by having a daughter of one of the original Sons of the Black Sword married to the Maharaja in the Capitol. We are cordial with them now, but it's been hard for them to forget centuries of abuse. Most importantly for the happiness and success of my son, I know her, and I know the character of those who raised her."

Jagdish nodded slowly, as all the pieces fit. "No wonder they call you Rada the Wise."

"I thought about having Rada the Merciless be my title, but it didn't fit quite as well."

He grinned at the idea. "Then I shall inform Shakti. She loves this sort of thing. Expect many letters full of poetry and compelling arguments."

Sometime after Jagdish had left to tell tall tales and buy drinks for his warriors, Karno joined her on the balcony. When he had answered her summons, he had been dressed in rough worker attire. Now he wore the finest robes, appropriate for a Maharani's consort. Though she suspected Karno deep down would still be more comfortable in gleaming silver armor than either worker or first caste garb.

The Librarian Queen was known for her wisdom, and that reputation had been well deserved. Rada understood that for her son to be a good ruler, he needed a proper father to teach him how to be an honorable man. She also needed a partner to help her weather the trials of her obligation, and a protector to keep her safe. Enough time had passed for her to mourn Devedas and, more importantly, for the people to mourn the loss of their idealized leader and hero. She had been repeatedly challenged, but once it became clear that her hold on the Capitol was firm, every great house had been quick to offer their best to compete for her hand.

None of those were good enough, because Karno was the most decent and honest man she had ever known...and she had missed him so very much.

Still a man of few words, Karno sat down beside her.

"So, tomorrow begins our wedding celebration," Rada said.

"I look forward to it."

Chapter 46

Many Years Later

"What is this place?"

The boy looked up from scrubbing the floor to see a very old man standing in the entryway of the temple. It was odd to have a visitor here so late at night. The boy usually had the place to himself while he cleaned.

"What do you mean, sir?"

"This magnificent building, what is it for?" The stranger walked inside. His hair and beard were long and white, his skin dark and wrinkled from exposure to harsh weather. His clothing was odd and unfamiliar, stained by travel and bleached by sun. He studied the elaborate carvings on the wall, which had been painted by the finest artists in Vadal City to be exceedingly lifelike. "I know who these images are meant to be."

"Everyone knows who they are," the boy said. "They're our gods and heroes, sir."

Pausing before the symbol of the meat hook, he asked, "Is this some manner of memorial?"

The old man must have just gotten off a boat from one of the mysterious foreign lands to not know about this place, because everyone in Lok made the pilgrimage here eventually. "This is the temple of Lord Ashok, god of justice."

The old man thought about that for a moment, and then he

began to laugh. He laughed as if that was the silliest thing he had ever heard.

"Don't laugh! This temple was built on the very spot he defeated the Night Father!" The boy got off his hands and knees and angrily threw down his rag. "Don't you dare mock Lord Ashok!"

"Calm yourself, lad. I intended no offense. I was simply unaware of the promotion." Then he noticed for the first time what the boy had been doing. "You scrub the floor?"

"That is my obligation to scrub the floor."

"Do they shed blood here often, then?"

What an odd question. "No. Why would they?"

"I was just wondering."

"It is tradition. Every night one of us is asked to scrub the temple floor."

"Do you know why?"

The boy shrugged, because tradition was tradition. It just was. "Thousands of dusty sandals walk on these sacred stones every day from all the faithful coming to pray for Lord Ashok's guidance. It is my job to shine the stones until they are so clean they reflect the light." The boy pointed at the glowing bulbs overhead. "The Keepers choose me for this duty a lot because I always do my best."

"To honor your obligation is an important thing." The old man surprised the boy by giving him a solemn, old-fashioned bow, then he surprised him again by asking, "May I help you clean?"

Nobody had ever asked the boy that before. "Sure, I guess."

The old man took off his shoes and left them in in the entrance, so as to not track more dirt inside. He got another rag from the bucket, wrung it out, got on his knees, and began to scrub.

"You are doing it wrong," the boy told him.

"Apologies. It has been a long time."

"Watch how I do it." The boy cared about his labor and wanted it done right. "See?"

The old man watched and copied him. "Yes. That is clearly the superior technique."

The boy just shook his head and kept scrubbing. "You don't even know what this place is for, so why do you come here?"

"I was born in this city. I've been away for so very long that I wanted to return one final time." He looked at the carvings again. "I suppose I wanted to see old friends before I die."

That made no sense. "My grandfather's grandfather carved those. Those are gods and heroes, not *friends*."

The old man chuckled and continued scrubbing. "Even gods and heroes have friends, boy. They all had love and hate and dreams and fears."

"Lord Ashok has no fear!"

"Is that so?"

The boy decided that this must be some kind of heretical unbeliever, so it was his solemn duty to educate him about the gods. "Lord Ashok fears nothing and he still watches over us, punishing the wicked and saving the righteous. All those obligated to keep the laws pray to Lord Ashok to help them make good judgments, so they do not go astray. Our warriors try to be fearless, just like him."

"Good for them... What do they believe about Thera?"

"Ah, so you *do* know some of the gods!" The boy had suspected the old man was playing a joke on him, for no one could be that ignorant. "She is Lord Ashok's lady. Her temple is across the river, where the great tower fell on the Rakshasa's evil head! It is said all our gods used to be forgotten, hidden away by the Night Father and his evil masks, but Thera is the one who taught us how to remember. She is mother to our people, and her love is what set us free. She waits in paradise for Lord Ashok to return to her."

"Then she should not be kept waiting any longer." He stood up, put the rag back in the bucket, and began walking away.

"Where are you going? The obligation isn't done yet."

The old stranger gave him a weary smile. "Mine is."